PRAISE FOR

THE GIRL KING

★ "Masterful. . . . Yu crafts a rich tale filled with detailed world-building." —*SLJ*, starred review

"Absolutely fantastic." —**Kendare Blake**, #1 *New York Times* bestselling author of the Three Dark Crowns series

"Engrossed me from the first page. Lu is a heroine for the ages!" —**Julie C. Dao**, author of *Forest of a Thousand Lanterns*

"Will draw you in and keep you guessing." —**Heidi Heilig**, author of *The Girl from Everywhere* and *For a Muse of Fire*

"Fierce and unforgettable." —**Marjorie Liu**, *New York Times* bestselling author and Hugo Award winner for *Monstress: The Blood*

"A delight." —**Cindy Pon**, author of *Want* and *Serpentine*

"Everything I want in a high fantasy." —**Samantha Shannon**, *New York Times* bestselling author of *The Priory of the Orange Tree*

"Yu crafts a tremendously stunning world with complex characters and a heart-pounding adventure." —**BuzzFeed**

"A cleverly crafted world that still feels completely believable, and, even better, *new*." —**Hypable**

"Riveting." —**Vox**

"This book has been pulling in the hype— with good reason." —*Paste* magazine

"A fast-paced, seamless fantasy adventure full of action, mysticism, and female empowerment." —*Booklist*

THE GIRL KING

MIMI YU

BLOOMSBURY

NEW YORK LONDON OXFORD NEW DELHI SYDNEY

BLOOMSBURY YA
Bloomsbury Publishing Inc., part of Bloomsbury Publishing Plc
1385 Broadway, New York, NY 10018

BLOOMSBURY and the Diana logo are trademarks of Bloomsbury Publishing Plc

First published in the United States of America in January 2019
by Bloomsbury YA
Paperback edition published in February 2020

Bloomsbury books may be purchased for business or promotional use. For information on
bulk purchases please contact Macmillan Corporate and Premium Sales Department at
specialmarkets@macmillan.com

ISBN 978-1-5476-0308-4 (paperback)

The Library of Congress has cataloged the hardcover edition as follows:
Names: Yu, Mimi, author.
Title: The Girl King / by Mimi Yu.
Description: New York : Bloomsbury, 2019.
Summary: When their father names a male cousin as next ruler of the Empire of
the First Flame, Lu must go on the run to reclaim her birthright, leaving her
younger, timid sister, Min, to discover her own hidden power.
Identifiers: LCCN 2017056221
ISBN 978-1-68119-889-7 (hardcover) • ISBN 978-1-68119-890-3 (e-book)
Subjects: | CYAC: Inheritance and succession—Fiction. | Princesses—Fiction. |
Magic—Fiction. | Shapeshifting—Fiction. | Fantasy.
Classification: LCC PZ7.1.Y9 Gir 2018 | DDC [Fic]—dc23
LC record available at https://lccn.loc.gov/2017056221

Book design by Danielle Ceccolini
Typeset by Westchester Publishing Services
Printed and bound in the U.S.A. by Berryville Graphics Inc., Berryville, Virginia
2 4 6 8 10 9 7 5 3 1

All papers used by Bloomsbury Publishing Plc are natural, recyclable products
made from wood grown in well-managed forests. The manufacturing processes
conform to the environmental regulations of the country of origin.

To find out more about our authors and books visit www.bloomsbury.com
and sign up for our newsletters.

FOR MY 엄마 AND 아빠,
WITH INFINITE GRATITUDE
AND DEVOTION

PROLOGUE

It was well before dawn when the Ana and Aba stirred the priestess from her bed. Had she been anyone else she might have been deep in slumber. As it was, she did not sleep much, and though she'd been still and supine, her eyes had been open. Gods did not bother with words, but they had their own language. When she felt Them surge like lifeblood through the stone walls and floors of the temple, she knew, and she rose.

The priestess was unsurprised to find her brothers waiting for her in the sanctum. The city's borders fell under Jin's purview as the Steel Star; he would have felt the disturbance at the gate in his blood, like the first distant rumble of thunder before a summer storm. As for Shen, little that happened in Yunis ever escaped his attention.

The men sat on their crystalline thrones before the fire. Shen was already staring into it, his face stern and tense. Jin stifled a yawn; soft and rumpled with sleep, he looked half a boy. He'd been young, no more than twenty, when the city fell and they'd been forced to flee into the Inbetween. Time flowed strange and uneven here. It had been seventeen years since, but he hadn't aged a day. None of them had.

"It's the lake gate again," Jin said, as though she didn't already know. "What do you suppose it is this time? Another deer? Maybe a mouse?" His tone was wry, but there was an eagerness beneath it he couldn't quite hide. It was his duty to oversee their army, but here that left him with little to do. A threat at the gates would give him purpose, at least.

"We should go in person," Jin continued. "Why waste Vrea's energy with a spirit projection? Let's just saddle up some elk—"

"It's nighttime," Shen said shortly.

"—and grab some lanterns," Jin added, undeterred.

"Last time I let you patrol the border in person, you went Below and were *seen*!" Shen snapped.

Jin's smile faltered. "That was an accident, I told you."

"Seventeen years we've kept ourselves hidden, and you spoil it all on a lark." Shen was always grumpiest at night; Vrea would never say it to his face but she found it endearing. A rare lingering human quality in their stoic elder brother. "You'd better hope this disturbance tonight doesn't have anything to do with your little 'accident.'"

"I don't hope for anything anymore," Jin shot back.

Maybe because he'd been so young when they left, it sometimes seemed Jin was still one foot in that place. Or perhaps it wasn't a foot Vrea was thinking of—something more vital, a mind, a heart.

"Let's go, then," Shen said as Vrea took her seat. "Whatever is at the gate, I'd like to deal with it before morning."

"Yes, let's not keep those deer waiting," Jin quipped, but his good humor was worn thin. He sat forward, brow creasing in concentration. A sweet, hapless simulacrum of his older brother.

Vrea held out her hands. The men took them. Shen's grasp was perfunctory, Jin's warm and affectionate, like that of a trusting child.

The priestess closed her eyes to the violet-black flames. Then she willed the three of them out and away.

They lifted from their bodies, light as a cool summer wind in the Below. When she opened her eyes again they stood, the three of them, at the edge of the lake. It was lit silver-pale by a young moon and permanently fringed with dense gray fog— a by-product of the high concentration of feral magic around the gate.

Tonight though, the fog was thicker than usual, swirling on the wind like it were agitated. Whatever was at the gate, it may not just be deer, after all. Something was off. The spirits were riled.

"Is everyone accounted for?" she asked. Her brothers stood on either side, translucent but stable. They clung to her hands carefully—releasing their grip would break the projection, pulling them back into the sanctum where their bodies rested in wait.

"Come on," Shen said. "We're not far."

They drifted through the fog. They could scarcely see arm's distance before them, and so hugged the edge of the lake to keep their bearings. An unnecessary precaution; as they neared, Vrea could feel the gate thrumming, calling her forth.

Still, it would have been easy enough for the naked eye to miss. The fog thinned out and there it was: just an odd blur, like haze off rocks on a hot day. An aberration in the air, shiny as new scar tissue, in the shape of a door. There were no obvious landmarks, no signifiers, no adornments. That would have gone against their purposes.

Vrea turned toward the gate and whispered under her breath, stripping away the protective spells—just enough to peer through from their side. As she tugged free another layer, she felt Jin shift at her side, itching to reach for his sword. She needn't remind him of the obvious: they weren't there, not truly. Whatever waited for them at the gate couldn't hurt them, would not even be able to see them. But she could understand wanting the familiar security of holding a weapon.

A final word off her tongue and another layer of magic dispersed.

The gate opened out onto the opposite side of the lake in the Below. Through the haze of the remaining protective spells, the Triarch could see a shore no different from the one upon which they stood: water-slicked rocks, cold gray water, swathed in the pale eerie fog of feral magic.

The only difference was the young man.

He stood opposite them, dead center in the gate, like a false reflection in a mirror. He was tall and handsome, well dressed for the elements. His hand was outstretched toward them, and in it he held a gun.

Vrea had a moment to marvel. She'd seen guns once before,

in a vision given to her by the Ana and Aba. It had been imperial soldiers then, clunky with unfamiliarity and hands more accustomed to crossbows. They were a new thing, even in the Below.

This gun was smaller than those, more elegant, its dark wood handle inlaid with shiny bits of mother-of-pearl, and its user held it with cool certainty. He did something with a finger and a bit of metal clicked. Vrea followed the sound with her gaze—

An explosion. Small but garish. She smelled burned steel and sulfur and sparkstone. That was to be expected.

What was not was where the bullet went.

The seal of the gate should have kept all matter that belonged to the Below in the Below. The bullet from the gun should have shot out over the open water of their lake before slicing into its cold, swallowing depths.

Instead, the bullet flew, fleet and dispassionate through the gate, into the Inbetween, and past Jin's ear.

Vrea's body was miles away, safe in the sanctum. Even so, she felt her heart stop.

Shen and Jin reached instinctively for their swords. "Wait! Don't . . . !" she began, but it was too late. They released her hands.

They were gone before the warning even left her mouth, yanked back to the sanctum. She felt the tug herself, but managed to hold on. Her grasp was weak, though, without the amplifying support of her brothers; she would be drawn back soon enough.

Hang on, she told herself. *Just a while longer. You have to figure out what just happened—*

"It worked!" screamed the young man in the Below. He was still holding the gun. "Did you see?"

For a moment she thought he was mad, that he was speaking to himself. But then another man emerged out of the fog behind him. He was much older, slight. His head was shorn, just like hers. A monk, then, though the dun brown of his robes did not resemble any order with which she was familiar.

"I told you this was the gate," the possible monk said mildly.

"Never mind that," the young man said, grinning. He had a beautiful smile, with straight, oddly even teeth. They looked like porcelain. "I can't believe the bullet is passing through."

"Using that northern sparkstone from the mountains makes all the difference," the older man told him. "It's just as I theorized. There's magic left in these mountains, even down here. Loose, in the water, in the rocks. It seeks its source. And where it goes, we will follow."

The young man lifted the gun and shot again. The bullet flew past Vrea. She heard it skitter against the rocks behind her.

"And where do you suppose it's going?" the young man asked. He stepped closer to the gate, as though hoping to catch a glimpse. "What do you suppose is over there, on the other side?" he asked.

"Power," said the monk, stepping in close behind him. "True power."

"Next time, we need to try the cannon."

"We need more than a cannon. We need an army."

"In that case," the young man raised the gun again and aimed, "it is time I write to my aunt."

He shot. This time as the bullet flew by her, Vrea *felt* it.

There was something familiar in its core—some entrenched thread of feral magic. She reached out her energy and felt it tug at her currents, at the fibers of the spells wound about the gate.

She looked up at the two men gazing through at her, oblivious to her presence.

Only not.

The older one, the monk, looked at her, and for a moment, as she shook loose the reverberations of the strange bullet, he *saw* her. There was comprehension on his face, and wonder, edged with hunger, avarice, jealousy. *Want.* Almost lustful. He saw her, and he knew what she was.

She was reciting the spells of protection before it even occurred to her to act, swaddling the gate back up under spools of gathered magic. She tore it from the air, from the stones beneath her feet so quickly it sparked and smoked as she bound it. The faces of the two men warped and paled, then disappeared behind the shroud she wove.

It took the last of her energy. She heaved out a final spell and collapsed onto the ground, felt the vague cold of the lake-smoothed stones beneath her.

"Vrea!"

She opened her eyes. Shen was gazing down at her. For a moment he looked so aged, she thought he had adopted Jin's slippery failing, his inability to stay in the moment, in his true body. But, no. It was merely concern that made his face so weary and drawn.

"Are you all right?" Jin was on the floor beside her.

"What happened?" Shen demanded, seizing her hands in his. "Who was the man with the gun?"

She stood on shaking legs. Her body felt sullen and heavy and foreign, the way it always did after a sending. Warmth fell across her face and she looked up at the small windows at the top of the temple walls. Each had become a muted square of cool gray light. The sun was starting to rise. Morning in the Inbetween.

"What was it?" Shen pressed. "What did you see?"

"Something new," she rasped. "And it saw me."

CHAPTER 1

The Girl King

*T*he sword cut through the air a finger's width from Lu's face. She suppressed the instinct to flinch. The thrust was meant to throw her off balance so her opponent could knock her to the ground. Once that happened, she would be done for.

She wasn't so easy. *Sorry to disappoint, Shin Yuri.*

Lu leaped back lightly, swinging her own blade in a hard, upward parry just as the sword master sent his crashing down upon her. She was ready for it. Their weapons met with a flat *thwack*. Wood on wood.

"Good!" her shin barked, dancing back from the blow. "Now, fix your stance!"

Lu darted a look down at her feet. Shin Yuri took advantage of her distraction. She barely had time to raise her sword before he fell upon her.

"Don't use your eyes to fix your feet!" he scolded between thrusts. "The body knows the body. Eyes are for the opponent!"

Idiot! A beginner's mistake. Hardly befitting a princess who had picked up a practice blade at the age of seven and spent the past nine years training daily. A princess who in a few short hours would be named her father's successor . . .

Yuri came at her hard, raining fresh blows on her. She shuffled back, taking him with her. His movements were violent, almost wild, but she wasn't fooled. His control was ironclad. Still, a man his age could not keep up this pace for long.

"Keep me moving!" Shin Yuri snapped. "Let me use up my energy."

I know that!

The shadow of Kangmun Hall's massive red walls fell over them as they danced along the perimeter of the Ring. The hall was named for the first ethnic Hu emperor—her own great-grandsire—who had led his army of nomad warriors south to conquer the failing last Hana dynasty. They had had the Gift of the tiger back then, allowing them to rend their enemies with tooth and claw. But that was long ago.

Yuri pushed her back another step. Lu imagined herself in the bronze-laced red wooden armor and orange tiger pelt of the old Hu kings, like those she had seen hung in reverent display in the Hall of the Ancestors.

She leaped forward and swung hard. The blood pounding in her ears became the thundering hooves of a thousand Hu warriors astride massive black war elk. The warriors screamed for victory—for *her*—their magnificent mounts foaming at the mouth in their toil.

"Reckless!" she heard Shin Yuri shout. "Control your strokes! Fewer swings, more *knowing*."

His words meant nothing to her. She was what thousands of years of warriors had wrought. She had the blood of the tiger in her veins. Who was he to tell her how to swing a sword?

She drove him back another step. As Shin Yuri raised his blade, she spun away from him, then reversed the motion, circling back toward him, raising her sword high above her head. She brought it down, hard, just as he completed his own stroke. The force of her unexpected blow knocked the sword clean from his hands.

Shin Yuri dove after the blade, but Lu kicked it out of reach. He hit the sandy ground, rolling away from her. He bounded back to his feet, poised to dash, only to find her wooden blade at his throat.

Lu kept the sword steady in one hand and used the other to pull off her leather practice helmet, the heavy black rope of her plait tumbling down her back.

"I believe there is a saying for this situation, is there not?" She grinned, wiping away the sweat brimming on her upper lip with her sleeve. "Something about the student becoming the shin?"

Pride and annoyance tugged at the old man's features, but before he could speak, applause broke out, sharp and unexpected as the ringing of a glass wind-chime.

Lu turned and saw three girls gathered just outside the chalked perimeter of the sparring ring. Against the sandy practice yard, the trio's pastel-hued robes gave them the misplaced look of flowers scattered in the dirt: Lu's younger sister, Princess Minyi, and two of her nunas, Butterfly and Snowdrop. Seeing the surprise on her face, they burst into pleased giggles.

Minyi's sallow face was sun warmed and flushed. She was dressed as their empress mother preferred her to be, in the old Hana way, her layered robes of pale pink cinched high at the waist. The empress had never tried to dress Lu this way, even when she was a young child. But then, between the two of them Min had always been the more malleable.

Butterfly and Snowdrop wore the yellow batik robes customary of palace nunas, topped with a hooded cape—a symbol of modesty. But Butterfly and Snowdrop had uncovered their heads to enjoy the late summer sun.

"Ay!" Lu hollered, striding over to them. "What are you doing here?"

"We overheard you sparring," Min said. Her voice was ever tentative, like the tip of a toe testing hot bathwater. "It sounded so exciting that they—we—wanted to watch. Just for a moment."

Lu blinked in pleasant surprise. It had been some time since Min had watched her spar—years, truly. She'd assumed Min wasn't interested. Her sister had always been a sensitive creature, flinching at even the clashing of practice swords.

"Don't be cross, Princess," Butterfly interjected, pulling Lu's gaze away. "We just wanted to see if the rumors were true, that you're as deft as a man with a blade." Snowdrop let loose a fresh peal of laughter.

"What's so amusing? You don't think I'm as good as a man?" Lu demanded good-naturedly.

"Oh no, it's not that!" Butterfly smirked. "Snowdrop was just commenting that in your practice robes and helmet, Her Highness cuts as handsome a figure as any crown *prince* could hope to—"

"You truly are the Girl King, just as they say!" Snowdrop interrupted, dissolving into fresh laughter.

Lu caught herself before she reacted, but from the corner of her eye she saw Minyi stiffen.

"Girl King" was the derisive nickname Lu had earned among both court officials and commoners contemptuous of her ambitions—as Snowdrop well would have known, had she the sense of a child half her age. She understood the language of awkward silences at least; she went quiet, sensing her error.

"The Girl King?" Lu said with a deliberate smile. The tension eased just slightly from Min's shoulders. "Perhaps I will be! We'll see soon enough."

Very soon. By the end of the day, she would have her new title, and finally put to bed all the rumors: that she was too weak to rule, that the Hu dynasty was on its last legs, that her father was planning to marry her off to her stupid, drug-addled Hana cousin, Lord Set of Bei Province.

"Yes," agreed Min. Her voice was rushed in eagerness, grateful to move past the discomfort Snowdrop had initiated. "We should probably head over to court soon."

"Court?" Lu repeated. She cursed, looking toward the sun. "Is it that late already? Why didn't you say so sooner?"

Min flushed as she always did when sensing the slightest displeasure directed her way. "Well, it's not so late yet—" she amended quickly.

"Snowdrop, take Princess Minyi to her apartments and get her dressed for court," Lu interrupted, her thoughts racing. It wouldn't do to be late today of all days. "Butterfly, run ahead to my apartments and tell my nunas to prepare a hot bath and lay out my clothes. The formal teal robes, and the plum underskirt with gold trim. Make sure to speak to Hyacinth directly. She knows the clothes and how best to prepare my bath."

"Yes, Princess."

Lu turned toward her sister. "I'll see you at court."

"Should we meet beforehand so we can walk to Kangmun Hall together . . . ?" Minyi ventured hopefully. Lu tamped down a sigh; Min hated making an entrance on her own. Most days Lu didn't mind playing the chaperone . . .

"Not today," she said brusquely. "I can't afford to be late."

"I won't be . . ."

"Best hurry now!" Lu flashed her an encouraging smile before turning away.

She hurried back to Shin Yuri, who had removed his sword belt and was now worrying the shoulder buckles on his sparring jerkin.

"I apologize for the interruption, Shin Yuri."

"Interruption?" he said blandly. "What interruption?"

A smile quirked at the corners of Lu's mouth.

Shin Yuri spat in the dirt, then turned to fix her with a tight frown. "Time for court, is it?" He didn't wait for her answer. "Well, before you go, allow me to do my duties as a shin and give you some notes on your performance today."

Lu sighed, hands on her hips, but Yuri was immune to her impatience by now. "I'm an old man, Princess. Half a century on this earth wears on the body," he told her, extracting a handkerchief from his tunic. He wiped his face, soiling the fine silk. "You did well today, used your speed to your advantage. But

you would not have succeeded against a man—an opponent—
the same age as you."

Lu bristled. Her arms rose to fold over her chest—a defensive
gesture. She willed them back down. "You can't know that."

"You have talent and strength on your side. Good instincts.
But that will take you only so far. If you're going to survive in
a battle, you need to develop your mind as well as your body.
Efficiency of movement comes from experience, keen observation, and observation can only be done with—"

"Patience!" she snapped. "Yes, I know. You've told me a
thousand times before."

"And I'll tell you a thousand times more if I think it will
help you survive." His eyes locked with hers, and Lu was struck
with the uneasy sense that he was speaking of more than just
sparring.

He is just being condescending, she told herself fiercely. Her
father was about to name her his successor; what did she have
to fear? One day she would be Yuri's empress, and yet he persisted in trying to put her in her place like she was a child. Why
were old men so tiresome?

As though hearing her thoughts, he said, "If you do not
trust my words as your elder, then trust my experience as a
warrior."

*A warrior who abruptly resigned from his post in the North for the
comforts of the capital,* a nasty voice in her head hissed. This was
the undercurrent of gossip that had been following Yuri around
since he had returned to court some five years ago. An odd
tension—to be labeled both the best and a coward.

"I trust you," she told him, scuffing the sand with the toe of her boot.

Yuri resumed the task of loosening his jerkin. "I should hope so," he said. "If you don't, I'd have no business being your shin."

He dismissed her with a wave. "Best get prepared for court. You have a long day ahead of you."

"Yes," she said firmly. "I do."

⁂

The drums heralding the start of court beat solemn and orotund, steady as blood. The theater of power. Standing with her sister and their nunas like actors waiting backstage, Lu peered through the seam of Kangmun Hall's closed front doors, out into the Heart. The massive yellow stone courtyard was made small by the scores of court officials, magistrates, prefecture governors, and Inner Ring gentry pouring in.

There would be more people outside the closed gates— unlucky lower gentry whose family rank did not warrant a seat within the Heart, and supercilious First Ring gossipmongers who bandied fresh information as currency. There might even be a few Second Ringers lucky enough to sneak through the Ring walls under some pretense or another. All of them waiting to hear secondhand tellings of the emperor's pronouncements.

Word of my succession will spread fast. Lu's chest tightened in anticipation. At long last, it was happening.

"Really? You can't even wait for them to open the doors?" The voice was low in her ear. Lu jumped, whirling to find her eldest nuna Hyacinth doubled over in silent laughter.

"Cut it out," she hissed. But she was unable to suppress a smile. "I'm just gauging the crowd," she said with exaggerated primness. "Reconnaissance."

Hyacinth snorted. "You look like a child sneaking into her birthday gifts."

"I think you mean I look like a future emperor."

"Certainly. A future emperor sneaking into her birthday gi—" She broke off into a strangled giggle as Lu poked her in the ribs.

"Oh!" Min exclaimed. "I'd forgotten. The pink men are visiting today."

Her sister was peeking through the gap in the doors. Lu leaned back in over her shoulder and glimpsed three foreign men in the crowd, their pale pinkish flesh and bulbous facial features marking them as the delegation from Elland.

Lu pulled her sister back from the doors. "Call them *Ellandaise*. Not 'pink men.'"

Min flushed at the admonishment. "Of course. The nunas call them that sometimes . . . It's just a bad habit. Forgive me."

"Commoners use that term. It does not do for a princess," Lu told her. Then she frowned. "It doesn't become a nuna, either. Well-bred girls from Inner Ring gentry with sky manses ought to know better. I'll see that Amma Ruxin has a talk with them." The stern old amma in charge of training Min's handmaidens would not stand for such behavior.

"I understand, sister. I'm sorry—"

"So," Hyacinth's effervescent whisper came in her other ear. "What will be Emperor Lu's first decree?"

"Stemming the northern expansion," Lu said, turning away

from Min. "We're bleeding resources needed for the city's poor into the colonies."

"It'll be difficult to walk back those mines. The wealth from the sparkstone they're dredging up—it's enticing. And popular."

"What is popular is not always what is right," Lu countered. "We've encroached onto northern land for too long."

Hyacinth tilted her head, considering. "It's not like there are any slipskin clans left to give it back to."

"Right," Lu snapped. "Because the few Gifted we didn't *kill* are languishing in the labor camps."

"It's time! Everyone into their places!" Amma Ruxin snapped, giving both Lu and Hyacinth a reproachful look as the doors began to open. Hyacinth rolled her eyes at the woman's turned back. Then she winked at Lu and stepped into place with the other nunas.

"*Good luck,*" she mouthed.

Lu took a deep breath and stepped outside, in front of the assembled court. Min trailed so closely it looked like she was trying to hide beneath her skirts. Even a regular court session left her little sister anxious; a crowd this size might kill her. Hopefully Butterfly would catch her if she fainted.

Their parents were already seated on the stone portico, side by side, though somehow they made the arm's-length distance between them look much wider. Theirs had been a marriage of politics, arranged to strengthen ties between the ethnic Hana aristocracy and the ethnic Hu royals, and they had never found reason to make it anything more.

"Come on, then," Lu directed Min. "Let's play our parts."

She said it with the edge of a shared joke—one only they in the whole world could share.

Her sister blinked, a surprised smile quivering across her mouth, chasing away the rictus of fear for a moment.

The sisters filed over and fell to their knees before their father, Emperor Daagmun, ruler of the sixteen provinces of the Empire of the First Flame. "Your child and subject bows before the Lord of Ten Thousand Years," they recited in unison.

"Rise, my daughters."

Lu stood easily; Min's heavy layered robes made the task more difficult. Butterfly and Snowdrop hurried over, heads still bowed in respect, to assist the younger princess.

Their father caught Lu's eye and smiled. He looked well today, resplendent in formal robes of saffron and gold—all signs of illness tucked away beneath silk and royal pomp. He looked every bit the strong and formidable Hu ruler he needed to be.

Lu stepped forward and dropped a warm kiss on his hand. It trembled in hers and she swallowed a pang of sadness. He could not hide his disease forever. From this close she could see the tired lines of a much older man around his eyes.

By contrast, Empress Rinyi looked ten years younger than her thirty-some years. Lu had always felt there was something almost urgent in the care she took with her appearance—all those oils and salves and meticulously applied powders. As though she were preserving her beauty for some later occasion. Lu nodded curtly in her direction, and their mother responded in kind, her fixed smile barely hiding a poisoned well of disdain and impatience beneath.

As Lu and Min took their seats the drums stilled, leaving in their wake only the sharp crackle of the First Flame, burning bright and eternal at the center of the Heart. According to Hana legend, the flame had been ignited by a drop of the sun thousands of years ago—a gift from the gods to their then-fledgling kingdom—and kept alive ever since.

Her father spoke: "Ours is the greatest kingdom this world has ever known," he began. For a moment, his voice cracked, and she flicked a sidelong glance toward him. Was he having one of his spells now? But, no. He remained steady and upright in his throne. She relaxed as he continued.

"Our kingdom comprises an empire the likes of which our ancestors could not have imagined. Beyond what even my bold, visionary great-grandsire Kangmun, the first Hu emperor, foretold. Each day our borders grow wider. Our colonies are hungry, thriving, like the topmost branches of a great tree, stretching ever closer to the sun. At the same time, our towns and cities grow more prosperous and efficient—the strong roots of the empire."

Her father went on to describe news from the northern front. The mines were dredging up enormous wealth from the earth—sparkstone enough to soon see the entire imperial army fitted with firearms. Settlements were sprawling, and soon they would make proper colonies, worthy of women and children, shops and cities.

There had been another—highly improbable—sighting by scouts in the Ruvai Mountains of a battalion of men clad in the white and gray uniforms of Yunis soldiers.

Her father did not mention the bandit raid on prison camp

eight two weeks ago that had sprung over fifty laborers and left her cousin Lord Set, General of the North, looking the fool. Everyone knew of it, though.

Lu hid a satisfied smile and parsed the crowd. The left side of the Heart was filled with officials, while on the right were the First Ring gentry. Each was ordered such that the most important among them were seated in front, closest to the emperor.

A few rows deep, she spotted Hyacinth's parents, the Cuis, and her nuna's three younger sisters. With them sat a boy of thirteen or fourteen she nearly didn't recognize—until she noted the small birthmark on his chin. Wonin, Hyacinth's younger brother. He must nearly be of age to begin his studies at the Imperial Academy. It had been some time since Lu had last seen him, and in the intervening moons he had grown into a tall, elegant-looking youth.

Another boy a few rows behind—older than Wonin, though considerably less well mannered—met Lu's gaze as it moved over him. He gawped at her as if she were some kind of court dancer, eyes traveling down the length of her body. She felt her face go cold, and he blushed, dropping his stare into his lap.

Soured, Lu closed her mind to the crowd. She had chosen today's robes not just for how their cut elongated her elegant figure, but because the teal gave her a cool, imperious air. Memorable, yet dignified. Smart. But in the end, would any man see that, or was she only a pretty thing for them to gaze upon? It irritated her that she couldn't say.

Beauty was a weapon—one that required honing and care, like a sword. But also like a sword it could cut both ways.

We will see who cuts whom once this is over.

A flutter of movement caught the corner of her eye; Min bent in her chair to scratch at her calf through the layers of her skirts. The beads dangling from her hairpins rattled from side to side with the movement. Lu bit her tongue; better not to draw further attention now. She vowed to speak to Min about it later and turned her attention back to her father's words.

". . . Even at the best of times, an empire must not leave anything to chance. A strong emperor does not just rule for the present—he plans for the future."

His words sent a trill of excitement traipsing down the notches of Lu's spine, like a series of bells, each amplifying the last until her body rang with it.

The future.

It was finally happening. She kept her face trained in a mask of assured solemnity.

"And so, today," her father continued. "I will announce my successor."

He was looking at her. Lu gazed back with the slightest of smiles.

And then it happened. He looked away, as though ashamed of himself.

An unfamiliar sensation seized up her insides, then released, like the black and spotted fronds of a dying fern unfurling in her gut.

Dread.

All pretense of poise and gravity evaporated. Lu was shaking her head in a mute "no" before her father even said the words.

"I hereby betroth my eldest daughter, Princess Lu, to Lord Set of Family Li, General of the Fifth Regiment in Bei Province. He will be your next emperor."

Stillness fell, tentatively placid as a newly frozen lake. The only sound was the murmur of the First Flame.

What happened next, Lu supposed, depended on one's belief in ghostly interventions. Either the hungry fires consumed a bit of still-damp kindling, or some greater cosmic force was stirred by her father's speech. In either case, the First Flame reared up high, then let off an excited pop that resounded through the walled Heart. A shower of sparks rained down in its wake, forcing those seated closest to it to lunge back in alarm.

The crowd took it as a sign. Their roar was deafening. For a disorienting moment, Lu thought they were angry. But then, no; she could make out the words. *Long Live the Emperor!* they shouted. *Long live the Empire of the First Flame!*

It was like hearing the ocean at a distance. Blood thrummed so hard in her ears it was as though the drums that had signaled her entry to Heart had taken up again.

Not Set, was all she could think. *Anyone but Set.*

The dread in her blossomed into outrage, its vines scrabbling at her guts and climbing into her throat, as though trying to escape through her mouth. Some part of her registered that if she allowed it out, it would come as tears.

So she choked on it, bit and swallowed it back down. Crushed the life from it until it was nothing more than a blackened pit.

How could he do this to me?

Lu looked to the emperor with beseeching eyes, but her

father was still gazing out at the cheering crowd. And then Lu noticed her mother and sister looking at her from their seats. Minyi was bent at the waist, hunched over; she had been scratching at her calf again when their father's pronouncement came and was too stunned to right herself. Their mother was as still as ever, her face unreadable.

You, Lu thought. Their mother had to be behind this, just as she had been when Set and Lu were children. Even after all these years, she had never given up on her heinous nephew.

The empress ever possessed a studied air of stern, benign dignity. At least in public. The only time Lu ever saw her speak sharply was in the closed company of her amma and her daughters—the usual targets of her ire. Some, like Lu, more often than others. Even in relative privacy though, Lu rarely saw her look excited or pleased.

But now, as the emperor called the meeting to a close, her gaze still locked with Lu's, the empress smiled. With teeth.

CHAPTER 2

The Apothecarist's Apprentice

A fat green fly lit upon Bo's haunch, pierced the mule's flesh, and began to suck. Nok smacked it dead.

A rote prayer for the loss of life rose to his lips, but he did not say the words. His mother had taught them to him when he was small—picking grubs off fruit, pinching fleas from his neck. Or had it been his aunt? It didn't matter. They were all gone now—his Kith and all the others—and Nok didn't pray anymore.

Bo continued eating, oblivious to both fly and boy. He was a dull, indifferent creature, but Nok didn't mind. Some livestock grew skittish around him, as though they could smell the residue of something predatory—something canine—on him. Something he'd rather not think about.

He rubbed his hands together, brushing off blood and bits of fly. The ropey scars crisscrossing his palms caught and chafed on one another. They used to hurt when he was tired, or sometimes when his dreams were especially bad, but that had been years ago. Now they felt nothing.

He stooped to pat his boot and confirm the knife he kept there was in place. The blade was made for cutting herbs from the garden, but it would go through a man's eye, if it came to that. Not that he had any reason to expect trouble—but experience taught him trouble didn't come only when expected.

He was triple-checking the saddlebags to make sure he had everything he needed for Market Day when Omair emerged from inside the house.

The house was carved from one of the many thick-bodied silver trees that dotted Ansana's sloping hills. The farmers along the northern periphery of Yulan City had built their homes like this for centuries, developing a method of hollowing out the tree so it still lived and grew around them.

"Oh, good, you haven't left yet." Omair sauntered forward, slowed by his perpetually swollen knees.

"Stay there, I'll come to you," Nok said, already hurrying forward.

"If I didn't know any better, I'd say you're treating me like I'm old," Omair groused, but he stopped.

Nokhai did not know Omair's exact age. At times, the apothecarist seemed almost gleefully ancient. Then, at turns, the decades seemed to slough off his stooped shoulders until he looked no older than forty, maybe fifty.

He was a short, stout man with a bald head he oiled until it gleamed. Barely visible beneath the hoary bracken of his beard, his brown face teemed with pockmarks and limpid trails of scar tissue. But his eyes were an odd, misplaced gift: a warm, lively red-brown shot through with veins of yellow, like rivulets of gold running through good earth.

He held out a poultice. "Do me a favor and give this to Adé. It's for her mother."

Nok frowned, not taking it. "Adé? I was just going to run the errands and come straight home."

"If you're going all that way you may as well see her," Omair tutted. "I worry about you, living out here with no friends. It's not healthy for a sixteen-year-old boy to be so lonely."

"I'm not lonely," Nok said immediately.

Most of Ansana's denizens were closer to Omair's age than his own sixteen years. Their closest neighbors, the Wangs, had two boys Nok's age; they ignored Nok on good days, and pitched rocks at him on worse ones. But Nok had never felt a lack for it. Solitude was safety. Trouble only happened when other people were around to start it.

It had been nearly seventeen years since Omair moved to Ansana and rehabilitated an abandoned house, filling the desperately empty niche of a village healer. But in towns like this, families went so far back it was as though they had emerged there, right out of the damp earth at the dawn of time.

"The old man's hiding something," they would mutter. *"Did you see how fast Peng's ax cut healed up? Unnatural. And he says that boy's an apprentice, but where did he find him? Just appeared one day, in the dark of night. Who—what is he really?"*

And if any of them learned the answer to that . . . but, no, it was better not to even think of it.

Omair pressed the poultice into Nok's hands. "Indulge an old man and be young, would you? Tell Adé to make you laugh. Talk to other people who aren't me for a change."

～⚬⚭⚬～

The crush of Yulan City felt denser than ever. Locals shouldered past farmers from the empire's rural outskirts, who cried out their offerings of fresh produce. Livestock lowed and brayed. Foreigners from every distant port—dazed travelers and seasoned traders alike—edged their way to and from the docks. Wooden carts wheeled in a dizzy, creaking maelstrom, piled high with squash and turnips and crisp greens, clanging racks of metal pots and pans, piles of combs carved of bone, and blanched wicker baskets. All of it pervaded with the aroma of a hundred different spices, and the damp, brackish breath of the Milk River.

Nok cut through the Scrap-Patch Row section of the Ring, so called for the way its denizens cobbled together their homes from spare bits of brick, metal, and cloth—whatever they could find. Perhaps once upon a time, it had even been a row as its name suggested. Now it engulfed nearly a quarter of the Ring, its untidy borders spilling ever outward. The city's population of poor folk was ever growing, and they had to live somewhere.

The crowds thinned as he entered the Silk Passage. The cacophonous shouts of merchants and grunting of livestock were replaced by gentle voices and the quiet murmur of a fountain located in the center of a wide, well-swept plaza. The pungent scent of spices gave way to refined orange blossom oil. Nok found his feet were no longer catching in wagon ruts, or open puddles of filth.

A man panting under the weight of a painted rickshaw passed him. The rickshaw bore two foreign women holding parasols to shade their pinkish faces from the sun. They stared curiously at Nok, their pale eyes moving from his long, uncombed hair down to his muddy boots. When he met their gaze, they quickly turned away.

Pink men everywhere these days. There were those who resented their foreign presence, their fancy sector of town, and the wealth with which they'd purchased that land. Nok had no feelings about them either way; they weren't the ones he had to worry about.

Nok came to a stop in front of a two-story dress and cloth shop. A weathered wooden sign bearing a carving of a peony hung over the door. He peered into the window, past the displayed bolts of silk and damask, a jade-green robe draped elegantly over a headless mannequin.

There were two shopgirls amid the throng of patrons, dressed in identical uniforms. The smaller of the two—the one he sought—had a pretty, heart-shaped face, warm dark brown skin, and a cloud of black curls bound tightly at the base of her neck in a chignon.

As he watched, she showed a bolt of blue ribbon to a well-heeled older woman. The shopgirl pulled out a length for the woman's inspection, smiling pleasantly, though the expression did not reach her eyes. The customer tested the ribbon between two suspicious fingers and, apparently displeased with what she felt, shook her head and departed.

Nok passed the woman on his way in. She stiffened visibly at the sight of him. Little brass bells tinkled over his head as the door closed behind him.

"Can I help you, sir?"

The shopgirl he had been watching through the window approached. She gazed down her nose at him the best she could—no easy feat, given she was a good head shorter.

"Yes, in fact," he said, playing along. "I've heard your shop boasts the finest blue ribbon in the entire Ring—"

Adé burst out laughing and threw her arms around his neck. He tensed up at the touch; she was always doing things like that. He brusquely moved her to arm's length.

"How long have you been spying on me?" she demanded.

"Just long enough to see you botch your sale—"

She swatted at him. "Oh, that lady's horrid! Always coming in here on Market Day and asking us to pull down this bolt and that silk and hardly *ever* buying anything. She's a nightmare. Acts like she's got a sky manse when she's some Ring-born butcher's wife. We all want to tell her off, but of course if we did that the Ox would have our heads—"

"The Ox?"

"Oh." Adé waved a hand as though she were chasing off a fly. "That's what we call the shop owner when he's not around. And he's usually not around . . ." She glanced about quickly before leaning in to whisper, "Word is, he's got a mistress half his age holed up in an apartment down the street."

Nok smiled and shook his head. "Listen to you. Talking like a real shopgirl."

"I *am* a real shopgirl!"

She did look the part, dressed in the Blue Peony's uniform: muted blue robes cut in the old Hana style to invoke a sense of nostalgic luxury. Silken slippers hugged her small feet, and from her ears hung dainty white pearls.

He poked at one, sending it jiggling. "These are new."

She yanked it off her lobe and held it up for his inspection. "Fake. See the clip? All of it's fake. But it looks very convincing, right?" She twirled. "Can barely tell it's not the real thing."

"I wouldn't know."

Adé laughed. "Good point. Me neither, I guess." She was always so cheerful; not an easy trait to retain after a childhood like hers. Nok still found it mystifying after all this time.

It was Adé who had helped Omair nurse Nok back from the dead, back when Omair had first taken him in. She'd been the old man's first apprentice. Once Nok had recovered, the two of them spent their days side by side, mashing herbs and beeswax into salves, until two years ago, when Adé's mother Lin Mak decided to move the family back to Yulan City.

"Where's Bo?" Adé pushed past him to peer out the window expectantly. She turned, horror dawning on her face. "Oh, heavens. He hasn't died, has he?"

Nok had to laugh. "No, he's still kicking. Literally. I stabled him at the Northern Gatehead this morning."

"So," Adé leaned in conspiratorially. "You must have heard the news."

He shook his head. "What news?" Outside of making Omair's purchases, he hadn't spoken to anyone.

"The emperor announced his successor today."

"Oh, that." He'd heard murmurs about the so-called Girl

King in the market, but he'd shut them out. Just the mention of the princess made him feel eleven years old again, even after all this time.

She'd been an aberration back then, drenched in scarlet, every hair in place, apparently oblivious to the desert heat. Even stripped of the jewels, the silks, she would have been unmistakable as royalty. That tall oaf Chundo had sneered she had a face like a sand fox; Nok had secretly thought if that were true, it wasn't such a bad thing.

Some traitorous part of him wondered what she might look like now.

Tall, probably, he thought, firmly putting an end to it.

"Makes no difference really who the emperor is," he heard himself say. "It's not like she's going to help people like us."

Adé's eyes widened in surprise. "Goodness, you haven't heard, have you?" She shook her head before he could respond. "The emperor didn't pick Princess Lu—he named her cousin. Lord *Set*."

The very name tore Nok from the present, and suddenly he was there again.

I'll kill you!

The girl's screams rent the still desert air. Her fists were flying, lashing the body beneath her again and again.

Mercy, mercy—

Back in the marketplace, Nok's scars began to throb.

"You know," Adé prodded, mistaking his silence for confusion. "Set, the Hana scion? The empress's nephew? Decorated general of the northern territories?"

"No—I," Nok said. His voice sounded weak. His father

would hate that. He cleared his throat. His father was dead. "No, I know. Just—surprised is all."

And how must the princess feel?

I'll kill you!

And she nearly had. For all the good it had done her, in the end.

"I think we were all surprised, but then, we've never had a woman emperor before, have we?" Adé sighed. "And now I suppose we never will. Not in our lifetimes."

She shrugged. "So, how long until you head back to Ansana? It's hot today. Let's go get some iced fruit—my treat!"

Nok looked around the crowded shop, regaining his bearings. "Are you not working? It looks like you're working."

She winked. "No worries. Mei will cover for me."

"Oh?" he said. "Does she know that?"

But Adé's mind was made up. "Mei, cover for me, would you?" she called out to the other shopgirl.

Mei's face soured. "I covered for you two weeks ago."

"I had to walk my brothers to school."

"That wasn't *my* problem."

"I'll take all of your Market Day hours next moon!" Adé pushed Nokhai toward the front door. "Come on. Go, go! Before she decides to rat on me. She *hates* me," she whispered confidentially.

"I can't imagine why," Nok said.

"Oh, who knows?" Adé sighed, letting the door slam closed behind them. "Some people are just awful."

༄༅༆

The crowd along Kangmun Boulevard had grown since Nok had run his errands; it moved like thick mud. Someone swore loudly at him to get out of the way. Nok jumped aside. An elderly woman hobbled by, pulling a wagon laden with knives that gleamed fiercely in the afternoon sun.

"Come on!" Adé seized his hand and lunged down the street. The noise and smells of Market Day always seemed to invigorate her as much as they exhausted Nok. "Come *on*," she repeated, tugging at his wrist like she meant to wrench it off.

"Cut it out," he complained, trying without success to shake his hand from her grasp. It wouldn't do to have someone see them hand in hand. People might talk. People always talked, even where there was nothing to say.

Adé wedged her way between the swollen belly of a free-roaming donkey and a cart of dusty yams. Nok had no choice but to follow.

"I'm not as tiny as you are!" he protested, jabbing the donkey with his elbow to avoid being crushed to death.

"Tiny!" she yelped. If she had more to say about it, though, he didn't hear. Her voice was drowned out by the mumbling drone of the crowd.

Nok caught up with her as she extricated a slippered foot from a dark, suspicious-looking puddle. "I should've changed out of my work clothes," she said forlornly. "If I get anything on this stupid dress the Ox will kill me. And if that happens, my mother *really* will kill me."

She sighed, shaking her foot. Foul-smelling muck splattered everywhere, leaving a sad gray stain on her shoe. "I'm supposed to see Carmine this evening, and Mama gets so worked up if I don't look perfect for him."

Carmine. So, Adé's Ellandaise suitor was still around, then. A sturdy, well-fed young man with pink skin, pale dun-colored hair, and an easy smile. Nice enough. His father was a merchant. Rich and well connected.

"How's Carmine doing?" Nok asked lightly.

"Good," Adé said, hesitant. "Actually, I wanted to talk to you about that. I—"

But Nok's attention was drawn away. A troop of soldiers had materialized up ahead, by the gate embedded in the wall of the Ring.

"Hey," Adé said, sticking Nok in the side with a sharp finger.

"Ow!" he snapped. "What is it?"

"About . . . you know, Carmine and all . . . ?"

"Clear the street! The gate is opening! Make way!" the urgent call came from somewhere ahead of them. Nok craned his head instinctively, searching for its source. The crowd was stirring, agitated—a beehive poked with a stick.

"Clear the street!" the call came again. *"Make way for the Ellandaise emissaries!"*

Nok couldn't see how it was possible, but the crowds seemed to intensify, as though a few hundred extra bodies had formed up out of the packed-earth streets.

"We should get off Kangmun Boulevard." Adé tugged anxiously at Nok's sleeve. "Is there an open turnoff anywhere? I can't see a damned thing—"

"Clear the street!" The call came again, now urgent, and close.

Nok spotted an opening beside a cart of persimmons. "There! We can—" Nok turned, but Adé had disappeared.

"Clear the street!" The crier was so close now it felt as if he were shouting straight in Nok's ears.

"Adé?" he called.

The faint cry of her voice came from somewhere far off to his left. He looked frantically in the direction of the call, but a heavyset man slid behind him blocking his view.

"Nok!"

He whirled again, but didn't see her.

"Adé!" Nok scanned the slowly thinning crowd for her face, but she had disappeared. Cursing, he ducked into the nearest alley. It was blissfully empty.

The crowd was beginning to stream southward, toward the harbor. If he ran, he might be able to outpace them using the city's alleyways, then scan the passing crowd for Adé. If she hadn't been crushed.

No. Adé would be fine, he told himself. She'd grown up on these streets, knew her way around far better than he did. He would find her again—so long as he didn't lose himself in the alleyways, which wound tight and numerous as capillaries around the artery of Kangmun Boulevard.

He headed in what he hoped was a vaguely southward direction.

"Mercy, young man . . . mercy." A beggar woman rattled a bowl of coins at him as he wended his way through a particularly narrow alley. Just a pair of skinny, leathered hands and ankles poking out of a pile of filthy rags; an unremarkable

THE GIRL KING   37

sight. Nok nearly ran on, until he glimpsed the face beneath her ragged cowl.

Dozens of dull blue dots formed trails of ink just beneath the skin of her cheekbones and down her chin—the unmistakable facial tattoos of a northern mountain temple shamaness.

He did not recognize her particular designs, but then, the mountains had once been full of unaffiliated lesser temples—usually practicing some unsanctioned amalgamation of Hana Mul rites, Yunian traditions, and local customs.

"Mercy," the shamaness repeated. She shook her bowl at him again hopefully; the coins inside clinking coldly against one another.

In spite of himself, Nok felt a stab of pity. How a mountain shamaness had come to the crooked alleys of Scrap-Patch Row, he could not fathom, but then, how he had gotten there defied belief as well.

He reached into his tunic and pulled two coins from the pouch strapped to his chest.

"Here," he said roughly, dropping the coins in the shamaness's bowl. She peered up at him gratefully. She was younger than he would've guessed, no more than forty. When their eyes met, her ingratiating smile vanished, and she drew back with a *hiss* of surprise. Before he could react, she reached out and snatched his wrist up in a surprisingly strong, gnarled hand.

"*Slipskin?*" she whispered.

Nok's heart dropped to the pit of his stomach. He'd been found.

CHAPTER 3

Duty

*L*u scarcely registered her father dismissing the court. She only knew that she had found herself in Kangmun Hall, the doors closed at her back, and her family and their respective attendants gone. The emperor hadn't so much as looked at her—just allowed himself to be swept away in a deluge of eunuchs and chattering inner court officials. Lu had watched him go, feeling as though she were looking at a stranger.

Someone cleared their throat. Lu looked up. Her dozen nunas stared at her with anxiety and embarrassment in their eyes. Hyacinth came to her side and gave her hand a squeeze, but Lu shook herself free. If she gave in to that bit of sympathy, that suggestion of softness, she would unravel completely.

"What are we waiting for?" she said, forcing a smile like baring her teeth. She turned in the direction of the Hall of the

Ancestors. "I still have my Analecta lessons, don't I? Let's not keep Shin Mung waiting."

In front of the double doors of the hall, twelve women draped in burnt-orange robes waited in two orderly lines. Ammas.

Lu stopped short. She knew who she would find inside, and it was not Shin Mung.

She could leave. Lead her nunas back to her own apartments, where—where what, exactly? She would bar the doors and crawl into bed? Weep and moan and tear out her hair, turn away food until the unlikely day her father changed his mind? Unthinkable. Some other girl in her position—Minyi, perhaps—might lower herself to that. But not Lu. She did not run, and she did not cry. If conflict came at Lu, she would rush to meet it.

She squared her shoulders and walked into the hall, nodding at the ammas in respect as she passed. Her nunas followed closely behind.

The empress was waiting for her at the far end of the hall's long, incense-clouded colonnade, gazing up at the ancestral portrait of Emperor Kangmun. Her head was cocked thoughtfully, as though she had never seen it before. She still wore the full ceremonial regalia from court, drenched in layers of floor-length muted-vermilion silk. The trim was embroidered with flowered vines that clambered up her bodice and high-necked collar. They looked like they were reaching up to choke her.

Lu cleared her throat. The sound echoed down the hall. Her mother did not tear her gaze away from the portrait. "Is that how you greet your empress? I know you were raised better than that. I saw to it."

"Where's Shin Mung?" Lu demanded.

Her mother finally turned, with a rattle of swaying jewelry and a disdainful purse of her painted lips. "Elsewhere. He had important matters to attend to," she said. The implication was clear enough: *Your lessons* aren't *important. Especially now.*

Lu smelled the bait, bloody and rancid and *old*. She wouldn't bite.

"Were these theatrics really necessary?" she asked instead. "Tricking me into seeing you?"

"It hardly seemed worth the effort, true. But I sent for you several times this past week, only to be told you were nowhere to be found. You're a difficult person to track down."

"Well, you found me. What do you want?"

Her mother raised one perfectly sculpted eyebrow. "To begin with, I want you to address me with respect."

"I'm sorry," Lu said. "What do you want, Your *Highness*?"

Cold fury flashed in her mother's eyes, but only for half a breath. When she turned her gaze toward Lu's nunas, it was placid and cordial. "Girls, go wait outside with the ammas. We won't be long."

Halting movement rippled through the handmaidens, as though the empress's words were a physical force prodding them to action. They glanced nervously at one another, then looked to Hyacinth. Hyacinth was looking at Lu, still and implacable as the figures of the ancestral portraits surrounding them. She'd been the only one not to respond to the empress's command. Lu loved her for it.

"Stay," Lu told them. It was stupid—a childish act of rebellion. But while she may have lost her father's love and the throne in one fell hour, Lu was still a princess. And a princess alone directed her own nunas.

She opened her mouth to say as much, but her mother spoke first, in clipped, irritated tones. "After the day you've had, do you really want to give them more fodder for gossip?"

Lu's jaw clenched. "They would never gossip about my affairs. I trust my nunas."

"That's touching, but I would rather not suffer for your lack of judgment," her mother replied. "And I do not have the day to sit about entertaining your misplaced loyalty."

"So go, then," Lu snapped. "I wasn't the one who ambushed you."

"Don't be dramatic. I mean to speak with you now, woman to woman. Though I wonder if it will come to anything. Time and again, you insist on playing the child."

Lu crossed, then uncrossed her arms. No one could agitate her like their mother. She wasn't certain if the reverse was true—her mother was easily agitated by so many things—but it often felt that way. At any rate, it was only a matter of time before one of them said something truly ugly. Perhaps it was better her nunas weren't around to witness that.

Lu glanced at Hyacinth and jerked her head toward the door. Her friend nodded once and directed the others back outside.

Once they were gone, her mother slipped a pale, elegant hand from one sleeve and beckoned Lu closer. "Come here. I won't have this conversation yelling across the hall at you."

Lu huffed, reluctantly closing the distance between them. Her mother's citrus perfume and musky powders cut through the hall's permanent fog of incense, and the combination turned her stomach.

"What do you want to speak of?" she asked.

"As your mother, it's my duty to guide you through the journey you're about to take." The trill of triumph in the empress's voice was unmistakable. It was as though she herself had been named heir to the empire.

For her mother, this was likely as close to power as she could ever hope to get: Set, her blood, her beloved nephew, her proxy on the throne. *Pathetic*, Lu thought. Until she remembered that the same was now true for her.

The empress continued: "The Betrothal Ceremony, your wedding, and all the duties you will have as the wife of the emperor, the mother of his children—the court will expect you to execute all of them seamlessly, as though it were in your very nature. But in truth, there is nothing natural about it; only hard work, planning, and practice will allow you to succeed."

Lu did her best to ignore the idea of bearing Set's children. "Is that all?" she sniffed. "Since it seems my lesson with Shin Mung has been canceled, there are other matters I'd like to attend to."

Her mother's eyes narrowed. "If you're thinking of running to your father to wheedle an appeal to his decision, I wouldn't bother. He indulged you—indulges you—far too much. It's made you ignorant to the ways of the world. Do you think his choice of an heir was all his own to make? Do you truly believe all it takes to rule an empire as vast as ours is one man with a blessing handed down from the heavens? Not even you could be so simpleminded, surely."

Her mother had never been kind to her, but she had never before been quite so openly cruel. Or so open at all. While she henpecked Min in a way that could almost be described as doting, her disapproval of Lu was largely one of silence, discernible through absence rather than action: the lack of touch, the emptiness in her gaze, the indifference to her joys and triumphs. Min was their mother's project, while Lu was their father's. No one ever said as much, but it had been the unspoken rule of their family.

"What do you know of me?" Lu demanded, the words lashing out of her. "You know nothing of what I am capable. How could you? You've never paid me any mind."

"I know more than you think," the empress said. Her eyes drifted toward the door, where a moment ago Lu's nunas had exited. "I have eyes and ears everywhere, child. They tell me everything. And I know far more than you."

A sour jolt of betrayal lanced through Lu's gut. It was known the empress had spies embedded in each department of the court staff, but it had never occurred to Lu that any of her own handmaidens might be among them.

Stupid, she told herself quickly. *She's lying.* Lu had no reason to suspect disloyalty among her nunas—and yet, like a poison, the idea spread hot through her veins. Uncertainty, once felt, could not be unfelt. Her mother was trying to throw her off balance. Lu saw it, but that didn't make the doubt any less acute.

Her mother sighed. "I suppose there's no harm in telling

you now that your father did speak for you, against his advisers. But," her mother shrugged, "he is easily swayed, easily shamed. He has no resolve. But he did have faith in you, even if it was misplaced." And then, with just a trace of bitterness: "He loves you."

"Love?" Lu spat. "He humiliated me. In front of the entire court! The entire city!"

"Yes, well, that is one thing at which he excels: humiliating others. You've learned that lesson today, and now it is time for you to learn another. This is the end of your childish aspirations. It is time to put away fantasy and focus on the life you have."

Lu barked out a laugh. "You're enjoying this. You love tearing me down, you always have. You never wanted me to succeed."

The empress sighed again. "Don't flatter yourself, child. This has nothing to do with you. I'm merely satisfied to see the empire set down the right path. That is what matters. Not your vanity, nor your hopes, nor your happiness."

"So, I should settle to be miserable and powerless, like you?"

For a moment, Lu thought the empress was going to hit her. Absurdly, she felt a sudden prickle of fear. They had come a breath away from blows before, but their mother always stayed her hand, as though she knew Lu wouldn't hesitate to strike back. Or, more likely, her father's favor had protected Lu like a shield. The fury with which her mother beheld her now, though, looked set to tear through it.

Instead, her mother stiffened, then folded her arms carefully across her chest. "Listen to me, girl: you will never rule. Men may derive some amusement from a spirited girl, but they will not tolerate a willful woman, let alone deign to be ruled by one. You were never destined for anything greater than what you have—far less, truly. You can bend to that reality, or you can be broken by it. I won't waste my time with you further. Come see me when you're ready to learn your place."

She strode across the hall, the clack of her high pot-bottomed shoes methodical against the floor. At the doorway she paused to call back:

"Do you know, when you were born, I came here and lit a candle before each ancestral portrait, from your late uncles to Kangmun. To thank them you were a girl."

Lu stared at her, met those glacial gray eyes in confusion. Her mother regarded her unblinking. "Had you been born a boy, you would have been so much harder to crush."

The doors swung shut hard behind her. At their close, Lu sank to her knees, suddenly exhausted. As though her mother had wound all the energy in Lu's body around her wrist like a ribbon, dragging it behind her as she left.

She cast her eyes upward, to Emperor Kangmun's portrait. Her great-grandfather's painted face gazed back down, ferocious and square jawed and unyielding, wreathed by a backdrop of stars and fire, a tiger pelt hanging from his shoulders.

"Help me," she whispered. No answer came but for the frantic thumping of her own heart.

Kangmun's effects were displayed beneath the portrait in a glass case: a slender sword in a beautiful scabbard of onyx, gold, and emerald, and close beside it, like two lovers lying side by side, a rather more crudely hewn blade of iron—his first sword, from his days as a slipskin king. A marriage of his two identities. Beside the two weapons were arrayed a handful of rings and seals, a scrap of paper that bore his calligraphy, and a lock of hair bound with gold thread.

Next to the case, on a dress form, hung a set of his emperor's robes, the dye of Hu imperial scarlet still clinging to their age-embrittled silk. Lu fixed her gaze upon them; judging from their cut, Kangmun had been a large man. Broader and taller than her father, even.

Infuriatingly, Lu felt her eyes well up at the sight of those robes. At the legacy and the honor they bespoke. She blinked the tears back fiercely. She had been so *close*. What had turned the tide against her?

She could not say how long she stayed there on her knees. Her mother was right. There was no taking back her father's decision, not when he had announced it before the whole empire. This was her life now. She would walk through the same unhappy motions of marriage, of childbirth, of managing palace staff and the small manipulations of gossip and whispers, like a hundred generations of women before her, starting with the Betrothal Ceremony, where again she would be paraded and humiliated in front of the entire court, and—

The Betrothal Ceremony.

Lu looked up sharply, eyes falling upon the broad, ghostly form of Emperor Kangmun's robes and tiger pelt. And an idea took root. A stupid, rash, *childish* idea. One that might just work.

Her mother's voice echoed in her mind: *You can bend to that reality, or you can be broken by it.*

Let them try to break her, then.

CHAPTER 4

Slipskin

*S*lipskin."

Nok's throat was closing up.

The shamaness studied him with bright, eager eyes. "Yes," she murmured. "Yes. And Ashina at that. The blue wolves. A strong people. But what you have . . . I never felt *that* in any of you before . . ."

His free hand dropped the morning's purchases and shot to his chest, as though to push away the massive weight crushing him—but of course, his hand grasped at nothing but his tunic.

I'll kill you!

The girl's voice cried out again. It was only in his head, he knew, and yet he could *hear* it, surer than the blood thundering in his ears.

The beggar woman's hand tightened around his wrist, her nails digging painful little crescents into the flesh, bringing him back to the present.

His breath came back to him with a gasp. "Let go!"

She released him. He stumbled back, and for a taut moment the intimacy of his secret reared between them, terrible and unexpected, like a trod-upon snake. Nok stooped and retrieved his bag, never taking his eyes off her.

He ran.

"Your secret is safe with me, little pup!" The woman's voice rattled after him. Her laugh was rough and sad. As he turned the corner, he heard her add: "We're both a long way from home, aren't we?"

Nok couldn't say for how long he ran, but he finally stopped in a narrow alley with his heart pounding like it was set to kill him. The alley let out down into the harbor; he could see the Milk River, hear dock workers shouting at one another, tossing crates of cargo.

I'll kill you!

He whipped a glance over his shoulder. The alley was empty—of course it was. He mashed a hand against his eyes. What was he expecting? The shamaness? Soldiers wielding steel? The whole imperial army at his heels?

Get ahold of yourself.

The only danger was his own fear, his own memories. And he knew how to control those.

"Nok!"

He jumped, but it was only Adé. She was smiling and waving, but as she neared the cheer drained from her face. "Are you all right?" she asked. "You look as though you've seen a ghost."

Her words almost made him laugh. He stumbled instead.

Adé leaped forward and caught his elbow. "Do you need to eat something? I bought an apple—"

"I'm all right," Nok managed to wheeze. "I'll be fine," he told her. "Just got a bit dizzy."

He threw up. Water yellowed with bile splattered the ground.

"Oh gods," Adé cursed. "All right, definitely no food then. Sit."

She led him toward a stack of packing crates. A trio of dingy chickens pecked at the dirt before them. Adé shooed them away, and Nok collapsed onto the crates gratefully, dropping his head into his hands. The scars on his palms and face were aching as they hadn't done in years, the pain quick and lancing and panicky. It was as though with a croaked word, the shamaness had released some sickness that had lain dormant in his bones.

"Nok?" Adé's voice sounded distant. She dropped down beside him.

His heart was hammering so loudly. Surely Adé could hear it. Surely the whole city could hear its pounding, screaming out who he was. *What* he was.

She rubbed his back, murmuring comfortingly in his ear, but he could not understand the words; the dissonance, the confusion of them made his stomach roil. He focused on trying to breathe.

"Dunno what's wrong with me," he muttered finally. "Guess I just got overheated."

Adé's brow furrowed. "Drink some water, then."

Nok fumbled for the bladder he kept slung over one shoulder and drained a few weak drops onto his tongue before offering it to her.

"You need to drink more than that," she told him matter-of-factly. "Finish it."

"Oh, what are you now? A healer?" he teased weakly. "Some sort of apothecarist's assistant?" She stuck out her tongue but watched him carefully to make certain he took another swig. The water in his mouth felt foreign and metallic and wrong. He forced himself to swallow.

He set down the bladder. Adé was staring off toward the harbor, where docked boats were bobbing lazily on the murky salt river. It was one of the rare things Nok had seen that made her sad: sailors and ships.

Her father, Tesfa Mak, had been a foreign mapmaker and navigator from the Western Empire, where the people dressed in silks of blazing white and deepest indigo, taking refuge from the heat in blanched palaces of marble, drinking iced nectar.

But now Tesfa was dead, along with Nok's parents, gone wherever it was dead parents went.

Adé seemed to sense his gaze and turned back with dark, nervous eyes. They held his for a moment, then dropped. It wasn't just melancholy for her father, Nok realized. Something else was on her mind. "Listen, Nok," she said, reaching out a tentative hand. "I was trying to tell you earlier . . . ," she trailed off.

"Yes?"

"Carmine's father is throwing us an engagement party next moon," she blurted. "It would be nice if you could come."

"A party . . . ?" He paused, shook his head. "Wait, did you say 'engagement'?"

She nodded.

"Con-congratulations," he said. His voice was still weak and hoarse, and it made him sound less than enthusiastic. He cleared his throat. "Congratulations."

"So, will you come, then?" she asked with a hopeful smile. "To the party?"

Nok wrinkled his nose. "In the Ellandaise sector? They'll kick me out before I got two steps in."

Adé laughed. "No, they won't. Just tell them you're looking for the Anglimn residence—they'll know where it is."

"Why do you want me to come?"

"It's going to be full of strangers, and rich pink people, and—"

"Perfect for me," he quipped. She poked him in the side.

"*And*," she pressed on, "it would be nice if I had a friend there."

"You have other friends."

"Not," she said, "like you."

A trio of Ring girls traipsed into the alley, a flurry of arms joined at the elbows and excited chatter. Nok and Adé stood to give them room to pass. As they did, one of them flitted a glance toward Nok, then whispered something to her friends. The three of them dissolved into giggles before hurrying away toward the harbor.

"What are they looking at?" Nok frowned. People his age were always *laughing*. It made him nervous.

"They're looking at you, dummy," Adé told him, crossing to the opposite wall of the alley, facing him.

"Why would they look at me?" he asked stupidly.

"They . . . well, you know . . ."

Nok looked at her, uncomprehending.

"They like what they see," she said, exasperated.

The color rose in his cheeks, uninvited and most unwelcome. Reflexively, he made to rub his scarred palms together, but he forced them back down. "They wouldn't look if they knew what I was really like," he muttered, looking at the ground.

"True," Adé retorted. She produced an apple from the folds of her robe and flung it at his chest, giggling as he scrabbled to catch it. "I can barely stand you myself."

He rolled his eyes, lobbing the apple back to her. "It's so charitable of you to leave your job in the middle of the day to spend time with me, then."

"I," she said loftily, "am the picture of charity." Then she threw the apple to him in an underhanded arc high in the air. Her aim was poor; Nok was forced to lunge forward to catch it, nearly colliding with her. Instinctively, he reached a hand forward to brace her around the middle with one hand as the apple fell neatly into the other. He caught the scent of vanilla and cedar in her hair as he pulled away.

"Sorry," he mumbled, releasing her waist and making to hand the apple back over. As he placed it in her palm, though, she closed her other hand over his, pulling him even closer.

"I'm not," she said. And when he looked up she kissed him.

It was soft and dry. Chaste, as far as kisses went. At least, Nok assumed it was. He didn't know much about kisses; this was his first. He wondered for a fleeting moment if he should kiss her back. What trouble it would mean if he did. A part of him wanted to, regardless.

He pulled away. As he did so, the apple slipped from their

hands and rolled down the street, coming to a rest in a wagon rut. Nok watched it go, guilt over the wasted food rising in him. Adé was still looking at him.

Someone else with Adé's past, someone who had once been so intimate with starvation that it was like a sister, a lover, might never be so careless with food. But that was how Adé had always been, he knew. Even in the throes of her family's troubles, even staring death in its gaunt, hungry face, she'd been distracted, looking expectantly for some brighter future that was inevitably around the next corner with those eager brown eyes. Not like him.

"You're angry," she said. It sounded like she was chewing her lip; he couldn't look at her to say for certain.

His hand was still in hers, a holdfast. For a dumb, animal moment, he felt a jolt of pleasure at the warm contact. When had he last been touched without violent intent? With gentleness and love? It had only been Omair, tending his wounds four years ago, and Adé—always Adé. She'd been holding his hand when he awoke that first morning in Omair's home, so far from the desert, and all he'd known.

A dozen sense memories surged to the surface of their stagnant pool: his mother's fingertip against his forehead, stroking a loose hank of hair back into place; his cousin Idri playfully scooping him and his sister into a bear hug as they squealed in protest. His little sister Nasan, toddling at his side when she was small, then running across the barren red flats together when her legs shot up and sprawled nearly as long and lanky as his own.

You could have that, and more. The thought whispered through him like a dry wind, and he knew with certainty that at his word, Adé would leave Carmine. *You could court her, marry her, have a family again,* the voice in his head insisted. And he could see it, feel it all, the knowledge of a hundred moments elapsed into one: Adé at his side shopping in the market for a supper they will share, Adé reaching a small hand up to cup his face and kiss him, Adé holding him close at night . . .

Adé knowing his secrets.

What would she think if she knew what he really was? Would she still want to kiss him? She was the best person he knew—and yet, he couldn't say for certain. He'd seen too much evil to trust the immutability of good in anyone.

I would only put her in danger, anyway.

He shook his hand free.

"Carmine is a good match for you," he said.

"I know," she nodded vigorously. "I know that. And I—he's a good person. He's kind to me, and he makes me laugh. I don't mean to . . . I just always thought that you and I would be, you know, when we were kids. I couldn't live with myself if I didn't at least ask." She paused, frowning. "Did you ever—?"

"No," he said, cutting her short. "I don't think about the future."

"Oh."

Nok rubbed his palms together.

Adé brushed one slippered foot over the other. "Does this mean you won't come to my engagement party?"

"I'll think on it," he said. He stepped away, not meeting her eyes. "I should get going."

Adé frowned. "Back to Ansana already?"

"Omair needs me," he told her lightly. "I've lingered long enough as it is."

"Do you want me to walk you to the Northern Gatehead at least?" Adé asked hopefully.

"No, it's all right," he said, forcing a tight smile. "I know the way."

He left quickly, before there could be any other objections. If she watched him go, he did not turn around to see.

CHAPTER 5

The Small Princess

*T*he unknown woman reached toward Minyi, tender as a mother.

She could not see her face, but Min felt she recognized her nevertheless. Deeply, down to her bones. She closed her eyes in the warmth of the stranger's arms. The woman's white silks were soft against her fingers. She smelled clean, like spring winds—but beneath it, Min sensed something unsettling. Sulfur and burning, like a candle that had just been snuffed out.

When she looked up, the woman's face was a chasm of writhing light and fire, horrible to behold.

Cold fear seized her, but the sensation quickened into an unbearable heat. The woman's robes turned to living flames, scorching Min's arms and neck and setting her hair ablaze. She opened her mouth to cry out and the stranger bent over her, sucking the scream out of her with a cruel, searing kiss—

Min awoke with a start violent enough to chase the

nightmare away. Even as she blinked the sleep from her eyes, it seemed to fly from her grasp like a pale gray bird, leaving only a lingering trace of dread.

She shivered, feeling both cold and hot.

Not today. I can't be ill today of all days. Their mother would be livid if she missed her sister's Betrothal Ceremony. Min sat up.

And felt a hot surge between her thighs.

She cried out at the sensation, already deadening into a cold, heavy wetness.

Across the room, Butterfly sat up. "Are you all right, Princess?" she asked drowsily. Beside her, Snowdrop's small feet poked out from beneath the sheets; she smacked her lips in her sleep but did not rouse.

Min just shook her head wordlessly and stumbled out of bed, grabbing at the silken hem of her nightgown.

Butterfly was up in an instant, kicking Snowdrop in her haste to assist Min.

"Princess, what's the matter? Are you hurt?"

Min slapped the nuna's hands away and hiked up her hem to her waist.

A bright scarlet spot was staining its way through her under wrappings.

Red. So red.

She thought of the first flame, no doubt crackling away in the courtyard at that very moment. In her mind's eye she saw a flash of white silk burst into flame. She blinked; where had she seen that before?

But the thought vanished as her body gave another involuntary contraction and yet more blood spilled forth.

She screamed.

Amma Ruxin rushed into the room, followed by the rest of her nunas.

"What's happened?" demanded the amma.

"It's all right. She has her first blood." It was Butterfly who answered. Who understood, even before Min herself.

Relief flooded Min's body, quickly chased by hot, diffuse embarrassment. She wasn't dying—only stupid.

Amma Ruxin was clucking at the nunas to refill Min's tub and fetch clean undergarments. "Hurry," the older woman snapped.

They did their best to tidy Min—scrubbing her thighs raw in the bath, then swathing her up in clean, lightly perfumed white wrappings, as though her body were a wound. Even when they'd finished, she felt ill.

Of all days to let this happen, she thought miserably, tears welling up in her eyes. Bad enough that she should embarrass herself looking a sweaty, repulsive mess in front of the whole assembled court, let alone in front of her cousin Set and his Hana entourage, too.

"It's all right, Small Princess," said Amma Ruxin, laying a firm hand upon her shoulder. "No tears," she added, wiping at Min's face with a handkerchief produced from deep inside the sleeves of her robes. "You're a woman now."

⚜

The empress was having her long black hair styled for the Betrothal Ceremony when Min shuffled into her quarters. Her mother's ammas flitted about her like hummingbirds around a trumpet flower. She was a beautiful woman: tall and graceful, with a stately elegance wrought through good breeding and years of practice. Today she looked especially striking in robes of deep cerulean embroidered with gold thread, and makeup that accentuated her high cheekbones, full lips, and gray Hana eyes.

Min curtsied as best she could in her stiff new robes.

"Mother," she said.

The empress cocked her head slightly to one side—no easy feat given the weight of her hair, dripping with jeweled pins and topped with a gold diadem. There was apprehension in her face—disappointment perhaps? *Is it the robes?* Min fretted, feeling the cold prickle of panic. *It's not fair. She's the one who picked the lilac . . .*

Min herself had favored a bolt of malachite green silk, but the empress had quickly dismissed it, reminding Min of how badly dark colors washed out her already pale face.

Her mother was correct, of course. Min *did* have a pale face—soft and round and bland as an uncooked dumpling. Her sister Lu could wear bold colors to striking effect, the jeweled tones intensifying her sharp, lively eyes and quick grin. But then, it seemed Lu could do anything she wanted.

Except be emperor, a little singsong voice inside Min whispered. Her gut clenched at the cruelty in it. Where had that thought come from?

Her mother held out a hand. "Come here, my sweet." When Min stepped forward, the empress enveloped her in a brief, perfumed embrace. The sharp smell of mandarin blossoms lingered in the air, and Min breathed in deeply to savor it.

"Amma Ruxin tells me you are a woman now," said the empress. She cocked her head, and the faint lilt of a smile strained her lips. Her face went soft like love. Just for a moment. "You look pretty. All grown up."

In spite of herself, Min felt a bloom of pleasure and relief in her chest. She indulged it for a cautious moment before forcing it back down. The empress was in a good mood this morning.

Her mother turned back to her mirrors. She frowned slightly at her reflection, touching a loose loop of hair. "This is out of place," she informed Amma Inga, a reedy woman whose head reminded Min of a lumpy turnip.

The empress cast a sidelong look toward Min as Inga sorted out her hair. "The robes will do. But I daresay you've grown since we had them cut—outward, if not upward. A hazard for anyone at your age, I suppose."

The relief she'd felt earlier flinched and contracted behind her breastbone. "Yes, Mother," Min agreed.

"You should take care to eat less, but don't worry about it too much," her mother continued, carefully watching the ammas work in the reflection of her mirrors. "When I was your age I tended toward stoutness myself; it is only a phase. And it means you will be plump in the correct places when you're a bit older."

"Yes, Mother."

Min secretly wondered if there could be any truth to the empress's words. All her life she had been told she would be beautiful one day—one day, one day—and all her life it had never happened.

"And for the time being, at least you have our Hana

eyes—no, *no!*" The empress broke off to scold Amma Inga, yanking the hank of hair from the frightened woman's hands. "This is atrocious. Ailin, come here and fix this savagery . . ."

Min bit back a sigh, sitting at her mother's dressing table as the ammas hurried forth to tend to the empress. There was a large polished mahogany box atop the vanity, gaping open to reveal a bounty of jeweled hairpins.

Min selected one and turned it over in her hands. The pin was yellow gold, adorned on one end with a fist-sized lily of mother-of-pearl.

She looked up and her face gazed back from the mirror. It was true she had the famed gray eyes of the old Hana Family Li—her own vague like vapor, while her mother's were bright and unyielding as wet stone. Apart from that, Min looked every bit like their father: the same round cheeks and anemic complexion. The full, downturned lips that should have been attractive but somehow lent her an anxious, dour air.

Not for the first time, Min wondered if her mother so emphasized her Hana eyes because she wished Min looked more like her—as though calling attention to that token similarity could eclipse the chasm of difference between them. Or perhaps it was simply that her eyes were the only feature pretty enough to comment on.

It was small comfort that Lu had not inherited their mother's particular beauty, either—she little resembled either of their parents. Instead, she was often described as their first uncle Hwangmun returned from the heavens in the body of a girl.

Hwangmun had been killed in a rock slide while on a tour of the northern front, along with their second uncle Hyomun, shortly before either Lu or Min were born. But Min had seen the uncanny likeness to her sister in Hwangmun's gilded portrait in the Hall of the Ancestors. The close resemblance was considered auspicious—their uncle had been a man of legendary grace and intelligence. Min couldn't think of anybody more graceful or intelligent than her sister.

Hwangmun had also been—rather unfairly, Min thought—very comely. So Lu possessed not only Hwangmun's caliber of character but also his lively copper-flecked eyes, canny face, and elegant build.

"*Min!*"

She sat up with such a start she nearly stabbed herself through the palm with the hairpin in her hands.

"Rise at once! What are you thinking, sitting in that gown?" Her mother gestured angrily toward her ammas. "Idiots! All of you! Allowing her to crush silk like that."

The ammas bobbed in staggered supplication, like flowers in a strong wind. "Your servant deserves death, Empress," they recited in apology.

"I am unworthy of your forgiveness, Mother," Min mumbled. She knew her lines, too.

The empress closed her eyes tightly as though the light were hurting them. A slight line materialized between her brows—the one mark of age upon her otherwise firm face.

"Min," her mother said softly. "You are a *woman* now. Do you understand what that means?" Before Min could respond, she continued. "You must act in accordance with your duties, and recognize and perceive those duties as they arise, without needing to be told what is expected of you. Do you understand?"

"Yes, Mother," Min said miserably. *Stupid,* she cursed herself. She'd gone and spoiled the empress's mood. Tears burned her eyes. But truly, what had she done? It wasn't her fault; she'd just wanted to sit.

It's not fair, another voice hissed, and with it came a flare of anger so strong Min jerked with it.

"Stand over there," her mother waved a hand at her, turning back to her mirror. "We can go to Kangmun Hall together once my hair is done." She frowned as one of the ammas stabbed a braid in place with a silver and jade pin.

"No, not that one, Wei. Bring the mother-of-pearl lily. That one is from my girlhood and bears craftsmanship local to the Family Li region. The Hana retinue will recognize it, no doubt . . ."

Wei went to the dressing table, breezing past Min as though she did not even exist. The amma rooted around gingerly in the pin box. "Empress," she said with some hesitation. "I do not see it here."

"Then look harder," her mother commanded, her voice taking on a sharp edge.

But again Wei came up empty-handed. "It is not here, my lady." She turned to the other ammas. "Have any of you seen it today?"

The other women shook their heads and Wei returned to the box, digging through it with renewed concern.

Min looked down at her hands and realized with a jolt she was holding the exact pin Wei sought. She opened her mouth to speak, but nothing came out. Instead, as though her feet belonged to someone else, she drifted over to a richly upholstered chair in the corner. As the ammas gathered around the vanity in concern, Min bent slightly and stabbed the missing pin through the plush underbelly of the chair.

"Forget it for now. We are late," her mother snapped finally. "Bring me the gold pin with the pink jade drops. But find the other later—it is my favorite."

Min glanced about; no one was even looking her way. She felt the pressure in her chest ease.

⚬

Lu was late.

The ceremony was set to begin, and all the guests in place, but for the bride-to-be. Min cast about for her sister anxiously but still found her missing. Had something happened? It wasn't like Lu to be late.

Min's legs trembled with the strain of her blood cramps and high ceramic shoes. She hugged herself about the middle help-lessly. She felt sore and emptied out. Surely by now she must be bleeding through her wrappings. She imagined a red stain spreading across the backside of her robes; at any moment someone would point it out in disgust and horror. She felt almost too feverish to care.

It was too *hot* to care. Even beneath the red silk canopy hanging over the dais, the midday light was punishingly strong.

Perhaps if I stand still enough, the sun won't notice me, she thought. Her knees buckled in response, as though her own body were chiding her for her foolishness. Butterfly broke from the ranks of nunas stationed behind her and took Min by the elbow until she regained her balance.

"Will you be all right?" the nuna asked softly.

Min flicked a nervous glance toward her mother, but her mother was looking for Lu—still conspicuously absent. The empress's normally full mouth set in an angry red line as she glared at the second, higher dais before them, as though trying to force Lu to appear, draped in modest black and gray betrothal silks, by sheer will alone.

Min had always thought the symbolism of the Betrothal Ceremony beautiful: the bride-to-be swathed in dull robes of gray and black, embodying the cold, unawakened state of unused tinder; the plain white dais upon which she was presented forth to her husband-to-be representing the transitional space she occupied, no longer belonging to the family she had left behind her, nor yet to the man come to claim her. The woman had to mount the dais alone and of her own accord—no family, friends, or servants could assist or even touch her. Once upon it, she belonged to the heavens alone.

And then—most beautiful of all, Min thought—came the moment when the groom-to-be mounted the dais with her. There, he would remove the betrothal robes to unveil the covenant gown beneath: deep, warm gold, like a new flame, to represent the heart that has begun to kindle. On the day of the wedding, she would come to him in the same gown, only now with a cape of brilliant scarlet—a fire stoked and burning and beautiful for him alone.

The line of servants behind them parted, interrupting Min's thoughts. A eunuch bowed low beside her father. Min heard him murmur to the emperor, "The ammas checked her apartments. There is no sign of the Princess Lu or her nunas."

"Tell them to look harder," snapped the empress, shooting

the hapless man a furious sidelong glare. Then, after a moment, "Check the abandoned shamaness temple."

Min blinked in surprise at that—no one ever went into the old shamaness temple, except perhaps the odd page boy on a dare. But, she supposed, that would make it an excellent place to hide.

"We have people searching everywhere," the attendant assured the empress.

Her mother huffed. "I swear to the heavens if the girl's run off, I'll flog her myself—"

"She won't have run off," her father interrupted, looking thoughtful. "What she could possibly be doing, though, I wonder."

At that moment, a ripple went through the crowd, beginning in the far west corner of the courtyard. Min craned her neck to see the cause of the commotion, for once grateful of her high-bottomed shoes. A group of monks was emerging from the Hall of the Ancestors. Only the monks wore robes of gray and white, and these figures were dressed in the warm orange silks of nunas . . .

"The princess!" Snowdrop squealed from behind her. The little nuna had all but clambered onto Butterfly's shoulders to afford herself a view.

Min looked to the front of the party and saw her sister, tall and magnificent in a new robe of scarlet silk. Not her betrothal robes.

"What does she think she is doing?" her empress-mother seethed between clenched teeth. "Daagmun, stop her. Stop this at once—Amma Ruxin . . . someone find Ruxin! Heavens above, what is she *wearing*?"

Min squinted toward where her sister was making her way—slowly, deliberately—toward the dais of betrothal. Her sister had many clothes of red silk, which favored her ink-black hair and copper-flecked eyes in addition to celebrating their Hu heritage, but Min had never seen her wearing these robes before. They were, she thought, rather ill-fitting—far too big, almost as though they had been cut for a full-grown man—and the silk ran thin and nearly threadbare at the elbows. Nevertheless, there was something familiar about them . . .

"The robes of Emperor Kangmun," her father murmured softly. "She must have taken them from the Hall of the Ancestors."

"Heavens have mercy," Butterfly whispered behind her.

"You," the empress hissed, pointing at a pair of her ammas. "Fetch the princess. Escort her back to her apartments and change her into the betrothal robes. Have the guards drag her if you must—"

Min didn't dare laugh—not in a situation of this gravity, not with her mother in such a state—but she nearly did anyway. They should have known her sister would not take her fate lying down. "It's too late," she heard herself say.

"What?" Her mother whirled on her, but Min pointed to where her sister was mounting the white betrothal dais. Lu's nunas knelt reverently against the stone floor of the Heart in two neat rows as the princess made her ascent.

Her fathered chuckled then, unexpectedly. "The little one is correct. Lu belongs to the heavens alone now. We must see what she does."

Her sister raised an imperious hand and the chatter in the courtyard evaporated. The only remaining sound was the omnipresent crackle of the First Flame.

"Open the gates. Let me look upon my suitor."

Princess Lu's voice rang out loud and clear over the hushed crowd. The guards started at her order, then hesitated. They exchanged glances before turning helplessly toward the emperor.

Her mother started forward, but the emperor grabbed her wrist and she froze in place, staring in disbelief at where they touched. She recovered quickly, though. "Stop this foolishness at once!" she hissed, yanking her arm away. The cold-burning fury in her voice made Min flinch, as though it had been aimed at her.

But her father ignored his wife, looking instead toward the waiting guards. Almost imperceptibly, he nodded. There was a breathless moment, and then the courtyard gates parted with the sonorous wail of iron.

"The ceremony has begun," the emperor said.

CHAPTER 6

The Betrothal Ceremony

Lu's cousin wore a broad, handsome smile when the guards opened the gate, but it curdled into a scowl the moment he saw her. There were no gaps in his teeth, Lu noted. They must have replaced the missing ones with porcelain.

The Hana had had wedding traditions of their own, but those of the Hu were known and practiced far and wide through the empire since their conquest. Set could hardly fail to notice she was draped in scarlet when she should have worn gray and black. Undoubtedly, Set and his advisers had rehearsed the steps of the ceremony so frequently in the past month that he could recite them in his sleep. But they hadn't taught him what to do should his bride refuse him, had they? A look of doubt crossed his face, swelling into panic.

And then Lu found it was *she* who was smiling.

She stood and clapped once to call attention. The sound resonated loudly against the red earthen walls of the Heart, stark in the silence. There was a muted shuffle as a half thousand bodies turned to acknowledge her.

"Welcome, my dear cousin; honored Hana guests!" she called to them. "We are delighted to host you. Please, approach." She gestured them forward.

Annoyance flickered across Set's face. According to the traditional Betrothal Ceremony, it should have been he who controlled the movements, *his* actions that held significance, while she just sat there like a stupid little fool and waited for him to steal her throne.

Lu's grin widened. *Unbalance your opponent's footing and take control of the fight . . .* She would need to thank Shin Yuri for his wisdom. Instinctively, she sought him out in the crowd but did not see his face among the gathered shins.

Her cousin grudgingly dug his heels into the sides of his massive gray destrier to urge the beast forward. He was a handsome sight, a Hu soldier's studded black leather vest emblazoned across the chest with the symbol of the First Flame fitted over a silk Hana-style jacket of deep, moody blue. Around his neck, he wore a thick chain bearing a single charm: a palm-sized chunk of crystal.

Set's retinue followed him, clearly as unnerved by her unexpected appearance as their leader: three hundred men on horseback looking nervous as little boys on their first day at the Imperial Academy. Lu smiled internally, then directed her attention to the unfamiliar old man riding at her cousin's side. He was small and meekly hunched, garbed poorly in drab heather gray, astride a discordantly handsome chestnut courser. At first, Lu took the old man's robes for cotton, or even burlap, but as he came closer she saw they were made of raw silk—soft and subtle.

So, this must be my cousin's so-called mystic, she thought scornfully. The magic monk who had broken Set's addiction to poppy tears. Supposedly. Could her cousin truly be abstinent, now? Many believed once addiction set in, it was nearly impossible to free oneself.

Aside from a spare white brow, the monk's head and face were completely hairless, like an infant's, but his eyes were canny. He would have to be clever to manipulate himself into such a high position. He was a person to watch, then.

Set reached the foot of her dais, the retinue stopping with him. He was close enough now that she could see his gray Hana eyes more clearly. Just like her mother's and sister's—the color of storm clouds and smoke—but his stare was even more penetrating than the empress's, and held within it was a fury the likes of which Min was incapable. He glowered at Lu with those eyes, as though he would have liked nothing better than to tear her down from where she stood.

She smiled placidly. He was welcome to try. It hadn't worked when they were children, and she was no child now.

"Welcome," she repeated to the Hana men. Then, opening her attention back to the rest of the courtyard she announced, "All of us gathered here today are familiar with the components of the current Hu Betrothal Ceremony: the bride-to-be upon her pedestal, and the three actions of the suitor:

"The slaughter of the tusked stag with the suitor's own blade, symbolizing his physical prowess," she listed. "Then, there are the recitations from the Analecta, symbolizing the intellect of the future emperor, and finally, the call-and-response of the bride's three riddles, to reflect the suitor's wisdom of the heart.

"Each of these acts represents a treasured part of our collective Hu and Hana histories, demonstrating the worth of an imperial suitor. However, we live in dire times. Our need for a Hu emperor of strength, intellect, and wisdom is greater than it has been ever before. My cousin Lord Set of Family Li stands before you now as a candidate who may well possess these traits"— she paused for a moment, breathing hard—"as do I!"

A shocked murmur rippled through the crowd.

Lu ignored it. She must not lose her confidence for even a heartbeat. Right now she had a captive audience following her lead because she had thrown all of them off their footing. She had to keep them moving, clinging to her sure grasp, her certain rhythm.

"In the days of old, Hu kings were chosen through rigorous contests of strength, intellect, and wisdom. These contests insured we chose the very *best*, the strongest and smartest among us, rather than merely relying on the inertia of bloodlines and a token good word. These contests are what made us warriors—conquerors. And emperors." She let the words hang in the air for a moment. Conquerors of the Empire of the First Flame, the silence thundered. *Your* conquerors. *Your* emperors.

Galvanized by the thought, Lu snarled with a passion that surprised even her, "And what have our traditions become? What have we degenerated into? *This!*" She thrust an accusing hand toward the tusked stag's makeshift pen. The three men tasked with guarding it started.

"This!" she repeated, making it a scoff. "This dumb, domesticated beast, bred for appearance alone. Yes, its wildly curling tusks—far larger and more ornate than those of its wild cousins—make it fearsome to look upon, but were it to try to run, it would fall upon its face! Generations of safety and comfort and inbreeding have made its natural weapons utterly cumbersome and useless in practice. Like a sword so heavily set with jewels and adornments it cannot be lifted."

As though sensing the attention turned upon it, the stag looked up, its eyes patient and docile, chewing on a fistful of hay.

"The empire does not have to endure such a fate. It cannot. We can still choose the best, the worthiest emperor to lead us toward the future. That is why I ask my cousin, my suitor, to dispense with the pretty gestures and symbolism and prove his worth against mine. Rather than assuming your superior wisdom, let us submit ourselves to the shins for tests of wit. Rather than slaying a caged domestic beast here in this courtyard— ride to the northern forest with me and let us see who can take down a real tusked stag! Rather than wearing a pretty sword at your waist, take it up and prove you can best me with it."

She could sense her words working—stirring and rousing the gathered crowd. She could *feel* the thrum of their excitement in the air, as dense as humidity and the flat trill of cicadas during monsoon season. And so, without giving Set a chance to respond, Lu turned to her father.

"I trust," she began, and for a moment, meeting her father's eyes—dark, interested, but hesitant, undecided—her voice faltered, breath catching in her throat. She squared her shoulders, steeled her bones, breathed. She did not risk even a glance toward her mother. "I trust," she repeated, "that my father, my emperor, leader of the great Empire of the First Flame, and the Lord of Ten Thousand Years, agrees with me."

Aside from the constant crackle of the First Flame, the courtyard was deathly silent. Of the five hundred or so advisers and gentry privileged enough to have station within the inner court, some had been on their knees, foreheads pressed to the ground, some unabashedly gaping up at her, while others were poised in mid-bow, uncertain of what they ought to do. At that moment, though, as one, they all turned toward the emperor in anticipation.

Please, Lu thought, beseeching him with her eyes. Willing him to look at her, to truly see her. *Be the man, the father, the* king *I know you to be.*

The emperor swept his imperious gaze out over the court, at the thousands of burning, inquisitive eyes staring back at him. He cleared his throat. Lu felt each body in the courtyard lean inward, as if that would allow them to sooner hear his decision as the words fell from his mouth.

Bright and glorious as polished gold catching the sun, her father laughed.

He laughed longer and louder than she had ever heard him before. Until tears welled in his eyes. The crowd was beginning to stir, uncertain of how they should react, but eager to know.

Lu's lips parted, as though her body were already preparing to rebut his rejection of her. With what words, though? None came to mind. This was all she had, and she had laid it at her father's feet.

The emperor looked to her, and in his eyes she finally saw something solid. Something warm and fond and awed. She saw his love. Good.

He nodded, expectant. As though waiting for her to return the feeling.

She made to smile—then stopped. Instead, she turned her chin up coldly and flicked her eyes away before she could see what hurt she had inflicted. *Let him be hurt*, she thought with a small surge of satisfaction. *Let him feel how I felt*. In truth, her father was giving her nothing more than she had earned.

Lu turned back to Set. "The emperor has agreed, then," she told him. Her cousin's gray eyes were murderous. The blood in her veins felt molten and desperately close to the skin, as though all of her were about to burst into a shower of flame and sparks.

"You and me, cousin," she said. "Let us see who the true emperor is."

CHAPTER 7

Magic

*T*he celebration that followed the Betrothal Ceremony was something Min had been looking forward to: a wine-soaked daylong feast that stretched into the night, with actors, gymnasts, singers, and jugglers providing entertainment. That had been before she'd received her first blood, and her sister had decided to turn the entire country upside down, though.

To make matters worse, the sky had darkened, forcing the festivities indoors. An inauspicious sign, several of her nunas murmured until Butterfly pointed out that it was monsoon season, after all. And, she'd added, considering how dry the summer had been thus far, rain wouldn't be a bad thing.

Perhaps so, though Min found herself wishing the dry spell had continued a bit longer. The banquet hall was unbearably crowded and humid. Her robes, which had been cut for a body far less bloated and cramped than the one she now inhabited, squeezed at her middle. She found herself wishing for a different

life, one in which she had never discovered how badly an oper-
atic rendition of the folk song "Damned Be the False Lover,
Damned Be the True Lover" could stoke a headache.

If only she could retreat to her apartments, close the curtains against the light, and sleep for the next week. Or at the
very least, loosen the cinching, oppressive ties of her robes. She
glanced at her mother, seated to her left, and decided neither of
those options were viable at the moment.

Her mother looked ready to murder the singer performing
before them. Instead, she cast her eyes away, as though repulsed,
and seethed into her plate of pheasant. This, too, proved an
unsatisfactory victim for her rage. A moment later she signaled for Amma Ruxin to help her down from the dais where
they sat.

"Where are you going?" the emperor asked her.

"What concern is it of yours?" her mother snapped back.

Min watched her disappear, but she was distracted when the
singing ended and a flush of servants arrived to clear their
plates and dish up the next course.

She tried to recall which course they were on, but she had
lost count somewhere between the braised ox fruit and the
salad of exquisitely arranged edible flowers. Her stomach roiled
at the sight of yet more food.

Tradition dictated that for the main course they would sup
on the tusked stag killed by the groom-to-be at the Betrothal
Ceremony. But then, tradition had dictated quite a number of
things, all of which her sister had chosen to disregard, leaving
them short a tusked stag.

Down the table, her cousin sat at her father's side with all the handsome, easy grace of any wealthy young man at court. But Min could see a tension in his back, a wariness in his gray eyes. Min had felt a stab of pity for him; Set had clearly forgotten in their time apart that when it came to Lu, everyone had to play according to her rules. On another day, the thought might have been fond; today it felt sour, simmering.

The entertainment switched to a large band of musicians that included—horrifyingly—four different drummers. People flooded onto the floor to dance, leaving the dais almost empty.

Beside his wronged nephew, the emperor seemed if not oblivious to the tension, then certainly not guilty for it. He watched the people before them with studied attention, as though he were seeing dancing for the very first time. Min wondered if he was beginning to regret the promise he had made to allow Lu to compete for the throne.

As for Lu herself, she appeared to be the only truly happy person in the courtyard. Her sister stood by the floor, watched the dancing with a pleased kind of impatience, as though she were enjoying herself, but also looking forward to whatever was next. The trace of a smile stained her mouth like the plum wine she was swigging straight from the carafe.

Min was struck then with fury, hard as a hand across her face. Anger at the sheer *unfairness* of it all. Lu did as she pleased, while Min donned a heavy mask of politesse over her pain. For what? The Betrothal Ceremony of which Lu had made a public mockery? It wasn't just herself Min thought of: Set had worked so hard to get where he was, only to lose that to the whims of an arrogant girl. And what of all the preparations by the ammas and nunas, the work by the palace staff Min had never even met or seen? Even their mother, who had made the day such an ordeal for Min, deserved better.

She watched her sister lean over to whisper what was undoubtedly a bawdy joke that had her nunas biting back barely stifled laughter behind their hands. It was too much. Her sister's lean, strong body and that incorrigible swagger with which she carried herself.

Min knew she was being petulant, but that chagrin burned away at her insides, too. What if she was right? She could be right. She could allow herself that much—

"Little sister!" Min started at Lu's voice in her ear, sudden and soaked with wine. Her sister threw her strong arms about Min's neck in a crushing embrace. "Why so dour? Today is a good day!"

She hadn't even had the chance to tell Lu about her woman's blood, she realized. The thought left her feeling almost as guilty as she was sad. It seemed there must have been a time when she would've told Lu before anyone else. Hadn't there? Perhaps sometime tonight, when they were alone, she could find a moment to confide—

"She has her first woman's blood," Snowdrop blurted from her station at the back of the dais.

"Your woman's blood?" Lu's head whipped back toward her, her voice perhaps a bit louder than she'd intended. "Well, this *is* a good day! Congratulations! Where is your wine—why have you no wine? We must drink to your new life as a woman! Snowdrop, hand me that cup there for my sister . . . that's a girl . . ."

Min's face flushed crimson and she whirled back at

Snowdrop, wishing with her whole heart she could strangle the little handmaiden. She wanted to scream, wanted to reprimand this foolish nuna, show that she *was* a woman, that her sister was not the only princess capable of fulfilling her role and commanding respect, but the anger welled up inside her throat, choking off her words. It felt like a living thing, hot and animal and roiling, surging forth toward Snowdrop—

Oblivious, the nuna shuffled over and proffered the cup of plum wine to Min. "Here you are, Small Princess—"

Her words broke off into a scream as the cup in her hands shattered. Pink wine splashed the nuna's face, the front of her robes, and bits of ceramic caught in her hair.

Lu cursed, brushing drops of wine from her face. "What on . . . Snowdrop, did you drop it?"

Snowdrop was already blubbering in shock, stammering apologies through her tears. "N-no! It . . . exploded! Right in my hands!" she squealed.

"It must have been cracked . . . oh gods," Lu cursed again. "Snowdrop, you're *bleeding*." She pulled a handkerchief from her robes and held it to the red spot welling on the girl's palm. "Go see the court physician," Lu told her. "Have him clean and bind it."

Min watched the scene before her as though from a distance. When the cup broke, she hadn't screamed like Snowdrop or jerked away in surprise like Lu. It wasn't that she had been expecting it, exactly. More that it seemed only right that it had happened. The natural progression of things. She felt oddly calm, watching Snowdrop walk off weeping with Butterfly in tow.

"That girl is an idiot," Lu said flatly, when the nuna was out of earshot.

Min's lips quirked into a smile. "I know."

Lu cast a searching look around the table. "Well, we should still drink to you—there must be an extra cup around here . . ."

Min leaned forward and snatched the carafe from her sister's hand, taking a deep swig and relishing the look of surprise on Lu's face. She smacked her lips in satisfaction.

"It's sweet," she said.

⁂

Two hours later, the wine's sweetness had gone sick and sour in Min's belly. The feast was in full swing: a raucous dance circle had formed at the center of the floor with Lu and her nunas at its center. Min's own handmaidens had left her side to join in, whooping and cheering loud as anyone. None of them noticed Min slip away.

The rain had ended, and the central gardens were eerily still but for the drip of water off the trees. Most of the servants had been reassigned to duties at the feast, and those that hadn't had likely slipped off duty to watch the dancing. Min was grateful for their negligence, scuffing her way down an empty covered walkway. The night air was cool against her skin, perfumed with jasmine and citrus and wisteria. Blissfully quiet. At this distance, the stomping cacophony of the feast was muted. Big, but soft. Like the roar of the ocean.

The covered walkway ended at the Courtyard of Prayers, at the center of which stood the Gray Temple. The building had been abandoned since shortly before Min was born, but before then it had briefly housed the last order of Yunian shamanesses—hostages of the empire following the Gray City's surrender of the Gray War. They had been Yunis's best beloved, the most powerful and secretive wielders of northern magic, if the stories were to be believed.

But they had been an uneasy feature in the court of the empire, regarded as foxes in a henhouse. It had been only a matter of time until those suspicions had calcified to accusations; they were executed scarcely a year after their arrival.

Min shivered. As children her nunas had whispered the temple was haunted. Even now many of them would not walk by it without a whispered prayer of protection. When Min had mentioned it to Lu, however, her sister had just scoffed that nunas could be as ignorant as peasants sometimes.

It's just an old building, Min told herself. Whatever magic the shamanesses had brought with them from Yunis had died along with them. And she was a grown woman now, too old to be frightened by ghost tales.

She hurried through the courtyard, though, slowing only when she reached the next covered path. It was lit by an overhead string of lanterns, but these were easily outshone by the full moon. She looked up at it, flinching at the toll the movement took. The world heaved around her, and she closed her eyes against it. Perhaps she'd had too much to drink.

"It's not like I've never had wine before," Min grumbled to herself. She had had a cup at her father's last birthday celebration. Nearly a whole cup. "At least half," she continued. "It's hardly—oh!"

Her voice broke off as a figure emerged from a stand of

well-trained willows up ahead and stepped onto the path. As it turned toward her, she recognized Set.

He stopped when he saw her, taking an apprehensive step backward. The odd crystal he wore around his neck caught a ray from the full moon and flared, hot and white. Min flinched, instinctively covering her eyes.

The light burned so strong it blanched the world. It seemed to bleed past the boundaries of sight and became a sound—a high, clear note like the ringing of a glass bell so deafening she could scarcely hear the ordinary world. The merriment of the feast carrying across the courtyard, vulgar by contrast, went mute.

As abruptly as it had appeared, the light winked out. Its song stopped as well, abrupt as a slamming door.

She moved the hand from her eyes and saw Set was walking toward her, brushing stray drops of rainwater from his shoulders.

"Good evening, Small Princess. I did not expect to see you here." His voice was cheerful, but she sensed it was forced.

"I . . . ," she hesitated, then curtsied. "Good evening, cousin."

The world seemed so ordinary. Had she imagined the way his necklace had caught the light? An effect of the wine, probably. Drunkenness. That was all. The thought left her oddly bereft.

"What is the Small Princess doing, wandering so far from a court feast on her own?" Set asked.

Min's heart dipped. Would he tell her mother he had found her wandering? Well, so what if he did? She was allowed to walk. Min hesitated before saying, "I felt faint, cousin. I did not wish to disturb the other guests on such a joyous—" her voice dropped off as she remembered that in fact, the day had been less than joyous for him.

He did not seem to register her folly, just nodded. "I am sorry to hear you are unwell. Allow me to accompany you back to the feast, so you might fetch your nunas. It does not do for a young girl to make her way in the dark alone . . ."

He is trying to get rid of me. Like she was some dumb child.

"No, I just . . . I wanted to tell you—" The words surged from Min's mouth before she could stop them. As though to chase after them, she took a step forward, then tripped. *These damned pot-bottomed shoes.*

But the ground rushed up toward her, and there was no time to explain. Then one of Set's hands was there, catching her own. His was warm and steady. He put the other on her waist, bracing her.

"The stones are wet. From the rain," she blurted. Set had removed his hand from her waist, but the other was still wrapped securely about her own. Her fingers were curled tightly about his. She did not remember doing that. "The shoes . . ."

"I think you mean 'the wine,'" he said. Min reddened, but when she looked up she saw he was smiling, and not unkindly.

"Forgive me. A joke," he said, releasing her hand. He stood with his arms akimbo, regarding her. "Now. What was so important that you should throw yourself to the ground in your haste to say it?"

"I just wanted to say that today, that my sister—"

"Embarrassed me in front of the whole court?" Set suggested. "Made me look a complete fool? Perhaps reminded everyone of the weak-willed failure, the degenerate drug-addled child I used to be?" He smirked around the words, but there was no humor to it—only something cruel and loathing barely kept at bay, straining against his politesse. Min sensed a single wrong word might topple the dam, send it flooding forth.

She winced. She'd brought this on. Why was she so *stupid?* "No, of course you're not those—things," she said quickly. "How Lu treated you. It was . . . unkind. You're not a drug-addled . . . you're not those things."

And he hadn't been—at least, not while he was at court the last time. She'd been little, but she still remembered first laying eyes on him. He'd ridden through the palace gates upon a gray stallion, proud and tall, the sun gleaming off his long, black plait. Looking back, he had been scarcely more than a child. Younger than she was now. At the time, though, he had seemed so grown up to her. So handsome and new.

There had even been a time when she'd dared to hope she might wed him in place of Lu. After all, she'd reasoned, her sister clearly wanted nothing to do with him, and she couldn't have imagined at that age that anyone—even their father and mother—could make Lu do anything she didn't want. Min cringed thinking of it now. She'd been such a stupid child.

Of course, that had all been before. Before the trip to the North, before Lu had—

"Do you know why I began taking the poppy tears?" he asked abruptly.

Min blinked. "I . . . it is said—that is, they gave you them to treat the pain. After my s-sister broke your teeth in the desert."

Her cousin smiled bitterly. "That is what they say, isn't it? You were there on that trip North. What do *you* recall?"

"I was there," she conceded, "but I didn't see the fight. I'd gone to bed right after dinner." It stung a bit that he so little remembered her, but then, it had been a long time ago. Besides, Min had been so young—what interest could Set have had in a dumb girl like her?

"Of course," he said. "Well, the story your sister spread isn't quite the full truth. She tends to leave out the bit where she and that Ashina boy she took such a liking to ganged up on me, two against one, doesn't she?"

Min's lips opened and closed. It was true; she had never heard that part before. Would Lu really do something so cowardly? She'd always been adamant about fighting her own battles, but still . . . her sister *did* have a fierce temper. It wasn't so impossible to imagine her taking advantage of the opportunity to teach Set a lesson.

"Can I tell you a secret, Min?"

She stared. No one had ever entrusted her with a secret before. She'd hear her nunas whisper to one another about crushes on page boys and the sons of officials late at night when they thought she'd gone to sleep, but they'd never shared them with her. They thought she was too stupid, too uninteresting to fully appreciate them.

"Yes," she heard herself say eagerly. "You can. Tell me a secret. I'd never—I'd keep it safe."

Set looked at her with appraising eyes. "Of course you would. You're Hana, like me. We're kin; bound by blood. We want the same things, don't we?"

He didn't wait for her answer. "Your sister caused some damage with her fists and her little wooden sword in the desert that night, it's true. But nothing lasting. Your mother wanted me to stay with your family. The court physicians were traveling with us—they could treat me. But your father . . . well." He moved toward the edge of the walkway, smiling wryly out onto the dark, rain-heavy garden. "Lu had shown she could not bear to have me around, and your father can't refuse her anything, can he?"

Min's lips parted, but she did not know what to say.

"I had come to the capital for grooming," he continued. "I left my family's home in glory—the future emperor in all but name. But when I returned North, I returned in failure. My father is a man who does not tolerate failure."

Min nodded uncertainly. She had never met Set's father— her mother's older brother. He was Hana, and wealthy, like the rest of that side of her family. That was all she knew.

"Do you know what he did to welcome me back, my father?" Set continued, oblivious to her ignorance. "He called me into the main hall of our manor. It was empty, save for him and his personal guards. I will never forget his exact words. They were: 'I would not have raised a hand to the future emperor. But you've failed, and now you are nothing. You are not even my son.' Right there in the hall of my childhood home, he ordered his guards to beat me within an inch of my life."

Her cousin disdainfully flicked a cluster of wisteria hanging by his shoulder. Rainwater and white petals showered to the ground. He shook the damp from his hand.

"Bei Province is cold," he murmured. "It is not a proper

home for us Hana, the people of the First Flame. The Hu exiled our most powerful families up there following Kangmun's conquest. Far enough away that we couldn't cause any trouble. It does something to men, I think, to be torn from their lands."

He sighed. "Exiled from our rightful center of power, we have grown dull, listless. We drink to endure the fog, smoke poppy tar to stave off the boredom. My father in particular is fond of spirits. Spirits can make the best of men mean and ill-tempered. My father was never the best of men."

"I'm sorry," Min whispered. Set looked up at her. "I didn't know."

"Few did," he said lightly. "My mother runs a tight household and kept the story quiet. They'd been giving me poppy tears for the teeth your sister broke. After that day, they gave me more for a broken jaw and cracked ribs. The deep bruises, two blackened eyes. My mother could not bear to see me in pain, and she insisted they increase my doses. And so, even after I was healed, I needed it. My body craved it—and my mind. Behind its veil, I did not have to look into this new world in which my father had renounced me."

"No one could blame you," Min said softly.

Set turned to her and lifted one eyebrow. "Couldn't they? It was a weakness in me. The poppy tears—and later, when I began to smoke it, the tar—protected me, made the edges of things soft. I was tested, and I chose weakness. Comfort. This is the person your sister and her ilk think I still am—but I've changed. I chose a different way. Do you know why?"

She shook her head.

"My father—perhaps he was ashamed of me, perhaps of

himself—he left a year after my beating for our family's summer retreat farther south. I've only been once in my life. It's a pretty bit of property, right on a small lake. A bit warmer than where we lived. A good place for relaxing and thinking on one's own. Which is what he did. He relaxed and thought . . . and drank. And drank. For four years now he's been doing this, never returning home once. Never sending a single letter."

"He—he was wrong to do it," Min murmured. Children weren't to criticize their elders, Min knew, but Set looked so proud and yet so devastated—what else could she say? "It was cruel."

Set sighed. "Do you know, Min, what it is like to hate your father? Your own parent?"

Yes, whispered a small voice within her. *No!* she corrected herself. She pictured her mother's face. Then, more vaguely, as though it were hard to recall, her father's.

Yes.

How could she think such a thing? *I don't hate anyone,* she told herself quickly. *I don't.* But it was too late. There were some thoughts so ugly and so true that once released they could not be unthought. Like a drop of blood spilled on white silk.

Set wasn't paying her any mind. Perhaps he hadn't expected her to answer.

"The Analecta, the monks, they tell us we shouldn't hate our parents," he went on. "That we *can't.* We came into this world to serve them, that it is our duty by the laws of man and heaven. But the day my father left, I swore I would never serve an unworthy master again. Not him, not his memory, not the pain he caused me, and not the poppy tar I had been smoking.

So I sought out the best healers and priests the North had to offer. Physicians to backwoods shamans, it made no difference to me what their pedigree was, so long as they could show me a way to stop. And Brother—the loyal monk who serves me—fresh from the labor camps along the front lines, he did."

"How?" Min asked without meaning to.

"How?" Set paused, then seemed to gather himself. He didn't move away, but she had the sense he'd stepped back several paces. "Perhaps one day I'll tell you," he said. "It is a complicated story, and not very interesting for a girl your age, I think. But the important thing was I made a *choice*. I chose to find what was true in this world—what was constant, and real, and unbreakable beneath the filth and noise of everyday life. I figured out what I wanted, and I chose to pursue only that goal. And one day, very soon, I'll make them all see that—my father, your sister, all those backbiters and naysayers in court. They'll all see who I truly am, what I am capable of, when I'm their emperor. I advise you to do the same as me, cousin. Find what is true, and live only for that."

But what could that possibly be? Min could never hope for the power to which he aspired. All she knew was an endless monotony of embroidery lessons, disrespectful servants, her mother's disapproval, her sister's ostentatious rebellions that she never saw fit to share with Min, and a thousand lovely silk robes leading up to the one they would bury her in. How could she ever expect to find truth when her existence amounted to little more than a politely stifled yawn?

Aloud she said, "I'll try my best. To do what you said."

"You're a good listener, Min," he told her absently. "A good girl."

"Oh, I'm not a girl," she blurted. "I'm a woman."

Set blinked in surprise, fixing his cool gray eyes upon her. "Oh?" he said.

She lowered her own gaze. "I know you don't think it, no one does," she said, her voice struggling to rise above its accustomed whisper. "But it's true."

When she dared look up again, his eyes reflected bemusement, and something else—curiosity?

He was *seeing* her. Truly seeing her. Before she had been like the mottled brown moth that blends in against the bark of a tree to hide from predators, but she had moved, and he had glimpsed the colorful undersides of her wings. He saw her.

Around them, the rain picked back up. Min shivered. She felt an odd kind of fear—not the jumpy sort that had sent her hurrying past the shamaness temple, but something new. Like taking two stairs down by mistake, but righting yourself before you fall. A small exhilaration.

"A woman. Yes," Set said, his voice soft beneath the steady beating of the monsoon rain. "Yes, of course. I see it now. A young woman."

"I am," she agreed, her voice high with relief.

He seemed to mull this over. "And yet, earlier, when I arrived, I presented you with a set of porcelain dolls—a gift suitable for a child half your age. Most inappropriate. I fear I've insulted you, and embarrassed myself in the process."

"Oh, no . . ." She flushed, remembering. He'd barely looked at her, placing the velvet-lined box of dolls in her hands before flitting off to speak with her mother. "N-no, cousin. Your gifts—they were lovely. Truly, I cherish them with all the affection and delight they warrant."

"Nonsense! I would not leave you so unduly insulted. Much could be said against the young scion of the Hana, but few have called me miserly."

"I would never—"

But he held up a long, pale hand. "You are in the right. Tell me what you would like, and come the morning you will receive your new, much improved gift, Small Princess."

"Minyi," she said. "Call me Minyi. If you wish." That was the polite thing to do, was it not? He was her elder, he ought to call her by her given name. True, she had the higher rank for now perhaps, but he was her cousin, and one day he would be her emperor—she felt a flash of guilt, as though the very thought were a betrayal of Lu.

Not that she would care. The thought pricked meanly at the skin of her nape. She could hardly deny the truth of it, though; what use did her sister have of Min's opinion either way?

"Minyi," Set was repeating slowly, as though weighing each syllable with his tongue. He reflected for a moment, then said, "Your mother always called you Min, as I recall."

"Min is only a pet name. A child's name."

"And as we established, you are no child."

"No," Min agreed. "I am not."

In spite of herself, she grinned. It was nice, this rhythm, this verbal dance into which they had fallen. Her nunas did this with each other sometimes, but never with her.

"Well, Minyi." Set quirked his lips into a smile that she thought really very pleasant, after all. "What should we do about finding you a more appropriate gift? What would you have of me? A pair of silver earrings dripping moonstones down to your shoulders? A carved hairpin of green nephrite?"

"I have earrings. And hairpins," she ventured coyly.

He grinned in encouragement. "Tell me what you wish for, and it will be yours."

"The crystal around your neck." She blurted the words out without thinking.

Surprise flickered across Set's still, handsome face, followed by a peculiar uncertainty.

"This crystal?" He laughed, but the sound was hollow.

Gods, what had she done? He could grant her literally anything within her imagination and of course she had asked him for the one thing he wasn't willing to give.

"Dear Minyi, this charm is only quartz. Worthless. You deserve fine, polished jewels. Aquamarine and amethyst to stoke your gray eyes. Veined agate and saltwater pearls nested in a setting of silver polished until it gleams."

She blushed scarlet. Things had grown so nice between them. Why had she gone and spoiled it? *That was the wrong thing, Min—no, the* worst *thing you could have asked for. Idiot! Look at his face. This crystal clearly means a good deal to him.*

"It was wrong of me to—forgive me."

He seemed to consider her carefully. It reminded her of the

way a sleepy cat might idly watch a bird. "Small Princess—Minyi," he said. "Tell me what attracts you to this trinket."

"I-I was only being foolish. I know so little of the world, I did not realize it was worth so little."

"But you admired it nevertheless."

"When I first saw you—that is, when I first saw it about your neck, it—it sang to me."

"It *sang* to you?"

"Yes."

He stared at her for what felt like ages. When he spoke, his voice was low. "Well. That is interesting. You see, this pendant is from Yunis. Brother and I recently investigated the ruins of their old city, and I came upon this fragment in the rubble. So I took a piece and had a jeweler turn it into a necklace. Just a keepsake from my travels."

Then he shrugged. "No doubt there is more where it came from. And we are soon to be brother and sister, so I suppose I can see it any time I wish. Just as I can see *you* any time I wish." He lifted the chain over his head, and with little ceremony draped it over hers, careful to avoid catching her hair.

Min looked down to where the crystal rested on the high curve of her breast, touched it delicately. It felt oddly warm and animal. Alive. Her robes weren't so constricting anymore. She felt as though she were floating, made of cool air and moonlight.

When she looked up, Set was watching her with bemused, attentive eyes.

"Now, if I may be so bold to ask, what did it sound like?" he asked.

Min considered the question, then the questioner. High above them, the sky darkened and reopened. Rain fell in a deluge. Where it struck, heat rose from the earth as steam. Under the cover of the walkway, the hanging lamps seemed oddly bright, blazing about Set's face like a corona. Fiery white and shivering. A thousand eyes staring down at her, sharing his same glowing curiosity.

Min's mouth was dry and thick, and the rice wine had left her throat scratchy, but her voice came out clear and strong. "It sounded like magic," she said.

CHAPTER 8

The Stranger

A dash of wet brushed Nok's cheek. Rain. He looked up. The sky had grown dark and marbled as a new bruise. He cursed under his breath. With luck, it would just be a passing summer shower rather than the first thundering downpour of monsoon season.

"Come on, hurry," Nok muttered, pushing Bo's stubborn bulk in the direction of Omair's house. It had been a long day of delivering medicines around Ansana, but Nok was grateful. Work meant doing rather than thinking, and after his encounter with the shamaness, Nok could do with less thinking.

A vision of the beggar woman flashed in his mind.

Slipskin?

His throat tightened, and unconsciously he scrubbed his eyes, as though to wipe the old woman away.

Around him, the village was still under the threatening sky.

Only Mother Wang was out, shooing a stray chicken into its coop. At the sound of Nok's approach she looked up, her face souring. Nok did not know the woman well. The closest they'd come to talking was last spring, when he had made the mistake of cutting through one of their fallow fields on his way back from the city. She had set their dogs on him.

Dogs usually liked Nok, but these were mean creatures. He had barely gotten away with the clothes on his back.

When he reached the path leading up to Omair's house, Nok noted light glowing from the small windows at the base of the trunk. A pleasant tendril of smoke, purpled in the gloaming, curled from the chimney. Omair would have porridge simmering over the waning fire. Nok's stomach growled in anticipation.

He pulled a reluctant Bo toward the stable. "Why we even keep you around, I don't know," he muttered. Then he gave the old mule a gentle scratch behind the ears, where the hair was surprisingly downy and soft. "Ready for dinner?"

Nok opened the stable door and froze. There was a horse inside. A big one, with a lean, proud build. The dirty saddle blankets draped over its back didn't quite manage to hide the lustrous black-brown coat beneath.

A Hana warhorse. Unmistakable. Nok had seen enough to recognize one ten lifetimes from now. A cold finger of fear scraped down his spine.

For their part, Bo and the strange horse snorted at one another with a look of mutual disdain.

"Well, Bo," Nok said, slowly backing out. "Looks like we have a guest."

Had Omair ever *had* a guest before? He occasionally received patients from neighboring villages and settlements. Farmers, mostly. Certainly no one who would be in possession of a horse like this.

Nok left Bo in the yard and made his way cautiously toward the rear of the house. The late summer night air had only the barest hint of autumn chill, but the sweat drying on his skin left him cold.

He lifted a hand to open the door. Muffled voices came through from the other side. Nok dropped his hand and crouched by the window instead.

The stranger was speaking. His voice was gruff, as though from years of tobacco smoking, but his accent refined, lofty. Definitely Inner Ring. At least. It matched the mystery horse in the stable. "I'm telling you, Ohn—"

"Omair."

A snort. "*Omair?* Is that what you're going by these days? What is that, southern?"

"It doesn't hurt to be cautious. They were looking for me a long time."

"To that end, you would do well to think less about your name and more about your reputation. How do you think I found you? A country apothecarist with your talents—word spreads."

The whispers of the villagers wormed their way into Nok's thoughts: *Unnatural.* Magic, its manipulations of energy, its sacred rites, had been banned within the empire since the Yunian War. But that didn't mean it went away. There were still places in the Second Ring where you could find fortune-tellers, vendors touting love spells, fast wealth with the swig of a potion.

But that wasn't Omair. Nok had always known the old man was special—a true healer among the usual crop of charlatans. Now, though, he wondered just who Omair—Ohn?—was. What he was. What he had been.

Nok wrung his hands together, felt his scars catch. It wasn't that these questions hadn't occurred to him; more that he didn't wish to know. Let dead things stay buried. That was the way it had always been with Omair—they didn't need to know their pasts to trust one another. Did they?

Absently, Nok palmed at the knife in his boot.

"Something tells me," Omair said pointedly, "I don't think you came all this way under the cover of dusk to talk about my name."

The stranger conceded with a grunt. "You've heard the emperor named that Hana boy his successor?"

"Indeed. And that Princess Lu has challenged him for the title," Omair replied. "We *do* hear things out here."

Princess Lu. Nok's stomach clenched at the sudden memory of her narrow face, hair dark and iridescent as the wings of a raven. He pushed the vision away. He'd hoped those memories were behind him, in the dust of the North, with the bones of his family.

"The princess has challenged him, it's true, but the boy behaves as though the throne is already his. I've been watching him—who he meets with, what he promises them. He's building support, mostly among the military. And there are well enough many in court who would sooner follow a Hana man—any man, any Hana—than her. Set knows it. Lu, she's too young to see it. Too sheltered. She thinks that her wits and pedigree and the love of her father will be enough to carry her. But Set's planning something. I just don't know exactly what."

Omair made a sound of acknowledgment. "It's hard to believe that Daagmun—that the emperor hasn't caught wind of this."

"You've been away too long," the stranger said. "You forget how the court works—secrets are both currency and weaponry. The clever ones hoard them until the right opportunity. And if you're not clever, you don't survive."

"Then how are *you* still around?" Omair retorted, but his voice was fond. Nok had never heard the old man speak this way—it felt not unlike how Adé teased Nok.

"That's good," snapped the stranger. "That's very funny. Well, here's another joke for you: Set believes he's found Yunis."

Nok frowned. Yunis. The Gray City in the North. Where rites and devotions and diplomatic meetings between the half a hundred Gifted Kith took place for a thousand years. Until the imperials razed it a year before Nok's birth.

It had been beyond a dark time for all the Gifted—Nok's mother often said he and Nasan had been born after the end of the world. But of course, she hadn't known what was yet to come.

"Yunis was destroyed," Omair said, as though echoing Nok's thoughts. There was a creak as he leaned back in his chair.

"The old city was," countered the stranger firmly. "There were always rumors of survivors—"

"Just rumors."

There was a long pause. "I still have friends in the North. Men I fought beside in battle. Men I trust my life to."

"And?"

"I have it on good faith that Prince Jin—the youngest of the Triarch—was recently seen patrolling their borders with a force ten thousand strong."

"That's *one* royal. If there's any truth to the story at all."

The stranger chose to ignore Omair's second comment. "That one royal is the one that matters—he controls their army."

"It seems unlikely there would be anywhere left for them to hide," Omair mused. "The colonies have grown so. I hear they're using sparkstone to crumble the mountains."

"Just the foothills, here and there. If anywhere could hide a city, it would be the Gray Mountains," the stranger said. Then he snorted. "And the situation up there is far more precarious than the emperor would like—than his advisers let on. I suppose you heard about the prison break earlier this moon? Fifty slipskins and convicts freed—"

Nok's breath caught in his throat. *Slipskins.* For half a heartbeat, his sister's face hovered in front of his own and something in him soared. *No,* he said, yanking it back down. It was a familiar feeling; how many times had he woken thinking the past year, then two years, five years, had been a terrible dream, only to remember it was all too real?

Fifty slipskins. He slammed down the spike of hope and

exhilaration and fear that surged in him at those words. They had nothing to do with him. *Everyone I ever loved is dead.* He'd *seen* them die.

"What does Set want with the Gray City, anyway?" Omair asked, drawing Nok back into their conversation.

"I don't know." The stranger sounded frustrated. "None of us seem to, except for his monk, and he's not telling. But whatever it is, Set seems willing to commit half the imperial army toward getting it, even if it means beggaring the empire along the way. If the girl doesn't prevail, war may be at hand again."

"The girl," Omair said. "That's why you're here, isn't it?" His voice took on a new edge. *Bitterness,* Nok realized. "You want me to make a new king."

"You did it before."

"And did you forget what happened then?" The pain and loathing that clung to his words was unlike anything Nok had heard from the old man before, but he recognized their shape nevertheless. *Shame. Guilt. Loss.* All things Nok himself wore like a second skin.

"This time won't be like the last. I've trained Princess Lu since she was a child," the stranger said, his voice vehement. Not angry, though; proud. "She's green, but strong. Smarter than her father ever was. And she has a good heart. She will need guidance, but I believe in her."

When Omair spoke again, his voice was soft: "Does she look like her mother?"

The stranger scoffed. "It isn't like that."

Omair lapsed into a weighted silence. Nok could imagine with perfect clarity the look on his face: the glint in his shrewd, appraising eyes, the way his mouth would turn down slightly at the corners in restrained disapproval, as though waiting for your shame to occur to you.

"Don't look at me that way," the stranger snapped. But there was something almost affectionate in his tone. "It's not going to work. I'm not eighteen anymore. I'm an old man."

Omair said nothing.

"There's something about the princess that recalls her, certainly—how not? But no, she looks nothing like her. And so what if she did? Like I said: I'm an old man."

The princess's mother . . . ? Did the stranger have romantic feelings for the empress? Nok recalled the radiant, stately woman with cold gray eyes. Eyes that to his mind inspired fear over affection, but then, he knew some men could be quite stupid about pretty women.

"I'm not accusing you of anything untoward," Omair said. "It's only, old men get sentimental."

"Do we?" the stranger scoffed. "All except you, I suppose. Always cold as stone."

"You'd be surprised," Omair said, sadness softening his voice.

Nok shifted uncomfortably, his knees popping slightly as he did so. It seemed wrong to eavesdrop on this strange, private turn the conversation had taken.

"Do you still think of her?" There was an edge of reproach to the question.

"Of course I do," Omair snapped. "I should ask the same of *you*. You know what happened to her, what *we* did to her, and you still dare to ask me for *this*—"

Something hot and wet and soft brushed down the back of Nok's neck. He toppled over with a yell.

"What was that?" The stranger's voice came closer, as though he were already on his feet and moving.

Nok scrabbled back on his elbows and looked up. Bo gazed back expectantly.

"Nokhai?"

Omair was standing in the doorway, framed in the warm yellow light of the kitchen lamps.

Nok scrambled to his feet, brushing off his legs. "I . . . fell," he muttered, as though that explained anything.

"Are you all right?" Omair asked, a smile on his warm brown face. "My, the time got away from me. You're very late— good thing you made it home before the rain."

The stranger sidled up beside Omair, allowing Nok to place a figure to the voice at long last. He was a tall, well-built man. A plain rough-spun cloak draped loosely over his head and shoulders. Nok squinted, but lit from behind, the man's face was just a shadow under his cowl. One hand slipped under his cloak to rest on something at his waist. Nok went cold. The man had a sword.

"This is the boy?" The stranger sounded skeptical. "I thought he'd be taller. His father was a big man."

The blood drained from Nok's face. This man knew—had known his father. What else did he know?

The stranger's arm snapped forward. He gripped Nok by the chin, tilting his face up. Nok caught sight of cool, intelligent eyes, a sharp brow, hard jaw, black hair laid tight around his forehead as though bound back severely. The stranger was close enough now that Nok's nose filled with his smell—dusty and horsey from his ride to Ansana, but beneath that, clove and well-oiled, costly leather.

The man squinted, then carefully, as though the wound were still fresh and not years old, thumbed over the silvery lick of scar marking Nok's right cheekbone, just below the eye. "That healed up ugly, didn't it?" he remarked.

And then Nok knew him.

The princess's voice hurtled out of the darkness cloaking the past: *"I'll kill you!"*

Nok shrunk within himself, as though trying to escape it, this fragment of time that ricocheted around inside his head like a wayward bat. He closed his eyes, but he could still see the blade swinging in a wild, crooked hack. The edge was so straight, so clean; it scarcely whispered across the length of his palms. The unsteady backswing planted the ghost of a kiss on his right cheek. His hands were wet. Something glinted blue-white upon the sand—

"For heaven's sake, Yuri!" Omair's voice erupted through the memory. "Let the boy go. You're frightening him."

The stranger's hand disappeared. Nok stumbled, as though his body had been lifted from the past, then dropped unceremoniously back into Omair's warm kitchen.

The stranger . . . no, Nok realized. Not a stranger after all. But not a friend. Not to him at any rate. But he was to Omair. There was no mistaking the affection between them. So what did that make—

"He's one of them," Nok blurted. "Did you know that?" His voice was shaking, louder than he'd meant it to be. "He's a soldier. An imperial. A guard for the prin—he's inner court. He's a servant of the *royal family.*"

A glimmer of surprise crossed Omair's face. "Ah. You remember him?"

Nok's heart skipped. Wildly, he thought about the knife in his boot. Omair seemed to see it happen, interpret Nok's fear. His face fixed into one of concern. Familiar and yet—

"Nok," he said softly, reaching for him. Nok flinched as the old man's hand touched his shoulder, reassuring, gentle—

A new voice arose in Nok's mind. One he had worked so hard to wall up, lock away brick by brick. Taut and thin as tendons, it broke through. *I won't let them take us—I won't . . .*

Nok knew what was to come next. The jumbled mess of blood and flesh and dark, browning fluids that his mind had mashed his family into: here, his father's sightless eyes gazed up at the stars, the red pulp of his unnamed baby brother seeped through his mother's cold, disembodied hands, and everywhere, under every flap of skin and jutting bit of bone, appeared his sister's mouth, screaming promises a child couldn't ever keep.

"I won't let them take us! I won't!"

"No!" Nok screamed, throwing the apothecarist's hands off. Desperately, he shoved past the stranger—the soldier—and ran outside.

He scarcely registered the thunder booming overhead, but he felt the rain. It came down in sheets, streaking his vision, running sopping tendrils of hair down his forehead. He ran regardless, ran from the stranger, from Omair, the memories. He ran until his legs and his lungs burned. He did not stop, he never stopped—he fell. His foot caught a furrow and he went down hard, knees planting in the saturated earth.

He righted himself, wheezing raggedly. The animal panic clutching his heart subsided enough for a more rational panic to set in: *Where do I go?*

Adé's face arose in his mind's eye, but he shut it out. No, she wasn't an option. He had no one but Omair. And now he'd lost even that.

A white flash lit the sky and he jumped. Lightning. It flashed again, and he saw he was in the Wangs' soybean fields. He rubbed his dirty palms against the thighs of his pants to dry them, but the cloth was just as wet. He was soaked through; he needed to find shelter.

That was when he heard the dogs. Lightning flashed again, and for that brief illuminated moment he saw them: three lanky, underfed mutts, goaded on by the Wangs' two eldest sons, brandishing sticks and whooping.

Nok ran, making for the edge of the imperial Northwood that crept in at the edge of the Wangs' lands. Slipping on the rain-slick earth, he reached the lip of the forest. Night had truly fallen by now and he hesitated at the dense, dark press of trees. But he could hear the shouts and barks growing closer over his own ragged panting, and so he plunged ahead, kicking up damp clumps of pine needles and moss.

He threw himself upon the first hospitable tree he saw, leaping to catch the lowest bough. The sleeve of his tunic caught on one of its branches and tore as he shook it free. His wet boots scrabbled for purchase against the slippery bark. He'd nearly hauled himself up when the first dog's jaw closed around his ankle.

A shout burst from him as he fell. The wet bedding of fallen leaves and brush did little to cushion him. His ears rung with the impact. The dogs were all around him now, nipping and snarling at his hands as he struggled to bring them protectively over his eyes. The dog that had pulled him down was still worrying his leg, though Nok noted dimly that it hadn't broken the skin.

He hazarded a look between his fingers, but saw no evidence of the Wang boys. One of the dogs, drawn by the movement, seized Nok's hand in his mouth. This time it drew blood.

The smell stoked them to a frenzy. As the teeth sunk deeper into his palm, Nok let out a panicked cry, wrenching his arm away. Stupid—the flesh tore, and blood poured from the gash. Heavy paws slammed against his back, sprawling him facedown against the ground.

I will die, he realized. *If I stay here, I'm going to die.*

Would that be so bad? He was never meant to live this long. Death had erred five years ago; it was past time to rectify the mistake.

No. Not like this.

He made to rise again, hissing as the pain in his hand flared to life. The dogs were back on him, leaping two at a time now, in waves, pushing him down.

Something else was there.

Nok sensed it dissonantly, like turning two pages of a book when he only meant to turn one—jerked out of his own sequence of events, and into a different reality. The dogs still bayed around him, but something in the air was different.

The rain had stopped.

The hairs on the back of Nok's neck rose as a warm, powerful wind swept through the forest. It settled right above him and the dogs. A fresh shower of pine needles and bark rained down from the trees and he blinked furiously to keep it from his eyes. The dogs were lowing as though they'd been struck.

Nok opened his eyes and saw them slinking away, eyes wide and liquid with fear. He rolled over onto his back, breathing hard. His hand was still bleeding, but he no longer felt it. Or perhaps he no longer cared. Rising above the pain, above the fear, he felt a sense of oddly sedate eeriness. The dogs gave a final whine—the bravest among them verging on a snarl—then tucked tail and ran, leaving Nok alone.

No—not alone. Someone was there with him. Some*thing*. Nok pushed himself up with shaking arms, turned to face it.

And looked into the wet, glowing eyes of a wolf.

The creature was massive, half the size of Bo. Larger than any ordinary wolf.

But its eyes struck Nok as most unnatural—instead of nocturnal glinting gold, they were black and vast as caves.

Its stare was a heavy, tangible pressure on his skin. Nok knew he should look away, that returning the creature's gaze would only agitate it, but he found himself frozen.

There were predators in and around Ansana. Foxes and coyotes and wild dogs. The odd cougar. But he'd never seen anything quite as large or majestic as the creature before him now.

Not since the Ashina had broken the Pact and lost their Gifts.

He felt no fear, strangely. He was too tired for that now. He was spent.

Fitting that this is how he should die: the last living Wolf, who never learned how to be a wolf, eaten by a wolf. He could have laughed in spite of everything, but something about the beast before him demanded solemnity.

The wolf advanced. Nok closed his eyes, waited for the blow of those tremendous paws upon his chest, the tearing of teeth on his throat.

I'm coming, Nasan. I'm coming, Ma, Idri. Ba . . .

Instead, he felt the creature still, standing over his body. It sniffed at his face, huffing, and its breath was a warm wind of earthy forest smells tinged with blood.

Nok opened his eyes. The creature was regarding him with almost human curiosity, appraising him in silence. A nighttime breeze sailed over them peacefully, lifted Nok's hair, playing like fingers through the ruff of heavy gray-blue around the wolf's neck.

Without quite knowing what he meant to do, Nok reached out and rested a shaking hand upon the wolf's head.

A cavalcade of visions ran through him with the swift violence of a sandstorm, strange and slippery and visceral as a dream:

A skinny girl screaming soundlessly, belly big, legs spread, pushing out a baby. Her life's blood—running red against sun-kissed skin blanched white, and when her eyes opened, they, too, were red.

A warm hand against his cheek, fingers petting idly at the gray fur there; his fur . . .

His own face—no, not quite, sharper, cannier and the hair longer, tossed carelessly over one eye.

A man of twenty, twenty-five, walking down a dark corridor, back stiff, step mouse-like and nervous. He turned back and looked at Nok with Omair's face, only impossibly, unimaginably young. The man pushed open a pocket door and Nok felt the dread that shook his hands, filled his throat . . .

The wide, implacable horizon of the desert. Setting sun spilling searing pinks and purples and violent orange across the sky, the sand still hot with daylight under his paws.

Abrupt as silence, a tableau of gray and white: a fog, a patch of cloudy sky, placid lake, a stony shore . . .

A voice, drifting down steady and deliberate from above him, a voice with weight and authority (*it is time*), her (was it a woman?) words equal parts question and statement . . .

A pair of eyes stared at him. Flecked with copper and familiar. A girl. Black hair. Shrouded from behind with a lush canopy of green, and beyond that, the sky so wide and blue.

He opened his eyes and found himself running, loping through the whipping underbrush swatting back at him—too slow, too slow. The wet ground tore beneath his paws, soft as moss.

Paws? Nok looked down, saw massive shaggy blue fur.

His body was gone.

He was inside the wolf. He *was* the wolf.

A spear of panic stabbed through him, and the creature came to a standstill, as though confused by it.

A high-pitched hysterical laugh caught in his throat, unreleased when he discovered that his mouth—no, the wolf's mouth—could not move to form it.

Bored by Nok's thoughts, the wolf focused on something small and legless sliding across the forest floor thirty paces behind him. Rainwater flew through the air in its wake, clinging to a stop amid the bracken. From far off came the senseless trilling of frogs.

The sky was still dark with night above him—and yet, impossibly, he could see as clear as though it were midday. The great barrel of his chest heaved as he panted—no, not his chest. The wolf's. His chest and the wolf's.

It occurred to him then that this was not a dream. Not in the ordinary sense.

The Gift.

They always said it would come, only it never had. Until now.

But that was impossible—the Ashina Pact had been severed, the gift lost forever to time and war and trampled beneath the feet of the invading Hu, buried under the imperial mining colonies. Only one chosen by the beast gods could carry a caul without a pact in place. Only a Pactmaker. And he was no . . . he couldn't be. Couldn't even bear the thought. It was too sick and cruel and absurd, after all these years. After he had lost anyone who would understand or care . . .

Those were Nok's thoughts. The boy's thoughts.

The wolf stamped its front feet impatiently. The wolf did not know irony. Did not care for the names assigned to things by men. It knew the dark of the forest—how to find clean-running creeks, how to cut the quickest path through the high grass. And it knew blood, not a hundred paces off, hot and alive and bound up in the bristling flesh of some small, soft creature. It knew hunger.

It occurred to Nok then that *he* was feeling all this, too. Through the creature's body, yes, but perhaps . . . he thought to lift the wolf's snout into the air, but it did not obey. This body wasn't his yet, he thought. Back home, the elders would've taught him how to integrate his mind with the wolf mind, but they were all gone now . . .

At the realization, he sunk deeper into the wolf, and his own concerns—those of a lost, scared little human boy—felt less real. As though before he had been hovering around the blood and tissue and muscle, and now he was a part of it all, diffuse and indelible.

Somewhere in the distance, a man yelled a name. *Nokhai.* Meaningless.

The smell of the forest flooded him then, overwhelmed him to the point where, were he still in his boy's body, he might've found tears stinging his eyes. Instead he huffed in the smells of damp bark and soil, of animal urine, and of rot. The musk of a thousand predators stalking just as many small, trembling deaths.

The wolf snarled in distaste, low and mild. *Fear.* It had an acrid, yellow smell. The wolf had no fear, but he recognized it. Knew it well, even: how to arouse it and just as well how to end it. They could do that. Both of them.

The wolf ran, taking Nok with it.

CHAPTER 9

Dawn

*L*u woke to darkness in the earliest hours of the morning. She had her nunas draw her bath, comb and brush her hair, then comb it again before pulling it into a series of intricate plaits. Her face was scrubbed and buffed and painted. Silly. She would sweat it off in a few hours, but ceremony was ceremony.

She exited her apartments to find Hyacinth waiting in the garden. The nuna leaned against a trellis, her face lit pale by the ghost of a heavy-bellied moon. Lu followed her tense gaze, but there was nothing there, just gardenias and tumbles of petunias. Last night's rain had left its damp fingerprints on everything.

"Why so glum?" Lu asked, making the nuna start. "Don't tell me you're worried I'm going to lose."

Hyacinth pushed a grin onto her face. "You? Lose? Never."

"I told you you're going to be the first head amma of the

first empress in our history, and I intend to keep that promise," Lu said with exaggerated severity.

"I believe you." The smile slipped from Hyacinth's face again, and she ran a hand thoughtfully over her tightly braided hair, dropping the hood of her robe. The moonlight bisected her face so that one half seemed to glow, while the other was shrouded in shadow. "A messenger came while you were in the bath," she said hesitantly. "Your father—"

Lu's chest clenched. "What's happened? Is he all right?"

Hyacinth nodded, raising a placating hand. "He's—well, he had one of his spells this morning, but the physicians are attending to him. He's resting. But he won't be able to join the hunt."

Lu felt her body go slack. "I should go to him," she said.

"I thought you'd say that," Hyacinth sighed. "The physicians insist he just needs rest and quiet. They said to check with them after the hunt."

"We're not returning for days," Lu protested.

"Your mother's with him," Hyacinth said, as though that were meant to be reassuring. Lu gave her a look and the nuna smiled wryly. "I know. But the physicians say he'll be fine. He's not going anywhere."

Lu frowned, then nodded. The last thing she wanted right now was to see her mother.

"Listen," Hyacinth said. "There's something else I wanted to talk to you about. I know it's poor timing, but I was thinking I ought to make a visit home soon. It's been months."

It often felt as if Hyacinth was more a sister to her than Min. It was easy to forget that she had a family of her own.

When nunas were chosen, they were assigned new names by the judges, based on their personalities and attributes. Over their years together, Lu had learned their birth names, but she only ever remembered Hyacinth's: Inka, of Family Cui.

"Wonin's grown so big I scarcely feel I can call him my little brother anymore," Hyacinth murmured, almost to herself.

"He looks nearly a man now," Lu agreed, recalling the lanky youth she'd seen in court.

"I know—" Hyacinth broke off as Min appeared farther up the path, flanked by her nunas. As they approached, Snowdrop tried and failed to stifle a yawn. It was catching; Min followed, covering her mouth hurriedly with her sleeve.

"Good morning!" Lu called out. "What brings you here at this fine hour?"

Min blinked back at her with distracted gray eyes, starting belatedly. "Sister," she squeaked as they drew closer. Her nunas curtsied. Min's gaze lowered swiftly, almost guiltily. It occurred to Lu that she hadn't seen her since the Betrothal Feast. Had Min been avoiding her? She did that sometimes when Lu angered their mother, as though worried she might contract the empress's ire by proximity.

"You look very beautiful," her sister mumbled politely, gesturing at Lu's deep, blood-colored robes, flecked with embellishments of gold thread and turquoise stones.

Gods, sometimes Min spoke to her as though she were a stranger.

"I know. You, on the other hand, look nervous," Lu countered. She'd meant it playfully, but the words came out sharper than she'd intended. "You're not the one being tested here, you do realize?"

"Mother says I have to stand with her while we see you and Se—Lord Set off," Min said meekly, as though that explained anything. "There will be a lot of people."

"And how *is* our dear mother?" Lu asked blandly. "I haven't seen her in days. Can't imagine why." Behind her, Hyacinth snorted, and Butterfly did a poor job of hiding a smile. Instead of laughing though, Min frowned.

"Oh, Mother's been in a terrible mood—"

"I'm sure she has." Lu grinned and lowered her voice, "Do you think she's more likely to murder me or Father first?"

"Don't say that," Min mumbled vaguely. "She cares about you . . ." Her voice trailed off, as though even she couldn't believe her own words.

Lu felt a familiar pinprick of annoyance. Sisters, she was fairly certain, were supposed to present a unified front against their parents. Min acted more like a twice-shot, over-burdened messenger, running ragged between Lu and their mother, trying to keep the peace. Their mother was a tyrant, true, but if only her sister would stand up for herself now and again.

"It was a joke," Lu said, nudging her sister in the ribs with her elbow. Min flinched, and Lu bit back a sigh. Her sister was only a year younger than her, but sometimes—often—she still acted like a timid child. "Jokes are *funny*, Min. You can laugh. And don't worry, I won't do anything to upset Mother further, so long as she doesn't try anything with me, all right?"

Min made a vaguely agreeable sound in her throat. A breeze

washed over them, scattering white jasmine petals from the vines overhead. Min winced as one kissed her eyelid.

"Do you want to walk to the gate together?" she asked.

Lu glanced back at Hyacinth. The handmaiden shrugged. "Oleander and Siringa are still dressing."

"No," Lu told her sister. "You and your nunas go on. We'll come soon enough."

Min nodded and turned away.

Lu watched the darkness swallow her up. The flesh of her arms prickled. The air was far from cold, but it carried something of the autumn; an underlying bite, a hint of frost and leaf mold. Golden and eerie and sad. Lu shook her head. She couldn't afford to be distracted right now. Not today.

"Shall I go fetch the others, Princess?" Hyacinth asked.

"Yes," Lu told her. She stretched her arms overhead and tossed a smirk over her shoulder at the other girl. "And get ready to call me empress."

⚜

The sun rose as the gates of the Immaculate City opened, creating a path from the palace Heart to the beginnings of Kangmun Boulevard within the First Ring. Lu guided Yaksun along it. She gave the elk an affectionate pat on his neck. He snorted and shook his head, the mantle of beveled jewels and copper bells decking his antlers jingling merrily.

Set was farther back in the line, surrounded by his fawning retinue and draped in blue Hana finery. She bristled and looked adamantly forward. It had been nearly a week since she had last seen her cousin. The day after the Betrothal Ceremony, her mother had cajoled her and Min into a private dinner with him. The evening had ended in a shouting match when Set began talking of expelling the Ellandaise from the city once he was emperor. Min had burst into tears when Lu shattered his plate against the wall.

The whole of the Rings had come to see them off, merchants staring from the doorways of their shops, and little children waving colorful silks out the windows of sky manses while their parents looked on. Everywhere there was laughter and excited chatter.

Everywhere but where her mother stood like a streak of gloom just inside the palace gate. She'd huffed in impatience when Lu passed by, as though the whole affair were a childish charade she could hardly stand to partake in. At her side, Min had looked slight and sleepy; Lu hadn't been able to catch her eye, so anxiously transfixed had her sister been on their mother.

Lu felt a tug of discomfort in her gut. Her father should be there with her. She recalled the last time she'd seen him—how he had sought her eyes during the Betrothal Ceremony. How she had looked away, the picture of contempt and spite. Who knew how long he had left? Not long enough for her to waste. Shame welled up in her. She resolved to see him the moment she returned.

Set rode up alongside her, waving graciously toward a group of Second Ring children gawking at them from a shaved-ice stand. When he turned back to her, though, his gray eyes were angry little chips of flint. "You've managed to rile the people up with this competition of yours, I'll give you that much," he bit out.

"You're welcome to end it at any time," she responded, her face a cheery rictus. "Just go back home."

They were approaching the Northern Gatehead separating the Second Ring from the sprawling country beyond. Built of wood and iron, the gate was as high as twenty men, and inscribed with auspicious tidings and protective runes. The captain at the lead of their party gave a shout to the posted guards. With a deep creaking of gears, it began to rise.

"A diversion," Set sneered, barely audible above the sound. "That's all this is, in the end. Isn't it?"

Lu bristled. "For me, perhaps. For you, it will be the end of your career."

The gate reached the peak of its ascent with a final screech, then let off a deep, metallic shudder as the guards locked it into place. The captain shouted once more to the guards who confirmed it was safe to pass.

Lu looked her cousin in his gray Hana eyes, narrowed with contempt and suspicion.

"Once this betrothal nonsense is over, I would write to your mother in Bei Province and tell her to prepare the household for your return," she told him lightly. "They'll want to restock the poppy resin, no doubt."

It was a cruel jab, but then beneath all his gentility and elegant silks, her cousin was a cruel man.

He stiffened visibly, then reined up. His stallion threw its head and gave a blustery snort. "We shall see soon enough, cousin, whose end comes first." Then he surged ahead.

Beyond the city walls the soft rolling land was blanketed in the greenery of late summer, flecked intermittently with tiny farmhouses of wood and stone. As their party maneuvered down Kangmun Boulevard, Lu noted distant men and women in the fields, hunkered down over low-growing bean shrubs and wading through rice paddies. To her right, a plowman drove a pair of yoked oxen through a newly fallow field.

Before them lay the northern forest, where the hunt would commence. Rising up from behind the trees, the harsh, snow-buffeted peaks of the northern Ruvai Mountains stabbed the sky. Miles of unknown wilderness.

She cast a sidelong glare at Set. Her cousin sat upon his white stallion with lazy elegance, joking with one of his Hana entourage. The other man laughed deferentially. Lu gritted her teeth.

A quartet of adolescent Hu boys upon elk fell in beside her, followed by a group of their Hana peers riding young stallions they seemed scarcely able to control. Royal hunts always meant the debut of a new crop of well-bred boys eager to prove themselves.

She recognized one of the Hu, Wonin—Hyacinth's younger brother. He met her eyes and gave a deferential nod of his head. She winked in response, watching as he made his elk prance delicate as a pony for the amusement of the other boys.

As the party reached the edge of the Northwood, the captain of the guard signaled toward his subordinates with a stiff gesture of his arm. Wordlessly, the men moved their elk into two meticulous lines around the party, one toward the front, and one toward the rear.

Normally her father would have spoken here, but today there was no mention of him. No one wanted to admit their emperor was ailing. Instead, the captain of the guard cleared his throat and announced, "Shin Mung, adviser to the Emperor, our Lord of Ten Thousand Years, will now recite an excerpt from the Analecta to initiate the hunt."

A thin, bookish man, Shin Mung slipped somewhat gracelessly from his elk and stepped forward. He recited in a quavering voice: "When the true king rules humanely, according in every manner with the Ways of the Heavens, then his kingdom will experience peace and prosperity . . ."

Lu passed her cousin a glance. Set was poised in his saddle, the trace of an idle smile twisting his elegant lips. But there was something new beneath its placid surface—something brimming, trembling. Anxiety, perhaps?

No. Eagerness.

"The true emperor is not he who holds the sharpest sword, but he who inspires his kingdom through his own righteous conduct," droned Shin Mung.

It had been five years since she'd seen Set swing a sword or string a bow. He'd been of unremarkable talent at the time— neither particularly good nor bad. But he'd become a general since. Even if it was nepotism that had won him that rank, he must have acquired some martial skills in the interim.

Lu flexed her fingers, itching to reach for her bow, her sword. Some weapon. Instead she took the leather gloves from her saddlebag and pulled them on.

". . . may your mounts be swift, and your aim be true," Shin Mung concluded.

And with that, they were off.

They rode deeper into the forest and prepared to split off into two groups. Sleek, athletic hounds laced artfully between the mounted horses and elk, alternating between efficiently sniffing the air for potential prey and nipping at one another in clumsy, puppyish discord.

Set raised an arm to call his men toward him, delegating and strategizing. Lu called over her own men. Yuri came first, reining up beside her.

"Princess," he said tersely.

Something in his tone made Lu meet his eyes. They were tight at the corners, and overly bright with some unspoken urgency. A cold finger of fear scraped down her spine.

"Shin Yuri," she said, leaning in toward him. "I'm glad you were able to come! I wasn't sure you'd be here. I haven't seen you in a few days." It was true—he'd disappeared after the Betrothal Ceremony. Had he even been at the banquet? She couldn't recall. Somehow the idea frightened her now. She'd overlooked something, she realized. What was it?

Yuri snatched her by the wrist, hard. He raised his other hand high; it held a knife. He brought it down, but she threw an elbow, hitting him in the wrist and knocking it from his hands. Just as he had taught her to do. Just as he must have known she would.

She met his eyes, wild and searching. His were grimly satisfied.

He hauled her close, nearly yanking her from her saddle. The coarse stubble on his face scoured her skin, and she heard him hiss a single word in her ear.

"*Run.*"

That was when the first arrow flew at her.

CHAPTER 10

Shamaness

A magnolia tree grew just outside the window next to Min's bed. She would track its changes through the year, watching the spring's crop of tight velveted buds soften and flare fuschia at their tips, then unfurl into fleshy stars spangling the bare branches. It struck her as sad in a way; each change so grand and lovely, and yet never final, always fruitless, always doomed to begin again.

Today, though, Min looked through the tree, trying to recall her dreams from the night before. Every time she grasped for them, they receded, as irrevocable as the tide. All she remembered was that her sister had been there, but when Min called out to her, Lu had turned around and it hadn't been Lu at all.

"I wonder what's happening." Snowdrop's high voice pierced Min's reverie. Min looked over to where her nunas were gathered in the corner of the room, chattering and eating candied haws from little bowls. Butterfly had unraveled her long black hair and was slowly running a comb through it.

"Oh, I *so* wish we could watch the hunt," Snowdrop chirped on.

Tea Rose laughed. "What do you know about hunting, Snowdrop?"

"I didn't say I wanted to *hunt*; I just wish I could *see* it!"

Min felt a stab of annoyance. "What time is it?" she asked. Not that it mattered. Her lessons for the day had been canceled.

"Princess, do you need something?" Butterfly swept over to her, reordering the bedding Min had disturbed. "Are you hungry?"

Min clung at the coverlet draped across her lap, drawing it down. A waxy streak of white powder and lip rouge was smeared across the edge—makeup from yesterday. For a moment she thought of how the nunas would be forced to strip the bed later for careful washing and felt a pang of panicked guilt, but she pushed it away. That was their *duty*. To serve her needs.

They should have done a better job of removing her makeup in the first place.

"Leave me!" she snapped, so suddenly that Butterfly dropped the blanket she was holding. It collapsed to the floor in a silken puddle.

"Princess?" the nuna asked hesitantly.

"I wish to be alone," Min said.

There was, she discovered, a mean pleasure to be taken in the other girl's uncertainty.

What is wrong with me?

Nothing. It wasn't her, it was them. Butterfly always seemed so sure of herself, but in the end she was only a servant.

The others were staring now. Min glowered back at them. It was time they recognized her as their mistress, not their charge. "Go! All of you!"

They filed out, wordless and radiantly uncomfortable. Snowdrop moved as though to close the pocket doors, but Butterfly yanked her along by the sleeve, leaving the doors open a crack.

Min collapsed back into her bed, scowling into the swallowing softness of the blankets. Outside, she could hear the faint, traipsing giggle of the stream in her courtyard garden, but that was all. It occurred to her that this was the most alone she'd been in a long time. Perhaps ever. It felt nice, just lying there by herself.

Except for the hard pain against her chest. Something was trapped between her and the wooden platform of her bed. She propped herself up onto her elbows and tucked her chin to her neck to look down. Of course—her quartz necklace, heavy on its chain. Set's necklace.

She felt a trill of excitement in her belly. Stupid, really. She wasn't some flighty little baby to be awed by a handsome boy, and he was a man grown, and most likely going to marry her sister . . .

Still. She sighed and flopped down onto the bed again, squeezing the crystal tightly in her palm. It was warm, just as it had been the night he'd given it to her. *The night that had felt like a dream,* she thought. Another rush of pleasure tickled her belly when she remembered how he'd called it their *secret*. And it was. No one else knew—not her mother, not Lu, not her nunas. It belonged to them—to her—alone.

Min lifted the pendant with one hand. It caught the shaft of sunlight streaming through the half-opened doors and flung scintillating motes of pinks and greens and yellows across the room, the color streaking down the papered walls. She pressed the crystal up against one eye, closing the other so that the whole of her world was contained within that iridescent prism. It was a nice idea: everything clean and tiny, a tinted and lilting pastel version of itself.

A shadow fell over the doorway, eclipsing the light and throwing her tiny glowing world into darkness. Min scowled. "Snowdrop, I can *see* you. I said I wanted to be left alone . . ." she began, lowering the crystal.

White silk robes flashed in the slivered doorway.

Min sat up. The heavy pendant dropped hard against her sternum, as though echoing her racing heart.

No one but she and her nunas and perhaps Amma Ruxin would be in her apartments at this hour. And neither nunas nor ammas wore white. Who would? White—the color of mourning. Of ashes. Of death.

Cautiously, Min stood. "Hello?" she called.

There was no answer. Then she heard a pair of pocket doors down the hall whisper open.

Min walked over and peered out of her room, fingers perched gingerly on the wooden frame of her own doors. She heard Butterfly giggling from within the closed room directly across the way, familiar and oddly distant.

Then she saw it: the doors at the far end of the hallway were opened, just wide enough for a girl Min's size to slip through. Shafts of sunlight wove their way through the woody vines and glossy green leaves of the jasmine growing over the open, trellised ceiling above, but Min shivered. It was strange, how an open door could frighten her so.

Something brushed her cheek and she nearly screamed. It was only a falling jasmine flower, though, from the vines overhead. Min glared at where it had come to a rest on the floor just beside her foot, snow-and-pink petals fringed in the sour brown of its waning. She made sure to step on it as she walked out the open door into the courtyard.

And found herself standing between the two guards stationed there. Of course—how could she have forgotten them. She opened her mouth to explain she was going for a stroll, then snapped it shut, her face flushing in panic at the flimsy lie. They were sure to fetch Amma Ruxin no matter what she said, but perhaps they could at least tell her who had come through—

"Would've loved to join the hunt," said one of the guards.

"Excuse me?" she squeaked.

The other man grunted in agreement next to her. "Would you want to be in the princess's party, though, or the general's?"

The first man gave a sly grin. "I'd want to be in the winning party, naturally."

"Which is . . . ?"

"Which is the winning party."

"Clever," his friend said, and snorted.

"Discreet," said the first man.

Min cleared her throat, shocked that they hadn't seemed to

notice her presence yet. "D-did someone come through here just now?" she asked in a voice that quavered far more than she would've liked.

But instead of straightening and stammering apologies, the guards just chuckled between themselves. The first one stretched, then twisted at the waist and bit out through a yawn, "Whatever the results of today are, things are going to get wild around here." He turned and raised his eyebrows at the other guard then, looking directly at Min.

Or . . . *through* her.

This time, she couldn't stop the cry of alarm that rose in her throat.

It hardly mattered, though—neither of them heard it. Instead, the second guard asked, "Listen, have you got some extra tobacco? I'm dying for a smoke."

The first one nodded, glancing around surreptitiously to make certain they were alone before pulling a rolled cigarette from within his belt pouch. Then, casual as anything, he handed it to the second guard.

His arm went straight through Min's chest.

She looked down in shock, a strangled noise emerging from her. When the man withdrew his hand, Min half expected something to happen . . . What, exactly, she wasn't certain. Would there be a gushing wound where his arm had been? Would her body disappear in a puff of gray smoke?

Instead: nothing. The second guard lit his cigarette with a match produced from inside his jacket and eked out a low moan of satisfaction.

Min looked down at herself, heart pounding, half a hundred

stupid children's ghost stories flickering through her mind. She didn't *look* any different than normal. She reached down and pinched herself cautiously, and felt the customary jolt of pain.

Only . . . she waved her hand in front of the second guard's eyes, just to be certain. No response.

Behind her, a girl laughed, rough and throaty.

Min whirled around just in time to see a flash of white robes disappear behind the groundskeeping cottage that stood at the edge of her courtyard.

This time she didn't hesitate, running after the glimpse of this unknown girl.

She was well ahead by the time Min managed to round the cottage, but for the first time Min could see her: a slight figure, running across the footbridge so lightly she seemed to float. Her long ink-black hair that was bound in a tight plait down her spine and her simple, gray-white robes were of an unfamiliar cut that struck Min as both foreign and old-fashioned. In her wake the girl left the scent of vetiver and wood smoke, and something that struck Min as the smell of stone—but no, that was ridiculous, wasn't it?

"Wait!" Her voice tore from her, but the girl did not so much as turn; she just crossed the footbridge and then abruptly turned off the path.

Min caught the barest glimpse of a pale, narrow face, like the sliver of a new moon. The girl's eyes were large and dark and unbearably sad, contradicting the low laugh she left hanging in the air as she disappeared into a building. It was only then that Min stopped and realized where she was.

The old shamaness temple loomed high over her.

Min felt an odd certainty then, that she could still turn around, could still wend her way back to her apartments, slip past the guards and down the hall, past where Butterfly and Dove and Snowdrop and Tea Rose were gossiping, could slip back into the soft silks of her bedding and close her eyes and pretend this was all a strange dream. But that would be a lie—she knew this in her heart.

She moved toward the vacant temple.

And felt a sudden flare of heat upon her chest, so fierce that it nearly took her breath away. She looked down at the crystal pendant from Yunis, Set's gift, and saw it clearly for what it was: a sign.

The unknown girl had left the temple door ajar. Min looked at that black gap and swallowed hard, feeling a trill of fear in her chest. No, not quite fear—anticipation. Excitement. Was this what Lu felt when she broke the rules? Was that why she smiled so brightly when she did it?

Min stepped into the dark.

It was cool inside, which might have been a relief from the summer heat were it not so musty. She blinked, willing her eyes to adjust, seeing nothing.

As if in response flame flared to life in the next room and Min followed it, no wiser than a moth drawn to a candle. When she turned the corner, she found the unknown girl sitting there, just as she somehow knew she would. The girl knelt on a silk pillow, tending a brazier and humming contentedly, as though she had been waiting there all morning just for Min to arrive.

"What do you want from me?" Min asked, her voice somehow both timid and much too loud in the silence.

The girl looked up, and for the first time Min could see her properly. The wan face she had glimpsed earlier wasn't exactly pretty up close but striking. A face like a fox, or some other feral thing.

The girl smiled.

"I have a gift for you," she told Min. And yet her lips did not move in accordance with the words. Rather her voice seemed to at once seep from the walls of the dark room and emanate from within Min's own head.

Who are you? Min wanted to ask. But something in the room—perhaps the musky odor of whatever herb the girl was burning in her brazier—was making Min sluggish, as if she were walking through water. Her head felt woolly and soft.

"You look tired," the girl said, again without speaking. "Please, sit." She gestured to where another silk cushion had appeared on the opposite side of the brazier.

Min stumbled forward and all but collapsed to her knees.

"Let me help you." The girl was at her side, though Min could swear she had never seen her move. She held out one small hand and Min took it, grateful. When she clutched it, she felt a jolt move through her arm, straight to her heart. It felt at once like a burn, and yet cold, so cold.

"Who . . . ," Min began, but her eyes were fluttering closed.

"When I was a boy, I sometimes wondered how I would die."

Min blinked. It was her father's voice. And there—there was her father, lying in his silken bower of pillows, far below her. Min gave a cry—she was in her father's bedchamber, and she was *floating*. Hovering in the air just below the intricately painted ceiling, like a spider suspended in an invisible web.

The girl was beside her, still clutching her hand. When Min met her eyes—somehow so familiar, that deep, earthy brown flecked with spangles of gold and copper—the girl raised a finger to her lips to gesture for silence. Then she grinned, as though they were just two naughty children waiting for a joke they'd played to unfold before them. Min clamped her mouth shut, though she sensed somehow her father would not be able to hear her, even if she were to scream.

"What did you say?"

Min looked down and saw her mother there as well. The empress had been stooped down beside a brazier, tending idly to its low-burning embers. As she spoke now, though, she rose, her voice stern and strong in contrast to the emperor's dry rasp.

It was strange, seeing her parents alone like this. A hidden passageway connected the emperor's apartments with those of his wife so they could visit one another with a sense of marital privacy, but nevertheless it was common knowledge that her mother rarely visited her father.

The emperor moved, and Min watched uncomprehendingly as he drew a long, thin silver flute away from his mouth. No— not a flute. She spotted the jade bowl affixed to its end, then the eerie, telltale blue smoke that unfurled dreamily from his nostrils, between his parted lips. He set the pipe on his night-stand beside a matching lacquered tray bearing an odd little lamp and some tools Min did not recognize.

Poppy tar? But it's banned! She could not understand. *Perhaps his physicians recommended it, for his pain,* she told herself. But wasn't that what poppy tears were for? And the physicians were always so cautious, so miserly in doling those out . . .

"When I was a boy, I sometimes wondered how I would die," her father rasped again, interrupting Min's thoughts. The way he said it, Min wasn't certain if he was responding to her mother or just speaking for his own benefit. He blinked furiously, as though his eyes were dry, and his gaze was vacant. For a moment, he cast it upward and looked straight at Min—or rather, straight through her.

"It was a childish thought, only half-formed—pale smoke curling around the edges of my mind," her father continued. "I could only understand death as being somehow apart from me. A thing that would happen only to some old man I might become, but never to me. You understand."

"I do not," her mother replied flatly. She was fiddling with one sweeping, embroidered sleeve of her robe.

"Only," the emperor continued as though she hadn't spoken, "only, it's not like that. I didn't see it until now. There is no mystery. There's no distance at all. All the days of my life were with me then, even then, as a boy . . ."

Her mother drew something from her sleeve then—a silken purse. She loosed its strings and withdrew a small white porcelain vial no bigger than one of her elegant fingers. Min watched as she pulled the stopper, walked to the emperor's bedside, and emptied its contents into a cup of tea.

"If only I'd been able to see, to truly see myself as I was, I would've seen my death there as well. Death has walked beside me all my days," her father murmured.

"Drink this," her mother said harshly, holding forth the cup of medicine and tea. "It will bring you relief."

Her father looked at the tea, then into her mother's eyes.

"I gave you what you wanted," he said. "You have Minyi."

Min jerked at the sound of her own name. What did he mean, exactly?

"I do." Her mother's words were fierce and taut.

"You remember what Tsai told you, about the girls' fates being interwoven." His voice was a whisper.

Her mother's face twisted into a horror. The look lasted only for a breath, though—then her mother's placid, beautiful face dropped back down like a mask.

Tsai? Min had never heard the name before. The unknown girl's hand clenched tight around her own, like a claw.

"I will never forget what that creature said," her mother said harshly, still holding out the tea.

"I'm dying," the emperor said, looking at the cup. "I won't be longer than another month. Maybe two."

"I know."

"Then, why?"

"You're in pain. And you're a coward. The going will be softer this way."

"I cannot," he murmured. "Lu. I must remain for Lu . . ."

At the mention of her sister, their mother went white. A horrible sound like a growl rose in her, and she flung herself upon her husband, one hand scrabbling at his throat and face. The tea sloshed over the cup she grasped in the other. Min held back a gasp. Her hand tightened in the unknown girl's.

"We have to stop them!" she cried. But then she saw the hungry, rapt stare on the other girl's face and understood she would receive no help from that quarter.

Below them, her mother had gained control over her father.

Min watched helplessly as she closed one hand hard over his nose and pried his mouth open, dumping the contents of the cup into his mouth. She held his jaw closed as if he were a fussing baby.

Her father flailed weakly against the soft, coddling cushions of his bed, then went rigid. Min saw the muscles of his throat—sagging and thin beneath the regal collars of his robes—working as he finally swallowed the tea.

Her mother released him with a satisfied sigh. A strand of hair had fallen loose from its fiercely clean upsweep. She composed herself, but Min couldn't stop staring at that bit of hair.

For a long moment, the emperor was so still he seemed to have stopped breathing. But then: "Would you stay?"

The dying man's voice was low, husky, and yet there was something of a child's plea in it. A whine, almost.

The empress stood, straightening her robes. "I've killed you," she told him coolly. "You know that much, don't you?"

"I know," he said. "Only . . . I don't wish to be alone."

"You are afraid."

"Yes."

Her mother leaned in close, her gray eyes regarding her dying husband with some strange mixture of tenderness and brutality. "Then be afraid," she whispered.

She righted herself, drew the tiny glass vial up inside the sleeve of her gown, and slipped out the hidden door without a backward glance.

The emperor's face went ashen. His breathing slowed, then quickened into a rusty rattle.

"Father!" Min cried, shaking herself from her shock, trying to comprehend the lie that was her family laid bare before her.

"Please," she said, turning to the girl beside her. "What's wrong with you? Why are you showing me this?" She tried to wrench her hand free, but the girl's grip was like iron, watching the man below them struggle and gasp and writhe. Her face no longer had the strange feral hunger it had shown before, but it was no less intense, no less rapt.

Min followed her gaze and saw her father staring wide at nothing—but, no. He was staring at them. He was staring back at the girl.

His body had gone slack, but for a moment his face contorted, a terrible collision of grief and longing.

"*Tsai* . . ."

The name was less spoken than pushed out of him, a long-held breath finally released. It was his last; he went still.

"Who are you?" Min demanded, whirling back at the other girl. Unable to extract her hand from hers, Min shook their arms in furious tandem. "What are you?!"

At that, the unknown girl started, as though only now, for the first time, hearing Min's voice. She turned slowly toward her and smiled.

"I am the death born inside you," she said. She embraced Min. Where their skin touched, it was like fire. Min screamed and threw her arms out, trying to push the other girl away, but it was as though she were melting, searing flesh to flesh, sinking down into her bones—

"Princess!"

There were hands upon her now—new hands, different hands. Stable and firm and warm. Alive.

"Princess!"

Min opened her eyes. Butterfly leaned over her, prying Min's wrists and arms away from her face. Behind her, Snowdrop was wringing her hands. "Princess, please. You must wake," Butterfly said.

"I'm . . ." Min saw that she was in her own bedchambers, lying atop her coverlets, fully dressed. A dream. It had all been a strange dream. A horrendous and ugly dream, but a dream nevertheless. Her mother, her father—none of it was real.

Oh, thank the gods.

"Princess?" Butterfly said, apprehensive. "Are you all right?"

Min blinked, felt the cold tension ebb from her muscles. The way the nunas were staring, Min could tell her face must have an odd look. She quickly rearranged it. "I'm awake. I'm fine."

Butterfly nodded and released her hands. The fear on Snowdrop's face did not fall away. If anything, it now intensified. Min felt suddenly more awake than she had been.

"What is it?" Min asked, her body going cold, as though Snowdrop's fear were so potent as to be catching.

"Princess . . . ," Butterfly began, for once seemingly at a loss for words.

"It's your father," Snowdrop blurted, tears welling in her eyes. "The emperor is dead!"

CHAPTER 11

Stalked

*A*nother arrow flew, this one so close to Lu's head she felt it whisper past her hair. It planted itself in the earth with a soft *thunk*.

Run.

Chaos broke. Shouts went up from her men—there was a flash of steel as weapons were drawn. A crossbow twanged and someone in Hu reds fell to the ground. Lu tried to track who it was, who had shot—who, if anyone, was on her side, and who was the enemy.

"Don't shoot, you idiots!" Set barked. "You're too close! We're going to hit each other!"

Set. The dissonant pieces of the puzzle fell into place. This was her cousin's doing.

Yaksun reared, nearly tearing Lu from Yuri's grasp, but the old man clung on with one hand, using the other to still his horse.

"You knew? Why didn't you *tell* me?" she hissed.

"I didn't know—not until just now. Listen. There's no time. Go North. There's an apothecarist named Omair in the village of Ansana. He will help you. Trust no one, not even your own men."

His words cut deep. "My own . . . ? They wouldn't . . ."

He growled and shook her hard. "I know you think you're invincible, but you can't fight them all on your own. Now, push me away, and make it look good. If you ever loved me, ever trusted me, you'll do what I say."

But *did* she trust him?

There was no time. No choice. She gave him a theatrical shove. The old man tumbled from his horse in a controlled fall; he hit the ground and rolled.

"*Ya!*" Lu yelled, digging her heels into Yaksun's broad sides. The elk gave a bellow and lunged forward in a full gallop.

Behind her, the clash of steel on steel rang an eerie song into the quiet wood. Not everyone had been part of Set's ambush, then. She hazarded a glance over her shoulder as six Hana men on horses broke out of the fray in pursuit.

"She's getting away!" Set screamed.

Lu urged Yaksun on. The elk picked its way over the forest floor; he was equipped to deal with this terrain. *The Hana in their arrogance had never given up their attachment to horses,* Lu thought with grim satisfaction. She yanked her reins to the left, urging the elk up an embankment, kicking up further distance between them and her pursuers. She cut a jagged path through the trees, pressing toward where they were densest. It was a risk; one misstep and they would be on the ground.

Yaksun ran until he was frothing at his bit. He stumbled,

and a lance of fear drove itself through Lu's belly, but the elk hadn't tripped, he was merely exhausted. How long had they been running? Lu looked back again, but there was only the stillness of the trees now. She reined up and the elk stopped. Had she lost them?

Something large moved in the undergrowth.

Lu froze, wondering if she had imagined it.

Keep going, stupid, she scolded herself, digging her heels into Yaksun's sides. If there was something there, better to present a moving target than to freeze like some witless deer.

It's only a boar, she told herself. *Or a badger, or—*

A silent blur of blue-gray advanced, then receded in the corner of her right eye. In spite of herself, she reined up and stopped. She was being followed. Stalked.

Around her, the wood was once more maddeningly, mockingly still. She could hear the diffuse, nebulous screech of cicadas in the treetops, the lazy fall of dead leaves and twigs. Nothing else.

Stupid, she repeated. *You're like a scared little child, turning shadows into ghosts.*

"Come on," she whispered to Yaksun, guiding him on, a bit faster now.

The elk stopped, let out a guttural low.

"Yaksun," she hissed, kicking at his sides. But the elk snorted in agitation, stamped backward, and threw his head, limpid brown eyes wide, ringed white and lolling.

The dam inside her broke, and all at once fear rushed down her spine in an icy rivulet. The thing was close. She felt its eyes on her from the shadows.

This time the streak of blue-gray came threading through the trees on her left, fast and close. She could see it now: thick fur, and flashing black eyes.

A wolf?

She whipped the bow from her back and scanned the trees, arrow nocked, heart thrashing against her ribs. *Could it truly be a wolf?* There hadn't been wolves in the Northwood since long before the Hu had conquered the Hana. Farmers had complained of losing livestock, and the king—she could not remember which, nor the dynasty—had initiated a campaign to have the creatures slaughtered. If it was a wolf . . .

They're pack animals, she thought with rising panic. Perhaps it wasn't just one wolf but several she was seeing.

A branch snapped to her right and she whipped her bow in the direction of the sound.

Not now, she thought, furious. She hadn't made it away from her cousin's grasp only to be felled by some animal, no matter how big.

The rage pulsing under her skin gave her an odd comfort. She might be at the precipice of losing all she knew, but she still had herself.

Another flash of gray. Lu instinctively shot, but heard nothing but the soft whisper of the arrow bedding itself amid the bracken.

And the animal was before her, claws digging into the rotted log upon which it stood.

She opened her mouth as though to yell, but the sound caught in her throat.

It was massive. Half the size of Yaksun.

But instead of crouching and leaping at her, the thing gave her a curiously intelligent look, then loped off into the trees.

She lowered the bow, cold sweat prickling her forehead, the back of her neck. What game was this? Was it toying with her? Where had it gone?

Lu hesitated, staring at where it had been. If she let it go now, it would likely return.

She patted Yaksun on the neck and directed him in the direction the wolf had disappeared. She would kill it before it killed her. That was the rule of the wood.

As she followed, she caught fleeting glimpses of it between the trees, emerging amid a clump of ferns, disappearing behind rocks, fleet as water. She flung an arrow at it, then another, but each fell useless to the wayside, as she somehow knew it would. It felt, she thought, as much like a dance as it did a chase.

Turn back, a voice inside her hissed. But something in her heart, something giddy and certain as the blood thundering there, propelled her forth. Even Yaksun seemed to have lost his fear, surging on as though he understood that she was now the hunter, and not the hunted.

The trees fell away, leaving them at the edge of a precipice. The wolf stopped at its edge, still and large and implacable as truth. Lu reined up quickly, scarcely more than a stone's throw away. Below them, she could hear the narrow trickle of a stream.

"Well met," she heard herself say, breath heaving in her

chest. She pulled the bow once more from her back and nocked an arrow, drew. For a moment, they stared at one another, the wolf and the girl. Its eyes were black, and somehow uncannily human. It seemed to be waiting for something.

What it was never came. She let her arrow fly.

Its course was true. She could almost see it sinking deep into the plush fur of the creature's chest, lacing delicately between its ribs, and finding the meat of its heart.

The wolf leaped over the edge of the cliff. Her arrow thunked safe and disappointed into the soft earth where the creature had only just stood.

Stunned, Lu leaped from Yaksun and ran to the precipice, slamming down beside her spent arrow to peer over the edge.

Below, she could see the little stream she'd heard, and lying prone, half in the water, was the wolf.

Dead, she thought, oddly bereft.

But then, it stirred. At first she thought she'd imagined it, the tremor was so slight. Then it lifted its head, rose on its front paws, and stood. Only—she gasped at the sudden realization— only now it was transparent as a thinning fog. She could see the stream and ferns and trees through the blue-gray haze of its body.

A ghost, she thought wildly, feeling dizzy. Feeling unreal, like she had taken leave of her own flesh. *Like in all the folk stories. Strange beasts and ghosts in the wood.*

The wolf shook its massive head, gazed up at her. Seemingly unimpressed, it turned and loped off into the trees beyond the stream, its form growing fainter and fainter as it went before dissolving completely.

She heard a low moan, and only then did she notice the body the wolf had left behind in the stream, like a cicada leaves its spent skin. Or a spirit leaves a corpse. Except what lay below lived, trembling and heaving. Flesh and bone. And it resembled nothing of the ghostly wolf that had abandoned it.

It was a boy.

CHAPTER 12

The Forest

*T*he world was spinning and Nok's mouth was full of metal. He rolled to one side and spat a gob of blood. He must have bitten his tongue in the fall.

The fall. The Gifting Dream. The wolf.

Wild, impossible memories surged over him like water . . .

Water?

Nok lifted an arm. It was wet. He was lying in a creek bed.

He rolled out of the stream, trying not to shudder. The forest swam drunkenly before him. He closed his eyes against it.

This isn't happening, he told himself. *In a moment, I will wake up in Omair's house. I'll see wooden walls and a dirt floor. The stink of fresh salve will fill the room.*

But no, that wasn't right. Omair wasn't safe anymore, and Nok had nowhere to go. He opened his eyes.

A massive bull elk stood over him, blinking inquisitively, blocking out the sun.

Nok opened his mouth to shout, but the sound shriveled in his throat. When he tried to sit up, the beast let out a blustery snort and stepped back. It turned as it did so, revealing the rider atop its back.

She was tall and athletic, wearing a plush cloak of scarlet and a look of guarded amazement on her tawny face. One gloved hand grasped the elk's reins, the other hesitating in mid-reach toward the jeweled pommel of the sword on her back.

Nok knew her the moment their eyes met.

Hers were contoured with an exaggerated line of black paint, emphasizing dark brown irises flecked through with copper and gold. Lively like fire. Twin mirrors reflecting his own shocked recognition.

She blinked.

Nok scrambled to a stand but slipped in the muddy bank. His body cried out in protest from half a hundred places. Ignoring it, he leaped back, instinctively putting a boulder between them. His wrist was already swelling from where he had wrenched it against the ground. When he flexed it, pain blossomed through his arm, but it moved well enough. Not broken.

"I know you," the girl said, her words hushed in wonder.

He licked his lips.

"I know you. I know your face." She had the lofty, imperious voice of someone accustomed to people listening to her. It was lower than it had been all those years before, but familiar nonetheless.

"I—" Nok shot a look to his right, spotting the telltale rutted dirt and tunneled bracken of a deer trail cutting through the underbrush. All at once his senses flared, as though part of the wolf were still in him. He was assaulted by the musky residue of the creatures. His eyes dilated, drawing his focus to a tuft of white-brown fur clinging to a branch at its entrance. A flash of images: hurtling through the wood, snapping at hooves, the clench of his jaws around a haunch of flesh, blood on his tongue that was not his own. Absurdly, his mouth began to water.

He shook his head hard and the world retracted. He wondered if the fall had not done some permanent damage.

"Will you say something?" the girl demanded, guiding her elk a step closer.

"I'm not—I'm not anyone you would know," Nok said, looking back up at her. *Focus. Stay alert.*

His answer seemed to displease her. She frowned and asked rather more impatiently, "Don't you know who I am?"

"The Hu princess." That much was obvious. Even if they hadn't met before, he'd know. Even if he hadn't tried and failed to forget her these past five years.

Could he run? He wasn't certain. Should he try? He flicked his eyes toward the deer trail again, then back to the princess's war elk. The beast's shaggy legs were thick as the trunks of young trees. If the princess gave chase she would overtake him, though he might be able to lose her in the dense brush.

"You don't remember my name?" She sounded almost disappointed.

Of course I remember your name—how not? he thought. *Your people were the most exciting thing to happen in all my young life. And the worst . . .*

The elk took another step toward him. "I remember your name, Nokhai."

He started. And when he looked her in the eyes he was drawn back to that day in the desert, under the high noon sky, when the emperor and his retinue had arrived at the Ashina's summer encampment. It had seemed to him in the years to follow that that was the moment his life had bent, as though over a knife's edge, and clove itself in two.

She had appeared in a gilded litter back then, rather than on a war elk. There had been two princesses: she'd worn scarlet, while her sister was swathed in a blue paler and thinner than the sky. Their hair was decorated with a bricolage of jeweled pins and golden combs and little white star-shaped flowers so fresh and crisp Nok thought only magic could keep them alive in the heat.

She had drawn his eye somehow. While her younger sister had fidgeted nervously, thin fingers of sweat creeping down her brow, the elder girl sat remarkably still, like a satisfied, imperious cat. Every muscle trained by perfect will.

Then, as though feeling his gaze—though how could she? Everyone there must have been looking at her—she had turned and met Nok's eyes. He had opened his mouth, then shut it when he realized there was nothing to be said.

A heartbeat and it was over; the princess had looked away.

She did not look away now.

His ears pricked. All at once, his senses—the wolf's senses?— flared back to life. He smelled saliva, hot blood, animal musk, and acrid sweat. He heard a murder of crows explode from the treetops half a league away. And beneath it, he heard barking.

"What is it?" the princess asked him, seeing the change in his face.

"Didn't you hear it?" But of course she couldn't. He shouldn't even be able to.

This cannot be.

"Didn't I hear *what?*" she demanded.

Recognition dawned on her face as the sound reached her ears.

"*Hounds,*" Nok said needlessly. He looked around for some mark of the landscape that might point him homeward, but all he saw was dense wood and shadow. He had never been this far into the forest before, he realized, fear quickening to panic.

"Get on," the princess said abruptly, closing the distance between them with her elk. Nok jumped back. "Get on," she repeated impatiently. Nok stared stupidly at her. She frowned.

"You're lost, aren't you? I can tell you are. They're hunting me, but they'll rip you apart just as soon. Either that or my cousin will capture and torture you until you tell them where I've gone."

The idea of being killed was bad enough, but to be killed for aiding her . . .

"I don't know anything about *you,*" he snapped.

"Maybe not," she agreed. "But they won't know that. And I doubt they'll stop to ask. At the very least, they'll arrest you for trespassing in the forest during a royal hunt."

She was correct, of course. With an internal growl of fury, he threw himself upon the elk's back. The animal stamped at his touch, trying to shrug him off.

"Don't you know how to mount an elk properly?" the princess demanded, looking far more irritated than someone in her position had time to be. "You sit like you're used to riding donkeys."

"A mule, actually," he shot back.

Would that Bo were here now, he thought. The fat, surly creature would never be able to outrun imperial-trained hounds, but he might have bitten a few, as well as the princess, before they went down.

"Hold on," she told him.

Where? he thought, sweeping his gaze down her back and reaching for her waist instinctively. Only—that didn't seem appropriate. A flush flowered up his neck and he quickly moved his hands back, finally settling them on her shoulders.

She turned her head, incredulous. "Oh, so you *want* to fall off?"

He gritted his teeth and wrapped his arms around her waist. The girl's belly muscles tensed slightly under his touch, but she seemed otherwise unimpressed by the situation. He supposed this was hardly the time for good manners.

"Ya!" the princess yelled, digging her heels into the elk. The creature lunged forward into a full gallop.

Nok's stomach dropped, and for a moment he thought he might fall off from fear alone.

"Hold on tighter!" the princess shouted. It took a moment for his fear-blank mind to understand she was speaking to him. He did as he was told.

They launched into the dark of the wood.

CHAPTER 13

Hunter

*N*ot fast enough.

"*Ya! Ya!*" Lu bellowed, urging Yaksun on with her heels. The forest became a green smear around them, but still the hounds gained.

She heard the Ashina boy gasp in her ear as the elk leaped over a fallen log. A moment later she thought she heard him do it again, but—no. This time it was the *hiss* of a crossbow bolt flying past, a finger's width from her head. Behind her came the yelling of men and the crash of horses through the brush.

"They're *here!*" the boy cried, his fingers digging into her waist.

Shin Yuri's voice rang in her ears. *I know you think you're invincible, but you can't fight them all on your own.*

"Time to find out, Shin," she muttered, reining up hard with one hand, using the other to yank her sword loose from its sheath. The elk let out a bellow as a blur of dusky gray hounds laced between his legs, nipping and baying. He kicked one in the head, breaking its neck with an audible *snap*, The hound's body sprawled across the grass. The rest backed away, bristling but newly cautious.

"What are you *doing*?" the Ashina boy hissed urgently in her ear. "Keep going!"

"Take the dagger from my hip," she ordered. They would both be killed, but she could grant him the chance to go down fighting. He tensed at her back for a moment, as though he were considering fleeing, but then his hand slid down her waist and she felt the dagger slip from its sleeve.

"*Stop!*" her voice boomed out.

Caught off guard, their pursuers reined up hard: two figures wearing hoods, so she could not make out their faces. One of them jerked a crossbow up and leveled it at her. She hardly noticed; she was staring at their mounts. Not horses. Two shaggy brown war elk.

Hu soldiers.

Trust no one, not even your own men.

"Is this how you cowards would dispatch of your future empress?" Lu demanded, forcing the quaver from her voice. "With a crossbow bolt to the back? If you wish to kill me, show me your faces and come fight me as men."

"I told you not to shoot," hissed the soldier without the crossbow. "Idiot! It's supposed to look like an accident, remember?"

His voice was that of a boy's, cracking like a hinge in want of greasing. They were both boys, she realized with a start— young and slight upon their massive elk.

The one with the crossbow hesitated, his weapon dipping. He quickly drew it back up. "They can messy her up afterward— maybe a boulder fell on her, who's to say?" There was the lilt of a smile in his excited voice.

"We shouldn't do anything without the others."

"Well, where *are* the others?" the one with the crossbow demanded, glancing behind them.

"They split off at the ridge," responded the other, sounding very much as though he regretted the fact. "I don't know what happened, but half the dogs broke off . . . I can't hear them anymore. Wait, I know! I'll blow my horn."

"Do that," said the one with the crossbow, sounding a little nervous now, the thrill of the moment worn thin. He turned back toward Lu. "You need to come with us, Princess. Dismount your elk and drop your weapons to the ground."

He saw the Ashina boy at her back for the first time. His weapon dipped. "Who the—"

It was enough; Lu seized Yaksun's reins and the bull elk charged. She raised her sword.

There was a *twang* as the boy with the crossbow fired. Panic shattered his concentration and the bolt flew low, whizzing past her thigh and planting itself deep in Yaksun's flank. The elk screamed, rearing into the air.

The Ashina boy's hands slipped from about her waist. Lu reached out instinctively to grab him, and then they were both falling. She caught a glimpse of tangled black tree branches overhead, the sun peeking bright white from between them. Motes of pollen and dust drifted in the light, lazy and scintillating.

They landed hard, in a tangle. The ground punched the

breath from both their bodies. Everything was upside down, and the air rung with a cold, dead, gray sound, as if she were trapped in some great metal drum. In this strange new world, Yaksun thundered away from her through the trees.

Lu sat up and a hound lunged at her—only to fall limp, impaled on the end of the sword she had thrust forth in sheer instinct.

She pulled the blade free, wiping the dog's blood upon the grass. The smell of it drove the others back in a frenzy.

There was a twang and a flitting sound; another crossbow bolt flew at her, but this time she merely tilted her head away to avoid the clumsy shot. She felt calm, her heartbeat steady and even. The world seemed to slow, as though each moment were awaiting her permission before it passed.

Lu stood and advanced, the edges of her world pulled tight around the boy rider upon his elk, and the weapon in his grip. Three steps; the Hu boy was loading a new bolt and cranking, cranking . . .

The crossbow was on the ground and he was screaming. There was blood upon her blade and blood spraying from the end of his arm where his hand had been, drenching his tunic, his saddle, his elk. The animal caught the scent, reared, and the boy fell, clawing at the air as though to call back the fleeing beast. He was screaming still, high-pitched and unrestrained, but he went quiet when she put her blade through his chest.

The other boy reined up and charged his elk at her, his sword raised. She leaped to the side easily and met his blade with a crashing blow of her own. His sword flew from inexperienced hands and speared itself somewhere deep in the brush.

He reined up and came back at her, pulling his bow from his back and nocking an arrow.

He should have run.

She could see his fear—in his halting approach, the way he clenched his knees tighter around his mount. He was not without skill, and he was brave—she would give him that much.

It would not save him.

She thrust her sword back into its scabbard and grabbed the throwing ax from her hip. The boy scarcely had time to register the movement before she had drawn back her arm and flung the ax in a horizontal arc across his path.

The elk realized its doom first and shrieked—an awful sound that shattered the air around them. A sheet of blood like red silk poured from the slash her ax had opened. The rider tumbled from the creature's back, tried to roll. Too slow. The elk's front knees crumpled, and it went down with all the weight in the world, crushing the boy beneath it.

He threw his arms out instinctively, pointlessly, and as he did so, his hood fell back. Lu saw his face for the first time: wide-set, honest eyes that were now filled with fear. A brown birthmark on his chin.

Her mind froze as Wonin of Family Cui let out an awful cry that rose over the crunching of his bones, his bravery finally broken.

The wood fell eerily still, as though the whole of the world were sucking in a breath. The quiet was punctuated by the violence of Wonin's terrible sobbing.

Lu stared at his face, trying to understand the horror before her. Wonin's legs were surely broken beyond repair, but he might still live if—no. She felt the flame of hope in her heart die as a bubble of shockingly red blood emerged from between his lips.

Unthinking, she stepped toward him. He had been writhing without aim, but at her approach, he thrust out a grasping hand. She raised her bow, fitting it with an arrow in a single motion, quick and soft as a gasp.

Blood burbled up between Wonin's graying lips as he mouthed wordlessly at her.

But then she heard it. "*Please . . . ,*" the boy whispered.

She lowered her bow just a hair's breadth, uncertain.

"Do it."

Lu whipped toward the sound, her bow instantly raised. She had nearly forgotten the Ashina boy. He was on his feet. "What did you say?"

He snarled and leaped back. "Don't point that thing at me!"

She frowned, but quickly lowered her bow. "What did you say to me?"

"The boy—he's going to die," Nokhai said, softer now. "He's already dead; he just doesn't know it yet. He's got a gut wound, and internal bleeding, too, most like. He could be dying for hours. I've seen—it's ugly, that kind of dying."

She looked back at Wonin. He had ceased writhing and stared at them with the frantic stare of a wounded animal.

"Do it," the Ashina boy repeated grimly. "Straight between the eyes; he won't feel a thing."

Lu raised her bow instinctively, then lowered it. When she looked in Wonin's face, all she could see was Hyacinth. She couldn't possibly have something to do with this, could she? She had wanted to make that visit home . . . *No.* Lu couldn't even allow herself to think it. Not her best friend. The one closer to her than her own sister, her own skin.

"I-I cannot," she said aloud.

"You can," the Ashina boy assured her. "I saw you shoot just now."

"It's not that," she said. "I . . . I can't kill this boy. Not like this."

"Why not?" He seemed annoyed. "You killed the other one without hesitation."

"That was different. I was—it was his life or mine. This one is . . . I know him. I know his family . . ."

The baying of hounds cut through her words. From the sound of it they were close, just over the ridge. They had the high ground; they would be riding downhill, toward where she stood.

She looked up at Nokhai. His face reflected the same terse realization.

"Kill the boy," he whispered, and she was surprised to see something like regret in his eyes. "Do it now. If he's still alive when they reach him, he will give away your position. *Our* position."

Lu raised her bow again. But whereas before the weapon had been a natural extension of her body, now her hands shook so badly she could scarcely keep the arrow nocked. Hot tears seared at the corners of her vision. She drew back, but her arms fell, and the arrow speared the ground.

She raised the bow again, the fletchings of her arrow bristling against her cheek. She took a deep breath and felt her heart slow, as clearly as she felt the dappled sunlight on her face, or the firm earth beneath her feet. The blood moved in her, steady and calm and sure.

Wonin's eyes widened, his indistinct gaze struggling to focus on her. He grasped at the air, still fighting what was already inevitable, what was as good as done.

There was the gasp of her bow. The fletchings of the arrow sprouted like a dark flower from between Wonin's eyes. He stared skyward, unmoving. He looked oddly at peace.

CHAPTER 14

Prey

*D*eath for the boy was instant, or so Nok hoped. He would never know. He and the princess were already gone—scrambling up the westward ridge on hands and feet, away from the baying of the dogs.

It was a shame, a boy that young dying alone in the forest. But he would've done no better by them had the situation been reversed.

The hounds were louder now. The princess had strapped her bow to her back in order to run unimpeded—a wise move, but one that left them unprotected. The uphill slope was hampering their speed, too; amid the dogs' incessant barking Nok could now hear hooves drumming the earth.

He could save them, he realized. If only—if only he could caul. Would the wolf come to him again?

He sucked in as deep a breath as he could muster and imagined the beast in his mind's eye: long legs, great shaggy head, fine white teeth long as a man's finger, the deep swell of its chest, robust like the hull of a ship.

Come to me. Come to me now.

It fell upon him suddenly, like a warm wind. He stumbled at the sensation, then pitched forward violently. But before he could hit the ground a pair of lean muscular legs reached forth and cushioned the fall. His hands crumpled inward before his eyes and unfurled again as enormous paws. All at once he was enshrouded in coarse blue-gray fur, each of his senses heightened—especially smell. It was as though humans experienced smell only in the pale, washed-out grays of ink and water, and the wolf smelled in shrieking, vivid color. There was no time to be bowled over by it, though.

Too slow, he called to the princess. All that came from the wolf's mouth was a twisted snarl. He cursed himself internally. *Stupid! Wolves can't talk!*

But the girl turned to him, eyes widening, and he realized she had heard him, after all. He tried calling to her again: *Get on!*

To her credit, she didn't stop to question the unlikeliness of his voice in her head. With a running leap, she was on his back, clinging on by two fistfuls of fur.

Here goes nothing, Nok thought as the wolf surged forward through the brush.

Her thighs cinched instinctively around his middle and she bent over him until her chest was nearly flat against his back. She was a talented rider—while his gait surely differed from that of a war elk, it took her only a heartbeat to conform to his rhythm.

The shouts of dogs and men—true men this time, no callow boys—came after them, followed by a brief burst of crossbow bolts and arrows. These were the soldiers they had lost up at the ridge, and their aim was true—Nok and Lu were spared only by the distance between them, which seemed to shrink with each bound he took.

"I'm going to shoot back," the girl announced, and reached for the bow on her back.

Not worth it! he shouted to her. *They're gaining.*

"The more I kill, the fewer are left to gain."

Won't make a difference. Too many, he insisted, his own voice taking on the heavy panting of the running wolf.

"All the more reason to—" Her voice broke off in a scream of pain and she jerked hard against him, nearly falling.

Are you hit? Fear lanced through him when she did not answer immediately. But he felt her fists clench tightly through his fur and knew she lived.

"I'm fine," she hissed through gritted teeth. "An arrow—didn't stick, just a scrape."

Ssss. Another crossbow bolt sailed overhead and landed with a *thunk* in the dry ground by Nok's thundering feet. *Sss.* Another bolt—this one taking a chunk out of the wolf's ear. The animal registered the pain with scarcely more mind than it would pay a horsefly, but Nok saw that the men were closing in.

"It's no good!" the princess shouted. "They're nearly on us!"

They were so close Nok could hear the shouting of individual men.

"Stop. Let me get off," the princess said in his ear, her voice thick with pain.

What?

"Once they have me they won't follow you. No sense in us both dying."

Don't be an idiot!

She cradled her head with both arms as she threw herself from his back, hitting the dirt hard and rolling before rising to her feet.

Nok slammed the wolf's paws down hard, the great beast's claws spearing the earth. He pivoted in time to see the princess rise from her crouch and nock an arrow into place. Her arm shook oddly as she drew back—the wolf smelled the wound before he saw it, her red blood hidden amid the torn scarlet silk of her tunic. The arrow had grazed her . . . but it had taken a chunk of her flesh with it. Nok could see red muscle clench and strain as she lifted her arm and took aim.

But it was too little, too late. A shower of black arrows had been launched by the men pursuing her, and he watched with the wolf's keen eyes as they fell upon her from the sky like diving birds.

The air *moved*.

Nok did not understand at first, thinking perhaps it was some effect of the sun, or perhaps the way the wolf perceived the wind. But then the air *vibrated*, like the surface of a lake that had just been hit with a boulder. The arrows that should have pierced the princess through half a hundred times were swept away by the air. One moment they were there, and the next . . .

The soldiers were shouting in confusion . . . and then they were gone, swallowed by a gray haze pouring down from the ridge overhead. It was as though all the fog from the mountain-tops had come to flood the forest.

"What is this? What's happened?" The princess still had her bow nocked, but she was whirling around, uncertain of the direction in which she should loose it. Their eyes met, hers demanding an explanation, but Nok just shook his head.

His head . . . He looked down and saw he had regained his human form. The wolf had fled once more. Nok stood nervously and went to stand beside her. He was defenseless in his boy's body, and she had a weapon at least.

Without warning, the ground surged and rippled beneath their feet. Nok went tumbling and found himself caught in her arms. The two of them hurtled and pitched forward as the ground gave another mighty tremor.

An earthquake? But he had never felt an earthquake like this before.

All at once the air and earth about them went still, and a bright pinprick of light appeared deep in the forest ahead of them. As though there were a narrow tunnel that went straight through all the trees and bramble from the forest's edge to the clearing where they stood.

The pinprick of light became a shaft, and then a tunnel wide enough to fit a mule.

"Do you see—"

They were moving, pulled toward the light, as though the earth beneath them was nothing more than a rug being yanked across the floor by some churlish giant.

Nok threw his hands up over his eyes, expecting to crash through thornbushes and broken underbrush, but the feeling never hit. He opened his eyes and squinted at the shock of sun-light, oddly bright, no longer inhibited by a canopy of trees.

Through his slitted eyes he saw mugwort swaying lazily beneath the open summer sky.

A familiar brown face peered anxiously over him, blocking out the sun.

"We have much to talk about," Omair said.

CHAPTER 15

Histories

*W*ho . . . who are you?" Lu's voice creaked in a most unregal fashion, blinking up at the man's face. She tried to rise but found she was pinned to the earth by the weight of the Ashina boy, who had come to a rest across her knees.

He seemed as stunned as she, but the sound of her voice returned his bearings to him with a start. He jerked away from her as though he'd been burned where they touched, scrabbling away on elbows and heels.

Lu frowned. She'd been trying to *protect* him.

She made to push herself up, then let out a cry as she put her left hand to the earth. The crossbow wound. Her arm gushed hot blood at the sudden pressure. Shock and momentum had kept the pain at bay, but now it seared through her. Her arm felt on the verge of splitting in half.

"You're hurt."

The stranger lowered down to his knees with some effort. Then, with contradictory grace, he parted the silken tatters that had once been her sleeve to better view the wound.

"This will need to be sewn closed; it is very deep. For now I must staunch the bleeding." He pulled a scarf from around his neck and wound it around her arm. Lu stifled a scream of agony as he pulled the cloth tight.

Desperate for something else to focus on, she cast her gaze toward where the Ashina boy was cautiously standing, testing his limbs and joints.

"Are you hurt?" she called to him, her voice strained.

"I'm fine," he said coldly, as though he thought she might be disappointed by this news. He turned to look at the old man tending her arm. "Omair, what *was* that?"

Omair! The name gave her a start.

The old man shook his head and waved them up. "Inside! We cannot linger out here where someone might spot us."

"Omair," Lu repeated aloud, grabbing ahold of one gnarled brown hand. "Omair of Ansana? Shin Yuri sent me to you!" she stammered.

"Let's go inside," the old man repeated, casting a wary glance about them.

"Inside? Inside where?" She looked around properly for the first time. They were no longer in the depths of the inner forest, but on a grassy hilltop. Farmland sprawled about them. A large silvery tree stretched high overhead, casting dappled shade across her upturned face. There was a door in the trunk of the tree.

"Inside," the man said as Lu took a step toward it. "Then we can talk."

⚜

But talking was deferred in favor of the more immediate tasks of stitching up Lu's arm, and—seemingly far less urgent in her mind—heating a large iron pot of porridge. At his prompting, the Ashina boy brought a bowl of it over to her with an air of hostile reluctance. Lu accepted it, but her stomach felt like a knot of twisted iron, heavy and sullen. Politesse required she take a bite, but looking at the pale mash, she wondered if she would ever want food again. She set the bowl down.

The man regarded her with keen, curious eyes. "Yuri was right," he said. "There's something about you that feels just the same as your mother."

There was a weight in his voice she didn't understand. How could this stranger know her mother? The empress did not make a habit of befriending rural peasant apothecarists, surely.

Lu stood, fighting off a wave of dizziness. Her arm ached at the sudden rush of blood. "I must go back. My cousin—I don't know what he has planned."

"Yuri told me to keep you hidden until he arrived."

Her hand twitched toward the sword at her waist. This old man couldn't keep her imprisoned against her will—he could hardly stand up straight. But then she remembered whatever it was he had done in the forest. And there was the slipskin wolf to consider. She glanced sidelong to where the Ashina boy sat moodily on a stool by the cook fire. She doubted he would put up a fight; he wanted her gone.

It was hard to believe it was him, but there he was: the same hard-angled ochre face, the coarse black hair forever falling across his black eyes. Those eyes, though . . . they had changed. Once they'd sparkled like midnight starscapes.

Now they were black like an absence.

She could imagine what he'd been through since. The only true mystery was how he'd survived to end up here. She knew well enough what had happened to his Kith—to all the Gifted who had fought back.

They shouldn't have fought at all, she thought with a sudden flare of anger. The slipskins had no business going up against the imperial army; what had they expected? And her father had offered them a way out. But they had been too proud for that, too in love with their land and their traditions and their magic.

She understood, in a way. It was the decision she herself would've chosen had she been in their position. Still, had they bent just a bit—

Someone gasped. Lu looked up in time to see the apothecarist pitch forward in a swoon.

"Omair!" The Ashina boy had been skulking around the edges of the room, passing uncertain looks at both Lu and the apothecarist before, but now he leaped forward. He caught the old man by the shoulders and guided him upright again.

There was an odd gentleness in his movements. Survivors of the northern expansion had been relocated to labor camps—and yet, this boy was here, just outside Yulan City. This Omair must have had something to do with that, she mused.

"I'm all right," Omair murmured. "I'm fine." He blinked,

shaking his head, as though to clear his eyes of some obscuration. "I'm fine," he repeated. "Only a bit depleted. The spell—back there in the forest. I haven't worked magic like that in many years."

Lu stared. This man knew her mother. And he knew magic. Not a few sleights of hand, or the recipe of some swindler's herbal elixir. *Real* magic. The sort that was supposed to have disappeared years ago, along with Yunis.

"Who *are* you?" she blurted.

He smiled wryly. "That would depend on who you ask."

"I'm asking *you!*" Lu snapped, more sharply than she'd intended. She'd had enough mystery to last a lifetime. "Why did Yuri send me here? How do you know him?"

If the apothecarist was offended by her tone, he didn't show it. "That's as good a place as any to start, I suppose," he sighed. "Yuri and I grew up together."

She frowned. "Yuri grew up in the court."

"So did I, after a fashion." He caught the skepticism on her face and smiled faintly. "I fit the part of the rural peasant well, don't I? Well, that is how I was born. Poor and coarse, in a town not unlike this one. But I passed the civil service exam and attended the Imperial Academy, where I met Yuri. After the core years, we were divided into specialized colleges based on our aptitudes. Yuri went the martial route to become an officer—no surprise there—while I reluctantly found myself in the monastic order."

"What you did back there," Lu interrupted. "Hana monks don't learn . . . that."

"What? Magic?" he supplied. "They did. And they still

do—of a sort. In the Imperial Academy we were initiated into lower-level, domesticated forms of magic—reading runes, energy healing, herbology; that sort of thing."

Was he being willfully obtuse? "What you did back there was somewhat beyond herbology."

"Yes," he agreed. "But all magics are related at their core. All come down to the manipulation of energies. What I did today would be considered the use of 'free magic'—a bit of a misnomer, really. Lay folk call it that, but in the academy our instructors felt 'free' lent the misconception that it was free of cost, which no magic ever is. They preferred the label 'feral magic,' to impress upon us that it had the strength and the unpredictability of any wild thing. Because it is used by an individual and not an order, it must be paid for by individual sacrifice."

"What kind of sacrifice?" the Ashina boy demanded warily. Lu had nearly forgotten about him, but he had retaken his seat on the periphery of the room.

"Blood, say, for quick, coarse bursts of magic," Omair told them. "Or for more skilled wielders, life energy. Each person has it—some more, some less. And it can fluctuate during certain events in one's life—childbirth, death, moments of strong grief or anger. Even menstruating can heighten a person's powers."

"That's what you used to save us earlier," Lu deduced. "Life energy. Your own."

Omair nodded. "In part. I wasn't sure if I had the strength left in me, but wild places—forests, mountains—are quite dense with their own loose magic, and I was able to draw from that as well." He sighed. "Cities have their own sort of magic, but it's more difficult to wield. People bring noise and disharmony. Makes it tricky, inconsistent."

"But," Lu pressed. "If you didn't learn to use free magic at the academy—"

Omair nodded. "Yes, well. I had—extracurricular interests. I learned from a friend. I suppose you know the history of the Gray Shamanesses?"

Lu started at the change of topic. "Certainly. Everyone knows that."

"Nok?"

The boy gave the barest affirmative nod of head. "Of course. *Everyone* knows."

Lu narrowed her eyes, but the boy ignored her and continued: "The Gray Order were the elite shamanesses of Yunis. They served the Yunian mountain gods for five thousand years. Then the empire invaded and murdered everyone."

"That is *not* what happened," Lu retorted hotly. This boy had suffered at the hands of the empire, she knew, but someone had fed him outright lies. "My grandfather tried to broker a deal with the Yunians for the shared use of northern lands, but they refused. In the ensuing Gray War the shamanesses were a savage force, using unnatural magics to violently slaughter Hana and Hu troops."

"Oh, right, while you noble imperials *civilly* slaughtered women and children using *natural* swords and crossbows."

Her body bristled like a too-taut wire he had plucked. "War is brutal. Casualties are inevitable." But even as the words fell from her mouth, she felt they came from someone else.

"It wasn't a war; it was a massacre!" The boy stood so fast his stool knocked back up against the wall.

"Oh?" she retorted. "It happened long before either of us was born—were you there, somehow?"

"I didn't need to be!" he snapped. "I saw what your forces did to *my* people."

"We're talking about the Gray War, not the Slipskin Rebellion," she reminded him. "Yunis had an army."

He ignored the last part. "Don't play stupid. Yunis was a peaceful city, and their army was less than half the size of yours. And it doesn't matter which war we're talking of; you imperials won't hesitate to attack defenseless people if they have something you want. You came after the Gifted Kith with your full strength, and we had no armies at all. You know that—you saw what we were with your own eyes!"

It was true. She remembered it still: the field of painted leather yurts dotting the northern desert, amid hunched scrub trees and stalwart yellow flowers scrabbling up through dry splits in the earth. Pretty brown goats led by herders; children chasing elders who taught songs and histories and crafts. A community, not an army.

She knew it all along, so why was she arguing with him? Was this how children grew to be adults who repeated the mistakes of their forefathers? Not by ill will, but by rote?

Lu felt suddenly very tired. "I'm sorry for what happened to you slipskins, but that—"

"Stop using that *word*. We're Gifted Kith, not 'slipskins.' Gods, my father was right—you Hu have no respect for us, or what you used to be. Despicable. You're *traitors*—worse than the Hana!"

Lu opened her mouth to counter, but Omair interrupted. "Enough," he said quietly, firmly. "Both of you."

Nok frowned but resumed his seat. Whatever hold the old apothecarist had over him was strong.

Omair turned to Lu once more. "Tell me what else you know about the shamanesses."

She nodded, trying to hide how flustered she was. "As part of the treaty at the end of the Gray War, in exchange for allowing Yunis to retain its sovereignty, the Yunians agreed to discontinue their order. The existing shamanesses were too dangerous to leave in Yunian hands, of course, so they were sent south as wards of the empire—"

"Hostages," the boy interjected.

Lu ignored him. "They were taken to the capital to live in the Immaculate City. There, the shamanesses were assigned menial tasks normally relegated to the lowest-ranking monks and nuns. Dressing bodies for burial, laundry duties, that sort of thing. Then, shortly after my birth, it was discovered the shamanesses had been plotting against the empire. In turn . . ."

She faltered, but forced herself to push forward. She did not look at the Ashina boy. "In turn, the entire order was executed."

Omair nodded. "I believe the shamanesses were innocent of the crimes for which they died. The victims of politics, warring court factions."

Lu opened her mouth to object, to demand evidence for this theory, but she hesitated. *The shamanesses were too dangerous to live,* she told herself. That was what she'd been taught. It had to be true; who would have innocent girls put to death, otherwise? She almost asked the question aloud, but Omair continued speaking before she could. She couldn't help but be relieved.

"I was taught magic by one of the shamanesses." The old man averted his eyes as he said the words, an odd flicker of shame crossing his face. "Tsai. She was . . . a good friend, to both me and Yuri. Slight, almost brittle to look at, but that exterior hid immense power. A star crammed inside a soap bubble, Yuri liked to joke."

Lu waited for him to continue, but he did not. "I'm sorry about your friend," she said finally, "but I don't understand what that has to do with what's happening now."

"Your grandfather thought that by removing the shamanesses, he was taking away the Yunians' magic: the one weapon they had that the empire did not. What he failed to understand was that the actual magic, the raw energy, comes from the city itself—locked away in the bricks of its buildings, the stone of the mountains upon which it was erected." He paused. "Yuri thinks your cousin knows this, and he seeks to take it for himself."

"Set?" Lu demanded incredulously.

"Yes," Omair confirmed. "His guru—that former monk he keeps with him?"

"The one he calls Brother," Lu supplied.

"Yes, that is the one." Omair nodded. "Long before he came into your cousin's service, Brother was a Hana mul monk, specializing in energy healing. Talented but arrogant. He was assigned as a physician at one of the first labor camps up north. Instead, finding no supervision, he began carrying out his own agenda. He . . . experimented on the children."

His sad eyes drifted past Lu then. "Nok, Yuri tells me you might remember him."

Lu turned. The color had drained from the Ashina boy's face. He looked small and faint.

"I remember him," he said, his voice distant. Lu could see thoughts racing behind his eyes—he was making connections and drawing conclusions to which she was not privy.

Omair refocused on Lu. "Brother's experiments failed, and he was soon removed from the camps. Too many healthy young workers dying on his watch. Yuri tracked him for a time, but the man disappeared. Then he reappeared at your cousin's side, whispering in his ear. He—they—want to find Yunis. They want their secrets. Their knowledge—"

"Their magic," she finished.

Omair nodded grimly. "The combination of the energy in the Ruvai Mountains and the Yunians' ability to wield it was like nothing else on earth. Had they used it to its full power during the wars, I suspect they not only could have won but also marched south and left Yulan City a smoldering ruin."

"So why didn't they?"

Omair shook his head. "I don't know. They were not a martial people. Perhaps they thought they could stay in place and withstand your grandfather's army. Perhaps they did not want that blood on their hands. More likely, though, they knew that magic of that scale, that power, could not be properly controlled by humans. That it could have unforeseen, devastating consequences."

"I don't think my cousin would have such qualms," Lu mused.

"No," Omair agreed darkly. "Yuri thought not, either."

Silence stretched between them. An ember in the cook fire popped and Lu jumped.

"So, what now?" the Ashina boy demanded. "She can't stay here. Somebody—either a patient or the Wangs—is going to notice we have a mysterious houseguest who happens to match the age and description of a missing princess."

Lu bristled. *This isn't any of your business,* she wanted to tell him. "I'll stay hidden," she said instead.

"Please. Keeping you inside is like keeping a tiger in a cage—"

"Oh, *now* you know me so well all of a sudden!" she scoffed, cutting him short.

Omair closed his eyes as though the two of them were making it very difficult for him to exist.

"Stop *yelling*!" Nokhai snapped.

"I'm not yelling!" Lu hissed.

The boy rolled his eyes. "Well *now* you're not, but you've already made enough noise to bring the entire imperial army down upon us—"

"The army," Lu cut him off. "An *army.* I need an army. An army to dethrone Set."

Omair opened his eyes.

"An army?" the Ashina boy repeated incredulously. "To rival that of the empire? Do you know how many men that is?"

"It wouldn't have to be as big," Lu countered, mind whirling now. She set her sword on the table and began pacing the narrow span of the room. "Smaller is better, so we can move covertly, maintain the element of surprise."

"It could be enough," Omair mused, dark eyes brightening. "If you were able to infiltrate the capital with them."

"Yes," Lu said, galvanized. "The royal guard is bound to come over to my side. Most of them are from Hu families, and they *know* me. They've watched me grow up. Set is an interloper—a stranger to them."

"That's all well and good," countered Nokhai. "But where do you propose to find an army in the first place? I don't know if you're aware of this, Princess, but the empire is vast, and it— *we*—all belong to the emperor. Set. Not you—you're just a pariah now. And you could travel for weeks in any direction and not reach a land where the empire doesn't have soldiers and subjects."

"Not any direction," she said, scarcely realizing the truth of it before the words left her mouth. "Not north."

"North?" the boy repeated. "Need I remind you again that you *killed* everyone up north?"

How many times do I have to tell him that wasn't me? she wondered. Aloud though, she said, "Not the slipsk—not the Gifted Kith. Farther north."

"Farther . . . *Yunians*?" He had the gall to laugh now. "Even if those sightings were real, I doubt they'd be happy to see you. You slaughtered them and razed their city years ago."

"Not me," she said, her heart quickening as the idea blossomed. "The empire did. And I'm a pariah now. But a pariah with a better claim to the throne than Set. And if the Yunians were to help me reclaim my rightful throne, I could facilitate very generous terms in their favor—especially if I warn them of Set's interest in them."

"It might work," Omair murmured. "The Yunian force can't be very strong. They would certainly welcome an opportunity to preempt a long, bloody fight."

"Yes, exactly!" she said. "It will work."

"Have you both lost your minds? Omair," the Ashina boy pleaded. "This is crazy. You must see it's crazy."

"It has to be crazy," Lu countered. "What's happened to *me* is crazy. Extraordinary. And it will take extraordinary measures to set things right."

"You know that expression 'fighting fire with fire'?" the boy said sarcastically. "I don't think it's meant to be taken as advice."

"When can we leave for Yunis?" Lu said, turning back to Omair.

"We?" the boy repeated. "No way," he said flatly, rounding on Omair. "She can do whatever she likes, but there's no way we're helping her with whatever crazy plan she comes up with."

Lu frowned. The old man did look unsteady now, but she suspected there was more to him than met the eye. "It's his decision," she told the Ashina boy. "If he wants to join me, it's his choice."

"Stay out of it," the boy bit back.

"This concerns me as much as it does you," Lu objected, struggling to keep her patience. "More so, even. The fate of thousands could rest upon this. Do you think your life will be better with my cousin on the throne?"

"It won't make an ounce of difference to me. Both of you are imperial swine."

The words stung more than they had any right to. "You met my cousin when he was just a boy. You know what a monster he was—is. Imagine that same monster with command over armies. You're not seeing the big picture."

The boy whirled on her. "And that's all you see, isn't it! Winning your damned throne. Not the people whose lives you'll ruin or end to get there."

It was too much. Her cousin's betrayal—the betrayal of inner court officials her father had trusted, who had known her since infancy. Exile. And now this wrathful boy, this specter from her past whom she could not seem to quite reconcile to the present, insisted on standing in the way of the one solution she had to any of her problems.

Without meaning to, she took a step forward so they were eye to eye. The boy glared back with steely resolve. Lu was pleased to find she was slightly taller than him. "What is your contention with me? What did I ever do to you?"

The boy laughed in her face. It sounded like a bark, spare and hard and devoid of mirth. "What did you ever do to me? What did . . . I'll tell you—"

Omair banged his cane on the floor. "Enough, enough! Nok, I am sorry, I know you must see this as a betrayal of sorts, but I will be going north with Princess Lu. Please try to understand. She is correct—our lives will not be better seeing Lord Set on the throne."

Then he sighed and cast his eyes out the window. The sun had set since they had arrived, Lu saw, the sky a middling cobalt blue, wavering uncertainly between twilight and darkness. Omair turned to her. "Princess," he said. "If you don't mind, I'd like to speak to my apprentice alone. We can go out into the garden."

Lu shook her head, glaring at the Ashina boy as she turned on her heel toward the back door. "No," she said. "I'll go. Far be it from me to displace anyone from their home. Again."

CHAPTER 16

Known

Nok clenched his fists, watching the princess storm outside. If only she were leaving for good.

"I'm sorry."

He turned and saw Omair regarding him sadly.

Nok swallowed. "For what?"

"For keeping the truth from you."

"You never lied to me," Nok said flatly. "I didn't want to know anything I didn't ask for." *Perhaps*, he thought belatedly, *Omair had taken advantage of that. Well, if so, he'd been a willing collaborator.*

Omair was studying his face. "I saw . . . I saw your caul," he said finally. "Magnificent. Have you ever done it before?"

"No!" Nok said immediately. "No, never. That was the whole . . . it was shameful that I couldn't. I was the son of a Kith father and I couldn't caul."

"And yet, today, you did. How?"

"I don't know," Nok sighed, running a hand through his hair in agitation. "First I had this strange experience in the woods—"

"The Gifting Dream?"

"I suppose that's what it must have been. But after that . . . I couldn't control it. It came and went of its own accord, really fast."

"Can you try now? Just to see if you can will it."

"I . . . I don't know," Nok repeated doubtfully. He closed his eyes, trying to imagine the feel of the caul descending upon him, soft as snow, warm as sun. Tried to imagine pacing the earth with massive paws, black-blue hair sprouting over his shoulders and all down his back . . .

He opened his eyes, shaking his head. "Just now, back in the forest, I think I sort of was able to force it, but maybe that was only because my life was in danger."

Omair considered the logic of this. "And you were in danger the first time as well?"

The memory of the Wangs' dogs snapping at his legs flooded Nok's vision. "Yes," he said, nodding. "But it kept hold of me even after the danger was gone. I only came out of it after I found—after I saw the princess."

The wolf had been looking for her, he remembered with an unpleasant jolt. Seeking her out.

He didn't share the thought with Omair, but the old man seemed to hear it anyway. "And how did you find her?"

"The princess?"

"Yes."

Nok didn't have an answer for that; he didn't want one. He

didn't want to think about her at all. Omair raised his eyebrows at Nok's silence but didn't press the question.

"Your Kith must have passed down ways to control the caul, from generation to generation," he said instead.

"They did. But children learned it from the elders upon receiving the Gifting Dream. No Gifting, no initiation." Nok barked out a laugh. "And now, there're no elders."

"Do you remember anything about the labor camp?" The question was gentled by the softness of Omair's voice.

Nok hesitated. It was nothing he wanted to think on, but he couldn't refuse Omair. He closed his eyes, trying in earnest to recall that time. See it fully, for the first time in four years.

They killed his sister first.

That small, soft-spoken man had entered their barracks. If he had a name, he didn't share it, only introduced himself as the camp's healer. He was accompanied by two soldiers armed to the teeth and carrying lanterns. Nok and Nasan had shared a bunk—the room was overcrowded, piled high with crying, unwashed children. Half of them didn't speak any common languages, but they were all united under the imperial slur: *slip-skins*. Most were ill, coughing and shivering with fever in their bunks.

The healer ignored them, though, only stopping when he reached Nok and Nasan. A soldier had held a lantern up to their faces. "That's the one," the healer had said. "The girl."

Nok's hands shook, recalling how tightly he'd clung to her, how she'd dug her fingernails into his arms and bared her teeth—her blunt, all-too-human teeth—and fought. She'd always been the fiercest child in their Kith. But how could the fists of a child compare to batons the soldiers brought down upon their hands and faces, separating them blow by blow?

He never saw Nasan again.

The next day, a burning fever caught in Nok and wouldn't quell. They brought him to the camp's sickroom—little more than a flimsy tent stretched over a pile of overheated, slowly dehydrating, slowly dying bodies. Periodically, someone would come through with a barrow to collect the dead. Finally they came to collect *him*, so Nok had assumed he was dead, too.

Only it hadn't been an undertaker who took him—it had been a soldier.

"Yuri," he blurted suddenly. He opened his eyes, tearing himself back into the present. Back to Omair. "It was Yuri who brought me to you. I remember now."

"He had just abandoned his post," Omair said. "He was sick to death of the killing, the senseless brutality. He grabbed you on the way out—I suppose he saw it as the least he could do, some gesture at redemption." The old man sighed. "He knew he couldn't take you to the capital, so he found me. I hadn't seen him in years. And then, there he was, at my doorstep, holding a half-dead boy."

Nok spread his hands helplessly. "So why did he do it? Why me?"

Omair looked him in the eye. "Whatever they did to your sister?"

Nok nodded.

"You were next."

Nok turned away, angry and ashamed. That was no good answer. "There must have been a hundred others on the list right after me. I wish he'd saved one of them instead. I wish he'd saved Nasan."

"I know."

Nok looked up. Dark shadows weighed heavy along Omair's cheekbones and under his eyes. The apothecarist was far from young, but he appeared to have aged about ten years in the last day. "I know," he repeated. "But, Nok, he didn't. He chose you. And now your Kith's wolf has chosen you. It brought you to Princess Lu.

The princess.

"Maybe that means something," Omair pressed.

"Maybe it doesn't."

"Perhaps not. But you're alive now. You have a chance to do something with that life. To help change the course of the empire."

Nok shook his head before Omair even spoke. "I need you," he said. "The princess does, too. I'm old; I won't have the strength—we won't make it without your help."

Nok stood, agitated. "You need someone brave, someone good. That's not me. That was Nasan. Your friend should've chosen better. He should've developed a conscience sooner."

Omair sighed, sitting back. "At least think on it over the next few days while the princess recovers."

Nok opened his mouth to object, but Omair held up a conciliatory hand. "You can just pretend to think on it. Do that much for me."

Nok set his mouth and stared down at his hands. "Fine."

Omair beamed up at him. "Thank you. Now, why don't you go tell our guest to come back inside?"

The girl was standing by the dense bracken along the edge of the forest when he found her. He felt a flush of annoyance. *She should stay hidden; anyone could see her out there.* Before he could call to her and say as much, she hunched forward and vomited.

"Did the porridge sit poorly with you?" he said.

She whirled around, startled. As she turned, he saw her hand was already upon the handle of the dagger at her waist. Strong reflexes; she might survive out in the world on her own.

"Not used to peasant food, are you?" he said.

The princess relaxed, hand dropping to her side. She used the back of the other to wipe her mouth, then spat. "I was thinking about earlier. That boy I . . . the boys I killed."

As he drew closer, his lamp cast long shadows across the girl's face. Her eyes were rimmed red and the skin below them dark as a bruise. In the low light it gave her a haunted, wary look.

He understood, suddenly. "You'd never killed anyone before."

"It was not what . . . it was not as I expected. Killing, I mean." A shudder seized her and she hugged herself around the waist. He thought for a moment that she would be sick again, but she closed her eyes and seemed to will herself still.

"What did you expect it would be?" he demanded. "Bloodless? Clean? Triumphant?"

"Not *bloodless*," she retorted. "Only, I was taught to fight the

Hu way—with pride. There is no pride in defeating, let alone in killing . . . slaughtering . . . someone weaker than you. A child."

"Is *that* the Hu way? My people would be delighted to hear it, if only they were around to." Nok laughed and was startled by the bitterness of the sound. "There is no pride in killing. Nor in fighting, nor in dying, nor in living. Not the sort you mean. There is only despair and blood and fear."

The princess shivered again, though whether from the chill night air or from his words, Nok could not know. Her eyes were a tumult of flint and outrage, and something like sorrow.

He turned away toward the house. "Come back inside before someone sees you out here."

Before he could walk away, she snatched his wrist, wrenching his hand upward until the fingers splayed open.

"Hey!"

Ignoring his protests, she examined the flesh of his palm. Just as abruptly, she dropped his hand and grabbed him by the chin, raising his face up so she could better see it.

"You still have the scars," she said, almost in wonder, tracing a fingertip over the twisted purpled flesh beneath his eye. "I could scarcely believe it's you, but those scars don't lie. You really are the same Ashina boy I met all those years ago."

He jerked away from her. "Don't touch me!"

"Why did you lie to me in the forest?" Her voice was full of accusation and something that sounded remarkably like hurt.

They glared at each other in silence until at last he said, "I didn't lie. That boy . . . he's not me. Not anymore."

"I'm sorry to hear that," she said. "I liked him better than whoever you are now."

"Then you shouldn't have killed him," he snapped.

Nok turned and left her standing there. For a moment he thought she might try to stop him, but for once she was quiet.

CHAPTER 17

New Day

*I*t was perverse to wear her funerary whites to a wedding, Min thought. Her *own* wedding, no less. A real ceremony, with all its pomp and cheer, was forbidden: in the one hundred days following the death of an emperor, while everyone was garbed for mourning, there were to be no celebrations of any sort.

But the empire would have an emperor. And in this case, for Set to claim that title, he needed to marry a direct descendant to the Hu line, of which Min was the only remaining option. A quiet, efficient ceremony would have to suffice.

And so, she found herself kneeling alone in front of her embroidery easel within her locked and heavily guarded chambers, clad in snow white from head to toe. Waiting.

All around, it did not fit with any of her fantasies. She'd never known *who* she was to marry—the groom had ever been a vague tall, handsome specter, a role her cousin did fulfill, to his credit—but she had known the how and where. Had relied on those exquisite details—especially the vermillion bridal robes they would drape over her, drenching her in color and expectation. A scarlet peony on the cusp of plucking for the court to marvel at. But her emperor father was dead—passed like smoke from this world on to the next—and this was now her life.

Her father . . .

Her father had lied, and so her sister killed him in vengeance. That was what they had told Min. What they'd told everyone.

The emperor had never meant for her sister to rule. His empty promises had been a diversion, a father humoring his favorite daughter. And Lu, learning this, had poisoned him immediately prior to the hunt—murdered him in cold fury.

Then, during the hunt, she had isolated and attacked her cousin, who managed to fend her off until his soldiers came to his aid. Lu had fled, a coward in the end.

She was driven mad with her lust for power. That was the truth on everyone's lips. *That is what happens when you give a girl too much allowance, too much to believe in.* This is what people said when they thought Min could not hear.

It was true. It had to be true.

Only her sister was many things, some good: loyal, quick-witted, vehement, almost violent in her loyalty and her affections. And some bad: arrogant, hot-headed, stubborn. But, Min could not stop the voice in her head from whispering, Lu was no coward. Never a coward. Not *wise* enough to be a coward, even when being a coward was the far better option. No, her sister burned fast and bright and golden, heedless of the consequences.

Lu did not sneak. She did not run.

And then, too, there was Min's strange waking dream. The slim, black-eyed shamaness in white who had taken her hand and shown her a very different version of events. Her mother standing over her father, the empty vial relieved of its poison vanishing up her tailored sleeve.

Min's heart trembled at the memory, and for a horrible moment the shamaness's black eyes flashed in her mind, like moonlight skimming dark water.

Only a dream.

A vivid one, brought on by the slight fever that accompanied her woman's blood, but not real. There was no such thing as ghosts, and there was no magic left in the world anymore. *Only a dream*, she told herself. *Only* . . .

Her father's funeral emerged in her mind's eye. Her mother had stood beside her, implacable and radiant. Min had studied her from the corner of her eye, determined to discover therein a tear, a tightness in the throat, some sign of distress.

But there had been nothing.

Good breeding; nothing sinister. Only a dream.

How would she even allow for it to be true? That her mother could murder her own husband, that she could exile Lu, her own *child*, was unthinkable.

And, whatever the cause, Min had lost a sister and a father.

Mother is all I have left. The thought made her stomach clench. *Do I want to lose her as well?*

The pocket doors of her room opened, and like magic, the empress was there. Min felt a jolt of guilt at the sight of her, as though her mother could hear her thoughts. Before Min could speak, though, Set entered the room behind her. Min's heart leaped.

He was also draped head to toe in mourning whites, though Min thought it made *him* look ethereal and striking. But his jaw was clenched, and he had a distant, preoccupied look that made Min's heart twinge with reflexive longing. She hated that look. Helplessly, she recalled how they had last spoken; he'd looked at her—no, *seen* her. It had felt unlike anything in the world, to be reflected by those gray eyes. Now, though, his gaze was not a mirror but a wall. Every bit of him cold and closed.

Be here, she willed. *This is our wedding. Be here with me.*

The empress, conversely, was beaming. It was, Min realized, the happiest her mother had ever looked. She looked years younger—almost like a girl. "Your cousin," her mother said proudly, by way of greeting, "has drafted his first decree. He will present it in court tomorrow morning after your union is announced."

Her cousin did not seem to register the glow in his aunt's voice. "It will hardly matter what I announce," he snapped, "if my claim to the throne is still in question."

"Once you and Min are married that will not be an issue," the empress said, dismissively, the barest hint of a characteristic frown line appearing between her eyes. "And once the mourning period is finally over, we can order a real ceremony before the whole court. No one would question your claim after that."

"We need to find her," Set continued stridently, ignoring

his aunt's words. "As long as Lu is free, as long as she is out there in the world, she will try to depose me."

"Let her try," Min's mother scoffed. "What is she now? Nothing. A criminal. She will be apprehended in time—you have enough men searching for her."

"You know how she is!" Set snapped. There was a wild, preoccupied gleam in his eyes. "She's—unnatural. Crazy. And now she has nothing to lose! She would use her dying breath to take me down—"

"Focus on rallying support from your court and presenting your decree tomorrow," interrupted the empress coldly. "It's certainly bold enough to command their attention for the time being—"

"Easy enough for you to say!" her cousin barked. "But you can't just wish Lu away like that."

The room was hot with tension; Min felt faint. *Stop yelling,* her heart pleaded. *This is my wedding.*

"What is the decree?" she blurted aloud.

Set seemed to notice her for the first time. His face rearranged itself with some effort and he smiled indulgently down at her. "The decree," he told her, "will rid our land of the foreign scourge. The Ellandaise will have ten days to vacate their sector and our ports."

"All foreigners? The Westermen, too?" Min said in surprise.

Set waved a hand. "Yes, though we plan to be more lenient with their kind, unless they deal in poppy tears or other degenerate cargo."

"The days of foreign influence in imperial lands is over,"

said a voice from behind them. Min gave a start, but her cousin and mother parted slightly to allow Brother to join the circle. She hadn't seen him enter.

"Emperor Set's reign will be remembered as a turning point in our history," the monk continued.

Something in his low, languid voice felt as though it were walking cold feet right up the notches of Min's spine. "Your husband will be exalted as a great hero, half a god. He will accomplish feats the likes of which no one has seen before." He smiled, showing a mouthful of small white teeth.

He took her hand in one of his. Min looked down. Her skin was soft and pale. His was paler still, though rough and cold beneath her fingers.

"Are you ready to serve your husband, Small Princess?" he asked.

Their eyes met. Brother clutched her hand tighter, pulling her close to examine her eyes. "I think you are ready," he mused, sounding slightly surprised. "Though perhaps you don't know it yet."

There was nothing in her breeding that had prepared her to respond to this. *Think*, she scolded herself. Lu would've had an answer.

"Don't scare the girl," her cousin interrupted, his impatience almost comforting. "Come on then, Brother. Let's get this ceremony done with. It's been a long day."

Min tried not to sigh in relief when the monk released her hand. Her mother guided her down to her knees across from her cousin. Set's eyes were a plush, stormy gray. Troubled.

How do I serve you if you can't even see me? she wondered. *How do I reach you?*

He smiled dutifully at her, then took her hands in his own as the monk began to recite their vows. His hands were warm and strong, steadying the tremble right out of her own. And when the ceremony was finished, he beamed at her.

"We are now man and wife. Emperor and empress," he told her. She smiled back at him, nodding perhaps a touch over-eagerly. He looked so radiant, so tall.

"I'm very ha—" Min began, but he had already turned away to speak with Brother. The words died on her lips.

A warm pressure at her back distracted her. Min found her mother hovering over her, her face conflicted between pride and—what was that exactly? Fear? Nervousness?

"You'll be fine," the empress said, but it sounded more like she was trying to assure herself. And why? Min felt a twinge of annoyance. Did her mother really trust her so little? She vowed she would show her—show them all. She would be the most constant, demure, supportive empress Set could ever wish for. They would see.

"And now," Brother's voice rose behind them. "I'd like a moment alone with the newlyweds. To bless their union."

The empress's jaw clenched just slightly. "I don't believe that is customary," she said.

"Perhaps not," Brother said affably. "But with a couple so young, it is sometimes easier to discuss . . . ah, intimate matters alone. Auspicious dates for conception—that sort of thing."

Min felt herself redden from the tips of her ears down to her collarbone.

"Aunt Rinyi, it's fine," Set was telling her mother, guiding her toward the door. "I told you, Minyi won't ever be out of my sight."

"You promised." Her mother's voice was a hushed, hurried whisper, even as she was hustled out the door. "Remember, Set, you promised me."

The doors shut, leaving Min alone with her cousin—no, her husband, and the monk. Brother looked keenly at her; Set was looking at him.

"Why don't you two have a seat," the monk said, gesturing to the pillows upon which they had knelt for the ceremony. As they sat, he fetched one of the braziers near Min's bed and drew it closer to them, using the coarse raw silk of his robes as a buffer between his palms and the hot handles. He pushed their wedding altar aside and replaced it with the brazier.

"This will do," the old man said to himself. Min noted his voice seemed more substantial than it had when her mother was still in the room. Less airy and dreamy, more . . . well, ordinary. Clipped and efficient. She watched as he began to stoke the embers in the brazier until they hissed and blazed red once more. Then from within one sleeve, he withdrew a pinch of green-gray powder and dashed it against the coals.

A spry green flame the color of young wood sprang to life in the iron bowl.

Min flicked her gaze nervously at Set, wishing he might give her some word of comfort, take her hand again, but he was still watching Brother. She followed his lead.

"Do not be alarmed," the monk told her. "I am using the flame to scry the promise of your union. This is a bit of my

MIMI YU

own make of magic—a sort of crossbreed between the old
Hana water rites and some indigenous northern spells. Nothing to be frightened of."

Min's heart fluttered. *Scrying?* As far as she knew, Hana
monks did nothing of the sort.

Brother smiled as though hearing her thoughts. "These
days I know your monks do little besides burn incense and pray
and sweep the Hall of the Ancestors, but there was a time, long
ago, when their rites meant something more. *Did* more." He
turned his eyes back to the fire.

"Is it working? Can you see anything?" her cousin asked.
He leaned forward tensely. "Has the prophecy changed now
that my bride is Minyi and not Lu?"

"Patience," the old man murmured, peering into the green
flame. "How many times do I need to tell you? *Patience.* In all
things."

Set's mouth was pursed. "You told me it didn't matter who
I married—that as long as it was a Hu princess, the prophecy
would hold. That under my reign the old ways and the new
would merge to create the most powerful empire—"

"Tell me," the monk interrupted, focusing his gaze upon
Min. "Are you on your monthly blood?"

"I-I'm," she stammered, looking at Set in horror, but he just
nodded encouragingly. When had her life descended into a
constant state of mortification? "Yes?"

"It's all right," the monk told her with a gentle smile. "Nothing to be embarrassed about. Set is your husband, and I am
a healer. You have nothing to hide from us." Then his tone
became practical again: "Is it your first time having your blood?"

"N-no," Min whispered. "Only my second, though."

"Ah," the monk nodded, satisfied. "That would do it. Sometimes disturbances in your normal energy flow will cause interferences in what I can see." He reflected. "However, they do present the opportunity for interesting solutions." Then he asked, as though asking for a cup of tea, "Min, do you have any of your discarded bedding and wrappings here? Something stained with your monthly blood."

Min supposed that dying of embarrassment must be impossible, as she continued to live. "Y-yes? Yes, probably. Normally my nunas would take it away, but I've been locked up in here all day—"

"Excellent. Would you bring me some?" the monk continued.

As though in a strange dream, Min rose and walked to the far side of the room, where a bin held her discarded clothing. She fished out a single wrapping, stained unevenly with brown, dried blood, and brought it to the monk.

Without ceremony, he tore off a small section of the stained cloth and threw it into the fire.

For a moment, nothing happened. Then, the fire began to eat at the frayed cloth, letting off the oddly damp smell of burned cotton. Min watched as its green tongues licked inward. The moment it touched the bloodstain, the flames *hissed* and spat, like an angry cat, flaring from green to an unnaturally deep blood red.

The brazier *popped*, flinging bits of char and coal over the metal lip, singeing the carpets beneath. One of the embers began to catch, flaring to a bright orange. Min gave a cry of alarm, but Set stamped it out before the fire had a chance to grow. Her cousin grimaced with the effort, but his face changed to one of shock as he looked up.

Min followed his gaze. There was a woman rising out of the brazier.

No, not a woman—more like the shadow of a woman. A body of flame wreathed in smoke rather than flesh and bone. Before them, she became more tangible, more concrete, the flames taking on the subtlety of her sunken cheeks, thin lips, pointed chin. Then her eyes opened—black, so black amid all that red and gray. And Min knew her.

The shamaness from her dreams. The girl who had shown her the death of the emperor. Min recoiled in wordless fright.

But the shamaness was looking only at Brother—glaring at him with unearthly fury. She opened her mouth as though to speak, but all that emerged was a rattling hiss, like that of dried leaves skittering across a stone floor.

Brother had risen to his feet in alarm with the rest of them, but now he sized up the fire-woman with calm fascination. Then he spoke a few words in a harsh language Min had never heard before. To her ears it sounded like blocks of wood being hit together. The fire-woman merely scowled, so he tried again. This time, she seemed to understand. The fire crackled and spat at them.

An undignified cry burst out of Min. Instinctively, she covered her face with her hands.

"It's all right," Brother reassured her, though he never took his eyes off the shamaness. "Don't be alarmed. It's just a *sending*. Not a real being. Think of it as a shadow that's been left behind by its owner—the one who left it inside you."

"Inside me?" Min squeaked. Stupidly, she pressed her hands against her abdomen now, as though she could feel something growing in there.

"Ssstupid little man!"

Min nearly leaped from her skin. The fire-woman lurched forward toward Brother, but she had no feet—her body merely tapered off into flame—and she was confined to the brazier. Set gave a start, moving swiftly in front of Min, as though to protect her. She clutched gratefully at the silk of his robes.

"You think you know anything?"

"It's only a sending, it can't hurt you," Brother repeated at Min, holding up a hand as though to keep the fire-woman at bay. "It came from within you. Min, you have been cursed by a witch. This thing before you now is only an echo of what she was. Think of it as you would an internal parasite. A worm."

"Charlatan!" the fire-woman roared. *"I am a shade. I am revenge."* The fire crackling at her feet blazed malevolently again, surging up through her like wind in an atrium, whipping her hair of flames into a wild frenzy. Another shower of sparks fell around them. Min cowered, clutching tighter to Set's robes.

"What do you know of sendings? I left this piece of myself inside the girl when she was only just conceived! A middling bit of flesh and salt in her wicked mother's womb! I took the poison, the curse of magic from my own child and sent it into her. As she grew, so did I, consuming all the seeds within her. I ate her children, all the life she had to give."

Min froze, her fingers loosening just slightly on her cousin's robes. "My seeds ... my children? Is she saying I won't ..." The thought was too horrible to put to words.

"That is right, little princess," the fire-woman purred. *"What you would have made life, I turned to death. The only thing you'll ever birth is me."*

The fire-thing launched itself from the brazier with a crackling roar, swooping toward her. Min threw up her arms before her face. Set was gone—had jumped to the side. She was exposed, this kinetic wall of fire crashing toward her. But then, Brother was there. He hollered something in the same guttural tongue he had used to speak to the fire-thing earlier, and he flung something wet from a glass vial he had produced from his cloak.

The fire-thing howled and leaped into the air, dangerously close to the painted ceilings of Min's bedroom. Where the liquid touched it, though, Min saw dark pits in the flames, and rising from them, smoke.

The fire-thing slunk back into the brazier, like a wounded animal, but it was too late. The embers there had cooled, and the thing rapidly shrank. It emitted a high, keening sound as it went, until all that remained was a narrow column of smoke. The room filled with a gamey damp odor, like wet fur. It stung Min's eyes, and tears sprung up in its wake.

They all stared in stunned silence at the smoldering brazier. Wordlessly, Min strode over to her bedside table and grabbed the gaiwan of cold tea that had been sitting there since the morning.

"What are you . . . ?" Set began, but fell silent when Min dashed the contents of the gaiwan into the brazier, damping out the remains of the fire.

"Good girl," Brother said pensively. Min tossed the porcelain gaiwan into the brazier as well with a shudder, backing away. "Brave girl," he added.

"What does it mean?" Min demanded into the silence. Her voice came out louder than she had intended, pitchy and high. "Is . . . what it said, is it true? I can't give the emperor children?" Tears stung her eyes. She'd scarcely been married an hour and already everything was ruined. *She* was ruined.

"My dear," Brother said eagerly. "Think hard, now. Has anything . . . unnatural ever happened to you? Inexplicable things? Predictions that came true or strange dreams? Things bending to your will?"

Her vision clouded and all at once Min saw her mother's hands upon her father's face, pouring the poison into his mouth, holding his mouth closed—

No. She could not share that. It was too impossible, too absurd. They'd never believe it. *And worse, if they did, that might mean it was true . . .*

"I broke a cup," she blurted. "At the betrothal—at the dinner to welcome Set to the capital. I-I got angry, so angry, and the cup Snowdrop was holding broke . . ."

When she said it aloud, it sounded crazy. But it was true, she realized. She couldn't admit it at the time, but she'd broken the cup with her fury.

She burst into tears.

"Is there nothing we can do? Am I cursed for good?" she asked, sobbing.

"Dear one, this is not a curse," Brother told her. "This is a gift." He leaned over and took her hand. His was firm and cold.

"A gift?" she whispered.

"For you, and for us all. Do you know why I came to serve Set? I had a vision, a promise from the gods. A prophecy that I would guide the Hana scion south to wed the Hu princess. That only then could we conquer Yunis, reuniting the old knowledge of magic with the new knowledge of firepower, to create a weapon unlike any the world has seen before. A weapon that will grant Set complete control of the empire—and secure its future forever. But in order to create that weapon, we must first take the North, and you will help us do so."

"North?" Min repeated. "Me? I am to go to the war front? But my mother will never allow it."

"I know girls your age tell their mothers everything, but you're a married woman now, so can you keep this confidence for your husband? Even from her?"

"Yes . . . I th-think so," she said, because she knew it was what he wanted to hear.

"Good," said Brother. "Then we will all go north. Your cousin will become the greatest emperor of the greatest empire known to man. And you are the key—you, in the service of your husband. My dear, are you ready to serve him?"

The monk's words were so lofty as to be meaningless. A hundred questions and fears sprang to Min's mouth, prickling and buzzing like insects. To ask them though would reveal her stupidity.

"Yes," she said instead. "I'm ready."

A lie. The accusation crackled within her like an ember flaring back to life. It sounded like someone else . . .

Min flinched. When she looked up again, Set's gaze was fixed upon her with a keen intensity she had never seen before—never warranted, she supposed. It burned with delight, with intrigue.

A lie, a lie, a lie . . .

"I'm ready," she repeated, hoping desperately against hope that somehow she could make it true.

———

But as soon as the doors to her apartments slid closed behind Brother and Set, the tears fell. They streaked hot down her face, falling from her chin to leave dark fingerprints on her white robes. Without the glowing attention of the two men, all she had left was herself, and her fears.

She would never bear children. Never give Set sons—heirs. And they wanted her to go north, ride into *war* with them. The very notion filled her with a terrible, wordless terror, consuming as fire.

She had scarcely left the capital in her life, save for summer visits to the palace by the lake, and that fateful trip up to the slipskin encampments when she'd been a little girl. But they'd traveled by carriage and palanquin then—luxurious gilded wheel houses with silk pillows and her nunas close by to fan her sweaty face and pour her cold drinks. She couldn't begin to imagine what riding into war would look like, but she suspected there would be no silk pillows.

She slid down boneless until her face touched the cool of the floor. *What will I do?*

Lu would know. But Lu was gone. And Min knew, with each timid beat of her despairing heart, that she was not Lu. Hadn't that always been the problem?

Help me, she thought. A desperate prayer—but to whom? There was no one left to hear her.

"*I am.*"

The other girl's voice slid around inside Min like oil in a glass. "*I'm still here.*"

Fear shot through her, pulling her upright. "You!" she cried. "But Brother, he . . . he—"

"*Killed me?*" the shamaness concluded with sweet scorn. "*I died long ago, before you were born.*"

Min frowned, rubbing at her eyes with the heel of a hand. "W-who are you? What do you *want?*"

The shamaness sighed, as though disappointed. "*The question is, what do you want, Min?*"

"I—I don't know," she whispered.

"*Liar.*"

"I'm not lying!"

"*Aren't you? You're a liar, Min, and that's what liars do.*"

"I'm not!" Stupidly, tears welled in her eyes again.

"*You are. Listen to me: in this world, there are only fools and liars. Fools are largely ordinary, but every now and then one will be born who is blessed—golden. Golden fools are beautiful, so they can afford to be honest. They float above the rest of us, wearing their pretty truths on their breast like a badge.*"

Lu, Min thought, and it was like a cold finger prodding the meat of her heart.

"*The rest of us aren't allowed such luxuries. We're too twisted and cruel and ugly. If people saw what we were—well, that is why we must lie, isn't it?*"

"We . . . ," Min repeated softly. Her tongue was thick and

slow in her mouth, like running in a dream. *Perhaps this* is *all just a dream*, she allowed herself to think. Stupid. She knew what this was, even if she couldn't admit it.

"*Yes, Min,*" the shamaness continued as though she had heard. Perhaps she had. "*We. You know what you are. You've always known.*"

"No, no, I'm not, I won't—"

"*Don't be* sad, *you silly girl,*" chided the shamaness, and it was so playful as to be scornful. "*Golden fools are all alike, but there are so many different kinds of liars. We're forced to toil, nothing is given to us that we don't tear our fingers to the bone digging for, but liars are so full of* possibility. *There's nothing that can't be won with a well-crafted lie. Why, in the right light, a liar might even glint like gold.*"

Her voice was beautiful and hideous in equal measure, a hoarse singsong both sweet as a child's and guttural as a death rattle, with none of the harsh crackle of the fire-creature in the brazier.

"What do you want?" Min whispered.

"*I want the same thing you do.*"

Min closed her eyes. Each word seemed to scrape and claw away at her, leaving her raw and open all over.

"But I don't *know* what I want," she insisted again.

She could see it though, even as the words left her: she would grow tall and elegant, her face shifting into a cool mask of beauty like her mother's. Her voice would strengthen with wisdom and her nunas would love her for it. She would use it to make clever jokes that would make them laugh. And every time Set looked upon her, her and the blessed golden children she bore for him, he would *see* her.

"*I want to be free,*" the shamaness sighed, almost wistful. "*Just as you long to be free of me, of yourself as you are.*"

Was that freedom she was imagining? It felt like power. Perhaps freedom was a sort of power. Or perhaps freedom could only be won through power . . .

"How do I do it?" Min's eyes were open now in the dimness of her too-small bedroom.

"Go north," said the shamaness. "Just like your beloved and his false monk bid you do. Go north. Take me home to Yunis. Once I am there, I will be free to leave you to your stupid little dreams of sons and beauty."

Could it be that simple? Her heart clenched, daring to hope.

"But," Min said as she realized, "Set only wants me because I have you." What could she possibly offer him otherwise? She was just a stupid little girl, slow-witted and plain.

"Find him Yunis, and he will love you for it," the shamaness said. "Grant him Yunis, and you will grant him endless power. After that, what is there he can't forgive?"

Like a conjuring, Set's face swam before her eyes, indistinct as water. He saw her and smiled, flooding her with a peculiar warmth. Warmth like safety, like certainty. It felt, Min thought, a lot like love.

Yes. If I give him Yunis, it will be enough. The hope surged through her, bright and urgent. *I'll give him Yunis, and I'll give him sons, and I'll be so clever and obedient he won't be able to help but love me, magic or no.*

Perhaps he would even let her pardon her sister. Lu could never rule, of course—oh, that would make her angry—but surely Set could find a place for her in the court.

"And I will be able to have children? Once you're gone?" Min pressed. She had to be sure.

"All the hideous little princes you can manage to squeeze out."

An unpleasant thought came to Min then. "But Set wants to destroy Yunis, doesn't he?" she asked, her voice catching on the words. "He just declared war on them."

"He does," the shamaness purred. *"He wants to gut it and use it and rend it until nothing remains but ashes and lost hope."* Min could feel the oily pleasure, the smile in her voice.

"But why . . ." Min frowned. She was missing something, but what? *Stupid, why am I so stupid?* "Why would you want to destroy your own home?"

"Tell me," the shamaness sighed wearily, as though speaking to a difficult child. "Tell me about your *home*, Min. What does the word mean to you?"

And she saw Butterfly and Snowdrop and Tea Rose, giggling together in a closed cluster ahead of her on the sidewalk.

And she saw her mother, so beautiful and severe and cold— always radiantly cold—sighing over her shoulder as they both gazed despairingly at Min's reflection in the mirror.

And she saw Lu. She saw her from behind, the swing of her long braid as she walked away. Always toward something else, some place Min couldn't quite follow.

And she thought perhaps she understood.

CHAPTER 18

North

*T*hey awoke to a pounding at the door.

They've come for the princess, Nok thought as he opened it.

"Adé?"

Nok gaped at the girl in the doorway. He glanced nervously over his shoulder but only saw Omair. The princess was nowhere in sight, hopefully heeding his instruction to stay hidden. "What are you doing here?"

"You missed my engagement party yesterday," Adé said, chewing her lip. "I was worried."

"Your—" Nok closed his eyes. "I . . . I forgot."

"Oh." She rocked on her heels, then thrust a parcel toward him. "It wasn't much fun, to be honest. There are all these wild rumors flying about the Ellandaise being forced to leave the city so no one was in the mood . . ." Perhaps mistaking his nervousness for boredom, her voice trailed off. "Anyway, that's not important. I brought you a slice of cake. Leftover from the party. Try it; it's nice."

He looked down at the parcel in her hands. It was wrapped in soft white cotton and tied with a string. "You can't be here right now," he blurted, regretting it as a flash of hurt distorted her pretty features. Just for a moment; then she was setting her jaw.

"What's going on, Nok?" she demanded, pushing past him. "You're acting strange—well, stranger than usual."

Helplessly, Nok moved to let her in. He glanced outside, but the view was clear. Not a person in sight. He closed the door behind them.

"Adé!" Omair was rising from his seat at the table. "What an unexpected surprise."

The girl favored him with a warm embrace. "It's so good to see you!"

"Look how you've grown! How are things in the city?"

"Well, it's complete madness this morning, of course." Then, seeing their blank stares: "Have you not heard about the emperor yet?"

Nok felt a prickle of heat on the back of his neck. "What about the emperor?"

"Oh!" Adé said softly. "He—he's dead." As she spoke, she set her parcel of cake on the table—right beside Lu's sword. The princess had left it out. They noticed it at the same time. Adé's eyes widened at the exposed hilt with its imperial insignia: a solid-gold tiger's head, the roaring mouth filled with harsh carnelian.

"Nok," she said slowly. "This sword . . ."

Her words fell away into a scream of shock.

He followed her eyes to where Lu stood in the doorway of his bedroom, bow drawn, an arrow pointed straight at Adé's heart.

"No!" Instinct threw Nok between the two girls. "Put that down!"

Lu's bow clattered to the floor. "She saw the sword."

"Have you lost your mind?" he barked at her.

"Is that . . . ?" Adé's voice was faint behind him.

The princess's voice was low and hoarse. "Tell me what you just said about my father."

"Get back in that room and stay!" Nok snapped.

She never took her eyes off Adé. "Tell me what happened to my father."

Adé looked between Nok and Omair before saying slowly, "I'm so sorry, but your father, the emperor—he's . . . he's passed."

Lu's eyes were wild but dry. "When?"

Adé shook her head. "Yesterday, I think. They're coronating your cousin today—"

"He has no claim!" Lu blurted hotly. "He was only ever going to be crowned if he married me—"

"If he married a *princess*," Omair corrected softly from behind her.

"Yes, exactly . . ." Her voice dropped off. "Min." The name fell from her lips, soft and terrible.

Adé hesitated, then nodded. "He's marrying your sister."

The princess closed her eyes. Her mouth trembled, and for a moment it looked like she might be sick. Nok almost felt sorry for her in that moment.

"There's more," Adé continued, and her voice took on a queer softness, as though she were approaching a feral animal. "They say it was *you*. That you killed your father and fled. They've dispatched soldiers to find you. There's a reward for your capture—dead or alive."

"That's a lie," Lu blurted. "I would never—that's a lie!" She took a step toward Adé, as though she had been the one to make up the story.

Nok could see the truth dawning on her now. She'd been set up. If her cousin could not kill her, he would do worse—turn her into a murderer, a traitor. Guilty of regicide and patricide—a criminal of unforgivable proportions. Who would be hated and hunted from one end of the empire to the other.

"So, what now?" Lu demanded. "It's not over. Set can't have won."

"Yuri may have underestimated him," Omair mused.

"Set underestimated *me*!" Lu snapped. She looked as though she were barely resisting the urge to hack Omair's kitchen table to pieces. "He can't think he'll get away with this! I have to *do* something."

"We will," Omair reassured her. "When Yuri gets here."

"And what about her?" Lu said, nodding toward Adé. "What if she tells someone she saw me?"

"She won't," Nok interjected.

"How can you be sure?" the princess pressed, looking past Nok to size up the other girl. "How can you trust her?"

"They can trust me!" Adé said hotly, glaring back. "Omair and Nok are my friends—I'd never do anything to hurt them." Then, almost as an afterthought, she added, "Your Highness."

Lu scowled, holding Adé's gaze for a moment longer. Seemingly satisfied by what she found there, she grabbed her sword from the table and retreated out of the kitchen.

Nok groaned, slumping against the wall. Beside him, Adé was trembling.

"Nok, what is *happening*?" she hissed. "What is Princess Lu doing in your house? You know half the imperial guard is looking for her."

Omair came in close and took her by the arm. He looked at her, eyes solemn. "You can't breathe a word of this to anyone, Adé. Not your mother, not Carmine—"

"Of course not!" She turned to Nok. "You know me, Nok. I would never—"

"You need to go," he interrupted harshly. His fear was wearing thin and only anger remained in its wake—anger at Lu, and at himself for letting things go this awry. "I told you, you can't be here. It's not safe. Please, go. Before someone sees."

He pulled the girl from Omair's gentle grasp and threw open the front door.

Five soldiers astride as many warhorses stood in the yard. Heavy swords hung from broad leather straps at their waists. The men's steel-studded uniforms were torn and splattered with dried mud that did not entirely hide the cobalt Hana-blue

cloth beneath or the red-flame badges of the Hu Empire emblazoned on their chests.

Nok's knees buckled.

The man in their lead slid from his saddle. "You, there! Is
this where the healer lives?"

Nok wanted to pat his boot, where his knife was sheathed.

"Boy!" the soldier called again, stepping closer. "We're
looking for the healer."

"Nok," Adé hissed through clenched teeth, panic rising in
her voice. "Say something."

"Might be he's mute," he heard another of the men say.

"Do you speak, boy?" the lead soldier demanded. He was
near enough now that Nok could see his eyes. Brown, nearly
black, like his own. Unlike him, the soldier had a beard. It was
growing in patchy. "A farmer told us a healer lived up this ridge.
Our friend here needs some help."

There was a sixth in their party. Injured. The man's leg was
wrapped in soiled makeshift bandages. He rode double with
another soldier, leaning against him for support.

"One more brave casualty fallen in service of the great
empire and its bloody fire pit," jeered one of the men, a hulking
wall of muscle with long mustaches and fast, mean eyes. Nok
despised him on sight.

"Omair's an apothecarist," he told the first soldier. He
willed himself not to look over his shoulder, where Lu had
been moments earlier.

"Well, does this Omair know how to treat a wound?"

No good came from imperial soldiers, but no good ever
came from refusing them, either. What would happen if the

next villager they came across directed them back to Omair's and they discovered he had lied?

"Come inside," he heard himself say.

The lead soldier instructed the others to help the injured man down from his mount. While they busied themselves, Nok turned to Adé, her arm still clutched in his own. His pulse quickened as their eyes met—she was here because of him. If anything happened to her—

"Go," he hissed, pushing her out the door. "Ride fast. Don't look back."

Her eyes were wide in fear. "Nok, what about you?" she whispered.

"It'll be all right," he told her, but the shaking in his voice did little to instill confidence. "They don't know she's here. Everything will be all right."

"Nok, I—"

"I promise. We'll see each other again soon."

The lead soldier and two others were approaching, carrying the injured man between them. *"Please,"* Nok said, pushing Adé lightly away. "For me. Just go."

He saw her look back just once, before she mounted her borrowed mare and disappeared over the side of the ridge, leaving him alone. *Good,* he thought. Whatever happened here, she would be safe.

"Omair?" he called back into the house. "Some soldiers need your help." He hoped they couldn't hear the strain in his voice.

"Of course. Come in, come in!" came Omair's immediate response. Nok hesitated, but only for a moment.

He ducked reflexively in the low doorway as they entered. The lead soldier followed his example, but the other three were not paying attention and the tallest of them bashed his head. His helmet took the brunt of the blow, but he cursed loudly anyway.

Crowded into the small dwelling with four big men, Nok was momentarily overwhelmed by their stink—stale mud and unwashed bodies. Out of the corner of his eye he scanned the room, but aside from Omair, it was empty.

"Welcome, good soldiers," he said, giving a little bow. "What brings four of the empire's fine warriors to our home?"

The lead soldier bowed brusquely. "I am Captain Sohn of the Bei Province imperial infantry. We are pursuing a fugitive in the area, but Soldier Lim here suffered a deep cut in his calf and we're concerned about infection."

"A fugitive?" Omair's eyes widened. "He must be quite dangerous to warrant such an elite search party. Should we be worried?"

"We're looking for a girl, actually," Captain Sohn said shortly. "A princess. Tall, pretty. Have you not heard of the emperor's death? Princess Lu is wanted for his murder."

"Oh my." Omair clutched a hand to his chest. "We've heard nothing. News travels slowly out here. My, my. We live in very dark times."

The lead soldier ignored the comment and merely said in clipped tones, "Please see to Soldier Lim's injuries. My apologies for the inconvenience. The heavens will reward you for your service to the empire."

Meaning, we won't be paying you for your work, Nok translated in his head.

Omair just smiled. "Injury and illness keep no one's schedule. A healer must keep everyone's."

Captain Sohn appraised the cramped quarters. "I'll wait outside with the rest of my men. Soldier Wailun, stay here with Lim," he told the largest of the men—the one with the mustache and mean eyes, Nok noted with dismay.

Sohn and the other soldier departed. As Nok filled a kettle with fresh water, Omair patted a cushioned chair by the lit fireplace. "Why don't you bring—Soldier Lim, was it? yes?—over here."

The bigger man, Soldier Wailun, crossed the room in two strides and unceremoniously dumped his injured companion into the chair.

"Ay!" yelped Soldier Lim, catching himself on one of the chair's carved arms. "My leg!"

"Suck it up," sneered the larger man, hoisting himself atop the kitchen table. He used one massive arm to plow a clearing in the clutter of herbs and jars, then reclined as though he were on a bed. He punctuated the movement with a guttural groan of relief so loud and vulgar it reminded Nok of the time he'd seen the swollen belly of a long-dead raccoon burst, sputtering forth stinking gas and bits of gut.

Noting his gaze, Soldier Wailun leered and said, "We've been traveling all night and morning, boy. I deserve to relax."

Nok went to Omair's side. He watched as the old man cut the soldier's pant leg to reveal unnaturally pallid skin, the color of a fish's belly, crusted rust-brown with dried blood. Lim let out a shuddering *hiss*.

Nok looked away. Not because he was squeamish; he had seen far worse. He didn't look because the sight would have sent a pang of sympathy through him, and he didn't want to feel sympathy for the Hu or the Hana. Especially not a soldier.

Omair turned to Soldier Wailun, still lounging atop the table. "I need your help. Can you hold Soldier Lim still while I sew the wound closed?"

Nok heated a needle over the open fire before handing it to Omair, along with the thread. After he located the salve and stood with the jar in his hand, he saw Wailun staring hard at him.

The man sat up, propping up the bulk of his body with his elbows. "Where's that boy from? He don't look a thing like you; can't be yours."

"Doesn't he?" Omair smiled quizzically at him. "Well, he is. Our family is from Ungmar, a little farming village just beyond the Southwood, near the foothills of the Gongdun Peaks. Nok, where is that salve?"

Soldier Wailun pulled at a leather strap across his chest until the water bladder attached to it emerged over one massive shoulder. He ripped the stopper from the bladder with his teeth and took a short, hard swig. "Southerners, eh? He looks an awful lot like the slipskins we see in the labor camps up north."

Thud. Nok scrambled after the dropped jar of salve. It rolled across the floor, the glass mercifully unbroken. His neck reddened, even as he caught the jar and handed it to Omair.

"How *is* everything going on the front?" Omair asked the soldiers lightly.

Soldier Wailun snorted. "Who knows. Haven't been there in weeks. When I was, my job was rounding up stray slipskins for the camps. Rumor is some of them can still caul, so we were ordered to kill every animal we saw on sight, even if it was just a marmot. Made for strange hunting—and even stranger eating." He laughed raucously.

Nok froze. *Don't do anything stupid,* he told himself. In any case, what the soldier had suggested wasn't even possible. Most Gifted lost their caul in death, returning to their human forms.

Most of them.

"It must be harder up there now, without Commander Li— that is, Emperor Set," piped in Soldier Lim. "He knew how to run things. We never would have been able to convince the Ohmuni to surrender and relocate without him."

"The Ohmuni?" Nok blurted.

Soldier Lim scarcely spared him a glance. "The last slipskin tribe still intact—they took on the form of these little yellow deer. Easy enough to kill one at a time, but hard to eliminate. They kept hiding in this chain of caves . . ."

Nok knew who the Ohmuni were—he'd spent enough sleepless nights thinking on the irony that a clan of pacifists with herbivore cauls were the last surviving Gifted Kith, when warrior stock like the wolves of the Ashina and the red bears of the Varrok had long since been massacred.

"Anyhow," Soldier Lim continued, "I liked serving under Commander Li. He will make a fine emperor."

"Better than that arrogant Girl King, that's for sure," snorted Soldier Wailun. "At any rate, it's about time we Hana retook the throne. I tell you, things were better back when we had the reins." He looked Omair up and down for a long moment. "Isn't that right, old man?"

Omair only smiled blandly. "I will administer the poppy tears now," he announced to Soldier Lim.

He fished inside his robes, extracting a small glass bottle strung around his neck by a leather thong. From the bottle he gingerly tapped three drops of milky-white liquid into a cup of tea. Then he proffered the cup to Soldier Lim.

Soldier Lim licked his lips, then tipped the steaming contents of the cup down his throat. He shook loose the last drops at the bottom of the cup before handing the empty vessel back.

"Just rest," Omair told him. "I will begin in a moment."

Soldier Wailun stared with his sharp, mean eyes. "You sure you two ain't got some northern blood in you? You look it."

Omair smiled. "Do you think? Well, who can know! Perhaps long ago our ancestors came from the North. Blood is longer than memory, as they say."

The soldier grunted doubtfully as though *he* hadn't heard that expression before.

Omair began stitching up Soldier Lim's leg while the man lolled his head against the back of the chair, nearly chewing a hole in his bottom lip to stifle a scream of pain. The poppy tears must have been working; there'd be no stifling anything if they weren't.

Nok could feel Soldier Wailun track his movements as he crossed the room. He knew this soldier's type: a natural bully. Stupid and uncurious, but with a sharp nose for weakness in others. Show any, and out his claws would come.

Everything in Nok wanted to flee, but to do so would only

arouse more attention. He settled for scooping a basket of mint from the table and sitting as far away as he could—not far enough, the room was so small, and the soldiers so big—to separate leaves from stems.

"Pretty herbs," the soldier sneered. Nok gave a noncommittal grunt and went about his work, trying to quell his growing panic. The man was bored, and he wanted something to torment.

"What kind of answer is that, boy?" The solider sat up, knocking over a glass bottle and sending it skittering across the table. It hesitated when it reached the edge, then tumbled to the ground and continued its sad roll until it hit the wall. "Don't you know how to address your betters?"

"Sorry," Nok muttered, still plucking at the mint leaves, their sharp sweet scent now turning his stomach. Out of the corner of his eye, he saw that Omair had stopped stitching Soldier Lim.

"Sorry, *sir*," the soldier corrected him with a sneer. "And look at me when I talk to you, boy."

Nok raised his eyes to meet the soldier's. *Disappear. Disappear. Disappear,* he willed himself. He could do it; drain the fear from his gaze. Make his dark eyes two black corridors leading nowhere.

"Insolent little shit, aren't you?" Wailun demanded, sliding his bulk off the table. His feet hit the floor with a *thud*, the metal ornamentation on his boots rattling. Nok clutched the mint so hard he could feel its crushed leaves leaking wet inside his fist.

"Answer me when I speak to you." The soldier drew up

dangerously close. He was quick for such a big man; in a blink his arm struck out and grabbed Nok by the collar, lifting him clean off the chair and pinning him against the wall behind it. Nok's feet scrabbled for purchase against the seat, but only the toes of his boots reached.

Disappear. Disappear. But his thoughts were laced with panic. He drew in a ragged breath and his whole world was drowned in the reek of Soldier Wailun's hot, sour breath, and the mint, pulverized in his own fist.

The soldier laughed and slammed him against the wall. His head took the brunt of the blow and a shower of stars rained in Nok's eyes. The big man's fist was pressed even tighter against him now, crushing his windpipe.

"Sir!" Omair's voice filtered in through the haze of his fear. "Please! He meant no disrespect. Please, sir! Soldier Lim needs calm and quiet while I sew his leg."

High-pitched laughter echoed through the little room. Soldier Wailun's head whipped around at the sound. His grip on Nok's collar loosened enough that the boy could turn, too.

Soldier Lim was dissolving into giggles in his chair. "Sew my leg! I'm not a blanket," he snorted convulsively. The poppy tears. Usually it just made patients sleepy, but sometimes . . .

Soldier Lim's giggles continued, and Soldier Wailun joined in with a harsh belly laugh. "Calm and quiet, eh? I think old Lim's doing just fine, aren't you, Lim?"

Soldier Lim grinned and nodded, then nodded again, then again, and suddenly his head slumped down to his chest and he was snoring. Soldier Wailun snorted, then turned back to Nok, pressed his fist harder against his throat.

"See? My friend agrees with me. Everything's good, isn't it, boy?"

He seemed to want an answer, so Nok choked out a sound that he hoped read as affirmative.

Behind the soldier's massive bulk, Omair was staring. The old man's eyes read fear and guilt. Grief. Involuntary tears filled Nok's own as he struggled to breathe.

Then, abruptly, the hand at Nok's throat was gone. He tumbled down, his tailbone taking the brunt of the fall. A keening sound filled the room; it took Nok a moment to realize it was his own wheezing as he struggled to pull air back into his lungs.

When his vision stopped swimming, he saw Soldier Wailun standing over him, his massive bulk silhouetted by the overhead light. A memory came to him, and he could smell the stench of the labor camp's sickroom, a soldier leaning in to wrench his sister away . . .

"Please," Nok heard Omair try again. "He's a good boy . . ."

Soldier Wailun grinned. "He's a good boy, is he? He's a weak boy. A *pretty* boy. Is that what you keep him around for, old man?" There was something new in his voice—some new, rabid thought that filled Nok with fresh dread.

The man's enormous hand was on him again, dragging him up by the hair. Nok's scalp screamed in pain. "Such a pretty boy. Such long eyelashes . . . and a mouth like a girl's."

"Sir!" Omair's voice was close now. He must've put a hand on Soldier Wailun because there was a jerk of movement, and Omair went flying across the room into the kitchen table, herbs and bottles toppling to the floor in his wake.

Nok was pushed against the wall again, this time face forward, his cheek slamming against the wood hard enough to bruise. He heard Omair cry out behind him, and Soldier Wailun unhooking his belt buckle. The click seemed to echo, the moment dragging on for longer than it possibly could. Nok had heard of soldiers abusing villagers in this way, usually women and young children, but sometimes . . .

Disappear. Disappear. Feel nothing. The words hammered in his chest, quick and brutal.

Soldier Wailun's grip on his shoulder went slack. Nok looked up and saw the arrow, like a black flower sprouting from the big man's throat. A single, orderly drop of blood dangled from its point, gleaming bright as a ruby.

Nok scrambled to avoid the man's body as it slumped against the wall. The arrow dragged through the wood, its head snapping clean off as Soldier Wailun crashed to the floor.

Behind where he had stood, the princess was still and languid as a panther, another arrow already nocked in her bow. Her copper eyes were flinty and cool as they tracked the fall of Solider Wailun's body.

"Go. Now." Omair's voice broke the silence, followed by a ragged snore from the still-prone Soldier Lim. "You must go."

"He's still alive." The princess's voice was close enough to startle; she stood over Soldier Wailun's body, toeing coolly at his ribs with her booted foot. Nok saw it was true. The soldier's mouth opened and closed wordlessly, filling with dark lifeblood.

"I had to get him in the throat," she said. "If I aimed for the head but didn't kill him straight off he might've screamed."

She pulled a knife from her boot and without ceremony, plunged its sharp blade through the man's temple.

It took some effort to pry the knife back out; the princess's face screwed up in disgust as blood slickened her fingers. When the blade was finally free, she wiped it clean against the dead man's tunic. Nok could see her hands were trembling. Perhaps she felt his stare, because she looked up to meet it. "I would do it again," she said ferociously. "He wasn't a true soldier."

"I think he was," Nok choked out.

"You must go." Omair was beside them now, shoving a full rucksack and small, densely weighted purse into Nok's hands. "Go. There is an old map of the known gates to Yunis in the purse. Guard it with your life. Now, before the others return—go!"

He felt like he was fighting to emerge from a dream. "What of you?" he managed to say, grabbing Omair's hand. Omair just shook his head. Nok's stomach dropped. "You have to come with us."

"I'm an old man with ruined knees, I'll only slow you down," Omair said. "Listen to me . . . take one of the soldiers' horses and ride for the North. Find Yunis. Don't trust anyone. Protect her. Protect one another."

"I'm not leaving you," Nok hissed, clutching at Omair's robes. A handful of pulped mint fell from his hands as he did so; he'd been holding it this whole time. The scent filled the room and his stomach lurched.

"You must. For the good of all." The old man kissed him fiercely on the forehead. "Go."

Nok felt oddly calm as Lu took the rucksack from him and led him out the back door. It was only when they crouched behind a scraggly bush to observe the soldiers' positions that he realized she was clutching his hand in her own.

"They're lounging below, eating," she whispered. "Horses are loose, grazing."

Nok nodded numbly. *We're leaving Omair behind*, he thought. *This is wrong. This is all wrong.*

"It's been awhile since I've ridden a horse, but as I recall it's not all that different from an elk," the princess muttered. How could she be thinking about that when they were leaving Omair behind? Oh gods, and with a dead *soldier.*

"They'll kill him," Nok whispered. "They'll think he murdered that . . . that soldier and they'll arrest him and—"

The princess's hand clapped over his mouth, sudden and warm. *"Shh!"* He opened his mouth against her palm to object, but then he heard it, too: the low mumble of approaching voices.

". . . taking a long time . . . ," one of them grumbled as the other knocked at Omair's door. Then knocked again.

The princess removed her hand from Nok's mouth. "If you go back now, we die. Don't waste Omair's sacrifice. This is our only chance."

You have a chance to do something with that life. To help change the course of the empire.

Omair's words came back to him like a command.

The princess stared at him with wide, solemn eyes. Nok nodded, just once.

A chance.

It should have been funny, how easily they were able to steal over the far edge of the hill and lure one of the Hana warhorses toward them with a few well-chosen apples from the tree they were hiding against. Nok thought he might never laugh again.

"We just need another . . ."

"Another what?" Nok asked.

"Another horse," she said as though he were quite stupid. "One for me and one for you."

"I can't *ride*!"

The horse they had recruited huffed against the princess's palm as she reached out to stroke it. Then it nosed at the rucksack on her back, as though prying for more apples. It reminded Nok of . . .

"Bo," he whispered. "We're leaving Bo behind."

The princess looked at him in disbelief. "You want to try to outrun a dozen warhorses on an old mule?"

"No, of course not! I just—"

A shout rang out from atop the hill.

"Now," Lu said. "Come on. Best to go before they see us." She slung herself over the horse and held out her hand.

A neighbor would surely take care of Bo until he returned. If he returned.

He took the princess's hand.

The horse bristled and stamped as Nok arranged himself in the saddle. Perhaps the creature smelled something on him that it didn't like; Nok thought briefly back to yesterday, his cauling. It seemed like that had been a hundred years ago. It seemed like it had been a dream.

"*Ya!*" the princess whispered into the horse's ear. Nok reflexively tightened his grip around the princess's waist and clenched his thighs into the horse's sides as the creature took off down the slope, bound for Yunis, leaving behind everything he'd ever known for the second time in his life.

CHAPTER 19

Mothers

A reward of eight taels of gold and the deed to a sky manse will be bestowed on the person who brings me Princess Lu, dead or alive," Set announced, his voice thundering in the reverent silence of the Heart. He was seated to Min's left, in her father's throne—*no*, she reminded herself. Her father was dead. Set was emperor.

Dead or alive. Min forced herself not to flinch, thinking of her sister. She would fix this. She would give him Yunis, and then he would love her enough to grant Lu her life.

Regicide. Patricide. These were the crimes leveled against her sister. Terrible words.

Lies, a voice inside Min hissed. She could not tell if it was her own.

"We will observe the customary one hundred days of mourning for the late emperor Daagmun," Set proclaimed.

A murmur of cursory prayers arose from the assembled court, but he cut it short.

"Now," he broke in. "Enough of the past. We must address our future." He paused, a furrow cutting into his handsome brow. "I have grave news to share with you: Yunis has declared war upon the empire."

Min's head whipped toward him before she could stop herself. He was still facing the crowd. Behind him, Brother nodded serenely along with his words. Seated on his far side, her mother was unresponsive, impassive. Had she known?

Of course she had, Min thought. *Likely everyone knew but me. Everyone who matters.*

The audience was murmuring, the noise a low roar. It was a sizeable crowd; this was Set's first public address as emperor, after all. Yet, Min could not help but note it was not as big as that on the day of Lu's betrothal. This morning's rain had likely cowed some people into staying home.

It's not raining now, the nagging little voice in Min's head pointed out. It was true: the gray flagstones of the Heart remained dark and slick, but the wan sky was beginning to perk again with blue.

Well, her cousin—*husband*—was certainly giving them something to regret missing.

Set continued: "At the end of the Gray War, we forced the armies of Yunis back within its gates and brokered fair terms for surrender. In our great mercy, we allowed them to live, under the condition they stay within their borders and allow our colonies to thrive. That mercy was foolish, we now see. For seventeen years, rather than rebuilding their own kingdom, the rulers of Yunis licked their wounds and plotted revenge."

He paused, letting that narrative sink in. Min's head swam with it.

For anyone her age or younger, Yunis was the stuff of legends. An otherworldly paradise, a tragic cautionary tale. The elegant northern city carved into the Ruvai Mountains, all stone and crystal. The hermit city that refused to open its gates to her grandfather's imperial forces. And in turn, the city that burned until it was nothing but broken rock and ash and smoke. But now, they were learning, some part of it had survived amid the rubble all this time.

"Just last month," Set went on, "Yunis perpetrated a raid on labor camp eight. I was there in the aftermath. More than fifty hardened criminals—slipskins and other degenerates—were set loose. And six of our own men were killed in the service of the empire."

Murmurs bubbled up from the crowd. Set held up a steady hand to settle them.

"I don't need to tell you that this was an act of war," he said grimly. His head dipped, just slightly, but then he raised his face to the crowd, a mask of stalwart grace and sorrowful burden. "Emperor Daagmun," he began. Min started at the sound of her father's name falling so easily from his lips. Then those lips hardened into a sorrowful line. "Before he was so cruelly struck down, Emperor Daagmun was weighing the evidence before him, weighing the decision to go to war. It does not do to speak ill of the dead, but I believe my beloved uncle would agree with me when I say he tarried too long in choosing to act."

Set stood then, pacing the front of the dais. Min half rose in her chair, as though to follow. Brother gave a quick jerk of his head and she sat back down, flushing red. She glanced at her mother, but the empress's eyes were transfixed on Set. Her face was eerily blank—Min wasn't sure whether to take that for a good or an ill sign.

"This is not a world for tarrying." Set's voice rose as he strode down the front steps, still slick with rain. His guards bristled uncertainly but stayed where they were. Her cousin continued on his own, along the path toward the First Flame.

"This is not a time for equivocating and hesitation," he said once he reached it. A stone pavilion sheltered the blaze, and Set paused, resting a hand against one of its pillars. He watched its flames for a long moment, seemingly oblivious to the puzzled silence of the assembled crowd. Then he reached into the pocket of his robes and withdrew something that fit neatly into his closed fist.

"We live in a dangerous moment," he said. "Our enemies encroach from all sides. Even from within. This empire—each of you—deserves an emperor who recognizes this. Who acts decisively. With strength."

Set lifted his hand high, then dashed it down toward the First Flame. Min craned forward to see, then jerked back as the blaze erupted into a brilliant yellow column. Like a living, vicious thing it shot toward the ceiling of the pavilion, arcing against the stone and pluming outward.

The crowd was on its feet, and this time their noise was thunderous.

"I swear to you, for every drop of imperial blood—both

Hana and Hu—that the Yunians sowed into the ground, they will reap a thousand of their own!" Set shouted above it. "We will not let the Northerners prevail!"

Applause filled the Heart. Min nearly rose from her seat to join in. Some primal response to such concentrated, powerful emotion.

In all likelihood, there was scarcely a person alive in Yulan City—be they the head of a sky manse household or a blacksmith working out of a hovel in the Second Ring—who had thought much about Yunis in the last seventeen years. Longer than Min's entire life. And yet, with a few well-chosen words, each person present seemed to believe with utter conviction that this war on Yunis was of the greatest urgency. As though it had been their own sons or husbands or brothers slain on the northern front.

She looked again toward Set's empty throne. Past it, her mother's face was frozen in a rictus of dismay. The anger and agitation radiating from her now was nearly palpable.

She didn't know, either, Min realized with shock. She had assumed her mother was as close to Set's plans as anyone.

Well, Min amended, perhaps not anyone.

Behind the empty throne, Brother smiled placidly into the middle distance.

❧

"I thought you were going to announce the banishment of the Ellandaise," Min's mother groused as they made their way down the corridor leading out of the rear of Kangmun Hall, flanked by Brother and Set's gaggle of eunuchs. "When did you decide—"

"I don't have time to run all of my plans past you, Aunt Rinyi," Set snapped.

"A *war* is a fairly significant omission!"

The empress shouldered past Min as she spoke, pushing her into the wall. Min pressed her palms against it to keep from falling, then lapsed into formation behind her mother.

"It went over well, don't you think?" Set mused. He turned to Brother. "You were right; people love a fight."

"They love a fight with a clear purpose," the monk amended mildly.

"What's next on my agenda for today?" Set asked the head eunuch.

The eunuch bowed, never missing a step. "The captain of the guard wished for you to, ah, inspect that prisoner he mentioned."

"Right, right," Set muttered. "Well, onward to the dungeons, then."

Min's mother stopped short. Min walked straight into her back, but the empress did not seem to notice. "The dungeons?" she repeated. "I know you don't think to bring Minyi."

Set looked back at her and blinked in surprise, as though he hadn't realized she were there at all.

"Actually," Brother said, stepping between them. "I'm heading back to my chamber now. It's in the same direction as Empress Minyi's apartments—perhaps I could escort her there?"

"Perfect," Set said quickly, seemingly satisfied his burden

had been relieved. Min's mother's full mouth shriveled into a hard line as she looked at Brother. Before she could speak, though, the monk was offering Min his arm. She took it.

≈≋⊙≋≈

But Brother didn't escort her to her apartments, after all. Once they'd departed from her husband and mother, he'd guided her back to his chamber—a room in a small outbuilding off Set's new apartments. Min shivered as they'd passed the front door leading to the bedroom in which her father had died.

"Just a moment, Princess."

The darkness in the room was absolute; the windows had been papered over. Min closed her eyes, then opened them again, but saw no difference.

There was a scrape, a puff of sulfur, a flare. Brother's face floated out from the void, wan and eerie. He smiled, the lines of his face cavernous and grotesquely exaggerated by the low light. He used the candle to light several more, illuminating the room.

Min blinked and found herself in a cramped study, not unlike that of a shin's. Stacks of limp, musty books lined the walls. Some were faced toward her the wrong way around, and all she could make out were the yellowed edges of their pages. Others bore their spines at her, but only a few were labeled—in fine, hand-lettered text. Min squinted at the closest, but she did not recognize the language.

"I apologize for the subterfuge," Brother said, lighting a fireplace against the far wall, then hanging a kettle over its crackling flame. He spoke lightly, as though she were a visitor dropping by for tea. "I mentioned to Set this morning that I wanted to begin your lessons. He and I both thought it best to shelter your mother."

Lessons? Min hesitated. "Yes, I suppose that was wise," she said softly.

"I'm afraid the empress does not fully trust me—or, rather, my abilities—yet," the monk continued. "Such is often the case with laypeople." He sighed, turning sorrowful eyes on her. "You will come to see this in time, I am afraid."

"Oh," Min said.

There was the sound of a scoff. Min recognized it with an odd twain of dread and excitement.

"He speaks of laypeople as though he's any different," the shamaness retorted. *"As though he knows anything."*

It was almost a relief to hear from her. The spirit-creature seemed to keep her own time. Min had tried calling for her over the past few days, when she was bored or lonely—often enough—but the girl never emerged, never spoke. Where did she go? How much did she hear and see?

Brother pulled a ceramic tea jar from a high shelf and shook its contents—a mélange of herbs she did not recognize—into a gaiwan. Then, he removed the kettle from the fire and poured boiling water over the herbs.

Min blinked. He really was serving her tea.

But what kind? This time Min wasn't sure whether the thought came from the shamaness, or from herself.

Brother poured the liquid from the gaiwan into a matching white cup, which he placed before her. Min stared down into its limpid, vaguely pink contents. He had been meticulous in straining the tea; no dregs had escaped into the cup.

"What is . . . " she searched for a more courteous way to phrase the question, but found none. "What is it?"

"My own blend of herbs. Some foreign. Nothing harmful, I assure you."

"Oh no," she said quickly. "Of course not."

"*Of course not,*" mimicked the shamaness.

I should tell him about her, Min thought. Did he know the shamaness was still in her? Was she truly there? How was anyone to know? She was the only one who could hear the voice. Perhaps she was losing her mind.

That thought frightened her more than she could say. Even if she did tell Brother, could he do anything about it? There was no telling what he might do: try to remove the thing or lock her away in a sickroom. In either case, she'd never reach Yunis, never grant Set his deepest wish—

"You don't need to drink it," he said. She started; she had forgotten about the tea. "You needn't do anything that frightens you, Princess."

She nodded, still staring down at the tea. And realized, too late, *Not princess. Empress.* But the moment to correct his mistake had already passed. Silence stretched between them.

A strand of hair slipped free into her face. Min made to push it back up, then jumped when she caught movement out of the corner of her eye—only to realize there was a mirror propped in the corner. What she had taken for a threat was just her own reflection.

Stupid. What was there even to fear? *You're safe here.*

She looked at the mirror, at the girl on the other side of the glass. A pale creature, vague in aspect, shrunken in stature. Her robes were new and a bit too large, making her look even smaller, younger. She shifted under the scrutiny of her own reflected gaze. There was something repulsed, almost contemptuous in the way it looked back at her. Was that the shamaness she was seeing? Was she there in the hate in Min's own eyes?

"Princess?" Brother broke the overlong silence.

Empress, Min thought again. Without answering him, she lifted the cup he'd set before her and drank the tea down.

It burned. Her eyes fluttered open in alarm—he'd poisoned her, after all! She coughed wildly . . .

Then—no. The tea was simply hot. She hadn't given it long enough to cool.

With as much composure as she could muster, Min rested the cup back on the table.

"What—what is it meant to do?" she asked.

"It will relax your conscious mind, freeing your unconscious to act in its full power."

Min nodded as though what he was saying made sense to her.

"It will take some time for it to take effect. In the meantime, let us start with what you've already accomplished," Brother said, laying a ledger and ink out on the table before them. He dipped a brush into the ink. "Now, when did you first begin to sense your power, what did you first notice? Please be specific."

"There was a dream," Min began. Her throat felt tight. Was she breathing correctly? Her lungs felt sluggish, as though they'd forgotten their purpose.

"A dream?" he prompted when she didn't continue.

"Yes. A red dream . . . and white . . ." Min squinted across the table at him. She ought to meet his eyes, she thought vaguely.

It was hard to focus, though, in the dim light. The candle resting on the table between them flickered, and she felt the sensation against her skin like fingers.

There was movement on the ceiling, directly above her. She whipped her head up to track it. *Just the mirror, stupid. Remember how you saw your reflection in the mirror*—only the mirror was on the wall, of course. The ceiling looked ordinary: dark wood beams, unadorned. Low. The beams undulated in sympathy with the dancing candlelight—

"Princess?" Brother whispered, far away.

Empress, she thought as her eyes, so heavy, like stones, slipped closed.

Some instinct in her called out for familiarity—she wanted safety. She wanted her mother? Was that what she wanted?

Find her, she told herself. *Find Set,* another voice murmured.

I've found them, the shamaness broke in, her voice a singsong. *Your mother, your husband . . .*

Min groped for them, like reaching out in the darkness.

They were walking side by side down a dank, narrow hallway, following an armed guard. It was dark; the walls were stone. She could feel cold radiating from them. They were underground, she could feel the pressure of packed earth all around them. Min squinted and saw bars. They were in the dungeons.

A new face swam into view. Pale and furious. For a moment, Min thought it was the shamaness, but her stomach clenched when she realized the truth.

Hyacinth.

The nuna's hair was in disarray, her yellow robes dingy and streaked with dirt and—

Gods, Min thought. Was that *blood?*

"Are these Lu's handmaidens?" Set asked, stopping short. "I'd like to question them myself. They may know Lu's plans."

Her mother shook her head. "They don't know anything—"

"I know Lu is innocent!" Hyacinth broke in, gripping at the bars of her cell. Her knuckles went red, then white.

This seemed to amuse Set. "Innocent, you say? The girl who killed your little brother?"

Fear flickered across Hyacinth's face, an uncertain quaver. "What?"

"What was his name?" Set continued. "Wonin? A brave young man. He only wanted to help his empire, his true emperor. And she cut him down like he was nothing. I'm sure she thought herself justified. Anything for the crown."

"Liar!" Hyacinth snarled, triumphant. "My brother wouldn't help *you*—"

"Your brother would do anything your father told him. And your father would do anything that improved his station."

For a stunned moment, Hyacinth drew back as if he'd struck her. Her pretty face twisted in confusion and grief. Then she lunged forward and spat. The emission struck Set's handsome cheek, streaking down toward his chin.

"You're a filthy liar, and a traitor. Lu would never hurt Wonin, *never!*"

The guard gave a shout, slamming a baton against Hyacinth's exposed knuckles. There was a sick splitting sound. The nuna let out a shriek.

Min closed her eyes against the sight. When she opened them again, a man was on the ground before her.

He didn't look like much. Short and stout. No hair, but for a filthy beard groping its way down his chest. Two soldiers in blue Hana tunics flanked him. They, and the iron shackles about his wrists and ankles announced him as a criminal, but nothing on his tired face or stooped posture suggested danger. Mostly, Min thought, he looked old.

"Who is he?"

Min jumped. Set and her mother stood behind her, just inside the heavy metal door of the tiny room—a prison cell. Set gestured toward the prisoner with a disdainful flick of his hand and Min flinched, shuffling out of his way—although, she knew, he could not see her.

Not this again. No, please, whatever it is, I don't want to see—

"*Lies.*" Min flinched and there she was, the shamaness in white. She hovered behind, her sharp little chin digging into Min's shoulder. When Min turned though, the girl had disappeared.

"Why have you brought me to see this creature?" Set asked the guards.

He was an uneasy fit in the tiny room. The gold silk of his robes looked unnatural, fussily bright against the old, stained stone walls.

The soldiers behind the prisoner bowed at the waist. As they straightened, one of them noticed the prisoner was still upright. He kicked the old man in the small of his back, sending him to his knees, hard. The man cried out—pathetic and thin. Min flinched.

"Are you simple?" demanded the soldier. "Don't you know to bow before your emperor?"

"Oh, is this the emperor?" the old man said. "I did not realize. I heard the emperor was a woman these days—"

"Why, you insolent old dog!" The soldier brought his gloved hand down against the prisoner's jaw with a sick, wet impact. A blood-slick tooth shot from between his lips and skittered across the stone floor, disappearing into the filthy rushes. Min closed her eyes and forced herself not to cry out.

"Enough!" Set barked. "Do you mean to keep me waiting all day in this disgusting cell? Who is he?"

"Your Majesty," the soldier said, quickly scrambling back into formation. "This man has information on the whereabouts of the Girl Ki—Princess Lu. We have reason to believe he was harboring her immediately after she murdered her father. He is also suspected of helping her slay one of our own company, a soldier named Wailun."

"How was this not brought to our attention sooner?" demanded the empress from Set's far side. Min started. She had forgotten her mother was there at all.

Set frowned at the interjection but nodded. "Yes, it's been days! How are we—how am I only hearing of this now?"

The other guard stepped forward. "If you please, Emperor Set, we tried to bring him before you as soon as he was discovered, but in the chaos—that is, the confusion of mourning the late emperor Daagmun, we were not permitted to enter the city. We had to hold him in one of the city jails."

"You should have informed the captain of the imperial guard!" Set cried.

"Begging your pardon, we did, Your Majesty," the second guard said. "But again, we were told no one was to enter or leave the palace grounds for the safety of the imperial family."

Set crammed agitated fists to his hips, turning as though to pace the floor of the cell, only to find the quarters too close to do so. Seemingly frustrated by this, he took a deep breath and refocused on the old man now hunched on the floor before them. "What is his name? How did he come to know my cousin?"

"The villagers in Ansana call him Omair. He is an apothecarist, allegedly. They say he appeared out of nowhere some years ago. He has no known relations, though there was a young man, an apprentice boy living with him—"

"And where is this boy?" Set demanded impatiently.

"He, ah, he disappeared, Your Majesty," admitted the guard. "We have men searching for him. He may be with the princess."

Set's mouth hardened into a red line. "Go," he managed to bark out. "I'll deal with you later. Out."

When they'd gone, Set whirled on her mother, almost accusatory. "You see?" he demanded. "Spies and conspirators everywhere. I told you Lu was plotting against me this whole time!"

"Lower your voice," her mother hissed. "You think the guards outside the cell can't hear? And what about him?" She gestured at the prisoner still cowering on the floor at their feet.

"You said she was just a dumb little girl," Set continued. He spoke more softly now, but it only seemed to intensify the malevolent sting of his words. "That she had no friends. And yet she has allies as far as Ansana!"

"This means nothing," her mother said with a dismissive wave of her hand. "Who is this man? A peasant. She likely coerced or tricked him into housing her."

Set fixed his gaze back on the prisoner. "Is that what happened, old man?" he demanded. When the prisoner did not respond immediately, Set seized a handful of his beard and yanked him to his feet. The man swayed, clearly unsteady, kept upright only by the force of Set's grip. "Who are you?" Set screamed in his face, slamming him against the wall of the cell.

Min jumped back, her whole body running cold.

The old man winced at the flecks of spit spraying his face. "If it p-please Your Majesty, your Emperorship, I am an ap-apothecarist. Nothing more." He turned his face to the side, like a nervous dog, mouth wet and trembling.

"An apothecarist, are you? A healer?" Set released his hold on the prisoner abruptly, sending him crumpling to the floor. "You're going to need a very, very good healer when I'm done with you."

Then her cousin drew back his handsomely booted foot and kicked the man in the ribs. Once, twice—the man yelped each time Set made contact, but the blows came faster, wild, uncontrolled, until his voice became a continuous shriek, and then a low moan.

Stop! Please stop! Min thought, but she wasn't sure if she meant it for Set or for the prisoner. Her heart swelled, squeezing the air from her lungs. She couldn't breathe, couldn't move. All she could do was stand there, pummeled by the man's wail. And beneath it the frantic, panted demands of her cousin.

"Where is she? Where is Lu? Where is the little bitch? Who else are you working with?"

It could only have been a few minutes, but it felt like hours later when her cousin stilled, breathing raggedly. Min stared at his heaving back and for the first time prayed he wouldn't turn around and look her way.

He thrust a palm against the wall, leaning heavily against it. A ring of sweat soaked the neck of his robes. The old man curled in on himself like burning paper. The acrid stink of fresh urine filled the cell.

Her mother drew back in revulsion. "He's soiled himself."

"Good," snarled Set. "That means he's afraid. As he should be."

"I don't know anything!" wailed the old man.

"If you're going to kill him," her mother said, "call the guards in to do it. This is a waste of our time."

"I won't kill him yet," Set said. "Not until I've wrung out every drop of information he has to give."

He delivered a final, disgusted kick to the man's side, but his aim was skewed by exhaustion; the toe of his boot merely glanced off the prisoner's ribs and hit the stone wall. He hopped back, cursing.

"This old peasant dog here couldn't have been working alone," he said. "He must have connections in the court."

"I'm telling you, Lu is relying on dumb luck," insisted her mother. "It will soon run out. I have spies everywhere—they would have told me if she'd begun covertly planning anything."

"Your spies are either useless or lying to you, Aunt Rinyi!" snapped Set. He turned away then, heading for the door of the cell. "I will get to the bottom of who can be trusted and who knows Lu's plans. And when we find her, I'll kill Lu with my own bare hands."

The cell door slammed hard behind him. For a long moment, her mother stared at it, as though contemplating the space where Set had stood. Then, without turning, she spoke.

"Omair," she mused, her voice low, but clear. Intentional. Both Min and the prisoner looked up sharply, as though her words were a lead tugging at their necks. "An unusual name. Sounds southern."

She turned back to where the prisoner remained crouched amid the dirty rushes scattering the floor. "Though, I suppose that's what you were hoping for, weren't you? Much less provincial than *Ohn*, I'll grant you that."

It was as though the name was a spell her mother had recited. The old man slowly rose from his defeated crouch. He winced, leaning his back against the wall, the pain still clear on his face.

But as Min watched, he slowed his breath, closed his eyes. She felt it—the way she could feel her own heart beating or a breeze against her skin. His energy leveled, drawing the pain from his side, his mouth, shifting it to a sustaining equilibrium. The change came slow and subtle, the way a new flower unfolds. When he opened his eyes, the weight of a dozen years seemed to slip from his shoulders. Gone was the slack, cowed expression— the mask of a frightened peasant replaced with the canny certainty of a man no longer out of his element looking royalty in the face.

"I thought perhaps you'd forgotten me," said this new man.

"How could I?" Her mother's tone was bitter. She did not appear to notice the man's quiet metamorphosis. "Pissing yourself. That was a nice touch. But, no. I didn't forget. Do you know how many years I spent looking for you? How much I paid, to how many mercenaries—all for empty promises of your swift, discreet death? You were my one loose thread."

"And here I sit," the man said lightly. "Ready to be snipped."

"Not quite," the empress said reluctantly. "My nephew grows more paranoid by the day. Do you know how many guards are standing outside your door? You have Set's interest now—you've become the key to his conspiracy. The thing that proves to his mind how dangerous Lu truly is. If I am the last person to see you alive, what would he make of that? What would he do to me?"

"And what of the princess? Are you not worried about her?"

"Lu? Please. She's more naïve than she is anything else. I may not be the girl's mother, but I did watch her grow up."

Min whipped around to face the empress. *Not Lu's mother?* No. She had misheard—

Did you? The shamaness's hiss echoed through the room, but when Min spun around to find her, she wasn't there.

"Naïve?" the prisoner repeated with a faint smile. "Perhaps. But I think you underestimate her other qualities."

Her mother sniffed. "Still playing the part of enigmatic savant, are we? Well, it won't work on me. I wasn't lying when I told Set that I'd been tracking her for years, that I have spies everywhere. If she'd had any wits at all, Lu would have had her own. She would have had the network of support, of loyalists that Set thinks she has. Even her beloved Shin Yuri—your old friend, wasn't he? What an opportunistic man he grew up to be. He's been in my pocket for years. She has no one."

"She has me."

The empress's eyes narrowed. "Maybe she did. But now I do."

"So, where does that leave us?" the prisoner asked, drawing himself up straighter.

Her mother shrugged daintily. "We find ourselves in a strange alliance, don't we? I intend to take the secret of Lu's parentage to the grave, and I imagine—out of whatever misplaced loyalty you still bear to Daagmun and that witch mother of hers—that you will do the same. Only, I fear you will reach the grave much sooner than I. Between Set, his men, all their combined paranoia, and your age, I needn't bother trying to kill you myself."

That seemed to amuse Omair—or was it Ohn? "I admit, I'm surprised you haven't told Set about Lu's birth yourself. It would delegitimize her entire claim. It's the answer to your nephew's problems."

"His problems, perhaps. But what of mine?"

Omair searched her face with keen, curious eyes. "What holds you back, exactly? It can't just be your pride."

Her mother flared. "Don't speak to me of pride. I have already given everything else I had—my name, my birth, my youth, my beauty, my *life*—to a husband who wanted none of it. I've spent the last seventeen years planning and plotting on my nephew's behalf. I deserve to keep this bit of pride for myself. Have you ever considered what it might feel like to have the entire empire know my emperor husband flouted our union for some lowborn foreign *shamaness*?"

Min's eyes widened. *A* shamaness? *Lu's mother was—she couldn't mean. No. Not the same shamaness . . .* She cast about again for the girl in white, but she had not reappeared. Somehow, Min knew she would not again, not here.

Her own mother inhaled sharply. "And what for? Nothing. It is all done and in the past. No one is left who can attest to the truth of it. All it would do now is cast more uncertainty, more instability into the court. They may start doubting Minyi's legitimacy—insist Set annul his vows to her, even. It's too risky."

The empress sighed, walking toward the door, picking a delicate path amid the soiled rushes. "I've worked too hard to secure Min's place in this world to chance losing it."

The man tracked her mother's movement with a sedate, cautious curiosity.

"You truly love your daughter," he said in mild surprise. "You would do anything to protect her."

"What mother wouldn't?"

The prisoner slumped against the wall of the cell, and Min once more felt the pain sparking from his side, the absence in his mouth where his missing tooth had been. He was powerful, whatever he was, but clearly even he had his limits.

"I think you and Tsai had more in common than you know."

"Princess?"

Min felt a sharp tug on her arm. She blinked. Before her eyes, the cell dissolved, taking her mother and the prisoner with it.

"Princess?"

Another tug. Harder now, almost painful. She winced, blinked—

"Princess Min!"

She opened her eyes. Brother kneeled over her. She was on the floor; she must have fallen from her seat—

"What did you see?"

"I saw . . ." She pushed herself up on shaky arms.

Tell him. Tell him about Lu. It will please Set. It will give him all he needs to secure the throne. Maybe he'll stop hunting Lu. Maybe he'll even let her come home and everything will be—

Her mother's words echoed back to her, though: *They may start doubting Minyi's legitimacy—insist Set annul his vows to her, even.*

"Princess?" Brother persisted.

"I saw—I was h-having a nightmare," she stammered. A thin, naked slip of a lie. "Amma Ruxin was angry with me. She was screaming."

For a breathless moment, Brother searched her face with those unyielding, temperate eyes. Then he sighed, clearly disappointed. "Very well," he said, helping her to her feet. "I fear I've overextended you. Let us get you back to your apartments."

She nodded, trying not to appear overeager.

He took her arm in his own, leading her to the door. She suppressed the urge to glance back into his mirror; she already knew what she'd see there. A girl who could be anyone. A girl who could be nothing at all.

CHAPTER 20

Exile

Crying was a weakness, and Lu was not weak. She would choose fury over fear, and her fury would sear away any tears that might well inside her. This was what she decided on the trail north.

She rode with the reins of the horse in hand, the Ashina boy seated behind her. He sat stiffly, as though trying to avoid touching her, but otherwise was so still, so silent she might have thought him asleep. The soft, lethargic sway of the wind-swept pines and the high trill of breeding cicadas had more to say than he did.

She let him keep his quiet. He'd been through enough. They both had.

Her father was dead. Her father was dead, and everyone believed she'd been the one to kill him.

Not Min, she thought. Surely her sister couldn't believe she could do such a thing, could she? Their mother, though . . . she wasn't so certain. But Min . . .

Poor Min. Sweet, innocent, simple Min. Sold off to Set by their mother like some prized mare. The thought slid through her, oily and repugnant.

Pushing away the thought, she looped the reins around a wrist and held up Omair's map, studying the browned paper rotely for the hundredth time.

As she folded it back up, Nokhai shifted behind her. Lu felt she ought to speak, but she could all but feel the mistrust radiating off him. How could this be the traveling companion the heavens had chosen for the most important journey of her life?

Omair trusted the boy to guide her, she reminded herself. And Yuri trusted Omair.

Did she trust Yuri, though? Even if his heart were loyal, he hadn't left her with much to work with. Was there anyone she could rely on?

Not anymore. Out here, I'm alone.

Fear sluiced through her gut as the horse stumbled beneath her. Horses, Lu thought in annoyance, were a decidedly inferior mount to elk. She yearned for Yaksun's broadness, his surefooted strength. This creature, for all its meticulous breeding, seemed to spook at every pit and root it stumbled on.

And there were plenty of pits and roots on this jagged, narrow forest lane. She'd wanted to take the well-maintained, slate-paved Imperial Road, but the boy had insisted—rightly, she had to admit—that they try a route less frequented by hordes of imperial soldiers.

The horse stumbled beneath her again. She frowned.

"You have a mule," she mused aloud. "Mules aren't so different from horses, are they? How frequently do you need to reshoe a mule?"

The boy at her back was silent for a long moment. Then he whispered, "Bo."

"What?"

"The mule's name is Bo. We left Bo behind," he said, sitting up straighter. There was now a panic in his voice that alarmed her.

"I know . . . ," she said. "We had to."

"Oh gods," he croaked. "*Omair.* We have to go back."

"Wait!" she cried, but too late. The boy slipped from the saddle and was running down the trail, back in the direction they had come.

It occurred to her for a frozen moment that she could leave him. Let him run back into the waiting arms of the soldiers probably still swarming the old apothecarist's house, searching the nearby fields for them . . .

Cursing, Lu turned the horse after him.

She overtook him in no time at all; perhaps horses weren't entirely useless. When she was close enough, she reined up and slipped from the saddle.

The boy was still running, but when she caught him by the shoulders he stopped, breathless. At first she thought he was winded, but then she realized he was having some sort of fit. He could scarcely breathe.

"*Omair,*" he hissed. "We need to go back for Omair."

"It was Omair's command for us to continue to Yunis alone. He saved us so that we could—"

The boy whirled on her at those words. "He saved us, and we *left* him. Oh gods, I left him . . ." He hunched on the ground, head clutched in his hands. Lu watched him quiver, tufts of coarse black hair peeking out between his clenched fingers. "Gods." His voice was so quiet Lu could barely make out the words. "I'm a coward. I've always been a coward."

Lu hesitated. She had never been very good at comfort. From an early age she had learned that to lose one's composure was unbecoming, so she had taught herself to keep hers wrapped tight around her like a cloak, to drape it over her unsightly pain. In turn, though, she had never learned how to soothe pain in others. When little Minyi had cried over some harsh words from Amma Ruxin or their mother, it had been Butterfly or Hyacinth who held her sister's hand, stroked her hair as she wept.

And when she'd made Set cry all those years ago in the desert, Lu had laughed.

Because he deserved it, she'd told herself. *And because he was a boy, and boys were supposed to be warriors, and warriors didn't cry.* She had learned that before she'd learned to swing a sword. She didn't get to cry, so why should he?

But here in the woods there was no Butterfly, no Hyacinth. And the boy hunched before her was not her cousin. He was no warrior, either. But perhaps that was all right.

"Nokhai," she whispered. The name felt at once forbidden and familiar in her mouth. She crouched down beside him. Her hand found his shoulder, clumsy and experimental. He flinched beneath her touch, but did not pull away. Her hand moved in progressively broader circles, until her fingers were tracing over his shoulder blades, the prominent notches of his spine.

"Omair knew what he was doing," she told him. "He made a choice."

"I owe him my life," the boy said heatedly.

She could feel the warmth and the sorrow coming off him in waves, and she wanted to touch him more, touch him *better* than a mere hand to the back. To press so close against his skin she could draw the hurt out like a poultice draws poison from a wound.

"We'll save him," she said fiercely. "If we go back now, there's nothing we can do. We'll just be prisoners—corpses, even. But if we can make it to Yunis, I swear to you I'll return with an army, and I'll free Omair. Once my cousin is defeated, it'll be the first thing I do."

Behind his tears, she saw something else: a flicker of calculation in their black depths sparking to life and burning away his tears. There was something familiar in it. Perhaps he was not so different from her, after all.

"Why should I trust you?" the boy asked, shrugging her hand off as though he had only just noticed it.

Good question. There were plenty of lines she could feed him. Pretty notions of honor and civility and the word of royalty. Promises from the empire that had murdered his family and razed all sign or substance of his home from the earth. None of which would mean a damned thing to him.

"You don't have a choice," she said instead. "Either we trust each other, or we have no one. Is that good enough for you?"

Surprise flickered over his face. Finally, he nodded, his mouth set in a grim line. This bargain of necessity, this acquiescence to the distasteful needs of survival—this was something he understood. An ugly language that they now shared.

Lu stood and offered her hand. "Come on, then. Let's save Omair."

Nokhai stood on his own, but when he was upright he took her hand and shook it grimly.

"Let's save the empire," he said dryly.

Then he dropped her hand as though he couldn't bear to hold it a moment longer. His face was still red and swollen, but his tears were gone.

⟡

They stopped for the night in a clearing far enough from the path that they wouldn't immediately be seen by passersby. The air was cool, so Nokhai built a small fire. Because they had scarcely seen anyone all day, Lu reasoned, the blaze was unlikely to attract any attention.

As Nokhai worked, she inspected the rucksack Omair had given them before they fled. Lu unpacked two wool cloaks, a small jar of strong-smelling salve—she would have to ask Nokhai about its use later—a few rolls of cotton bandages, a sack of roasted chestnuts still in their husks, several sachets of dried teas and herbs, and a stack of some sort of fried flat-cakes bound in a clean cloth.

She kept the cloaks and the flat-cakes in her lap, then

carefully replaced everything else. When she held up the flat-
cakes in victory, though, she found Nok had moved from
building a fire—now a pleasantly crackling blaze—to rubbing
down the horse.

He had already removed its saddle and blanket and slung
them over the low branch of a nearby tree, and in lieu of a comb,
he was rubbing his fingers in a circular motion through the
stallion's coat.

"It's all right, boy," he murmured. "You can rest now."

The sound of his voice was so unguarded that Lu found
her shout of "Dinner!" dying upon her lips.

He must have sensed her stare; when he turned, the mask of
suspicion had dropped down once more over his face.

"Omair packed . . ." Too late did it occur to her just hearing
the name might inflict pain. "There was food in the bag," she
finished awkwardly.

Nokhai came over and examined the bundles. "Turnip
cakes. Good."

"There were some nuts, too. I thought we should save those
for later."

But the boy had set down the bundle and was now fingering
a cluster of softly lobed leaves on the ground by his feet. "Sweet
purple."

"Sweet what?"

The boy worked his knife under where the leaves joined,
and with a grunt, he pried a fat wine-colored tuber from the
soft earth. He faced her with grim satisfaction. "Dinner. Goes
well with turnip cakes."

Lu frowned doubtfully. "Is it edible?"

"Would it be dinner if it weren't?"

"But it's from the forest."

He stared at her. "What do you eat when you're out on a hunt?"

"Whatever game we catch," she responded, folding her arms across her chest.

"And what if you don't catch anything?"

"The cooks make a meal from the food stores we bring with us—"

"And where do the food stores come from?"

"Our crop fields."

"And where do you think those crops came from?"

"Not the forest!"

"Maybe not, but they came out of the mud same as anything. Same as these sweet purples." He shook the roots. Clods of dirt rained to the ground.

"I suppose you're correct," she sniffed.

"Of course I'm correct."

As he cooked, Lu polished the edges of her sword until the blade gleamed white in the firelight. Nokhai's back was to her, but when she leaned to the side she could see the purple tubers resting on a raised bed of stones around which he stacked pine needles and twigs. He lit the kindling with his flint.

The air soon filled with a warm, nutty smell and he announced that the tubers were done. He handed her one, swaddled in a rag. She pulled the cloth apart and yelped when the skin burned her fingertips.

"They're hot," the boy said.

"That's very helpful!" she snapped.

She watched and did as he did, licking her fingers and using them to pull apart the crackling wine-purple skins to reveal the yellow flesh beneath. A swipe of her knife cleaved a chunk into her waiting hand. As she dropped the hot meat into her mouth her eyes widened in surprise.

"It's sweet."

"Hence the name."

She looked up. Nokhai was—not quite smiling, but it was close. It gave her a start; jerked something hard in her gut to see him like that. With his face lit, he looked a good deal more like the bashful child she had met in the desert.

When he caught her gaze in his own, though, his smile slipped.

"What?" he asked.

She shrugged, taking another chunk of sweet purple in her fingertips. It was cooler now. "I thought you'd forgotten how to smile. It's nice. You smiling, I mean."

His ears reddened. "Haven't had much reason to smile."

She wasn't sure how to respond to that, but it seemed he did not expect her to. He turned back toward the fire.

"Needs more kindling," he said. "The bigger logs aren't staying lit."

As he bent by the fire, red light danced across his face, accenting the hollows under his cheekbones and the edge of his jaw where it drew up sharply to meet his ear. Lu stared at that juncture, watched it clench as he worked.

He'd been the first friend she'd ever made on her own. It

was different from Hyacinth and the other nunas—she loved them as well as anyone in the world, but they hadn't chosen one another so much as they were chosen for one another. She'd seen Nokhai in the crowd when their retinue arrived, and right then and there she'd known . . . what, exactly? Only that there was a familiarity in him, like finding some precious thing that she hadn't even known she'd lost.

They spent that single afternoon wending their way through a chain of caves in the hillside while their Elders and her father convened in the Ashina encampment below. When they came across a nest of scorpions, Lu had wanted to crush them with rocks. But Nokhai had convinced her to let them be.

Aren't you afraid? she'd asked.

He hadn't understood. *Yes, of course I am.*

And she'd thought, *Here is a boy that is soft as flowers.*

They hadn't known then that the evening would end in curses and vows of war; they'd only been children.

⚜

"You know," she said. Nokhai looked up from the fire. "Even if the rumors about Yunis aren't entirely true, there might be some of your kind left. Not your Kith, maybe, but others . . ."

Nok's face closed off to her so swiftly as to be brutal. "Just because *your* kind thinks we're all the same doesn't mean we see ourselves that way."

"I only thought, since we are going to the outer territories, maybe we could ask after your Kith. See if anyone . . . you know, if they—"

"Survived both the slaughter and the labor camps?"

She hesitated at the choice of words, but his tone was no more hostile than usual. "Yes."

"No."

She frowned. "No, you don't think they did, or no you don't want to ask?"

"No, I don't want to know. No, I don't want to talk about it."

"But if there's any chance . . . you could have a home again."

A spasm of anger seized his face. "There is no home without . . . ," he broke off. "You killed my home when you killed everyone I knew."

Lu shook her head. "I don't understand. You were a princeling; if you had the chance, wouldn't you want to rebuild your people?"

"We don't—we didn't have *princes*. We weren't like *you*."

"But your father was a prince—"

"He was a Kith father. It's not the same thing. We didn't have *princes*."

"Still, he was important."

Nok stood abruptly and seized their pail. "My family is dead. My home is gone. I'm going to get water; sweet purples are dry eating."

She watched him stalk off down the slope toward the river.

She scrambled to her feet. "Nokhai!" Her voice seemed to tear out of her at its own volition.

He stopped, but did not turn.

"I'm sorry." The words wrenched from her, guttural and

haggard and absurd in how useless she knew them to be. "I'm sorry about your family." *I'm sorry about everything.*

His back stiffened, almost imperceptibly. Finally, at length, he said, "I'm sorry about your father."

It took her by surprise. In truth, she'd been doing her best not to think about her father. But she thought of him now, like a wound reopening at the soft brush of Nokhai's words.

"No . . . I mean, it's not the same thing," she said quickly. "I'm sorry. Truly. I wish . . . I'm sorry." She wished she could will him into believing her.

"I understand," he said. Then he slipped off into the night.

While the boy was fetching water, Lu began unpacking some of the supplies that their stolen warhorse had come laden with. They'd dumped some of the heavier items before fleeing, but she came up with a small silver hatchet, a grooming kit with scissors and a comb, and a sack of coins. She wasn't sure what it might buy them; she'd have to ask Nok. One of the saddlebags contained a musty woolen blanket and a stretch of thick, roughly hewn canvas bedding that had had been coated in wax to keep out the wet.

She had laid out the bedding beside the fire by the time he returned with the water.

"For sleeping," she told him, gesturing unnecessarily toward the bedding.

He nodded. "I'll take first watch," he said, sitting down against a tree.

"It's cold," she told him, climbing under the blanket. "You could just sit up next to me. Put your half of the blanket over your lap. We'll warm each other."

Was it a trick of the firelight, or did his face flush? "N-No," he stuttered. "It's fine, I'll just sleep here."

"Don't be stupid," Lu said before she could think to temper her words. "The ground is damp; you'll catch cold. The last thing I need is a sick companion to take care of."

"I'm fine." He scowled, crossing his arms across his middle. "We peasants are a little hardier than you royals."

"Maybe you could try cauling again—I bet you'd be warmer in that wolf body," she suggested.

Something almost like guilt—shame?—flared in his eyes. Finally, he mumbled, "I already tried. I think—I think it's lost. I haven't been able to do it since that first day."

"Oh," she said dumbly. She couldn't know what it would mean to lose the promise of that power, the Gift, then gain it back . . . only to lose it once more. She could guess.

"Well, give it time," she said weakly. "I'm sure it'll return to you." She winced at how stupid, how useless she sounded. "Are you sure you don't want the blanket?"

But he merely settled back against his tree and closed his eyes. "No."

Lu wanted just a little bit to shake him.

CHAPTER 21

Bandits

*A*ww, does my cousin love her little puppy?" Set cooed, his eleven-year-old's voice creaking rustily on the words.

"Shut up!" Lu screamed. "Stop calling him that!"

"Didn't your mom tell you to stay away from him? She said he's dangerous. Just to be safe I had better—" The Hana boy drew back his leg suddenly and landed a solid kick to Nok's knee.

His boots were hard black leather tipped in a point of ornately tooled bronze. Nok's bones screamed as he went down into the sand. The sun was falling, but it was still hot.

Stupid! How could you not see that coming?

Set was turning back toward the Ashina boys Mitri, Chundo, and Karakk with a smirk when Lu's fist caught him in the left eye. He stumbled backward with a yell.

"You want to fight someone, fight me," Lu snarled, raising her hands.

"You! Y-you should not have done that!" Set screamed at her. "Do you forget who I am? Do you forget?" Nok heard the terrible sigh of steel against steel as Set yanked his sword free and began waving it at her.

"No!" Nok gasped.

"Don't worry," Lu told him. "A sword's no good if you can't use it properly." But she was eyeing the metal blade uneasily.

Set fixed narrowed, red-rimmed eyes on her. "Watch your tongue."

"Not for you," she retorted.

He lunged toward her. Lu darted forward, easily dodging his clumsy horizontal swipe, and yanked the wooden practice sword free from his belt as he pitched forward. She turned and brought her foot down hard on his lower back. He dropped face-first into the sand.

She helped Nok to his feet as her cousin floundered. "Are you okay?"

He grimaced. It didn't feel like anything was broken.

"Bitch!" Set was spitting like a cat as he scrabbled to his feet, as furious as Nok had ever seen anyone. "Bitch!" He ran at them, sword raised high.

Nok raised his hands as Set slashed wildly at them. The blade was so straight, so clean, that Nok barely felt the tip of it whisper across the length of his palms, then plant the ghost of a kiss on his right cheek.

"Nokhai!" he heard the princess scream. He looked down at his hands. They were painted red as a setting sun.

Lu ran at Set, swinging his wooden sword like a club. There

was a horrible crack, and suddenly Set was reeling across the sand.

"I'll kill you!"

The princess was upon her cousin. She flung away the wooden sword and pummeled him with her fists until she drew yelps of *Mercy, mercy, mercy!* Something had dropped from the boy's body, glinting pretty blue-white against the sand. Jewelry?

No—teeth. Three of them, slick with blood.

"Nokhai! Nokhai!"

He closed his eyes against the sight.

"Nokhai!"

"No," he protested. *It will end,* he told himself. *Even the worst dream always ends. Just a bit longer, hold on, feel nothing, it will end . . .*

"Nokhai?"

A hand was on his shoulder, his face. He flinched, closed his eyes. But the touch was gentle. He wanted to surrender, sink into it. *Don't,* he thought deliriously. A trick.

"Nokhai!"

He jolted awake. Coppery eyes gleamed in the faint dawn light. The princess. His body flooded with relief, followed by an odd tenderness, misplaced across time.

"They stopped bleeding," he stammered, throwing up his hands. "I'm fine."

She narrowed her gaze at the puckered scars crisscrossing his palms, and he remembered where he was.

The princess shook his shoulder again, insistent. "Wake up!"

The dream slipped away, taking his tenderness with it.

"I'm awake!" he snapped, sitting up. "Clearly."

"*Shh!* Keep your voice down. Someone's watching us."

He was on his feet. "Where? Soldiers? How many?"

"Not soldiers," she said. "I went to make water, and when I was coming back I saw someone following me through the trees. They disappeared, but I took a roundabout way back here in case they were still tracking me."

Nok frowned. "It's pretty dark; are you sure?"

"Of course I'm sure!"

He licked his lips before glancing into the shadows around them. "It could've been a deer or something."

"I know what I saw," she snapped. "It was a person. A girl, I think. And she was definitely following me. Doing a good job of it, too. Stealthy. I think it was a bandit."

"A bandit?" he repeated incredulously.

"The northern foothills are rife with them," she continued, ignoring his tone. "We keep getting reports of them in the capital—some of them even infiltrated a labor camp. Caused a riot. They're said to be migrating farther south. We're probably right in their path."

Nok shrugged doubtfully. "Well, whoever it was, either you lost them or they decided we weren't worth robbing."

She shook her head. "Whoever it was, they gave me a bad feeling. Omair's map says there's a town not too far up the road. We should stop there, stay at an inn tonight."

"Absolutely not," Nok countered. "We don't know the area. If the town's too little, we'll draw attention."

"We need to stop soon anyway," she argued. "We're almost

out of food. We may as well see what's around, and if the town feels big enough for us to pass unnoticed, we can look for an inn."

"If it's big enough for us to pass unnoticed, I guarantee you it'll have just as many thieves as are in these woods. More, probably," he said stubbornly. "And soldiers, to boot."

"Well, what're we to do?" she retorted. "Ride until the horse gives out, then eat it? Walk the rest of the way to Yunis and arrive shortly before the birth of my cousin's third son?"

"Fine!" He sighed. "We can load up on some basics."

"We need warmer clothes, too," she pointed out, seizing on her victory. "The air's getting cold and the mountains will be colder. And if by chance Omair's map is wrong about where the gates are, we don't know how long we'll be wandering before we get to Yunis."

"If it even still exists," he muttered.

"It exists," she said firmly. "And stop trying to change the subject."

"Fine. Warmer clothes," he allowed.

"And a blanket for you, since your modesty would sooner have you freeze to death than share bedding with me."

"Modest . . . ," he said incredulously. "I'm trying to be polite, *Princess*."

"Polite is declining once, then acquiescing to common sense," she snorted. "You act like *you're* the princess."

He just glared. "Fine. A second blanket. Woolens. Oats for the horse and some grains for us. Anything else you want? Embroidered silk capes? Furs? Steel pots and pans? Rugs?

Maybe we should just build a house here and stay forever while we're at it."

"Don't be sore just because I was in the right," she said primly, taking the horse's reins and turning her back to him.

"Wait!" He grabbed for the reins. She turned and met his eyes just as their fingers brushed. He jerked his hand away.

She watched him do it, but only said, "What?"

"You look too . . ." He gestured in her direction and wrinkled his nose. "Too rich. People will definitely notice you."

She looked down. She was wearing her own black leather breeches, but she had one of his own rough-hewn knee-length gray tunics thrown over a cotton shirt, belted with a rope.

"Right," she scoffed. "I had forgotten how coveted rotting wool is these days."

"No, not your clothes . . . although I think we ought to dirty up the leathers a bit. It's more . . . " He paused. "Your hair. And your teeth. And your face."

"What's wrong with my face?" she demanded, her tone growing dangerous.

"Nothing's *wrong,* you look . . ." He shook his head. "It's just, no one besides a royal or maybe a First Ring lady would have hair that long. It's impractical. And you stick your chin up too high; try to look more . . . tired. And like you don't want to be seen. Yes, no, that's better."

She gave an exaggerated frown and lowered her face toward the ground.

"Should I furrow my brow and pout like you, too?" she asked.

"I don't . . ." He broke off, unsure if he was being teased or not. He caught the barest hint of a smile on her lips.

Ignoring it, he muttered, "Wait here." He slipped around the other side of the horse and dug through one of the saddle-bags there, extracting a little grooming kit Lu had found in there days earlier. It must've belonged to the soldier whose horse they stole, though none of them had appeared particularly well-groomed in his memory.

He searched the kit until he found a small pair of scissors.

She regarded them suspiciously. "Are you going to give me a scar or something?"

He rolled his eyes and thrust them toward her. "No. *You're* going to give yourself a haircut."

"Fine." She took the scissors and held them limply. "How do I do it?"

He stared at her.

"You look like I just asked you how to breathe."

"You've never cut your own hair?" He groaned. "Of course you've never cut your own hair."

"I'm a princess," she confirmed. "I have handmaidens."

"Oh, for heaven's . . . ," he grumbled, grabbing the scissors away and waving them toward a fallen tree. "Go sit there."

He cut her black hair in deft broad hanks, then more judi-ciously, so it fell in a straight, even line just beyond her shoul-ders. She sat stiffly but made no fuss when he used his fingers to turn her chin from side to side, measuring his work. Like many apothecarists, Omair occasionally provided barber services—cuts and shaves—out of their home, so he'd learned a bit here and there. He'd never cut a woman's hair before, but the rhythm of the work was familiar enough, and he relaxed into it.

Her fringe was blunt and immaculately sculpted, and he used the points of the scissors to coarsen it with a few nicks and notches. She flinched, blinking rapidly as bits of hair fell, clinging to her eyelids and cheekbones.

"Thank you," she murmured as he blew them away, looking up through the short dark trim of her lashes.

He grunted and ran a hand through her hair to shake it out. When his fingernails grazed her scalp, he felt her shiver under the touch.

He was suddenly aware of how close they were. It was the closest he'd ever been to a girl—to anyone, really. Besides Adé, when she'd kissed him.

Had Lu ever kissed anyone? Had she shivered like that beneath their touch?

Nok felt his face grow hot.

Remember who she is. What she is. Remember who you are.

He pulled his hand away, then stepped back to regard his work. She stood, pinching at the newly shortened ends.

"How do I look?" she asked with a self-deprecating tilt of her head.

"Better," he said shortly. "Except for the teeth."

"You're not doing anything to my teeth," she said firmly. "I'll just keep my mouth shut."

He turned to replace the scissors and grooming kit. "Not likely," he muttered, hiding his smile.

CHAPTER 22

Loyalty

They had installed her father's coffin in the main throne room in Kangmun Hall. It would remain there for the next hundred days. Afterward, a procession would escort it to its final resting place in the Imperial Mausoleum, outside Yulan City's Eastern Gatehead.

The rituals had become the most interesting part of Min's day. At first the very idea of them had frightened her. Her father's coffin was magnificent: constructed from multiple layers of black wood, the surface inlaid with mother-of-pearl, crystal, and gold, and draped in cascades of silk and fresh flowers. Still, despite the meticulous trappings, how could she ignore that a dead body was only steps away? Even one that was, or had been, her father.

It must smell, she'd thought. Corpses smelled right away, especially when the weather was hot. The first few days she kept her breathing so shallow she nearly fainted. But afterward, a perverse impulse drove her to seek out any odor of death beneath everything else: the incense smoke, and the perfume of oils, and garlands of roses and jasmine draping the coffin. She never found it, though. The coffin was well sealed.

After that, the rituals were easier. And, she discovered, they were the only time she had occasion to see her cousin—*my husband,* she reminded herself, though that part scarcely felt real.

On this day like most, Set arrived late, taking his place between Min and her mother as the water monks chanted and waved their censers. Was it her imagination, or did he seem paler than usual? Certainly she was not imagining the dark circles beneath his eyes or the way his fingertips twitched impatiently, all but drumming against his thighs. Not once did he look her way.

He has duties, Min chided herself, forcing the strain of disappointment from her heart. *Remember the burdens he bears.*

She shivered, recalling the way he'd drawn back his foot and kicked that old prisoner, Ohn, over and over.

That wasn't real, idiot. Just a dream. It was just a dream.

Liar, whispered another voice.

"Princess," hissed Butterfly, stirring Min from her thoughts. She started. The monks were signaling the end of the ritual. Min lowered herself in a bow.

Set was gone before Min's nunas had finished helping her to her feet.

⚜

Afterward, the handmaidens gossiped and entertained themselves in the main rooms of her apartments, but Min retired to her bedchamber for a nap. She found herself increasingly exhausted of late, as though the panicked, helpless circles she was running in her mind were taking a toll on her body.

She collapsed across her bed, staring up at the ceiling. When they were little girls, Lu used to make up elaborate stories about the abstract shapes painted up there: great battles between the blue blobs and lavender swirls of smoke, or a doomed love between a red triangle and a green circle. But then Lu had grown out of that, and out of sharing a bed altogether, and Min found the stories she came up with on her own were never as entrancing. Now she was too old for them, too. And Lu . . .

Lu was gone. Disappeared. The whispered consensus was that she was lost somewhere deep in the Southwood, but she could just as easily be hunkered down in some farmer's rice field or dead in a gutter in the Second Ring.

That final thought made Min's stomach clench, but she told herself for the hundredth time it wasn't possible. Her sister—but was she really her sister? she pushed the thought away—had always been invincible, a force of nature. Resolutely, defiantly bursting with life. And hadn't she gone on hunting trips with their father and his men, even when they were little girls? Spent days tramping through the forest, flushing hideous boars out from the underbrush, drinking from streams with her own cupped hands?

Min wondered at that now, though. The occasional hunting trip aside, her sister—*it was just a dream, just a dream*—was raised much in the same manner Min had been, with a staff to prepare their meals, shins to schedule their days, nunas to wash and dress them—even cut and file their fingernails. For all her swordplay and athleticism, the life of a princess had prepared Lu for life outside the palace walls as little as it had for Min.

No. Her sister always just seemed to know how to do new things, or was quick to learn.

Lu is special. She's always been special, she told herself, unable to keep the bitterness from pulling at the edges of the thought.

Hours later, when she emerged from her bedchamber to dress for supper, she found her nunas gone, and a note calling her to her mother's apartments.

Her mother was waiting by her dressing table, comb in hand, when Min arrived.

"Where's Butterfly? And Snowdrop?" Min blurted, unable to keep the wariness from her voice. The past few days had taught her that the unexpected usually meant something bad.

But her mother just smiled. "Amma Ruxin had some tasks for them. We've scarcely seen each other these past few days, so I thought I would help you dress, like I did when you were little. Won't that be nice?"

What do you really want? Min wondered. That wasn't the answer she was meant to give, though.

She took a seat at the vanity and allowed the empress to draw her comb through her long hair. It was as unkempt from her nap as it had ever been, but for once her mother did not chide her for it. Min tried not to flinch as the comb tugged at a snarl.

"You're very quiet," her mother murmured. "Are you unwell?"

Min thought of her father, dead, murdered. Of her sister— *sister?*—lost. She thought of a woman born of fire and spite.

The curse within her body. The husband who scarcely saw her. The husband whom she'd seen kick a man half to death without hesitation. And her mother whom she had seen standing uncomplaining at his side. Her mother who had gone to her dying father and—

No, she told herself. *You don't know what you saw. Dreams. Only dreams.*

"I'm fine," she whispered, her voice still creaky with sleep. She cleared her throat.

"I never had the chance to ask, what exactly did that old monk say to you after your wedding?"

There it is, Min thought. She'd been right to be wary of this sudden, unannounced audience. Her mother never did anything loving without some underlying, calculated reason. Maybe no one ever did.

"I know girls your age tell their mothers everything, but you're a married woman now, so can you keep this confidence for your husband? Even from her?"

Brother had said this to her after she'd doused the fire-thing with tea, after he and Set had consoled her tears. Min had nodded mutely, though at the time she had secretly wondered if she would have the strength to keep the truth from her mother, even if she wanted to.

She blinked rapidly, trying to keep her lies straight—so many lies, to so many people—too late remembering she did so when she was nervous. It was a tic her mother would be sure to notice.

"Min?" her mother prompted, the comb going still in her hair.

She'd been silent for too long. Beads of sweat sprang up along her hairline, the back of her neck. *Say something, idiot!*

"Brother? H-he taught me . . . some things," she said weakly. "Prayers and rituals," she added.

Her mother pursed her lips, but the comb resumed its brusque, artless sweep through her hair. "What sort of rituals? We have the water monks and nuns for that purpose. What does an empress need that they do not know?"

"It pleases Set for me to know them," Min said. That was good—perhaps the mention of her cousin would serve as a bulwark against her mother's disapproval.

It seemed to work. Her mother set down the comb and began plucking apart strands of hair to make a plait. Min resumed breathing, slow and even, trying to keep her relieved exhale from rushing out.

But when her mother spoke again, it was of a much different subject: "You know that as empress, you will be expected to provide your emperor with an heir."

Min felt her face heat in spite of herself. "Yes, of course."

"You're still young yet," her mother reassured her. "Things being as uncertain as they were, it was necessary to wed you immediately. But it will be at least a year, likely more before you're expected to even attempt to conceive. The physicians will first examine you, and the water priests will consult the stars and their vision pools to determine the most auspicious dates for conception." Her mother sighed. "They did the same for me, though they were wrong about you by a good two months."

"What about Lu?" Min asked, so lulled by the stroking in her hair and the rhythm of her voice that she forgot herself.

Her mother's fingers stuttered for a heartbeat but then resumed their steady plaiting.

Careful, Min scolded herself. What perverse impulse had driven her to ask that question?

"Lu," her mother said tightly. "The monks did not see her coming at all. Perhaps Set is right to bring in that Brother of his. Perhaps the old mul ways no longer serve us as well as they once did. People say in the early days of the Hu conquest, when they still had their own religions, they would enlist their shamanesses for the job. Apparently, they were more accurate—"

"Shamanesses?" Min blurted, a flash of red obliterating her careful calm. "Like the Yunian shamanesses?"

Her mother's hands stilled in her hair. "Yes, I suppose they were similar. Why? What do you know of the Yunian shamanesses?" The empress's voice had gone odd and quiet, but it wasn't dangerous, not yet.

"Just a bit, from my history lessons," Min said quickly. She hadn't had the exhaustive education that was granted her sister, but Amma Ruxin had taught her enough to hold a conversation.

"Is that all?" The empress reached the end of one plait and tied it off with a thong. She let the heavy rope fall. The hairs were laid less artfully than Min's nunas were capable of. A few were pulled too tightly, and they tugged meanly at her scalp.

"Yes. That's all," Min forced her voice to be strong, as though saying a lie louder might make it true.

"*I know girls your age tell their mothers everything,*" Brother's voice echoed in Min's head.

Was that really so? Even before, she hadn't told her mother

everything, not truly. Not the contents of her dreams or how much she loathed her painting classes. Not when she ate an extra egg tart at dinner. Not the bawdy jokes Butterfly whispered to the room after the nunas had blown out the lamps.

She saw then in her mind's eye the hairpin she had accidentally stolen off her mother's vanity, the day of Lu's aborted Betrothal Ceremony. A beautiful trinket of agate and pearl shaped like a lily. Butterfly had told the other nunas in hushed tones about how she'd heard from a maid that the empress had Amma Wei flogged for losing it. Min had felt terrible for a moment. But servants were terrible gossips, weren't they? Everyone knew what they said wasn't always true.

Min had threaded the pin into the plush underside of a chair, where not even the chambermaids would see it. The chair was scarcely two paces away from the empress. That was a secret. She had secrets.

Stupid trivial things, she told herself dismissively.

But how stupid and trivial were those things, really? If you piled enough little things together, they could grow quite big.

Maybe all those little things together were bigger even than what her mother did know of her.

What *was* it that her mother knew of her? Just her too-round face and unkempt hair. That she was milder than her sister, more obedient, kinder, slower. Younger. Smaller. In the end was that really anything at all? A daughter understood only in relief—defined by what she wasn't.

Her mother's hands moved over her hair again, lacquered nails combing down loose hairs, scraping lightly against Min's scalp.

"I was thinking," the empress murmured. "With things being so hectic in the capital now, it might be nice for you to take a trip somewhere, before it gets too cold. Maybe the summer palace out east, or my family's manor in Bei Province. You've never met my side of the family. It's about time."

Min turned in surprise. "Would Set come?"

"No, of course not. He has duties here."

"I," Min hesitated. "I heard he would go north again to lead the fight against Yunis."

"That is one idea *some* people are insisting on feeding him." Min had a good idea who those some people her mother was referring to might be—one person in particular. "It's absurd. He needs to stay here. Things being as they are, everyone is still gauging whether he is deserving of their loyalty. The court is full of snakes, and he must put in time courting those he can sway, and excising those he cannot. Controlling the empire means first controlling the capital. But there's no reason why you and I can't enjoy some time away while he settles things here."

"But . . . I've only just married. I'm not supposed to—I can't leave my husband so soon. I need to stay here and help him"— Min's voice faltered—"don't I?"

Her mother turned toward the vanity, setting the scattered bottles and combs there to right. "Like I said, Set is very busy, child. He has much to attend to."

If I leave, I can't go to Yunis. And I won't be there to help, and I'll never be rid of this curse, this spirit, and I'll never give Set an heir. But of course, she couldn't begin to tell her mother all that. If her mother knew of the curse, what would she do? Min wasn't sure, but she suspected it would not be helpful.

"I don't want to leave Set." Her words came out thin and petulant.

"That's sweet of you, dear, but I worry the stress of all that's happened is weighing on you. You do look so pale . . ." Her mother brushed the backs of her cold fingers down one of Min's cheeks. "Some time away would be good for you, I'm certain of it."

The thought of leaving Set sat like a stone in her gut. It was silly, she knew, given the other worries on her mind. How little attention he paid her. Would he even notice her absence?

I love him, she thought for the first time, and was pleased to find it felt right. What other words could explain the keening stretch of her heart, the thrumming want in the marrow of her bones? Her longing. Her loneliness. *I love him,* she repeated. Because she could. *I love him.*

Yes, but are you ready to serve him? Brother's voice whispered in her ear.

"I can't leave before Father is interred," Min blurted, amazed at her own quickness. "That wouldn't be proper." She resisted the instinct to make it a question.

A flicker of something rippled over her mother's still, self-possessed face. It was gone, quick as a bird, before Min could grasp it.

"Perhaps you're right," the empress sighed. "I will consider it further, but I think it will be for the best to send you away. Just for a time."

No, no, you don't understand! Min felt fury burn her throat like bile. Her mother would *consider* it? What of what she, Min, wanted? Wasn't she the empress now, after all?

Lu would have fought. She would have shouted and swept the perfumes and hairpins and combs from atop the vanity. Perhaps broken the mirror had their mother persisted. She would have fought, and eventually, she would have won.

Min's eyes flicked over to the chair where she'd hidden her mother's pin. Stabbed that lily of agate and pearl into the softly upholstered underbelly. Her mother followed her gaze, but saw only a chair.

I can win, too, Min told herself. *In my own way.*

CHAPTER 23

Capture

*T*he little ones are worth the least," Nok said, pointing at the coins arrayed in his palm. Lu followed his finger with her gaze and frowned skeptically.

"Half of them are the same size."

He considered. "Similar. But not the same."

"Didn't you just say one of the bigger ones is worth less than the smaller ones, though?"

"Well, they're worth less than these smaller silver ones, but not the smallest." He struggled to keep his voice patient and calm, well under the dull hum of the small marketplace. Even in a tiny village like this, flashing any amount of money around was unwise.

They were standing in line waiting to purchase grain—the last item in Lu's long list of supplies. Nok shifted uncomfortably under the heavy sack of woolens tossed over his shoulder.

He'd removed the stitches from Lu's arm in the morning and offered to carry their supplies to let her rest it.

"I want to order this time," the princess informed him. "I'll buy the grain."

"You won't even know how to pay!" he hissed.

"You can pay," she shrugged, all casual generosity. "I'll just order."

"I don't think that's a good—"

". . . The coronation was just last week, but already Emperor Set passed a new edict to expel the pink foreigners within a year." The conversation of two old village men at the next stall overtook their argument; Lu turned sharply at the sound of her cousin's name.

"Didn't I tell you he would make a strong emperor?" the second man was smugly saying to the first. "Frankly, I think it's time we Hana reclaimed power. From the stories my great-uncles used to tell me when I was a boy, things were better under our control."

"Can we really consider this a coup for the Hana, though, I wonder?" said the first man, scratching under the red cap sitting snugly on his head. Nok watched with vague disgust as he pulled out a louse the size of an almond, then flicked it dispassionately into the street. "He's an outsider coming in. How strong can his command over the court be?"

"They say now that the coronation's done, Emperor Set is coming back up north to the front, to lead the war against Yunis," the second man said. "If that's not a show of strength, I don't know what is."

Nok looked sharply back at Lu, hoping to stop her before she did anything—

"Excuse me?" she demanded loudly.

—Stupid. Nok suppressed a groan. They were supposed to keep their heads down, mumbling and shuffling like bored peasants—attracting as little attention as possible. He fought to keep the rising despair and annoyance off his face.

"Did you say the new emperor declared war on Yunis?" Lu asked the two men.

They stared at her, gaping toothlessly.

"Why, yes," the one with the red cap and the louse said at length. Then, he chuckled. "For that raid on the prison camp. You young people should pay more attention to the affairs of state."

"When exactly is he coming?" she pressed, ignoring his condescension.

"Well," Red Cap's friend said. "He hasn't left the capital yet. But he'll come soon enough. Everyone's saying as much."

Nok and Lu exchanged dark looks. Did this mean he knew Lu's whereabouts? Or did he simply mean to accelerate the pace of the war with Yunis? Either way, no good could come of it.

"You call it strength," Red Cap was saying to his friend, "but how can we have faith in a Hana reign if their scion immediately abandons his post? He's all but leaving the capital to the Hu. The heavens only know what plots his new wife will get up to in his absence . . ."

"I wouldn't worry about that," his companion assured him. "From what I've heard, this younger princess is little more than a child. Soft as down. No father killer like the Girl King."

Then he spat in the dirt, as though to express exactly how he felt about father killers and girl kings.

Nok grabbed Lu's arm. "Let's go," he said lightly. She whirled on him in mute fury, but he just pulled her closer as though in affection and forced a bland smile onto his face. "This line's taking too long, darling." He nodded back at the two old men in a manner that he hoped seemed natural.

"I'm not done," she protested.

"I think you are."

When they were a safe distance away, she tugged her arm from his grasp. "You shouldn't have done that. I don't need you watching over me."

"Tell me," he said, shifting the bag of woolens to his other shoulder, "that there was no chance you were going to hit that old man. Go on. Tell me, and I'll apologize."

She glowered at him but said nothing.

"That's what I thought," he said, and sighed. "Come on, let's get back on the road before it gets dark."

⚜

They picked up the horse at the stables, only to discover the town gates were closed, barring their exit. A wagon hitched to three massive, rickety wooden caravans stood in the central roadway, blocking the flow of merchants with their carts and farmers leading oxen. Nok craned his head to better see and glimpsed a row of men, all chained to one another, being prodded into one of the caravans.

"What's going on?" Lu asked a woman standing beside them. Nok frowned at her—could she go a minute without attracting attention?—but it was too late.

The woman looked them up and down. A live chicken dangled upside down from one of her hands. "They're clearing out prisoners from the jail to bring to the work camps up north," the woman grunted. She was middle-aged, portly. The chicken was utterly still save for its yellow reptilian eyes, which flicked beadily toward them. "Good riddance, I say," the woman continued. "Jail's full, and they might as well put the criminals to work."

"But why's the gate closed?" Nok pressed. Their low profile was a lost cause by now, anyway.

"In case any of 'em makes a run for it," the woman said, as though he was being intentionally stupid. "They'll open it back up once they're done. 'Til then, we can't do nothing but wait."

A group of men in matching orange tunics stood at the edge of the road, overseeing the traffic lazily, like well-fed cats watching mice stroll by. Nok's gut went cold. "Are those imperial soldiers?" he whispered to Lu. He didn't recognize these particular uniforms, but perhaps they were some rank with which he wasn't familiar.

Lu's head whipped around to follow his gaze, but her shoulders relaxed slightly when she saw them. "No," she said, shaking her head. Her newly shortened hair flicked about her chin. "Well, not really. They're local police. They must be helping out with this prisoner transfer."

Nok chanced another look their way. A mistake. Soldiers, police, it made no difference. They were all predators by training if not by nature. And like any predator, they could sense when they were being watched.

The orange tunic closest to them locked eyes with him, then turned to whisper something to the officer next to him. Nok looked away, but not before the first man started toward them.

"Dammit," he cursed. "They're coming this way. Walk faster."

Lu surged forward, pushing into the crowd. Nok grabbed her by the elbow.

"Walk faster, but don't *look* like you're walking faster," he hissed.

She narrowed her copper-flecked eyes at him. "I hope you just heard yourself," she muttered. "What do we do?"

"Just . . . act like everything's fine."

"Everything is clearly *not* fine—"

A heavy hand landed on his shoulder.

"Hold up, there," the orange tunic said, spinning Nok around. Lu stopped beside him, clapping one hand protectively around his wrist, the other still clutching the horse's bridle. They were blocking the road, but the crowd moved around them, indifferent as a river flowing around a rock.

Not their business, Nok thought bitterly. He couldn't blame them, though; he would do the same in their position. Would happily trade places with any of them right now.

"Stay," the officer told him, all lazy, casual power. He lifted the horse's head by the chin, inspecting its eyes, its teeth, before passing an appraising glance down the lean length of its body.

"This is a fine stallion," he said when he'd finished, deigning now to size up Lu and Nok. "Far too fine to belong to two village kids. Who'd you steal it from?"

"It belongs to our master, sir." Nok bowed his head, playing the part of the cowed peasant that he was. He glanced at Lu, willing her to do the same, but she was looking boldly at the officer with a disagreeable set to her jaw.

The officer noticed, too. "You're a pretty little thing, aren't you?" He caught her face in his fingers and held it up for evaluation, just as he had done with the horse. "Who do you work for?"

"Wen, the cobbler," Nok said quickly, praying the town was large enough to have more than one cobbler, or at least one coincidentally named Wen.

"Wasn't talking to you, boy," the officer said. He snorted, smirking at Lu. "A cobbler's servant, eh? Waste of a nice girl. Why don't you come work at our barracks instead? Do you know how to cook and wash?"

"No," Lu said coldly.

"Well, I'm sure we could find some other use for you," the man leered, patting her hard on the cheek before running a dingy gloved finger over her lips.

Lu's eyes ignited in outrage. Nok held his breath, waiting for her to draw back and punch the man in the throat, or maybe snap his errant finger in half. Instead, he saw the fire in her eyes temper, then dim. She lowered her gaze, swallowing hard.

Nok should've been relieved; he felt sick.

"Come on, now," the officer cajoled, stepping in closer. "Don't be shy." He grabbed her chin again, wrenching her face up toward his own. "How about a kiss and I'll let you go?"

"Don't touch me, you dog," Lu snarled, her patience worn through. She twisted to the side and pulled from his grasp.

The man's face went from slimy to metallic in an instant. "What did you say to me? You thieving little bitch; I should arrest you right now."

His fist came down toward her.

Nok's hand shot out and grabbed the man by the wrist. He knew he'd made a mistake before he even felt the man's coarse leather glove beneath his fingertips, but it was already too late.

The officer was bigger, stronger, but Nok caught him off guard and he faltered. For half a heartbeat, none of them moved.

Nok dropped his hand like he'd been scalded.

The first blow took him on the cheek. It was more a swat than anything; the man hadn't drawn back far enough for it to hurt much, but the second caught him on the ear hard enough that his whole head rung with it.

Run! he tried to shout at the princess. Maybe he said it aloud; it was hard to tell. If she had any sense, she'd know to—

"Leave him alone!" Lu jumped between them, pushing Nok behind her. The officer's closed fist caught her full in the face. She cried out, but rolled with the blow and somehow did not fall.

Nok closed his eyes against his own pain, and when he opened them again he saw that the other orange tunics were rushing toward them, plowing through the crowd. The officer leading the way looked older, seasoned. Someone in charge.

The men yanked them apart. One pushed Nok to the ground, his face sliding in thick mud, flesh catching on stones, tearing. Then he felt the stark, unforgiving cold of manacles going around his wrists.

"*Go!*" he shouted with the last of his breath.

A boot stomped into his back. He struggled to look up, caught a glimpse of Lu putting up her hands as two other men approached with manacles. *Crazy girl,* he thought in despair. *She should have run while she had the chance.*

"You're both under arrest," the initial officer snarled. "For stealing the horse and for striking an officer."

I didn't hit you; you hit me, Nok wanted to say, but instead he heard himself choke out, "Which prison are you taking us to?" The urgency in his voice betrayed his fear—quivering, pathetic.

He knew the answer. He could see it again, see it all. The work pits, the endless rows of soldiers flashing steel and whips and manacles. The dirty gray canvas lean-tos the soldiers had erected to house their prisoners, dotting the barren land like a cruel simulacrum of the tent villages he had grown up in. He remembered now, too, the smell . . . crudely dug latrine pits full of human waste and rotting garbage. The vaguely fungal stink of the gruel they were forced to eat. And beneath it all, the faint gray malevolent tinge of death, tightening his throat, making him gag, choking him.

He was dying, he thought in panic. He was going to die before they even got there, before they got the chance to kill him.

He knew the answer before it came, but he had to ask.

Which prison?

"Prison?" the officer laughed roughly. "Boy, you're not going to any prison. We're on our way to the labor camps, and we're gonna offer you a ride, free of charge."

CHAPTER 24

Ghosts

*L*u probed the skin around her eye with her fingertips, gingerly. Her face was beginning to swell. The officer had punched her good and hard.

The caravan hit a pit in the road and her hand jerked, forcing the heel of the palm right into the epicenter of the bruise. She winced, dropping her hand back into her lap.

The heavy manacle looped about her wrist jangled against its twin, shifting the short, heavy length of chain connecting them. The bedroll hiding her sword lay across her thighs, and she clenched it with both hands now, feeling for the hard line of metal through the fabric. She'd pulled it from the horse as they were corralled into the caravan, and the harried officers hadn't bothered to take it from her. Not that she could use it with her hands bound, anyway. Still, it was a comfort to have.

The first two caravans had already been loaded with prisoners and sealed by the time the officers dragged her and Nok over, so they'd been thrown into the third, alone save for a few wilted heaps of soiled hay. It was a relief, albeit a small one, Lu thought.

She glanced over at Nok. He was sitting in the corner, an arm's length from her, his head resting against the caravan's rear wall. Each bump and pit must have sent a hard knock to his skull, but he seemed not to notice. They'd been on the road for a while now, though how long or how quickly they were moving, she couldn't say. Their rolling prison was windowless, and whatever landscape they were moving through was silent, giving away nothing. Nok hadn't said a word the entire time.

Lu stood, crouching low to keep her balance, and shuffled over to him. She did her best to ignore the stinking muck the toes of her boots dug up along the way.

"Hey," she said softly. He looked at her, black eyes so distant that she couldn't read them, even if she squinted.

"You don't know what the camps are like," he said flatly.

She sat slowly beside him, leaving space between them. "No, I don't."

"We're never getting out of there, you know," he told her.

"We'll find a way."

"No one gets out of there alive."

"You did."

"Did I?" The words should have been hostile, but his voice sounded vague, unstrung. Come apart. As though he didn't quite remember who she was.

Lu frowned. "You did," she insisted. "You survived. You escaped."

"No," he said softly. "Someone—that man, Yuri—he's the one that saved me. He was there."

"Well, I'm here now. You've got me."

"Do I?"

Not knowing what else to do, Lu slid one arm down in the narrow gap between their bodies as best she could given the narrow width of her chains, and took his hand in her own. Nokhai looked down, startled away from the edge of his terrible, empty reverie. For a moment she thought he would pull away, but he just rested his head back against the wall. Sighed, swallowed.

Lu's gaze went to his throat, watching the muscles work. Then she looked away, squeezing his hand in her own, hard enough for it to hurt. Just a little. Just enough. Like a fraying rope thrown down that familiar well he kept falling into.

She had almost given up on getting a response when he squeezed her hand back. She met his black eyes, watching her almost curiously. Questioning. Like he was seeing her for the first time.

"Did you know?" he asked, his voice catching on the hoarse edges of his words. "When your family toured the North, when you met my Kith, did you already know?"

He didn't have to elaborate; she knew what he meant.

"No," she said quickly. "I was only a child—"

"But your father knew," he threw back. "He came to the North and made us promises—but all along, he knew we were all going to die."

"I don't know," she replied honestly. Had he? She'd never really asked herself that question in the five years since.

Perhaps she hadn't wanted to know the answer. "I think that he believed he was offering you a choice between leaving and fighting. But maybe he was too afraid to recognize that wasn't really a choice at all."

"He was a coward."

The words should have hurt, but Lu found herself nodding. "I suppose he was."

"What did you say when you learned what had happened to us?"

"I wept," Lu said, surprising herself with the memory. "Min cried, too." She'd nearly forgotten. "It was odd—she'd been so shy around you all. I think perhaps she was afraid. But when we learned what—she cried."

"Tears are easy," he said. He looked down at their joined hands as he spoke. She expected him to pull his away, but he didn't. "Tears don't cost anything."

"No," she agreed, following his gaze. "I suppose not."

He was silent for a moment. Then in a different sort of voice, he said, "You could have run, back there. Why didn't you?"

It hadn't even occurred to her. She wasn't sure how to answer. "We're . . . we have to stick together."

"No, we don't," he said flatly. "You're a *princess*. You could leave me any time."

"I need you," she said honestly. "I won't make it to the North alone."

"You could," he insisted. "You're strong, and even though you don't always act like it, you're smart. You don't need me."

"Well, who would cut my hair?" she said lightly, but her

voice held an edge of embarrassment. For what? She wondered. A compliment? *Stupid.* "I won't leave you."

"You might once you see the camp." His voice was dry, but there was a tremor in it.

She frowned. "Nokhai, I won't leave you."

"Why not?"

"Why would I?"

There was a long pause. He didn't respond, but she could hear the answer all the same. *Everyone else has.* She opened her mouth to protest, but—what did she know of it?

"Not me," she said at last, her voice more ragged than she'd intended.

He looked up then and something in his gaze shifted. His eyes were bright and curious, and being held by them was like falling into deep water on a moonless night. She stared back, feeling as though she were floundering, swimming against the current. For the first time, she noticed a little freckle of red-brown in his left eye, an island in all that blackness, just below the pupil.

She caught his mouth against hers. It wasn't much, just the barest brush of their lips. Then they broke apart and it was nothing at all.

He didn't move, though. He was so close she could feel his breath quiver through the loose strands of her hair. Blood moved in her belly like the ocean.

The caravan slammed to a halt, sending them tumbling toward the front in a tangled somersault. The chains of Lu's manacles flew up and slapped hard across her bruised face.

In the still that followed, she heard shouts from without,

blunted by the caravan's wooden walls. All at once, a volley of thuds hit the wood. Lu jumped up, her heart leaping.

She'd recognize that sound anywhere.

"Crossbow bolts," she hissed.

"Did we arrive?" Nokhai asked uncertainly. "We weren't on the road for long enough, were we?"

There was more shouting now, and Lu was surprised to hear higher voices, replacing those of the guards.

"Something's not right," Lu said needlessly. "We're under attack."

"By who?" Nok demanded.

There was no time to respond, though. Lu heard shuffling at the rear of the caravan. She looked sharply at Nokhai. His eyes no longer held their dead, haunted look. He was alert, calculating.

Good, she thought. He was here with her. She made up her mind.

"We charge them," she told him quickly. "Whatever happens, if you get out, run. I'll catch up."

"You're crazy," he whispered. "Between the guards and whoever—whatever—else is out there? We're not getting out alive."

Lu flashed a smile that she didn't feel. "You have to stop thinking that."

The door creaked open.

CHAPTER 25

Pact

Nok blinked owl-like in the sudden light. A figure stood in the doorway, hazy and indistinct to his unfocused eyes.

A blur at his side. Lu charged at them, absurdly clutching her bedroll between her raised hands.

The sword, he remembered. That would give the bedroll some weight, at least.

It was enough. That, and the element of surprise. Lu hit the figure at a full run, catching them against the head with the bedroll. They both tumbled from the doorway, out into the light of day.

Nok leaped after them.

The caravan was tall. He miscalculated the drop, stumbling as he landed, pain lancing through his buckling calves. Casting a wild glance around, he registered that they were on a narrow dirt road, fringed on either side by pines and dry bracken.

"Come on!" he yelled, perhaps at Lu, perhaps at himself. He could see the princess atop the figure from the doorway— another girl of age with them, small and compact. Lu had the bedroll still clutched in her chained hands, bashing the other girl's face as best she could. Another figure staggered around the far end of the caravan, this one tall and clad in orange. A guard.

Lu glanced the man's way. The girl beneath her used the distraction to curl her legs up and kick the princess off. They both scrambled to their feet, looked at one another, then to the guard, who looked back. For a moment, no one moved.

"Help!" the guard shouted. "There's another over here—"

The girls looked at one another for a moment. Then, in apparent wordless agreement, they both flew at him. Lu bashed him across the face with her bedroll. The other girl scooped a carved staff as tall as a man from the ground—she must have dropped it in the fall—and joined in. The guard went down with a crash.

Sunlight caught something metallic at his waist as he fell. *The keys!*

Lu must have had the same thought. While the other girl was busy choking the man with her staff, pressing it across his throat so hard he sputtered and quickly commenced to turning purple, the princess snaked her bound hands down to his belt.

"Here!" she hollered, flinging the keys as best she could toward Nok. They fell in the grass yards away from him. He darted forward.

He fumbled with the keys, pushing one into the lock on his

chains. The first didn't work—nearly snapped off, his hands were shaking so badly—but the second clicked, and the manacles fell away from his wrists.

When he looked up, the girl from the doorway had stood and was binding the guard's hands behind his back with a torn piece of his own tunic. He was conscious, but choking and wheezing into the dirt.

Lu dove for her fallen bedroll, but the other girl was faster, and unencumbered by chains. "Oh, no you don't!" she shouted. She grabbed the princess about the waist and flung her back to the ground.

Lu pulled her legs in tight and launched them into the other girl's knees, toppling her.

"Lu!" Nok shouted, running toward her as she scrambled to her feet.

She turned to meet his eyes.

"Go!" she roared. "I'm right behind you. *Go!*"

He stopped, pivoted, making for the forest. He dove into the bracken, throwing his arms up against the low branches flinging at his eyes. Stumbling over stones and fallen logs.

On he went, until the only sound left was his own ragged breathing. No more shouting. Just the trill of cicadas and an odd falling branch here and there—the slow, immortal heartbeat of the forest. Quiet. He stopped. Where was he?

The sharp, sweet smells of eucalyptus and pine filled his nose. Young fir trees fought for sunlight in dense packs hugging the trail, their black trunks slick from a recent rain, skeletal limbs garbed in wooly sleeves of pale green moss. He could be anywhere.

Could he summon his caul? He closed his eyes against the world. Tamped down his panic. *Come to me,* he willed, envisioning the wolf. *Come,* he pleaded. *If you won't come now, then what good are you at all?* Still, he felt nothing, save foolish and lost.

He cursed, turning back toward the road.

When he made it back to the edge of the wood, Lu was on her stomach in the road. The other girl had bound her feet with what looked like more torn strips of the guard's orange tunic. The guard himself was trussed up similarly a few yards from the princess, awake and alert, but no longer shouting. Whoever the other girl was, her side had won this fight.

Indeed, she stood over her captives, looking pleased.

"Gods," she cursed delightedly. Then she spat on the ground by the guard. She had excellent aim; it missed his face by the length of a coin. The man flinched.

"You didn't even know what you had, did you?" the girl continued, a smile tugging at her lips.

She strode over to Lu, grabbed a handful of hair and yanked her face upward. And then she smiled in earnest. "Princess Lu, it's an honor to finally meet you. My name's Ony."

"You!" Lu shouted in recognition at the girl called Ony. "I saw you in the forest! You were following us . . . ," her voice broke off. "Following me."

She was giving him an out, Nok realized. If they hadn't seen him, they wouldn't know she had a companion, might think he was just another prisoner in the caravan. Might not look for him. It was generous of her. And she couldn't even know he was watching. For all she knew, he could be halfway back to

Ansana by now. Given how quickly he'd run before, she likely thought he was. Shame roiled in his stomach.

"The princess?" The guard gaped, astonished. "*That* princess?"

"That's the one," the girl called Ony agreed cheerfully. She released her grip on Lu's hair. "Wait 'til my captain gets here, Princess. She was so disappointed when I lost you in the wood. She's going to *love* this."

Nok cursed internally. They had been saved from the camps only to be captured again. And this time by who, exactly? This girl and her people were clearly no friend of the imperials, but that didn't mean much. Most likely they were thieves, Lu's bandits in the trees. Ready to sell the princess off to the highest bidder—no doubt her cousin.

Lu must've been thinking the same. "Tell me who you serve," she said quickly. "I am going to win back my throne. If you help me now, take me to the Yunian court, I will find ways to reward you beyond your wildest imagining."

Nok looked about. Aside from the girl Ony, and the bound guard, they were alone. He could hear others on the far side of the caravan, though the sounds they made were far more subdued now, as though they'd finished rounding everyone up.

The guard wouldn't be a problem, if he could keep him quiet. That left only the girl herself.

He had to act quickly. He pulled the little paring knife from his boot, thanking every god in the heavens that the imperials hadn't found it when they'd shackled him.

His heart skipped wild like a rabbit. He didn't even know

who or what this girl Ony was. Could he really hurt her? Kill her?

Omair, he reminded himself. Lu was the key to saving Omair. And Lu herself was—what exactly?

Maybe I can just overpower her, he thought, focusing back on Ony. The girl was small but powerfully built. And he'd seen how quickly she'd moved. Still, he would have the element of surprise on his side, like Lu had when she'd barreled the two of them out of the caravan.

It would have to do.

He surged out from the bracken, knife in hand.

Ony saw him before he made it halfway to her. In the time it took him to raise his knife, she'd yelled out a warning to her friends and hefted her staff up in both hands.

Quick as a blink, she slammed it into his stomach.

He all but ran into the blow. For a searing, breathless moment he folded over the staff like a fallen scarecrow, the pressure in his gut leaden and so big it felt beyond pain. The knife slipped from his hand.

Ony retracted the staff, winding up for another strike. No need. Nok's knees gave and he went down hard. That pain he did feel, splintering and keen and absolute.

Ony's friends were there in an instant, pouring around the corner of the caravan, raining down upon him like a storm. The first to reach him crashed a kick into his chest, laying him flat. The back of his skull hit the dry earth and he saw sparks.

He blinked hard to clear them. The world was a smear of movement around him—he counted two, no, five, no, too many attackers. Most were his height or smaller—children. Only children. But they moved fast, fluid, certain. Experienced.

A movement behind Ony caught his eye. Lu. Her hands and feet were still bound, but she was rolling toward the bedding where her sword was still hidden. Two of their assailants caught her by the shoulders and yanked her back. They held her tight, but suddenly one of them—a girl no older than himself—was reeling away, crying out in pain. Nok saw a flash of red against her hand; Lu had bitten her.

Nok struggled to his knees, fumbling for his fallen knife. If he could reach Lu, cut the bonds from her feet . . .

Something hard cracked across his skull with the force of a charging ox.

The world around him went quiet like numbness. A heavy blanket falling over him. White stars burst, spectacular and searing before his eyes.

As they dissolved, he found himself on the ground, staring up at his attacker.

And that was when he knew he must be dead.

His own face stared back at him. Same black eyes fringed with dark lashes, same sharp jawline. Its expression, though, was an inversion of his own fear and pain: fierce and gleeful, like a cat playing with a mouse.

When their eyes locked, the look vanished, replaced with naked shock.

"Nok?"

He would know that voice anywhere. The voice that cried out in his dreams for the past four years.

I won't let them take me! I won't!

"Ay!" she hollered over her shoulder, waving at the others, whistling sharply. "Stop! Stop! Someone come help me over here!"

She bent over him now, shaking at his shoulders. He saw her clearly now. Not his face, not exactly. She had their father's nose; he had their mother's. That was what they'd been told growing up.

"Nok!" she repeated, urgently.

"Nasan," he murmured.

Then he slipped into darkness, never knowing if his sister had heard.

CHAPTER 26

Baby

*C*oncentrate," Brother instructed. "Close your eyes if you think it will help."

Min didn't think it would—he made the same suggestion every day.

What's the point? Nothing ever changed. *She* never changed.

But she did as he suggested, shutting out the monk, her bedroom, the table between them, arrayed with crystals and browned ledgers, a hand mirror, several odd metal contraptions she did not recognize, and disconcertingly, a small knife with a blade that looked hewn from glass. Brother's "tools."

"Perhaps one of these will work, since the tea did not," he had said when he'd arrived. That had been hours ago.

She'd had to bite her tongue to stop herself from telling him that the tea had worked. But if that were the case, she would have to explain why she'd lied, all the things she had seen, what

Set had done to that old man, what her mother had said about her sister—

"Think of what it felt like when you broke the cup at the Betrothal Feast," the monk pressed. "Try to conjure what was going through your mind. What you felt in your body, and where."

Min furrowed her brow. She'd been annoyed. At Snowdrop, at her sister. She searched for something deeper, something more meaningful, but all that surfaced was anger, harsh and red.

"I need her with me!" Set bellowed. The sound was close; he was in her apartments. He, and her mother with him. Min winced. *They're fighting again.* She flicked her eyes toward the red-lacquered pocket doors that stood between her and their chaos.

Brother smiled encouragingly, as though he hadn't heard anything at all. "Pay them no mind," he told her. "Concentrate on—"

"In a war zone? On the front lines of *battle*?" her mother countered. "Have you lost your mind?"

"On the contrary, I see more clearly than ever."

"Then you're going to have to explain it because all *I* see is madness."

There was a heavy thud, as her cousin—no, her husband— struck something. A wall, perhaps. Min flinched. Brother sighed.

"Let us see what they want." The monk leaned back in his chair.

"Stop lashing out," her mother scolded the emperor. "You're acting half a child! How am I to trust your word if you can't behave like an adult?"

Min resisted the urge to clap her hands over her ears. Instead she rose and walked toward her windows, gazing down onto the garden where her nunas milled like pigeons. Brother had sent them away for her "lesson."

He made them leave so they wouldn't gossip. Well, all this shouting certainly would give them something to gossip about.

Below, Butterfly stroked the seven-stringed zither, laid across her lap like a cat. The others sang along, their voices coming through the window muted and somehow sad, though the lyrics were happy.

Min felt so far away. As though they were in a world apart from her. She lingered there like a mournful phantom, half waiting for one of them to look up and see her. They wouldn't, though.

They never really liked me, she thought, not for the first time, but still, it stung. *No one does. Not truly. I could die and they would all weep dutifully, but not one of them would miss me.*

Min might have accepted this as the way of the world—the natural order between servants and those they served—had Lu's nunas not hung on her every word, fought for her sister's attention and praise. Loved her as a friend. A sister. Even having to sort her laundry and wash her hair had not dampened their enthusiasm.

For all the good it did them, murmured a voice in the back of her mind. *Now they're locked up. They'll be tortured, kicked and beaten—*

No! She shook her head as though to knock loose the thought. *That was a dream.*

But she found herself imagining Hyacinth, her knuckles bloody, her skinny ankles draped in chains—

Who cares about her? a voice within hissed. *Who cares about any of them?*

Lu's nunas, her own, it didn't matter. They didn't matter.

They're just maids, anyway, the voice sneered. Was it hers or the other? It was so hard to tell, lately.

"We need to leave soon. Brother says . . ." Set's voice rose in the other room, penetrating the doors and overtaking her own.

"As though what that *creature* says matters to me," her mother snapped.

Min glanced anxiously toward where Brother was still sitting, hands crossed in his lap. He didn't *seem* to have heard, though of course he must have.

"There is a *prophecy!*" Set raged. "My reign over the empire will only be secure if I can take the North, and I can only take the North if I have Yunis! Brother has *seen* it!"

"What do you really know of that man?" her mother demanded. "You should hear the things people say about him, Set, when you're not around! And you leave him alone with my daughter to do heaven knows what!"

"He *saved* me!" Her cousin's voice thundered, his rage so palpable it hit Min like a fist. She backed toward the windows. "He showed me there is still magic in this lousy, worthless world. Don't you ever, *ever* speak ill of him!"

"Magic . . . ? This is absurd. Minyi is my *child.* My only child. I won't have you and some quack monk telling me what to do with her."

They went quiet. For half a ragged breath, Min wondered if they'd left. Then her door burst open and her mother strode into the room, making straight for her as though Brother wasn't even there. Min flinched as her mother swept down upon her, wrapping her arms around her shoulders, her belled sleeves settling like wings.

"Min, come with me. We are leaving for the Eastern Palace. You went there once as a child, do you remember? You loved the lake."

Min did remember, but she hadn't loved the lake, which had seemed a vast, swallowing maw. It had been Lu who stripped down to her waist, splashing around in the shallows with Hyacinth, then swimming out farther than the others would dare, until her head was just a speck of black in the silver water. Min had stood on the rocky shore and wept in fear as Amma Ruxin shrieked for Lu to return *this instant, the gods help you, child.*

How had her mother so misremembered things?

"That wasn't me," Min whispered, but no one seemed to hear. Perhaps she hadn't really spoken at all.

"What you're proposing is treason," said Set. "I order Min to come with me, and if you take her away I swear I will have you locked up, Aunt Rinyi. No one is stopping me. Not Lu, not the court, and not you."

Her cousin filled the doorway, leaning heavily against the rounded frame with both hands. His handsome face was stiff with frustration and spite, blazing eyes locked on her mother. A hank of black hair had fallen loose from his plait.

Brother stood, holding a steadying hand up in Set's direction. "Let's all calm down—"

"Why, Set?" her mother demanded over him. "Tell me what on earth you could need Min for. She's just a girl, and she belongs with her mother."

I'm no girl, Min thought in outrage. *You told me yourself, I'm a woman now!*

"Minyi."

Set's voice was still and even, ringing in cold contrast to her mother's ragged yelling. He straightened, released his hold on the door frame with some effort. Then he smiled—false and faint—and held out his hand.

"Min, come here," he said.

Her mother's arms tightened, pulling Min against her chest so hard she could feel the give of the empress's flesh beneath the layers of her robes. Instinct and discomfort made her move to pull away, but her mother did not let go.

"We're going, Min," the empress said. Min could feel the vibration of her voice, and in it the tremor of doubt undercutting her words.

She looked up at her mother's face, then to Set's. One taut and self-righteous, the other frenzied and furious. Both pale. Both expectant. Waiting for her to choose.

Between what, exactly? What were they each offering?

Nothing, she realized, in that voice that was hers, and also not.

They were each *asking* something of her. Demanding.

The choice between the dangerous unknown, and the stifling, unbearable familiar.

She had to go to Yunis, didn't she? For Set. But how to make her mother see? *What do I do?* she asked the no one within her.

In the end, she didn't have to do anything. Set strode across the room and seized her by the hand. With one firm yank, she

THE GIRL KING   313

was torn free from her mother's grasping embrace and tumbled into his own.

"Tell her, Min," he said, his voice wet and overeager. "It's time. Tell her what's inside of you."

Min's whole body trembled. *I have to stop. I'm not a little girl, I can't be scared* . . .

"Be gentle, my emperor," Brother said, his voice still inappropriately calm, as though he were in some other conversation.

"Why, Set?" her mother said, and Min was astonished to hear how small and broken she sounded. How defeated. "Tell me why. You promised me you would protect her."

"Min can protect herself. She has strength beyond what you can imagine. It was foretold." He shook Min's shoulder, sounding absurdly cheerful. "Come on then, cousin. Wife. Tell her what you are."

"You've gone mad," her mother was saying, shaking her head. "You want her to tell me what she is? She's a *child*."

"Show her," Set insisted. "Show your mother what you can do." He prodded her forward.

Min looked between them again, both so rattled, so weary, and looking oddly young. She glanced at Brother, but he was still standing behind her cousin, hands at his sides. He wouldn't—couldn't—do anything. No one could stop this now.

No one except . . . *Help me,* she thought. A silly futile prayer.

You already have everything you need, you stupid girl, said the voice that was hers and also not.

She didn't, though—she didn't have anything. "I . . . I can't," she said, turning pleadingly to Set. "I don't know how to do it yet on my own. I don't . . ."

His face softened, as though he only now registered her terror and uncertainty. What this was doing to her. "Min, I'm sorry," he said, and something like shame welled up in his voice. "Of course you can't . . . I'm sorry. Come here."

In spite of herself, she felt gratitude flush through her veins. At last, he recognized what he was doing. He saw. She stepped forward, allowing him to tug her once again into a gentle embrace.

She sensed the change a heartbeat before it happened, felt the warning in her blood, her bones. Too late. His hands were hard, viselike around her shoulders and he whipped her around until her back was flush to his chest.

"I really am sorry," he said, his words fluttering against her ear like a kiss. "I was hoping it wouldn't come to this." Then he pushed her forward. "Brother? As we discussed."

Min stumbled, but the monk was there to catch her. Like a magic trick, the glass-like knife appeared in his hand. She stared at it uncomprehendingly.

The monk yanked her hair back and drew the blade across her throat.

Her mother shrieked.

She shouldn't do that, Min thought vaguely. *The nunas will hear. They'll talk . . . Everyone knows nunas are terrible gossips . . .*

The pressure on her shoulders was gone. Brother had released her. She stumbled toward the windows. Below, Snowdrop and Butterfly and the others were still singing, though now the song had turned sharp and eerie, more like sobbing than music.

No, Min realized. *That's me. That's me singing.*

Her hand went to her neck and came away slick with blood.

She sucked a breath to draw a scream, too late remembering that would only pull the blood in, down her throat, down into her lungs, drowning her in her own red waters . . .

Only the feeling never came. Just a pain, sharp and fine and bright as the first moment of dawn. *I'm still alive,* she marveled. The cut was shallow, just breaking the skin.

Set stepped toward her, but her mother was faster, pushing him away. The empress was upon her, catching hold of Min's face with her cold hands.

"Let me see!" she cried. "Let me see, baby." And whirling on Set, "What have you done? What have you *done?*"

Set's face was raptly curious, disappointment fraying the edges. He stepped forward, cautious, and the light from the windows caught the hollows of his cheeks, making him look stern, old.

"What were you thinking?" her mother screamed, whipping her head between Set and Brother. "You could've *killed* her! You still might! Oh, my baby . . . my sweet only baby . . ."

I'm not your only baby, Min thought distantly. *I'm not yours, I'm not a baby at all . . .*

"And look at her!" her mother continued, gently pulling Min's head to the side, inspecting her throat. "Gods! Think of the scar it'll leave! My sweet only baby . . ."

It was the wrong thing to say. Wrong. All of it wrong.

Not your only. I have a . . .

"My only baby," her mother repeated, as though to refute the thought. Her hands fluttered about Min's shoulders like pale doves.

"Get away!" Min shrieked. "Get away, get *away* from me!" She moved like an animal, flinging her arms wildly. Her hand caught, leaving a streak of blood across her mother's mouth. It looked like she'd smeared her lip paint.

"Empress Minyi," Brother said, stepping forward. "You're in shock, we need to fetch the Court Physician—"

No, Min thought distantly. *I already have everything I need.*

"Don't you dare touch her!" her mother was screaming at the monk. "I'll see you hanged—I'll see you flayed and forced to crawl through the streets of the Second Ring . . ." She moved to seize Min.

"Get *away!*" Min threw out her hands, and in that moment felt a new power course through her. Or perhaps it was the same power she had felt before, now swollen, amplified, transmuted. Gold and fire and heat and something like joy surged in her veins—and burst from her outthrust palms, invisible to the eye, but real. So real; the realest thing Min had ever felt.

Her mother flew backward, fast and impossible, as though lifted clear off the floor by a pair of unseen arms. She opened her mouth as though to cry out, but if she did, Min never heard. At that moment came a much louder sound—big and physical and *wrong.*

There was a great, ceaseless wind roaring behind her. The air surged, filled with scintillating floating bits of light. It was everywhere—cold little silvery flecks catching the light as they blew past. She could hear her mother screaming then, and Set, too. Did Brother cry out? She couldn't hear him. All three of them were cowering, tucked in on themselves, covering their faces.

Snow, Min thought deliriously. *It's snowing inside . . . Why be afraid of a little snow?*

One of the flecks caught her cheek. It was cold like snow, but hard. *Ice?* Then she felt the kiss of pain blossom in its wake. *Glass.*

She turned, and with a strange calm she understood she had shattered every window in her room.

A few remaining shards fell from the emptied frames as she walked toward them, tinkling merrily to the floor. She took another step, heard the glass crunch under her slippered feet, crisp as autumn leaves.

She looked out onto the garden. This time, every nuna below looked back, standing frozen with wide eyes. The zither lay in the grass at Butterfly's feet; it must have tumbled from her lap when she stood.

Min lifted a hand to wave, then realized her face was wet. When had she started crying? She touched her cheek. This time, when it came away red she did not shriek. She was not afraid anymore. Not of a little blood.

Everything is different now, said the voice that was hers and also not.

She heard stirring behind her and turned in time to see her mother stand, flecks of glass raining from her shiny black hair. The backs of her hands were bleeding from shielding her face, but she seemed otherwise unharmed. When she looked at Min, though, her eyes were vacant and unknowing as that of a doll.

"Min?" she whispered.

Min looked about her ruined bedroom. Brother was still standing by the table, his face aglow with something like awe. No—not quite. Hunger. Want.

She felt Set step in behind her, rest a hand upon her shoulder. She didn't look at him, but she could feel his shock, his exhilaration, his fear, radiating like heat from his body.

This is what he wanted.

"What have you done?" the empress said, and her voice was pale with horror. At first it wasn't clear who she was addressing, but then her bright eyes fixed upon Min. "What *are you?*"

Min felt her face move, the skin crying out from a hundred cuts she hadn't felt before. She smiled, anyway. And when she spoke, her voice sounded like someone else. "Don't you know me, Mother? I'm your baby."

CHAPTER 27

Deal

Sometimes in Nok's dreams, his sister lived. These were the worst kind; they meant he would have to watch her die.

But this dream was young yet, and Nasan scanned the horizon from atop a gnarled scrub tree, all ferocity and focus. She was the child she had been when he'd last seen her, looking vulnerably small against the milk-white sky. The northern plains were flat and barren, but Nasan was always clambering up what few trees and peaks she could find. *Are you a wolf,* Nok would tease, *or are you a sparrow?* Her fists like little stones would find his arms and belly until they were both on the ground giggling with it.

They're here! she cried.

The visitors arrived in their cauls: the golden eagle of the Iarudi, the red bear of the Varrok, the cream-yellow antelope of the Keian, others whose names Nok did not even know. He watched with an envy like hunger as each creature passed through the welcome arch of the encampment. Then, as sand pours off flesh, the cauls fell away to reveal the man or woman who wore its form. Glossy feathers and coarse fur melted into desert-burnished ochre skin. Talons elongated into tapered fingers. Snouts retracted and reformed wide noses, full mouths. A gift from the gods. Elegant. As natural as breathing.

But not for Nok. Not—

He's awake.

The men and women froze in their half-cauled states. As one, they turned and looked his way. A hundred pairs of eyes gleamed silently at him.

He's awake.

He turned, and Nasan was in front of him, close enough, real enough that he could feel the heat of her, could smell sweat and worn leathers and unwashed hair. He didn't think he could bear to see her die, not again . . .

"He's awake."

Warm fingers touched his face. His mother? Who else would be so soft with him?

But, no. His mother was dead. They were all dead. All except—

"Nok?"

He opened his eyes. His sister stared back down at him. Her face was older, worn. Odd, that had never happened in his dreams . . .

A dream. The worst sort of dream.

"Nasan . . ."

She was crouched beside him, concern and trepidation etching her face. "He's awake," she told a girl standing beside her. "Go tell the others."

His sister spoke with stern authority, though the other girl couldn't have been much younger than she. Nevertheless, she nodded and disappeared through the only door in the room.

No, not a dream.

Nok struggled to sit up. "Where am I . . . how . . . ?"

"Don't get up," Nasan scolded. The tone of her voice was so familiar as to hurt. Breathless, he complied.

"How are you here?" he asked, his voice cracking. "It's not—I saw them . . ." Words were not enough. He seized at her wrists, pulling her hands to his face. They were whole and warm and solid. Her fingernails were dirty. "How are you alive?"

"How are *you*?" she shot back.

Not without a great deal of help. A cold thought seized him. "Lu . . . the girl I was with . . . ," he said frantically, scrambling back upright.

"You mean the *princess*?" Nasan countered with a raised eyebrow.

He studied his sister. There was a challenge, a prodding in her voice he wasn't sure how to interpret. He nodded. "Yes. The princess. Is she all right?"

"Relax. She's fine. Not a scratch on her. I'll take you to her when you're up for it." She pushed him back down. "Just rest."

"I don't need to rest." Where were they? Nok craned his head to look, but all he could see out the room's single window was a dense thatch of greenery.

Nasan sighed. "In that case, I have some questions. First off, what are you *doing* here? How did you get out of the labor camp?"

"An imperial officer," he said, experimentally propping himself up on one elbow. "He got me out."

"*Why?*"

He considered explaining the extent of Yuri's past, the old man's connection to Lu—but, no. *Later.* When he better understood the lay of things.

"I got sick after you . . . after they took you," he said instead. "Really sick. They tossed me into the medical tent with the other lost causes. But the officer, he seemed to think I could be saved—I don't know; I guess he felt sorry for everything they'd done. He was on his way back down to the capital, so he sneaked me away with him. Left me with an apothecarist friend of his—I've been the apothecarist's apprentice ever since."

Nasan laughed. "In the capital? Right in the belly of the beast?"

"Not quite," Nok corrected. "Little farming town just to the north."

Thinking of Omair flooded him with restless urgency. It hadn't been long—less than a moon's pass—since he'd last seen him. But it felt a lifetime ago. Had the old apothecarist been relegated to some palace dungeon this whole time? Had there been a trial? Was he even still alive?

There was no way of knowing. All Nok could do was press on, move forward with Lu's plan. But Nasan and her friends had plowed through their path with the grace of a sandstorm.

What was the plan now?

In lieu of family, Nok had had Omair. Once he had had Adé. And now he was stuck with Lu. But—a smaller, uglier voice in the back of his mind thought—now he had Nasan back. Didn't he?

"Nok?" Nasan was watching him with careful, catlike eyes. "Are you all right? Do you need to rest?"

You owe Omair a debt, he told himself harshly.

"I was just . . . it's a lot to take in at once," he said. "I assumed you must be dead—that monk killed all the children he took, didn't he?"

"Almost all of them," Nasan said. "The same night they took me, we left the camp. Me and ten or so other specially chosen kids—anyone who retained any hint of the Gift. We were loaded into a wagon and traveled for miles. They kept the windows covered so we couldn't see where we were going, but I could tell the air was getting drier, colder. We were in the Gray Mountains. The monk had some sort of cottage set up there. Full of cages."

"The others said he peeled the skin off the kids he took," Nok murmured. "That he was looking for magic under their skin."

"Not quite," Nasan said. "He took three of us the first night we were there—me and two boys. I was the only one who came back. He took us up into the mountains. H-he had this map, marked with a location he thought might be a gateway into Yunis."

"Yunis?" Nok repeated in surprise.

"Yes," his sister confirmed. Her face took on a closed, careful look. Anyone else might have missed it, but there were some things siblings never forgot.

It was the same look that she used to get when their mother accused her of making off with the last dessert plum. Nasan had been clever enough to know she could never convincingly mime innocence, so instead turned deceit into a game of endurance, sustaining her lie louder and longer than her opponent was willing or able to deny it. Persuasion by exhaustion, Nok had called it.

The look had grown subtler over their four years of separation, but Nok still saw it for what it was.

What was she hiding?

"The monk had this notion that the city was—what was the word he used?—'slumbering.' That the Yunians had magicked it into hiding, and with the right combination of spells and sacrifices of his own, he could worm his way in."

"And then what?"

Nasan shrugged. "Damned if I know. He didn't share it with us. Anyway, when they got there it didn't look like anything special, but he seemed sure that it was that particular spot."

"So, what happened?"

She sighed. "He killed the other two right there, trying to use their blood to open the gate. When that didn't work, he tried to make me caul on the site. Right there on the ground, on my knees in the other kids' blood. Thought he was going to kill me when I couldn't, but he just took me back to the cottage. The next night, me and four of the others ran."

"And now you're here," Nok said.

"And now *we're* here."

"Who are all your other . . . friends?" Nok gestured around, referring to the other children he'd seen earlier. "And how many of you are there?"

She smiled, a hint of affection lighting her face. "Sixty-eight of us. Mostly Gifted, though there are a few ungifted who were also displaced by the colonies. Some are Gifted orphans we found wandering the woods after their Kith were slaughtered, a few are escapees like me, and about twenty are rescues from when we raided a labor camp a few months back."

"That was *you*?" Nok asked, dumbfounded.

"You heard about that?"

"They were talking about that all the way down in the capital," he told her.

"I looked for you, you know," his sister told him. "We raided the same camp we were taken to—number four, they call it. Creative."

"I wasn't there anymore," Nok said, thinking again of Omair.

"No," Nasan agreed. "Neither were any of the others. Karakk, Mitri, Chundo, Ammi, Moha, and Dohti . . . all the kids taken from our Kith. I didn't see any of them."

"Dead?" Nok asked.

Nasan just shrugged. "Probably." Her voice wasn't cold, exactly. Just unconcerned.

The unreality of seeing his sister sitting here, breathing, radiant, thriving, was beginning to wear off, replaced by a growing sense of unease.

"Lu—the princess, can I see her now?" he asked.

"I said she's all right. Don't you trust me?" His sister grinned at him, but behind the flash of teeth she was all cautious calculation.

Lu was a valuable commodity; what did Nasan want with her? Her face gave nothing away.

"She's quite the fighter, your princess," continued his sister. "Pretty, too. She nearly took out my best lieutenant's eye."

"She's not *my* princess," Nok said, pulling himself up to his elbows. This time she didn't try to stop him. "And your best *lieutenant* . . . ? Nasan, who—what *are* you?"

A wall went up over Nasan's face. "That depends."

"On what?"

She didn't answer the question but instead asked, "What are you doing with the Hu princess, Nok?"

"Helping her get north. To Yunis." he admitted.

"Why?"

"To—to get an army, regain her throne. If I help her, she'll free Omair, the apothecarist who saved me."

"You're helping an imperial—a member of the very family that killed our parents, our Kith—for some peasant doctor."

"Yes." How to make her understand what Omair meant, what Nok owed him?

Nasan's eyes, so like his own but so different, narrowed in suspicion.

Nok felt a prickle of fear. On instinct, he reached down to pat for the knife in his boot. He wouldn't use it; just wanted the assurance that it was there.

It wasn't. Of course; he'd dropped it in his botched attack on Ony.

His sister's eyes flicked down to where his hand was grop-ing for it and she raised an eyebrow.

He'd kept a knife there, too, when they were children. She understood.

"I *need* her," he said. "To get Omair back. What are you going to do with her?"

"That depends on what she's willing to do for me." Nasan's tone did not invite further questioning. "Do you think you could convince her to help me?"

Nok very much doubted anyone could convince Lu to do anything she didn't want to do, but his sister didn't want to hear that.

"I guess we'll have to find out."

He licked his lips. This was his sister, as sure as the sun rose in the east, but what could that mean stretched so thin over four years of separation? There was a lot Nasan wasn't telling him; more than he even knew to look for. He was sure of it. The way they were talking, it was like two dogs circling one another, unsure of the other's strength.

He almost laughed; if only his father could see how hard he'd turned out. The old man would never believe it.

"I'd like to see Lu now," he said decisively.

Nasan sat back on her heels. Something in her posture slackened, tentatively. "Are you sure you're up for it? You look terrible. Your face is all messed up."

The irony of her words cut through the fog of his suspicion. "Yes. Because *you* messed it up."

She smiled at that, all fierce joy and sharp teeth. "It could've been worse, big brother. At least I didn't kill you."

⁂

Nasan led him out the door, then abruptly swung an arm back to stop him in his tracks. When he looked down he saw why: they were a good thirty feet above the ground, standing on a narrow platform in the massive boughs of a tree. So, his sister didn't want him dead. At least not yet.

"I've been living in a tree, too," he told her when his shock wore off. "What a coincidence."

She gave him a quizzical look, like she wasn't sure if he were joking or not, but just pointed to a massive wooden basket hanging on an elaborate pulley of rope that swung all the way down to the ground. "We'll ride down in that," she told him. "I don't think you could make the climb in your state."

"Right," he said with a snort. "It's only because of me. Otherwise you'd be scampering down to the ground, no problem." Then, seeing her solemn face, "Wait, you're not serious?"

"I make that climb every day," she told him. "These are my quarters."

Quarters? He stared at her again, wondering for the hundredth time since he'd woken exactly who his sister had become. It was strange, how familiar she felt—it was so easy to slip into their old roles like they hadn't missed a day. But he had to mind the massive gaps between them, precarious holes of missing time and knowledge he kept threatening to fall through.

As they climbed into the basket, he wanted to reach out to her, say something to bridge the maw between them, but all that came out was, "I always knew you were part sparrow."

When they reached the ground Nasan turned to the girl who helped them out of the basket—a lieutenant, perhaps? Nok wondered—and asked, "Where's the princess?"

"She's in the lockup," said the other girl. "No one wants to get nearer to her than we have to." Nok peered more closely and noticed long scratch marks raking one side of her face. He smirked; Lu's work. The girl saw him looking and scowled, then spat on the ground.

"She's bound, isn't she?" Nasan demanded.

"Yes," the girl agreed. "And gagged. Still."

"There're dozens of us. I think we can handle one royal," Nasan snapped. "Bring her out to the lower clearing. Tell Ony to do it."

Nasan walked forward, tapping Nok lightly on the back to suggest he do the same. At least *he* wasn't bound and gagged. Yet.

He followed his sister into a clearing where children of various ages—mostly girls, but some boys—were gathered in clusters, honing weapons, cleaning root vegetables, or darning clothing. Nasan led them past a troupe of little ones turning some small rodent—a squirrel, most like—over a cook fire. The smell of roasting meat made Nok's stomach growl.

Many of the children looked up and saluted as his sister passed. Nok noticed that many of them bore crude tattoos of animals upon their upper arms. Not just animals, he realized, the Kith gods. Here, he saw the red stag of the Fonti, a tulip clutched in its mouth, stars tangled in its antlers; there a golden eagle of the Iarudi, resplendent against the corona of the sun. And as his sister swung her well-muscled arms in sync with her long stride, he saw the stark blue wolf of the Ashina, fierce and hard under a crescent moon, peeking out from beneath the sleeve of her tunic.

"The tattoos are meant to show what Kith each person is from," he blurted as the realization came to him.

Nasan nodded. When she spoke, it was with a heaviness—a sense of pride wounded. "Since we don't have our cauls anymore, we inscribed the memory of them on our skins. Maybe we should do you, too."

The Gifting Dream. He'd forgotten to tell her—or had he just neglected to? He'd have to tell her eventually.

"Funny thing—remember how when we were kids, everyone assumed I was defective, a weakling, a disappointment to our family lineage? Well, it turns out I may actually be a Pactmaker, the one to bring our Kith back from the dead!"

He cast his eyes upward to the canopy instead. They were in a denser, older part of the forest than he and Lu had been captured in earlier. Here, the trees were regal and massive, arching up toward the sky, centuries bound up within their trunks. Nok saw dozens of little tree houses like the one Nasan had referred to as her quarters dotting their lower boughs. A system of pulleys and rope lines connected them.

They came to a stop.

"Here she is!"

Nok jerked his head toward the voice and saw three of Nasan's people prodding Lu forward. Behind them, Ony had Lu's bow strapped to her back. In her hands, Nok saw with a flutter of his heart, Lu's sword gleamed.

Lu's hands were bound behind her back, and a stretch of white cotton tied around her mouth. Her captors used a long stick to prod her forward.

One of them gave her a hard shove with the butt of it. Lu went down to her knees. She huffed with the effort, but her eyes remained active, alert. Defiant.

Nok didn't realize he had moved toward her until Nasan's hand shot across his chest to stop him.

"Stay here," his sister said in a low voice. Then she walked forward and tugged the gag down around Lu's neck. "All right then, Tigress. Nok here wanted to make sure you were safe. Are you safe?"

A flicker of confusion passed Lu's features—did she recognize Nasan? As far as Nok could recall, they hadn't interacted back when the emperor visited the Ashina; they'd all been young enough at the time that their difference in age had seemed more significant.

The princess seemed to wrestle with how to react, but the look resolved right before she spat in Nasan's face.

A cry went up among the crowd, and a few of the assembled began to whoop, as though anticipating a brawl.

"Lu!" Nok cried out. Lu whipped her head toward the sound of his voice. "It's Nok! I'm here!"

"Nokhai!" she called out, the relief in her voice palpable.

He pushed his way through the crowd and crouched at her side. "Are you all right?"

"I'm fine!" she snapped, sounding more annoyed than frightened. "What is happening? Why does this girl have your face?"

"It's . . ." He looked at Nasan. "Can I untie her? I promise she won't run." Then he glanced back at Lu. "You won't run, will you?"

"Well, since you promised," she said tartly.

Nasan nodded reluctantly and a girl stepped forward to slit a knife through the ropes tying Lu's wrists. She surged forward and Nok flinched, but she just threw her arms around his neck, holding him tight. "They wouldn't tell me anything. I thought they'd killed you."

He froze at the weight of her body pressed against his. His hands had gone up instinctively, raised at shoulder level. For a moment he had thought she might kiss him again. He wasn't sure if he'd meant to push her away or return the embrace. It might look like either; the thought sent a flush up his neck.

Looking around the circle of strangers, he saw more than a few pairs of eyes had softened. The Tigress was human, after all. Nasan, though, just looked baffled. Nok lowered his hands.

"I'm fine," he told the princess as she released him. "Really."

His sister shook her head as though to clear her confusion. "You're fine, she's fine. We're all fine." She stepped forward. "Are you satisfied, big brother?"

"*Brother?*" Lu repeated, eyes widening. "This is your little sister? *That* sister? You said she was dead."

"It would appear I was mistaken," Nok said. Lu left a hand on his shoulder, as though she were afraid the others might try to tear them apart again.

Ony stepped forward toward Nasan. "You wanted to see her weapons?"

"Bring them here." Her voice tapered into a low appreciative whistle as Ony placed the sword in her hands.

A breeze stirred the trees overhead and a pale glimmer of light fell through, dancing along the length of the blade. The steel flared white like a flame set to oil. Around them, the others fell silent, as though their voices had been sucked out of them.

"Well, this is a pretty thing," Nasan said. She lifted it, her movements delicate, almost reverent. Even so, Nok could feel Lu's body seize up beside his as his sister swung the blade in a slow, languid arc, testing the weight of it.

"The craftsmanship is incredible, Princess." She stroked a finger along its edge and hissed delightedly when it drew a bead of blood. "I wonder how many of us you could cut down if you got your hands on it—"

"She wouldn't," Nok interjected.

"Wouldn't she?"

Nasan looked up at him curiously. She pointed the sword skyward and cocked her head as though considering it. Then without warning, she tossed it toward him.

Instinct took ahold of Nok and he leaped aside, the cold weight of steel cutting through the air where moments ago his ear had been. A cry went up through the assembled, though whether it was one of dread or amusement he couldn't tell. The sword, still upright, fell toward the ground—

And landed hilt first in Lu's hand with a reassuring smack.

For a moment no one moved. Then, all at once, a hodge-podge of makeshift and scavenged weapons materialized in the hands of his sister's people.

"Ay!" Nok yelled, instinctively leaping toward Lu and pushing her sword hand down. "She means no harm!"

He turned to Lu and hissed, "Put the sword *down*. Down now. On the ground."

The urgency of the situation, it seemed, had not yet dawned upon Lu. She looked positively livid, though she at least had the wherewithal to whisper as she rounded on him. "This is a four-hundred-year-old sword. One does not throw it on the *ground*."

"They do now." Nok grabbed her by the wrist and her fingers opened. Down fell the sword, impaling itself in the damp earth. "Nasan, call them off. She meant no harm! It was just an accident."

"An accident?" Nasan was looking at Lu. There was something shivering behind her eyes—a hungry infant thought, clawing its way toward the light of day. Then she smiled, looking pleased as a cat. He knew that look. No good had ever come of it.

"Clear off," his sister called abruptly. "Everyone back to work, except Lieutenants Ony and Matton. You're coming with us."

Two of the others—Ony, and a boy who must've been Matton, moved forward as the rest of the crowd dispersed in a flurry of excited whispers. He got a better look at Ony now, small and stocky, with a black plait streaked red and gold falling down her neck and the clever face of the Ungor fox etched upon her arm. She grabbed Lu roughly by the collar and shoved her in the opposite direction—back from where Nok and Nasan had come.

The boy Matton took Nok's arm, almost companionably.

"Where are we going?" Nok demanded. Matton grunted in response.

"He's not being rude," Ony said. "The imperials cut out his tongue."

Nok looked sharply at Matton, who opened his mouth in an exaggerated manner, waggling a scarred pink stump.

"Oh," Nok said politely. Matton had no tattoos—perhaps he was one of the ungifted orphans his sister had mentioned.

Nasan led them back toward a large, central tree house. She immediately began climbing, swinging herself up barely visible footholds carved into the trunk. Nok and Lu were taken up in the pulley basket by the others.

As soon as they were safely inside with the door closed, and Matton and Ony stationed outside, Nasan rounded on the princess.

"My brother tells me you're headed north."

Lu's eyes flicked toward Nok. She seemed to weigh her options, but he knew she wouldn't try for denial or weak deception—it wasn't in her nature. "We were. What does it matter to you?"

Nasan was pacing, regarding her with wary, calculating eyes.

"My brother also tells me you've got no love for our new emperor, this Set," she said. "Rumor has it, he's coming up this way with some forty thousand troops to help 'expand' the northern territories. Within a month, this whole encampment—our home—will be nothing but a wasteland. The trees fodder for your factories."

"What does that have to do with me?" Lu asked warily.

Nasan rolled her eyes. "You're the 'Girl King.' Even around here, everyone knows you were bent on being your father's heir. And I don't know if what they say is true—that you killed him to take the throne—"

"It's a lie!" Lu growled. "I loved my father."

Nasan held up a bored hand. "Frankly, I don't care either

way. What I care about is that you're ambitious, and you have a chance at overthrowing your cousin. Now, if you're up this far north, I can only imagine you're running away, or you're looking to find an ally with an army. You don't seem like the type to run away, and the only armies around here belong to the Hana—not a chance they'd back you over their favorite son—and the Yunians."

Seeing the flicker of surprise that crossed Lu's face, Nasan smiled. "It *is* the Yunians, isn't it? Interesting. You're more desperate than I thought. You think you can convince them to give you an army if you call a cease-fire and withdraw the mining colonies from the steppe, don't you?"

Lu frowned, reluctant to give Nasan anything. "And if I am?"

"I can help you get there," his sister said, dangling the bait. "If you can help us keep our home."

Lu stared, expressionless. "Why not just turn me in to my cousin? Try to barter for your lands in exchange for me?"

Nasan snorted. "My brother here tells me that raid on the labor camps a few months back made waves in the capital, yes?"

Lu nodded.

"That was us. Me."

"What does that have to do with selling me to my cousin or not?" Lu's voice was light, but Nok could tell she was impressed.

"Princess, we killed twenty soldiers and made the administration in Bei Province—including your cousin—look pretty foolish. They know it was us; they're too embarrassed to admit it publicly. I don't think Emperor Set's going to forgive us anytime soon. Plus," she said with a shrug, "I don't trust imperials."

"I'm an imperial," Lu pointed out.

"Yes." Nasan grinned. "But you're the imperial that happens to be in the palm of my hand. Right now? You live or die at my say. That tends to make people compliant. It would take a little more work to get that kind of control over your cousin."

Lu glanced at Nok. For a moment, he saw a glint of uncertainty in her eyes. She was wondering where he stood. This was his sister, after all.

"Look," Nasan said impatiently. "Like I said, you haven't got much of a choice, here. I told you what I'm after, now you tell me what you want. I help you, you help me. Simple."

"What makes you think we need your help?" Lu said guardedly.

"We captured you, didn't we?" Nasan demanded. "That means half an army of trained imperials can, too. And there's a lot of them between here and Yunis. Smarter than the men that were bringing you up this way, that's for sure. I know which routes to take to avoid their encampments and which passes in the steppe are unguarded."

"We have a map," Lu countered. "With that, and a little sharp thinking, we—I can manage."

"It's not that simple," Nasan said flatly. "There's a reason no one's seen a hint of the Yunians for the last seventeen years. No one finds Yunis unless Yunis wants to be found."

Nok felt the hairs on the back of his neck prickle, as though his body sensed a secret, a hidden danger that his mind did not yet perceive.

"What makes you so sure you can find it, then?" Lu asked immediately.

"I've been there before," Nasan replied simply, letting the words hang in the air before she continued. "The city didn't fall, you know. They just hid."

"So why'd they show themselves to you?" Lu demanded.

Nasan shrugged. "The ties between Yunis and the Gifted go back thousands of years. Our altars to the beast gods were kept in the city. Of course, we lost contact with them after you lot went to war with them and burned the city. But I guess they heard about us, our group here." She gestured about as though to indicate the camp. "One day, they sent a messenger to me. He brought me to the city gate and told me to wait. Then, he brought us some supplies—medicine, food, that kind of thing."

"So," Lu said impatiently. "You know where the city gate—the real gate—is, then. Tell us, and in exchange, when I win my throne, I give you and your lands protection."

"Thing is, the gates of Yunis aren't the easiest to find, direction-wise," Nasan said with grimace. "I can't just tell you where they are."

Lu rolled her eyes in a rather unregal manner. "I thought you said you knew? I imagine the direction is north, for starters."

Nasan shook her head. "Don't think north. Think up."

"Isn't north the same thing as up?" Nok said. "On a map, at any rate."

"Not 'up' as in that way," Nasan replied, gesturing with an arm in the vicinity of north. "'Up' as in . . ."

She pointed up to the ceiling. To the sky.

Lu barked out a laugh. "Is this a joke?"

"I'm deadly serious," Nasan said. "I know you Hu lost the old magic, but it's still common as ice up north."

"So," Lu said doubtfully. "How do we get there? Fly?"

Nasan rolled her eyes. "It's not quite like that. When you get to the gate, you have to be invited in. The place where the Yunians have hidden the city . . . it's like, we're here, right? And there are the heavens above us. Well, there's a space called the Inbetween."

"And that's where Yunis is," Lu finished for her.

"That's where Yunis is."

"Have you been in?" Lu pressed.

Nasan shook her head. "Like I said, only to the gate. They come out to see us when they want to meet."

"Then how do we get them to let us in?" Lu demanded.

"That's up to you to figure out," Nasan said blithely. "I just said I'd show you the way."

"You're asking a great deal in return for what amounts to mostly talk."

"Look," his sister said. "You don't get what you want, neither do I. Do we have a deal, or not?"

Lu watched her through narrowed, reluctant eyes. Then, she nodded. "We have a deal."

Nok sighed as the two girls shook on it, not sure whether to feel relieved or wary.

CHAPTER 28

The Inbetween

Nasan turned Omair's map over in her hands. She frowned and squinted at it.

"It works better if you look at it right side up," Lu told her, fighting to keep the impatience from her voice.

"The route you two chose was pretty inefficient," Nasan replied, ignoring the comment. "You must have walked east for three days straight at the Keian Bend, then doubled back again. Stupid." She folded the map up and handed it back.

Lu slid the folded paper into her satchel and tried not to bristle. "We had to stay off the main roads," she pointed out. "We chose safety over speed."

"Should've shot for a little less of one, a little more of the other," Nasan said. "All in all, it looks like you added a good week or more to your travels."

Lu bit her tongue. They'd done what they had to do, but she couldn't argue that they were making slower progress than she'd like. As it was, they'd had to spend two extra nights at the Gifted camp to let Nok heal and rest.

They had set out three—maybe four?—days ago from Nasan's camp. Lu frowned. Time was running together in her head, blurred by the monotony of the trail they struck. Lu had started out the journey trying to track the roundabout route Nasan led them on, but with no way to write it down, she found herself forgetting more and more of where they had begun. It worried her a bit. She didn't think the girl would betray them—she was Nokhai's sister, after all—but she didn't like the loss of control.

Each morning, the three of them rose early, fetched water if a creek was nearby, or otherwise took tiny sips from their skins until they found one. After an all-too brief breakfast of smoked squirrel and stale hotcakes, they were on the road again.

At night, they kept their fires small and discreet and took turns keeping watch in rotation: Lu, then Nok, then Nasan. They slept little, no more than they strictly needed. Most of their time was spent walking.

It was dull going, Lu thought as they trekked down yet another nondescript hillside scattered with stands of towering pines and eucalyptus. An old, narrow goat path—probably created by a Gifted Kith for their livestock long ago—helped them to pick their way through the parched, tall yellow grass here.

Lu spotted a rust-colored rodent darting in and out from one of the burrows that dotted the path like pockmarks. It was slight, no longer than her forearm, with a sweet face like a kitten's, but it followed them so persistently and with such keen, brazen eyes that she started pulling out her bow until Nok assured her it meant them no harm.

"Just a weasel. They're curious is all," he told her.

She frowned doubtfully but re-slung her bow and asked, "Did it dig all these holes by itself?"

"These holes?" He pointed to where the little creature had disappeared. "No, those are from ground squirrels. The weasels move into the abandoned burrows."

"How do you know so much about the animals around here?" she asked, falling into step beside him.

"I don't know much about this particular kind of weasel," Nok replied. "But there were similar ones along the autumn route our Kith took, through the steppe."

It was the first time she had heard him speak so freely about his childhood home, and his words conjured a memory of her own: "You told me," she said. "When we were children, you told me about those weasels. You said sometimes the older children would make a game of catching them with their cauls."

To her astonishment, a smile split across his face. "I remember that," he exclaimed. "You asked if they were good eating, and I said I didn't know, because no one ever caught one, far as I saw."

His words flooded her with effervescent warmth. It churned in her, then burst forth as a laugh. It wasn't funny, but that didn't matter. It felt like weeks since she'd had anything to smile about.

"Ay, lovebirds! Keep it down!" Nasan's voice came unexpectedly close and loud. Lu jumped as the other girl cackled in her ear. "Thought you were supposed to be a skilled hunter,

Princess," Nasan said smugly. "That's twice I've snuck up on you."

Lu huffed in annoyance. "I was *distracted*."

"Yes," Nasan agreed. "By my brother."

"If you tried even a little, Nasan, I bet you could be less of a pain," Nok muttered, face flushing.

"I'm sure I could," Nasan agreed amiably. "But what would be the fun in that?"

⚜

Lu took the first watch that night, sword unsheathed across her lap. Sleep came reluctantly to her lately, and when it came at all it was marred with dark, bloody dreams.

The wood was silent save for the even breathing of her sleeping companions, and the whine of the occasional mosquito. As they drew higher into the Yunian foothills the air had grown chillier—hard on their fingers and toes, but making for far fewer insects. It was an exchange Lu was glad to make, at least for now. She might be less glad of it if it got any colder.

"Hey."

The voice came soft beside her. Instinctively, her grip tightened on the hilt of her sword, but her fingers fell away when she looked through the dark and saw Nokhai's face, wan and starkly shadowed in the moonlight. The worry of danger passed, but her heart quickened anyway.

He closed the distance between them and sat, near enough that she could feel the warmth of him radiating through his wool tunic. "You should sleep," she whispered.

"Can't." He didn't sound too concerned, though.

"Not surprising," she said carefully. "You must have a lot on your mind."

It was hard to know how far she could wander into his thoughts before he pushed her back out, but tonight he just shrugged. Let her stay.

"That's one way to put it," he said.

A pale slash of his face was visible in the moonlight, just enough that she saw the smile quirk quick across his mouth.

"I can't help but feel like all of this means something, you know?" she said. "You finding your sister like this. It feels like . . ."

"Fate?" he said.

She looked sharply at him to see if he was mocking her, but the black pools of his eyes were wide and open. Earnest.

"Yes," she said, her mouth dry. "Fate."

She moved closer. He watched her with quiet interest but didn't object, so she pressed her shoulder to his. She felt his breath puff against her cheek, in the shell of her ear, waiting for her lips to seek his. She didn't make him wait long.

He kissed her back. She pulled him closer, surprised at the hunger with which he met her. He touched her, just below her ribs, then his hand jerked away when he realized what he'd done.

"Sorry," he whispered, the words warm against her lips.

She shook her head, making a wordless sound of frustration as she guided his hand back to where it had been. He opened his mouth in surprise and she covered it with her own.

A ways off, Nasan snorted and mumbled something blearily. They froze, but she lapsed back into deep, even breaths.

"Do you think she's really asleep?" Lu murmured.

"Nasan?" He pulled back and made a face. "Do we have to talk about my sister right now?"

Lu laughed, nudging his chin with her nose before burying her face against the heat of his neck. "She doesn't seem to like me much."

He stiffened. "Did she say something?"

Damn. "No," Lu said quickly. "No, of course not."

"Not everything is about you," he told her. He pulled back, the cold of the night air quickly filling the void left by his body. "Nasan's been through a lot."

"I know—"

"You don't," he cut her off. "You can't."

Lu pursed her mouth and stared at him, but he either didn't notice her gaze through the dark or refused to meet it.

Later, bedded down sleepless on the cold ground, she would think: *He is a boy covered in hidden wounds.* Each time she thought she had figured out how to safely embrace him, her fingers probed across his skin and found a new break.

⚜

Two days later, Nasan halted their trek to tell them unceremoniously, "There's a lake over the next ridge. The gate is along its shore."

"You're certain?" Lu pressed.

"Of course," Nasan retorted, clearly offended. "I know where I'm going, Princess. Don't expect to see much, though. Like I said, Yunis only appears when it wants to."

Lu rolled her eyes. "So you've mentioned a few hundred times."

Nok interrupted before Nasan could respond, as though sensing a spat coming on. "Maybe we should stop here and one of us can go scout to make sure the way is clear."

"I'll go," Lu and Nasan said immediately, in unison. Then they turned to one another and glared.

"You're not going together." Nok shook his head. "You'll kill each other before you even get to the top."

"There's no way I'm not going—no one is as familiar with imperial scouts as I am," Lu said at the same time that she heard Nasan protest, "I'm the only one who's been here before, you wouldn't even know what to look for!"

Nok put his face in his hands.

"Forget it," Lu said. "Let's all just go."

Nasan frowned grudgingly. "Fine by me," she said.

The trees had become sparse and thin as the days passed—staggering pines transitioning into bent scrub trees, until those too became few and far between. As they scaled the ridge, whatever remained of the forest fell away into a jagged landscape of barren foothills.

"It's very desolate," Lu said.

Nasan smirked and bumped Nokhai's shoulder with her own. "I think it's homey, don't you, brother?"

But Nokhai's eyes were far away. He was chewing on his lip so hard it looked like he might draw blood.

"Are you all right?" Lu whispered, touching his arm. He started, as though he had forgotten she was there.

"I'm fine," he said. "Just . . . feels strange here."

"Well," she said carefully. "Lot of memories for you, probably."

"No," he said quickly. "I mean, yes, but it's not that . . . it's physical. Like . . . like, there's something humming just below my feet. Like it's shooting straight up into my bones."

"I feel it, too." Nasan was looking over her shoulder. "Happens every time we get this far north. It's the ghost of the Pact, brother. The land, or rather, the magic in the land. We might've lost our cauls, but a trace of it will be in us always. Our blood remembers."

Nok shivered. Lu saw in his eyes that he still hadn't told his sister about his Gifting Dream—none of it.

Well. That was his business.

They fell into silence as they approached the top of the ridge, the ground now so steep that they were forced to their hands and knees. Lu thanked the heavens she'd held on to her leather hunting gloves as she searched for handholds in the rocky earth. She was panting now, her breath ragged.

Beside her, Nok seemed to grow stronger and surer the higher they climbed. At one point, she slipped in the dirt, and his hand shot out to grab hers before she had scarcely fallen at all.

She gave him a questioning look and he shrugged, looking just as surprised. "Maybe Nasan is right . . . something in the earth makes us stronger. Like it recognizes us."

For her part, Nasan barely seemed to register the change in their surroundings. She reached the top first, to Lu's chagrin, casting a wink back at them before peeking over the other side.

Immediately, her face changed. Gone was the glib amusement, replaced by fear. She ducked back and put a finger to her lips, then motioned them forward. Lu glanced at Nok, who shrugged, his face taut and dark with worry.

When they reached the top, Lu peered over.

There was the promised lake, placid and eerily blue as the sky. A mirrored bowl set in the center of the dry valley. And along its shore, a writhing mass of metal.

Soldiers. Hundreds of them.

In their gleaming steel-plated armor, they looked like a stream of glittering beetles amassing on a corpse. Close enough that she could nearly make out the faces beneath their helmets.

Then she noticed the tents, and the central flagpole flying the flag of the Hu Empire—and just below that, the blue banner of the Family Li. Set's men.

"Gods," Nok breathed beside her.

In unison, they ducked back down and turned to Nasan.

"I thought you said this gate was unguarded!" Lu hissed, just as Nok growled, "What is this, Nasan?"

"Keep it down," the other girl snapped, but her dark eyes gleamed uncertainly. "Obviously something changed. You think I just overlooked a thousand imperials the last time I was here?"

Lu bit back a retort and instead peered over the ridge again. "The far side of the slope is more densely wooded. Do you think we could make it down that way?"

Nasan frowned. "There's some cover down at the shore . . . but I don't think we can make it undetected."

Lu nodded reluctantly. "Maybe we could go one at a time. They'd be less likely to see us if—"

The blast of a horn rang out from below.

Lu knew the sound right away: a military scout. It took her a moment to realize it had come from the wrong side of the ridge—back from the direction they had come. She whipped around.

"Watch out!" Nokhai hissed, grabbing Lu's arm.

Before she could respond, the first of the crossbow bolts whipped past her ear, where her face had been a moment earlier. She turned in the direction it had come from and saw them: five imperial scouts in blue.

"Get down!" she bellowed as the riders unleashed another round of bolts. Nasan and Nok were already scrambling back in the direction they'd come, but two of the riders broke off, forcing them back up the ridge, toward the valley. Cornered, they leaped over the side, tumbling and scrabbling for purchase.

Lu half crawled and half fell after them, her knees scraping against the hard earth. She came to a rough stop a short drop below.

"We've got to get back—"

But Nasan grabbed her wrist.

"What—?"

Before their eyes, Nok seemed to grow. One moment, he was scrabbling down the ridge on hands and knees, and the next there were claws springing from his fingers, thick blue-gray fur sweeping easy as a wind across his face and back.

"Nokhai!" the cry tore from her, but the wolf that had been Nokhai was hurtling away from them, impossibly fast.

Lu saw the glittering blue and chrome armor of near a dozen mounted Hana soldiers cut through the scrub trees below, their swords flashing in the eerie northern light. Then she caught a blur of gray-blue fur knifing through them, lightning quick, leaving a wake of bucking horses.

"He's not . . . this can't be," Nasan whispered. She was still clutching Lu's arm as if she were set to wrench it off. "It's not possible. The Pact was broken—"

"He's done it before," Lu admitted. "When I first met him in the forest, he was like that. He hasn't been able to do it again since then, though. He can't control it yet, but—"

"Gods," Nasan breathed, dropping Lu's wrist. "My brother is a *Pactmaker.*"

A shriek drew Lu's eyes away.

Below them, two soldiers were on the ground, one very still and seeping red-black out of his eyes; the other screaming horribly, dark blood making a geyser from his arm. Something glinted in the sun—the fallen man's sword. Still clutched in his severed hand, yards away.

Nokhai, Lu thought, seeing the jagged edges of the man's torn arm. No weapon had done that.

She fit an arrow into her bow. Beside her, Nasan hefted her staff in both hands.

Lu's first shot took a soldier in the side. He flew from his horse. Another shot back at her, but she ducked. The arrow thunked hard into a narrow little scrub tree behind her. She ran, heart slamming in her chest, but before her assailant could follow, she caught a blur of gray and the man was torn from his saddle. Nok's massive wolf clutched him by the throat, gave him a single hard shake, throwing the mangled body to the ground. The other soldiers circled the wolf warily as the creature bared its teeth.

Lu started toward him, but Nok cried out to her in thought-speak.

Don't. I can distract them. Get to safety—both of you.

There *was* no safety.

An arrow speared the dry earth just to Lu's right. Another one flew at her face . . .

Nasan knocked it from the air with her staff. Behind her, Lu saw a horse that had lost its rider. The creature reared, and Lu darted forward, seizing the reins and whispering rapid nonsense until it stilled. She spun toward Nasan. "Can you ride?"

Nasan stared. "Ride?"

"A horse!" Lu shouted. "Can you ride a horse?"

"How hard can it be? Try not to fall off, right?"

"Ride down to the copse of trees we saw over the ridge," she yelled. "Find the Yunians and tell them to open the gate. Nokhai and I will meet you."

Doubt rippled across Nasan's face, but she was already scrambling into the saddle. "There's no guarantee they'll answer my call."

"We're all guaranteed to die if we stay here."

"Can't argue with that," Nasan said, and then she was gone.

Lu!

She spun at the sound of Nok's thought-speak. The boy's wolf was surging toward her. Lu's heart dropped; its long gray fur was streaked dark with blood. Behind it, a tangle of soldiers lay on the ground, their throats a hopeless seeping mess of red gore. Three were still on their horses, though, closing in behind him.

Lu nocked an arrow and took one of the men in the throat, striking him clear from his horse, but not before a second loosed a crossbow bolt straight into the wolf's ribs. It hit home with a hollow thunk. Nokhai jerked hard at the impact, letting off a yowl of pain.

"Nok!" Lu screamed, but he was still coming toward her, determined.

Get on! he shouted at her.

Madness. He would collapse with the added burden of her weight. But he was approaching fast. *Madness,* she thought again as she seized a hank of fur about his ruff and swung a leg over the beast's broad back.

"I sent Nasan ahead," she gasped out, then bore down close against his back as a crossbow bolt whizzed past her ear. "Trees by the lake. Meet her there."

Nasan—he repeated, breaking off as another crossbow bolt narrowly missed his flank and embedded itself in the dirt where a moment ago his paws had been pounding.

"She's fine," Lu panted, hoping it was true. "She'll be fine."

The short *blat* of a scout's horn came from behind them.

"There's only one of them now," she said. "Where did the others go?"

To get reinforcements?

She groaned. "Most likely. If that's the case . . ."

We only counted about a thousand soldiers, he cut in, pain pulling taut at the edges of his words.

They broke over the ridge and plunged into the paltry trees spangling its face. Nokhai cut through them, wending a deft, jagged path, trying to shake their attackers. The scout's horn blasted again, but this time it came from farther away, as if he were losing ground.

Listen, Nok said, and she was alarmed to hear how ragged

he sounded. *If I can't make it all the way with you, you have to go on, all right?*

"Shut up!" she snapped.

No, he said, and his voice was coming thin and terse now. *You have to protect Nasan, and you need to keep your promise to her, and all those kids of hers. And you have to get Omair—*

"Shut up!" she repeated.

Please promise me, Lu. Omair. Do you promise?

They were so close. "Shut up, or I swear I'll—"

The wolf's legs gave out.

They skidded hard down the remaining distance of the slope, carried by its momentum, kicking up stones as big and hard as fists. Clouds of yellow-gray dirt blew across Lu's face, stinging her eyes shut. Distantly, she felt the flesh of her left forearm split like wet paper, but she felt no pain. Not yet.

They jolted to a stop in a settling cloud of dust and gravel. Lu swiped at her face to clear it and felt wetness in its wake. Blood from her mangled palms. She smelled copper, smelled salt. Someone was moaning, low and ragged, and she recognized her own voice. She blinked hard, forced her swollen eyes to open.

They were at the edge of the lakeshore. Another thirty feet and they would be in the water.

A dark violet-gray fog rolled in over the lake, curling and swelling toward them. The ghostly form of Nok's wolf loped down the shore into it, paws skimming the surface of the open water.

Lu squinted her dust-stung eyes, trying to focus, but they welled with tears. When she managed to open them again the wolf was gone, but the fog remained.

Then she saw the boy's body lying on the shore. His broken, all-too-human body.

"Nokhai!" She flew down toward him. He was still moving, but his breath was ragged, and she saw that every wound and mark carved into the wolf was now left upon his own skin. The shaft of the crossbow bolt had snapped clean off in the fall, leaving only the ragged point lodged into his ribs.

His eyes were distant, but they focused on her when she touched him.

"Go," he rasped. "Get out of here."

"I am *not* leaving you," she hissed. His eyes . . . he was having trouble focusing, but they fluttered at the blast of the scout's horn, much closer now. Another horn responded in kind. Then another. Close. She heard the hard clip of a thousand hooves on stone, rippling toward them like a wave. She looked for them—the soldiers—but the fog had grown too dense around them.

All she could see were her own bloodied hands, clutching at Nokhai's pallid face, smearing red across his skin.

"You have to go," he told her.

"Don't be stupid."

"They're coming." And beneath the pain, the fear, she felt his iron, his mettle. "Go now."

"Not without you," she said. She hauled him up onto her back, struggling to stand. She made it to a crouch before her knees buckled and she fell back against the stones.

The soldiers were upon them. She could hear the shouts of men over the slamming hooves against rock, the labored huff of the beasts.

"Over there!"

The call came behind them, unexpected, from the direction of the water. Lu half rose, her hand poised on the hilt of her sword. But then she recognized the voice.

"Nasan?" she cried out, her voice cracking with hope and disbelief. "Nasan!"

Something large cut through the smoke-gray fog over the lake, as if it were pushing its way through a curtain: a scow with a hull carved into the likeness of a dragon, painted ivory-white. Then, no—it was a blushing fuchsia, then the palest blue. Impossible. Lu drew in a sharp breath. The boat was hewn entirely from crystal, scintillating in the low light.

A hooded figure was poling the boat along. Nasan waved frantically from its prow.

The blast of the Hana scout's trumpet came again, and it should have been close, closer, but it sounded impossibly far away. The air was oddly still. Something had changed.

The horses, Lu realized. The thundering of hooves had disappeared.

"Nokhai," Lu whispered, bending to pull at his shoulders. His eyelids fluttered but did not open. "Nokhai?" She shook him, frantic now. "We're here. We're saved. Please . . ."

The boat bumped against the edge of the shore, and the tall, hooded figure within emerged. They walked strong and upright, but as they advanced, Lu glimpsed beneath their cowl the face of a very old man, his skin spotted with age, eyes and mouth drooping not unpleasantly at the corners.

"Please!" she called out to him. "My friend . . ."

The man bent over Nokhai swiftly, touched his throat, his

temple, his chest. "He lives," he assured her. "We must hurry—bring him to my sister. But he lives."

He withdrew the cloak from his shoulders and wrapped it around Nokhai's limp frame. Lu looked up to thank him—but the face she had glimpsed before was gone, replaced by that of a young man no more than two or three years her senior. He stood, lifting Nokhai in his arms as though he weighed no more than a cat.

"Princess Lu?" the young man said politely, his eyes searching her face with a curious, almost boyish wonder.

"Yes, I . . ." She blinked, baffled at the sight of his dark, unhooded eyes, and soft, affable features where the old man had been moments earlier. "And you are . . . ?"

"My name is Prince Jin," the young man said. "Welcome to Yunis."

CHAPTER 29

The Gray City

*N*ok's eyes fluttered open.

He saw a high-flown arched ceiling carved from stone. All around him, silence. He blinked, and the pain came rushing in.

Even as it knocked the breath from him, he knew it was a good pain, a healing pain. His hand went to his ribs, felt clean bandages wrapped taut around his middle. The air smelled sharp and medicinal.

He sat up as slowly as possible, resting heavily on his left side to do so. It took him what felt like an hour to rise, but at long last he pressed his feet to the cold stone floor. He wasn't sure that he would be able to stand, but he tried it, anyway, and found he could.

He was thirsty, and desperate to make water. He shuffled about the room until he found a chamber pot and relieved himself.

As he cast his eyes about for where he might find drinking

water, there was movement in the doorway; a swift, gray blur pushing past the white linen curtain that hung there.

Nok jumped, then flinched in pain. When he looked back, whatever had been there was gone, though the curtain still swayed in its wake.

He took an exploratory step forward. Then another.

Behind the curtain, the hall was empty and massive and gray, so gray. The side of the corridor on which he stood was punctuated with curtained doorways like his, while the other was let with open archways taller than trees. Each had a delicate, spindly banister carved at its base like stone vines.

The ceilings here were higher than they had been in his room, and it struck Nok that they looked not so much made from stone, as cut into it. As though the building in which he stood were carved in relief out of the side of a mountain.

He went to one of the archways. Sticking his head out over the balustrade, he saw he was at least partially correct: the building was embedded in a steeply ridged mountain. Close to the base of the mountain, a manmade section flared out, connecting to a temple erected just below. The temple was blocky and four-sided, with sides that sloped slightly inward toward the top. A tepid breeze tousled his hair, threw it almost playfully over his eyes. He brushed the strands back, flinching at the pain that shot through his side when he moved his arm. The air felt neither cold nor warm, as though it were the exact temperature of his body. He felt light-headed.

He backed away from that dizzy edge, then froze.

At the end of the hallway stood the wolf.

His wolf. He couldn't say how he knew for certain, but he did, sure as he knew his own name, or the back of his hand, or the sound of his sister's voice.

For a long moment, neither of them moved. The wolf blinked at him, black eyes languid and peaceful, and Nok... *felt* it as though he himself had blinked.

Come to me, he thought.

Footsteps rang out from the other end of the hall, voices bubbling in their wake. Nok whipped his head around just as Nasan turned the corner, followed by a tall young man whose face Nok recognized but could not place. They stopped short, seeing him.

His sister looked him over once and grinned. "Brother," she said. The young man just inclined his head politely.

Nok looked back to where his wolf had stood, but it was gone.

"You slept long enough," Nasan said as she and the young man walked toward him.

Nok stepped to meet them. "Where's Lu? Is she all right? Did—"

"Nokhai." The young man was smiling as though he hadn't noticed Nok's panicked rudeness. "I am Prince Jin of the Yunian Triarch. Princess Lu is fine."

Relief swept over his body like cool water. "Can I see her?"

Prince Jin's brow furrowed. "Certainly, at some point, though right now I think it may be difficult to—"

"*Why?*" Nok demanded, the word emerging harsher than he intended.

Nasan placed a reassuring hand on his shoulder. "Don't worry. I've been with her this whole time. She's just being dressed by some waiting ladies—"

"Ladies in waiting," Prince Jin supplied helpfully.

Nasan cast him a wry look. "—or whatnot. Anyway, she's not wearing clothes, is what the guy's trying to tell you."

Prince Jin blushed at her assessment but continued, "Princess Lu has requested to speak in open court before the Triarch."

Nok frowned. "That's you, you said."

"Me," the prince agreed. "Well, one of three. I'm the Warrior, my sister Vrea, the Oracle, and my brother, Shen, the Steward. The Steel, Silver, and Gold Stars, respectively."

Nok touched his side gingerly. Like all Ashina children he had learned something of the Yunian government growing up. Right now, though, with his head swimming, and no grasp on how he had gotten where he was or how long he'd been there, he was having a difficult time recalling the finer points. "Are we your prisoners?" he asked warily.

Prince Jin's eyebrows shot up. "No, certainly not."

"Is Princess Lu a prisoner?"

"Not at all."

Nasan's hand squeezed at his shoulder. "Relax, brother. They've been nothing but good to us. Fed us, let us bathe in their hot springs, gave us an apartment big enough to house our entire Kith. Patched you up faster than I would've thought possible, too, with their energy healing. You've only been out for a couple days, you know."

"I didn't know," Nok mumbled, rubbing his head. The

surprise of waking up in this place was wearing thin, leaving only exhaustion in its wake.

"Prince Jin here was just giving me a tour of the grounds," his sister continued. "We passed the hospital wing of the palace, and I thought I'd check in on you."

"If you're feeling well enough, you could join us," the prince suggested. "We can locate you a wheeled chair if you'd like."

Nok gave a quick shake of his head. His side hurt some, but his legs ached worse from lying still for two days. "It's fine. I want to walk."

"Excellent." The prince nodded. "It's been a long time since we've had visitors."

Nok studied Prince Jin guardedly. He was young—most likely no more than a few years older than himself—tall, handsome. He had the most open, earnest face Nok had ever seen. It was almost unnerving, the way the other boy's sun-warm brown eyes sought his own, seeming to beseech him for his trust. And won it almost instantly.

Nok held back a sigh and nodded instead. "Let's go see some gardens, then."

⁂

Prince Jin led them down a stairwell conneting Nok's hallway to a lower level. Here, gardens were planted on dozens of stepped tiers cut into the side of the mountain, small pathways connecting them. The prince kept pace with Nok, acting as though his slowness were completely normal. Nasan had no patience for such coddling; she forged ahead on the stone path, pausing to gaze up at the ornate buildings cut into the face of the mountain in skeptical wonder.

Nok found looking up made him dizzy, so he kept his eyes trained to the path, or at whatever plant Prince Jin was directing his attention toward. The gardens the Yunians grew had little of the sharp, neat order Nok had glimpsed in those of the more upper-class homes of the Second Ring. Rather, they grew in a pleasant, languid sprawl of blue-green vines, some of the leaves stiff and needlelike, others plump and succulent.

". . . of course, we had more variety in the old days, but since we moved into the Inbetween, we no longer have spring—or seasons at all. As far as flowers are concerned, we are limited to what the Nima trees can provide," Prince Jin was telling him, gesturing to a cluster of trees, their mournfully drooping branches spangled with clusters of pale ash-white flowers.

"They are named for a lesser goddess who fell in love with a spirit of the Inbetween. So enamored was she that she watched him daily from a port in the Far Beyond—what you might call the heavens—until finally she leaned too far forward and fell. She died in her love's arms, and her last gasp was filled with such longing and sorrow that it washed over him like a perfumed wind. Where they rested her body, the first Nima tree sprung up. The blossoms that adorn their branches carry the scent of her breath, and they wear mourning shrouds of white petals."

"That is . . ." Nok fumbled for a polite word. "Quite a story."

Jin smiled in the same easy, unabashed manner he seemed to do everything. "It's only a myth, but it is my favorite because it is so romantic. We don't have a lot of romance in our myths, otherwise."

"He didn't love her back, though. Didn't even know her, did he?" Nasan interjected from below, making Nok jump. "Seems like a waste."

Jin's eyebrows vanished beneath his thick fringe. "To die for love? How could that be a waste?"

Nok shrugged uncomfortably under Jin's wide stare. "I suppose," he said, if only to end the conversation.

They wended their way down two more garden tiers. Nasan left them again to plow ahead.

"I would like to know Princess Lu better," Prince Jin blurted once Nasan was out of earshot. "Is there an activity I could engage her in? Would she take well to an invitation for a private walk around the palace grounds, do you think? I fear I am not very familiar with your Hu customs; I don't wish to seem overly forward."

Nok frowned. "I . . . I'm not Hu, either."

"My apologies! Of course, you are Ashina. But, you know the princess well," Jin said. "Tell me, what is she fond of? What does she enjoy?"

Hunting. Fighting. Aloud he told the prince, "I . . . I think she would walk with you?"

"Is there a particular gift she might enjoy? Certain foods? Flowers?"

Nok tried to imagine how Lu would respond to an offering of flowers.

"You are smiling . . . Did I say something amusing?" Jin asked quizzically.

"What? Oh no . . . it's just . . . well, nothing."

He is trying to court her, Nok realized with a shock. Was this boy—this young man—such a fool that he would be taken in by a pretty face?

He doesn't even know her.

Well, the prince was likely to be disappointed. He was amiable, but clearly a bit simple. Dull. Lu was not likely to be impressed. Was she? He *was* very handsome.

Jin surged on, heedless to Nok's discomfort.

"Perhaps no gift, then? But you think it would be acceptable for me to ask her to take a private walk. Just the two of us?"

The thought made Nok uncomfortable. He needed to sit and rest. "I . . . I think that would be fine," he heard himself say.

"My apologies for asking so many questions," Jin said. "I have never met anyone quite like Princess Lu." He smiled shyly. "Everything around here is so still, so quiet . . . like stone. She is truly a child of the fire—so alive. Even her eyes, they dance like flames."

Nok felt a twinge of annoyance in his gut. *Why is he telling me this?* He shuffled his feet, eager to move along. How did one politely sidestep a prince's interrogation?

"I'm sorry," he said. "I don't know anything about the princess . . . or, really, princesses in general. I'm just her guide."

Jin's brow furrowed. "She referred to you as her friend. My apologies, I assumed from the way she spoke of you, you knew her quite intimately."

Before Nok could reply, they were interrupted by the sound of a massive bell being struck. Its ring was low and subtle to the ear, but it thrummed through Nok's body with such force he felt as if he were caught in the gentle current of a river. Up ahead on the path, he saw Nasan look up as though she'd felt it, too.

"Oh!" Jin exclaimed. "Court is being called to session . . . I lost track of the hour."

"Court?" Nok repeated. "So, Lu will be there, right?"

"Yes," Jin affirmed. "Would you like to come? It just occurred to me that Princess Lu will have no one seated in her corner of the audience, and your support would look . . . ," he hesitated, gesturing limply toward Nok.

Nok looked down at the crinkled gray robes the healers had provided him, the obvious hitch in his step, the way he favored his left side. He was certain his face was a mess—dark circles running beneath his eyes, cheeks hollowed out with hunger and pain.

"Better than nothing?" he suggested.

"Possibly," Prince Jin said charitably.

⚜

Nok had never been in a court hall before, but it was hard to imagine that any in the world could be grander than the one he stood in now.

It took a moment for his eyes to adjust to the dim lighting, but when they did he saw that, like the hospital, the hall was cut into the side of the mountain. The ceilings here were even taller though, and lavished with vast, deliriously colorful murals. The murals were interspersed with hundreds of massive stalactites, each as tall as a grown man, stabbing down toward the floor. A closer look revealed that the stalactites were covered in carved patterns—each line chiseled away by careful, uniquely skilled hands.

As he and Nasan followed Jin down the central aisle, Nok realized that a soft, orange glow was rising from within the stalactites, turning each into a lantern. By the time they reached the end of the aisle, the hall was cheerfully lit. Nok wondered how it would compare in Lu's eyes to the court she had grown up with.

"The section there on the left is the guests' gallery," Jin said, interrupting his thoughts. Nok followed the direction of his nod and saw a slightly raised, gated box within which stood three empty tiered stone benches.

"I wish I could join you, but I must take my spot on the dais." The prince gave him a friendly, apologetic pat on the shoulder, then left them. Nok looked around at the slow-filling hall, its stone walls beginning to radiate back the heat and buzz of several hundred bodies and voices. A wave of nausea hit him, and he grasped at Nasan's arm instinctively.

"You all right?" she murmured. "We can go if you want— I'll take you back to the apartments they have us in."

"No, I want to be here for this." Righting himself, he made his way to the guest gallery and took a seat beside his sister.

Nok felt rather than saw Lu enter the hall. The noise of the gathered crowd pitched in volume—a flurry of hisses and whispers to "look, look!"—and just as abruptly, it fell ringingly quiet. He turned with the rest of them and there she was in the doorway, resplendent in red robes. A white fur mantle hung over her shoulders and was cinched about the waist with a heavy pendant of jewels. She looked like fire and snow, a sole flare of color against the uniform pale gray of Yunis.

A guardsman at the door stamped his cane and announced, "Princess Lu of the Empire of the First Flame." The crowd stood in unison.

A small smile played across Lu's red-painted lips, and she nodded graciously before stepping down the central aisle, accompanied by a trio of Yunian handmaidens. She looked as tall and strong as ever, but the size of the hall shrunk her—a princess, yes, but also an outsider amid a sea of strangers, very far from home.

When she reached the foot of the dais, Nok saw her hesitate before stooping upon the cushioned kneeler placed there for her comfort. The handmaidens came forward to fix the drape of her robes. Nok shifted, uncomfortable. She felt somehow far away, as though the regal trappings had built a wall around her.

"Your princess cleans up nice," Nasan whispered.

"She's not *my*—"

The guardsman stamped his cane again. "Rise for the Triarch of Yunis!" he called, his voice filling the hall. "Prince Jin, the Warrior, our Steel Star. Mother Vrea, the Oracle, our Silver Star. Prince Shen, the Steward, our Gold Star!"

Everyone around them stood instantly, heads bowed in reverence. It took Nok a moment to catch his bearings, but he scrambled to his feet, pulling a somewhat more reluctant Nasan up with him.

At the front of the hall stood Prince Jin, and behind him, a woman and a man.

Both were tall and stately, and both struck him as far more otherworldly than Jin. The woman in particular, Vrea, seemed to float. Draped in hooded robes of silvery-gray that swept the aisle in her wake—the slightest whisper of silk against stone—she looked like a slow-moving rainstorm. As she ascended the dais, she lowered her hood, revealing a serene, tawny oval face with deep-set eyes, a flat nose, and wide, pleasant mouth. Her hair was shorn close to the scalp.

Behind her, the Steward-King, Prince Shen, followed. Tall and regal, he drew the gaze with intelligent, searching dark eyes. His night-black hair was combed severely back from his face and tied into a plait that fell down his back. His features were strong and even, but there was something so stern about them that it made one shy away from thinking him handsome. His beauty was an objective one, neither sensuous nor pleasant. Awesome like that of a mountain, and just as impassive.

"That Shen's going to take some convincing," Nasan murmured in Nok's ear as Shen passed. "Hope your princess has more charm in her than she's shown so far."

"Lu's perfectly charming when she's not being antagonized at every turn," he shot back. "And she's not my princess."

His sister rolled her eyes. "Well, she certainly got to you. Maybe there's hope, after all."

CHAPTER 30

Proposal

The Yunians' white fox fur stole was beginning to slip from Lu's shoulders. She tugged it back up, then smoothed the thick, wooly skirts of her robes. They were dark red—as scarce a color as any in these parts. It seemed Yunis was called the Gray City not merely for the steely peaks of its mountains; its citizens appeared to wear no other color. Lu wondered fleetingly which had come first, the name or the clothes. Presumably the mountains predated both.

In any case, the Yunians had found some red cloth to mark and honor her Hu heritage. Nasan, of course, had immediately pointed out that it was the *wrong* red. Not that Lu would ever say it aloud, but the Ashina girl was right. The tone ran too dark and cool, more crimson than scarlet. But she appreciated the gesture.

It wasn't just a color. It was a symbol, and symbols were important. The red marked her as Hu, a royal of the Empire of

the First Flame. Moreover, the effort that had gone into pro-
curing that symbol signaled to the court she was of value to the
Yunian Triarch.

The stole she could have done without, she thought as it
slipped once more down her shoulder. The fur dulled the damp
mountain chill, but keeping it on seemed to require some skill
she had never learned.

Hazarding a glimpse out at the gathered Yunian public,
Lu wondered how they saw her. A spark of violence in their
hard-won solitude? Some of the hostile eyes looking back at her
seemed to suggest so, while others were more sedate, skeptical.

Vrea the Oracle, Shen the Steward, and Jin the Warrior
ascended the dais. It was strange, seeing these figures from her
history lessons come to life. They looked just as they'd been
described in the remaining accounts from Yunis—unchanged
all these seventeen years. Eerily preserved by the stasis of the
Inbetween.

According to Yunian legend, before the city fell, every
time one of the Triarch died, they would soon be reborn anew.
The Yunian gods, the Ana and the Aba, would send a sign to the
surviving siblings, and the baby would be found and taken to
be raised to fulfill its role in the Triarch. Allegedly, the families
of those chosen had been greatly honored to lose their sons and
daughters in this way.

Vrea and Shen took their seats upon identical thrones cut
from stone. Prince Jin went to a smaller chair located at his
brother's side. It made him rather look like a child sitting with
his parents. The prince caught her gaze and smiled, though, so

perhaps he didn't find the arrangement diminishing. Lu returned his smile briefly.

Out of the three, she'd spent the most time with him. Shen was aloof, Vrea evasive and odd, but Jin was friendly and startlingly ordinary. She'd even grown accustomed to the way his face would seem to shift ages when he was excited or distressed—"slippage," he called it. It had happened to him ever since they'd entered the Inbetween. No one knew why, though Vrea hypothesized it was a manifestation of his nostalgia, his homesickness for the world they'd left behind.

On the dais, Prince Shen gave a quick, spare nod, and the crowd took their seats.

Lu took that for permission to speak and bowed low. "I, Princess Lu of the Empire of the First Flame, come seeking audience before the Triarch of Yunis."

"The Triarch of Yunis welcomes Princess Lu of the Empire of the First Flame to its court," Prince Shen announced. "What is your purpose here?"

"I come before you today the rightful heir to the throne of my empire. Through the machinations of a few evil men, I was usurped by my cousin, Lord Set of Family Li of the Bei Province."

Lu winced internally, hearing beneath the lofty polish of her words a hint of nervousness, a tremor in sync with the anxious skip of her heart.

Keep on, she told herself. *No one else has noticed.*

She straightened the fur stole over her shoulders and continued. "Since taking the throne, Lord Set has instituted policies for the empire that spell certain disaster and violence for our neighbors to the north—including the city of Yunis. In his greed and hubris, Lord Set put in motion a false war, based on lies, in order to take your land, your resources. He would see anyone who stands in his way obliterated. His reign will bring you nothing but a continuation—no, an intensification—of war and loss. Suffering and violence like never before."

Kindly ignore, Lu thought, *that it was my grandfather who initiated that war and violence, and my beloved father who kept it alive.*

She looked up to see if the irony had registered among the Triarch, but the priestess merely stared back with that bemused, neutral face of hers. Prince Shen gave little more, and Prince Jin looked almost pitying. How was she meant to reach them?

Perhaps it wasn't them she had to reach.

If she could not get what she wanted from the Triarch, maybe she could appeal to their people. She turned to face the audience, and caught a flash of annoyed surprise illuminating Prince Shen's stoic face. It was a brief thing, but it gave her some satisfaction.

The audience looked no less hostile than the Triarch, though. A thousand scrutinizing eyes raked over her face, tugged at the hem of her skirts. The only familiar face was Nasan's . . . and beside Nasan sat Nok, skinny and drawn and beautifully alive.

His shoulders were anxiously hunched; it couldn't have been easy for him to be there, with his broken body, his distaste for crowds, his suspicion of royalty and politics. But there he was. Her breath hitched as his gaze settled on her.

He nodded encouragingly. A smile trembled across his lips and it was a precious thing.

"Citizens of Yunis," Lu heard herself say, tearing her eyes from his to refocus on the crowd. "Set is marching here, right now, with the imperial army at his back. I come before you now as a messenger, an exile—but also as a potential ally and friend. I beg you: give me an army. Help me reclaim my throne and overthrow the false emperor Set. Only I know his weaknesses, his flaws."

She stepped forward, her voice full of fire. "As emperor, I will end the war and colonization ravaging the North. I will bring strength and friendship and prosperity between us. Grant your people the security and freedom to open your borders once more. Give me an army, and help me bring peace upon both our lands."

Her words rang in the stillness of the hall. Then, she fell back to her knees in a deep bow before the Triarch, her forehead pressed to the stone steps.

The Yunians began to murmur.

"Could she really do it?"

"What of the cost to our people?"

"It's too great a risk . . ."

Prince Shen stood. "Enough! The Triarch will have silence."

The voices evaporated.

She looked up from the floor and met the prince's hard gaze. "You speak well, Princess Lu of the Empire of the First Flame," he said. "What you promise—peace between our lands—is, naturally, of utmost importance to us." His mouth set in a firm line, he continued: "However, I fear we cannot give you what we do not have. Our army is but a small garrison, barely three hundred men and women. And each is needed to protect what is left of our city, especially in the wake of your cousin's impending false war." He turned his back and walked toward the end of the dais, as if to signal that was the end of it.

"Please!" Lu cried, reaching out after him. It was pathetic, but she couldn't care about that now. He was walking away with what little hope she had left in all the world. "I beg you, give me two hundred soldiers and when I win my throne, I will furnish you with a trained force of five thousand."

The prince stopped, but did not turn. "No. My sister protects us here. She is all we have, and she is all we need. I cannot risk what is for what might be."

"It's as good a chance as—"

"*Chances* do not interest me, Princess Lu. I am a steward, not a gambler. You have a good claim to the throne, but nothing else. No army, no allies. Not even the clothes on your back belong to you—"

"She has *my* army."

As one, the room turned to seek the voice, like the tide following the moon. Lu whipped her head around to see Nasan standing alone and tall in the crowd.

"Oh, indeed, does she?" Prince Shen retorted, his dour gravity giving way to something new—a glimmer of arrogance, of tired cynicism. "And what pretty promises did she pay you for it, Ashina Child?"

Nasan shrugged, refusing to be baited. "The return of our lands—the Gifted lands—in the event of her victory. No more than we are owed."

Lu felt the controlled mask of her face slip and threaten to crash to the stone floor. If Nasan had wanted to support her in her plea, they should have organized a plan beforehand, presented themselves as a unified front.

"Brother," Prince Jin rose from his seat at the side of the stage, interrupting her thoughts. "Perhaps we could consider—"

"We cannot!" Prince Shen snapped, whirling on his brother, sending the younger prince back into his little chair. Then, in a quieter voice, "The risk is too great."

Prince Jin uttered a sound of frustration. For half a breath he looked torn, but then he sprang back to his feet. "Perhaps a risk like this is just what we need now!"

"One that could destroy us entirely? I think not."

"Is it better to live in this limbo? This stasis? Each day our numbers dwindle. Our people grow older, more isolated. What sort of life is that for us? For them?"

"It is better to live in this 'stasis,' as you call it, than to die out completely," countered his brother. "We cannot trust these imperials—"

"Prince Shen," Lu rose to her knees, voice quavering. "The empire is here, at your doorstep. You can receive it either as Set—death, destruction—or me, offering friendship, hope for all our futures. You have every reason to be wary, but I am not my father, nor my grandfather. I give you my word."

"How can I trust your word? You are not bound to us by any tangible means. You are not one of us," Prince Shen replied coolly.

"What if," Prince Jin said slowly. "What if she *were* one of us?"

"What do you mean?" his brother demanded.

Prince Jin strode from his seat now, down to where Lu

knelt. At first, his step was tentative, light, but he seemed to grow more confident the closer he came to her. "Princess Lu, your plea has touched my heart. I will vouch for you in any way that I can."

He extended his hand.

"Thank you," Lu said cautiously, accepting it. He drew her to her feet.

"What if," Jin said, his eyes never leaving hers, "we were to unite our kingdoms through family."

Family? Lu frowned, caught off balance. "I-I'm afraid I don't understand."

"Marry me," Prince Jin blurted. For a moment, he looked years younger—a boy no older than twelve. Then, quick as it had appeared, the child in him blinked away, replaced by the handsome young man.

"I will be your husband, your consort, live my days in your southern city. I will be the eyes and ears and wisdom and trust of Yunis, at your side. Surely my brother cannot ask for a more tangible bond than his own flesh and blood. Marry me, Princess, and you will have our army. *Your* army."

There was a ringing silence, as though Prince Jin had sucked all the air from the room with his words. Then came pandemonium. Shouts of outrage mingled with shouts of shocked glee and hushed, rapid whispers. Lu had the distinct impression this was the most excitement the people of Yunis had seen in a very long time.

There must have been a thousand eyes on her, but she turned and found Nokhai's at once.

His were black and still and faraway. The smile was gone from his lips. She thought frantically: *I would do anything to bring it back.*

A lie. She already knew what she was going to do.

Prince Shen seized the heavy poleax from a guardsman's hands, banging the butt of it against the dais. "Quiet! Quiet!"

As the crowd went still, Lu turned away from Nokhai and took care not to look at him again.

Prince Shen was glowering at his brother. "Jin, what you propose is unprecedented."

"Yes," the younger man agreed earnestly. "And why not? We live in unprecedented times."

Prince Shen's brow furrowed as he stared at Jin, searching his face, looking for some hint of—what, exactly? Weakness? Doubt? But Prince Jin looked back boldly, chin held high.

"Do you really wish this, little brother?" Shen's voice was softened with disbelief.

"I wish for hope," Prince Jin responded, his voice quavering now, not with fear, but with fervor. "Hope for a better future for our city. Hope that our people might someday flourish, rather than just cower and merely survive."

"Prince Shen!" Lu cried out. She walked to the top step of the dais. The room was so quiet she could hear the rustle of her crimson robes—*wrong, the wrong red.*

Prince Shen turned to watch her ascent. How did she look? Proud, defiant, tall? A woman grown? She could only hope.

"Will you honor your brother's proposal?" she demanded. "If Prince Jin and I marry, will I have my army?"

There was a long silence. Then, "You will," the prince said at last. "If you would have my brother, and the terms of our future peace, you will have our army."

Lu lowered her head. "Prince Jin," she began, and found it was not as difficult as she might have thought to keep her voice steady. "I accept your offer."

CHAPTER 31

Emptiness

*P*rincess Lu was the sole still thing in the room, the eye of a storm, the axis upon which the winds turned. She was staring at Prince Jin as though seeing him for the first time.

The gathered crowd kicked back into an uproar. Five hundred different opinions seeking to be told at once. Nok flinched at the cacophony, the voices clashing and breaking over one another like soldiers in battle.

"Clever," Nasan mused beside him. "A marriage binds Yunis's fate with Lu's. Yunis is desperate for a chance to become a real city again, and the princess is desperate for an army. This way, win or lose, they're in it together. She's smart to take the offer."

Too late, Nok realized he should say something in response. He nodded.

He never heard Prince Shen dismiss the court, but suddenly everyone was migrating toward the doorways at the rear of the hall. Nok stayed where he was, far away from all of it. Perhaps it was some quality of the Inbetween that spun his head so, made him feel as though he were drifting on the edge of a precipice, dizzy and strange. The hole in his side throbbed tender and overly warm.

"Come on." Nasan nudged his leg with the toe of her boot. "It's over. Get up. Let's go."

"What?" he said.

"I'll take you to the apartments they gave us," his sister said. Then she peered down at him. "Are you all right? You look even paler than before."

Prince Jin emerged from the crowd before them and Nok blinked, looking at him much as Lu had: as though for the first time. He tried not to recoil.

"Nokhai?" the prince said. He was polite as ever, but his eyes were lively and distracted, scanning the faces of the audience— perhaps to gauge their reaction to his proposal? "My sister, Vrea, would like a word with you."

Jin gestured to where the priestess stood, long and solemn and gray upon the dais beside Prince Shen. Lu crossed in front of the two of them just then, directed off the dais by a group of ladies-in-waiting. She didn't see Nok at all. He forced his eyes not to follow her. What was the point? He felt a lance of self-hatred in his gut.

Everyone always leaves me, he'd told her. And why should she be any different?

"Nokhai?" Prince Jin peered anxiously at him.

Nok looked from him to the priestess to Nasan. His sister just shrugged, as if to say, *it's up to you.*

"All right," he said uncertainly.

Nok looked back at the woman called Vrea. She nodded almost imperceptibly when Nok met her gaze. She walked off the dais, toward a door leading out the back. He followed after her.

The door led out onto a wide stone balcony, large enough to accommodate a garden with a pair of bubbling fountains on either end.

Nok felt a presence at his back and turned. Vrea was standing by the edge of the balcony, just outside the door. He'd walked right past her. At her side stood a wolf.

His wolf.

"That's mine," Nok said stupidly.

"It is," she agreed. Then she cocked her head. "You hurt."

"I . . . excuse me?"

The woman smiled and gestured for him to come closer. He did so, not without trepidation. In the pale, overcast light of the Inbetween, she looked even paler than she had inside, almost translucent. He had the strangest sense she was somehow drifting out of sight, impossible to catch in his focus. Like trying to look at someone under the slippery duress of twilight.

He thought of the ghost stories whispered among the Kith children in his youth—demons in the dunes, tricky ghouls emerging like vapor from the walls of caves. Eerie women like smoke in the night, coaxing foolish young boys to their deaths. A shiver tripped down the notches of his spine.

She's just a woman, he told himself. *Just a very tall, very pale woman. Don't be stupid.*

He took another step toward her, as though to prove to

himself that he was not afraid. He focused on the wolf—his wolf—at her side. It was not afraid; why should he be?

Vrea stroked an idle hand over the animal's broad head, and Nok felt the tips of her fingernails on his own scalp. "You hurt," she said again.

"No," he protested. "That is . . . what?"

Vrea smiled her slow smile. "Allow yourself to feel it, Nokhai. The hurt."

"I—"

The priestess slid closer, soundless and solemn as night. He willed himself not to take a step backward. The wolf stayed behind, and for a moment he thought he saw it flicker, like a mirage.

"When you have lived as many lives as I have, you start to understand hurt differently," Vrea told him. "Hurt and loss. And love. You recognize how short it all is, in the entirety of everything. But nevertheless, hurt is still hurt. Love is still love. They are real—insistently so—no matter how brief. And they must be heeded."

"I-I don't know what you're talking about," Nok said, flinching.

She stared with eerie, bottomless eyes, not unkindly.

"Forgive me," she said, her voice languid and low. "I'd forgotten. Humans have such shame about their feelings, don't they? And yet, they have so many of them. It must be very tiring."

"I . . ." He frowned. *Humans? What was* she?

Just a woman, he reminded himself. A tall, pale woman.

"I don't mean to be rude," he said tentatively, "but why did you want to speak with me?"

"Of course," she mused. "You must be exhausted. Your body is still healing. I will be direct."

"Thank you," he said.

"Nokhai, you are an odd creature. The only one left of your kind."

"The Ashina?" he blurted. "I'm not the last. Nasan, my sister. There's two of us. And there are a bunch more Gifted—"

"No, Nokhai. Not an Ashina. A Pactmaker," Vrea said. "Do you know what this means? The magnitude of your importance?"

"No. That is, yes, I know what it is. But, I . . ." He thought of his mother. His father. They never would have—they wouldn't believe it. Tears stung his eyes. He was suddenly bone tired. "I-I don't want it," he said, hating how young and small he sounded.

"People rarely want the things they get," Vrea said, her voice never losing its evasive, lilting quality, borne between cheer and melancholy. "But nevertheless, that gift is yours, and you must choose what to do with it."

She sighed. "These are the final days of Yunis. It has been foretold by our Mother and Father, the Ana and the Aba. Shen was displeased, troubled, when our little brother offered to leave this place, this Inbetween, to live among the earthbound, but I was not surprised. He is the third of the Triarch, closest to the earth, and I think he specifically, our little Jin, has always longed for it. He tires of this place. And humanity intrigues him."

"What do you mean these are the last days of Yunis?" Nok demanded. "Are you saying you're going to lose the war?"

And does Lu know?

"Will we lose the war?" Vrea repeated, smiling faintly. "That has not been told to me, not in so many words. What I do know is we should be prepared for the end, whatever that may mean. And that is in part where you come in."

"Me?"

"After the imperial scouring of the North, and the breaking of all your Kith Pacts, the beast gods—the Gift Givers, as you called them—came back to the Inbetween, their ties with the earth and its people—your people—broken. The gods are like ghosts, here. It is not where they belong. They need a people. That is their purpose. And once the days of Yunis are over, I fear their spirits will be lost forever. Perhaps this means they will return to roam and haunt the earth as phantoms. Or perhaps they will die, as only a god can. Which is to say . . . ," she paused, cocking her head. "Very painfully. It has been a long, long time since a god has died. Longer than the stretch of my memory. From what I understand, it pulls a great deal of energy from all the realms when it happens. It can be quite . . . cataclysmic."

"Cataclysmic?" Nok repeated. "Like, an earthquake?"

Vrea considered. "Perhaps. If an earthquake could happen not only to the ground, but to the water, the air, the very blood in your body."

"What . . . what would that look like?"

"It is best if this does not happen." She refocused upon him shrewdly. "When we leave this place, someone will need to lead the beast gods to a purpose. A home. Someone will need to be their steward. Someone with your particular gift, Nokhai. How convenient you should stumble across our threshold."

He ignored the pointed look she gave him. "When you say you're leaving . . . what does that mean?" he asked. "Why don't you just take the beast gods with you?"

"Where we go, they cannot follow."

"What's stopping them?"

"If a cloud asked you to follow it up into the sky, could you do it?"

Nok looked to see if she were joking. She was smiling again, but he'd already learned that meant little. "You could not, am I correct?"

"Where is it exactly that you're going?"

She was silent for a long while, then said, "What do you suppose is beyond the sky, Pactmaker? This mantle of white and gray you see above us?"

He shrugged. The question made him think about things he'd rather not. "My people said the heavens."

"And you? What do you say?"

"More of the same, I guess," he said. "A lot of nothing."

"Oh, but you can't mean that. A boy with your gifts, your depth. Do try again."

"What does it matter what I think?" he demanded.

"You asked where we are going. I believe it is customary to supply a question with an answer, no?"

"Where I come from, answers generally don't come in the form of new questions."

"You grow impatient. Very well. Where we go, we cannot fathom until we are there. Does a fish comprehend the land before it has been plucked from the sea? Or, better yet, does a tree comprehend a house before it is cut and hewn to form the walls? Who we are, here, now . . . we are like the tree. Unknowing, unformed, unused."

Nok's head swam. "I think you're better off the way you are now. Who wants to be cut up and turned into something else?"

"Sometimes uncertainty is better than languishing in the familiar—my brother Jin was not wrong about that."

Nok shrugged. "Better safe and bored than dead, I'd say."

"Do not mistake cynicism for wisdom, child; it's very tedious," Vrea tutted. "Where we go is unknown. It is endless. The emptiness. That is what lies beyond the sky."

"Like I said: nothing."

"Emptiness is not nothing. It is a space waiting to be filled. It is all possibility. It could be anything, so it is everything."

Nok did not know what to make of that. He leaned heavily against the balcony.

"I've exhausted you," Vrea said.

"No," he replied. "My wound exhausted me. You just . . . confused me."

She laughed—a strange, almost perverse sound. "You're funny. That's interesting."

"Is it?" he said, gazing past the edge of the balcony for the first time. To his surprise, they were overlooking water. For a moment he thought it must be the lake where they had encountered the imperials, but, no, he realized. Small frothy waves curled up along the edge of the shore, ceaselessly dashing themselves apart against the sand. It was no lake at all, but a sea. Farther out, the mirrored surface reflected the gray, cloud-dense sky above.

There was no smell, he realized. No brackish fishy tinge to the air the way there was along the harbor back home.

Was Yulan City home, now? *Home*. Where was that?

"I can't stay," he said. "I owe a debt to someone."

"Omair is welcome to join you."

He looked at her, surprised.

"Princess Lu," she explained. "She told my brother Jin of your quest. Your obligations to him. But after Omair has been freed by your princess and her new army, return here. Claim your rightful place."

"My rightful place?" He stifled the urge to scoff. "I wouldn't know what that is. I-I'm no one. I've been no one—"

"For far too long," Vrea said firmly. "You are the only one of your kind, Nokhai. The only one who can restore the Pacts, bring order back to your gods. Bring life—real life—back to what remains of your people."

Something cold touched his hand; he looked down and saw the wolf nosing at him. He ran a tentative hand through the blue-silver hairs behind its ears, sunk his fingers into the plush ruff of its neck.

"See how it longs for you?" Vrea murmured. "The bond you have with it is insistent—a force of nature."

"So why can't I control the caul?"

As though understanding his words, the wolf pulled back. Vrea held out her hand and maddeningly, the wolf slid toward her, slunk behind the sweep of her robes, peering out at Nok reproachfully.

"Your people had ceremonies for binding people to their cauls, did they not?"

"Yes," Nok said. "People did them when they came of age. But I don't know what they entailed, since I didn't have the Gifting Dream back when I was supposed to. Nasan had the Dream early, but she was too young for the ceremony. And now everyone who knew what to do is dead."

"We could help you find an equivalent means for the bonding," Vrea mused. "I am certain I could convene with the Ana and the Aba to work out a solution. If you stayed, we could do this for you."

Nok bit back a sigh of frustration. "The wolf seems to understand you. Can't you—I don't know, tell it to come to me?"

"I can no more force its will than I could your own. And I would not, even given the opportunity. One's caul is their own; that bond is sacred. It is a part of you, a part of your spirit. Your heart."

"So why won't it *listen* to me?"

That seemed to amuse the priestess. "Often we do not listen to ourselves. Forgive the expression, but it's only human."

He watched the wolf. Again it seemed to dim—fading just slightly, retreating a step, and then another. Then it turned and slipped straight through the stone balustrade of the balcony, dissipating like fog in the morning.

Nok stared at the space where it had been.

"Can I think about it?" he said finally. "Your offer?"

"Of course. In the meantime, you are our honored guest. We've given you and your friends an apartment right in the Heart—I think you will find them comfortable. Heal, relax. Think. It is a serious decision you make." Then she smiled in her vague, neither-here-nor-there way. "Take all the time you need. Ours is running out, but what we have left we are happy to share with you."

⁂

When Nok pushed his way back into the hall he ran headlong into Nasan.

"You're in a hurry," she said. "Do you even know where you're going? Come on, I'll take you back to our apartments."

He fell in step alongside her.

"So, that Vrea's a strange one," Nasan said as they descended the stairs leading out of the throne room and into the Heart. Her tone was light, but he could hear the curiosity girding her voice. The asking without asking.

"You were eavesdropping," he said flatly. It wasn't an accusation, but it wasn't a question, either. "How much did you hear?"

His sister shrugged, utterly unabashed. No less than he expected from her.

"Everything, then. Well, go on," he said. "I'm sure you have an opinion."

"No opinion." She shook her head. "What're you going to do?"

He scrubbed the heels of his palms against his eyes. "I have no idea, Nasan. My options are either to try and become this . . . this mythological hero of old, this *savior* like they want me to be, or to let down the entire pantheon of gods . . . ," he broke off. "This is madness." He barked out a laugh. "Can you imagine what Father would say if he were here? His failure—his mistake of a son. He'd never believe it."

Nasan stopped in the dead of the empty Heart, and spun to meet his eyes. "Don't say that."

"It's true," he countered. "You know it's true. He saw—he thought I was worthless."

"Ba, he . . ." Nasan sighed, for the first time seeming to struggle with her words. "I loved him—"

"And he loved *you*." The words wrenched out of him, harsher and more accusatory than he'd intended.

"I loved him," Nasan repeated firmly. "But he was wrong about you, Nok. What he did to you was wrong. How he saw you was wrong. I think if he were here now, he'd see that, and he'd be sorry. He'd be proud."

Was it true? Was that even what he wanted, after all this time? "It doesn't matter," Nok muttered. Tears stung his eyes. He blinked them away, forced them back down. "It's too late. What good is it, finding out I have that . . . that power, when everyone who was worth saving is dead and gone?"

"There are others, other Kith," she reminded him. "Wandering the deserts, lost without their Gifts, lost without the Pact. And there are my kids—Ony and the others."

He looked sharply at her. *If I said yes to Vrea,* he thought. *This would give Nasan everything she wanted. A second life for the Gifted.* He felt a flush of shame at the thought. *She's my sister. Don't be an idiot. She wants what's best for you.*

Didn't she?

"Maybe," he said aloud. "Maybe it would help them. But it would still be me. I could—I don't know, I'd find a way to muck it up. I'm just . . . gods, Nasan. How am I supposed to carry the weight of all those people? I couldn't even take care of you, back at the camps. All I had to do was keep you safe, and I failed!"

"It wasn't your fault, Nok. You know that, right? We were kids. *You* were just a kid."

"But I was older. I was supposed to protect you—"

"And you did. For as long as you could. You did good, big brother."

"It wasn't enough," he said. Her screams echoed out from the past, from all those years ago . . . *I won't let them take me!*

"Listen," said the Nasan that stood before him now. "If you need me to forgive you, I forgive you. You did your best. And you succeeded—I'm alive."

He looked up. In her face he saw both the mischievous little child she had been and the cagey, sardonic girl she had become, and the years lost between them. She reached forward and gave him an affectionate tap on the shoulder. It felt rather like a punch, but he understood she meant well.

"I lived, Nok," she told him. "It's time you did, too."

CHAPTER 32

The Key

*T*here was no sign of Lu along the gray lake. The water was placid, unremarkable. But when Min scuffed the toe of her boot against the shore, slivers of iridescent crystal surfaced amid the flat gray stones. She raised the pendant around her neck for comparison. It caught the pale overcast light, throwing rainbows across her chest, the silk of her skirts. The shards at her feet certainly could be the same material.

She stooped to pick one up, choosing a large piece unlikely to break. "Butterfly," she called.

"Yes, Pr—Empress." The nuna was instantly at her side, her pretty face nervous. Set had told Min she could select one nuna to join them on the ride north, and Butterfly was the clear choice—clever and resourceful.

Truly she seemed the only choice after the incident with the windows—after the *change,* as Min had come to think of it. The other nunas had scarcely been able to meet her eyes afterward; Snowdrop quailed when they were even in the same room, as though Min might strike her.

Stupid girl.

Aloud, she told Butterfly, "Put this crystal in my saddlebag."

"Yes, Empress." Butterfly took the crystal and all but fled. Even bold, witty Butterfly was afraid of her now.

That might have upset Min once. Before. Or would it have? In a way, fear was preferable to the other girl's usual patronizing affection—as though she thought Min couldn't see through it.

Min's mother had taken to bed in shock and grief for days after the change. She'd been unable to rise even when Amma Ruxin came to alert her of Min's departure north. That seemed a bit much, but it was just as well. Min wasn't quite ready to face her; not yet.

She will understand when I return. She'll see. Set will be pleased and no longer so quick to anger. And then I will give him sons, and we'll raise them to be just and honorable heirs. And Lu . . .

She faltered, casting a glance down the shore. Set was there, dismounting his horse to speak with Brother. Her cousin—her *husband*. She watched him warily, trying to gauge his mood.

The day before, a frantic messenger had told them imperial scouts had spotted Princess Lu in the hills around the lake—and lost her. Set had thrown a lit oil lamp at the man in fury. It missed, but it set a featherbed on fire where it landed. It had taken three servants to stomp out the flames.

Afterward, Brother's eyes had widened hearing the soldiers' account of how the princess had been cornered at the edge of the lake along with an utterly massive wolf, only to disappear in a strange, sudden fog. Their own party—Set, Brother, Min, and an additional two hundred troops—had ridden through the night to reach the lake.

They were all tired, but the journey seemed to be wearing on Set especially. He was calm now at least. But his anger could rise quickly, she knew. She remembered how he'd grabbed her, given her to Brother to slash with a knife like a pig—*no*. She didn't want to think about that. She wouldn't.

The wind changed direction and motes of Set and Brother's conversation floated down the shore toward her.

". . . Perhaps they allowed her in? Is that even possible?" Set was asking, accepting a rolled cigarette from one of his men. He lit it, waving smoke from his face. That was a new thing, Min noted—she'd never seen her cousin smoke in the capital, but now he inhaled cigarettes like a thirsty man downed water.

Brother eyed the cigarette in her cousin's hands now and pursed his lips, but he merely said, "The Inbetween is a place of mystery, and the mountains hold great power. Old power. Those who were born of it may exercise some control over its boundaries. In my research—"

"If there's a chance . . . if there was *any* way, I guarantee you she made it in. We need to find her," Set said testily.

"You have the sister," reassured the monk. "Your claim is safe. Lu is a fugitive. She's finished."

"You don't know her!" Set snapped, tapping ash from his cigarette. "As long as there's breath in her body, she'll come for me. She's *obsessed*."

"Your exhaustion is making you paranoid," Brother chided. "And I don't like all this smoking, Set. You must keep your energy focused on the goals ahead. If this expedition comes to naught, so be it. We can return to the capital, you can build up coalition support there. And I can continue to train Min. Learn to cultivate and harness her powers."

Set exhaled a flume of smoke. "What she did with the windows . . . she has power, that much is clear. But do you really think she'll be able to learn to control something like that?" The uncertainty on his face was so muddled it took Min a moment to see it for what it was: fear. Revulsion. It felt like a slap, followed by an odd gnawing emptiness in her belly.

"Patience. I told you, the girl must have time and instruction. She is your greatest asset whether you can see it or—"

"Yes, yes," her cousin said dismissively. "Do what you need with her. I'm going to send my men to search the perimeter of the lake for Lu." He stamped his cigarette out beneath one dust-hoary boot, then stared down at the crushed husk of paper and char. The harsh light of the steppe threw into relief his sallow skin, the violet-gray exhaustion pooling beneath his eyes.

"What of the wolf she was with?" he asked. "That couldn't have been an ordinary animal. I thought we killed all of that slipskin Kith—whatever they were called."

"The Ashina," supplied Brother. "And yes, their Kith was destroyed. A few of their children made it into the labor camps, but none of them retained their cauls. I tried to find some way to rebind the Pact, discover where in their bodies that linkage was hidden, but to no—"

"You appear to have missed something."

"It's possible that this wolf the scouts saw was an escapee or a deserter. Or perhaps it was only a dog, and the men were confused." The monk shrugged. "Of course, there is always the notion of an original slipskin. A Pactmaker, according to their myths."

"Yes," Set said irritably. "Myths."

"Myths are what common men call history distorted by time."

"No matter." Set shrugged, throwing his shoulders back and sniffing. "Whatever it was, I'll find and kill it, too. Myth or not." Then he put his foot into a stirrup and gracefully leaped back into his saddle.

"It may be of use to me alive," Brother said thoughtfully. "For my research."

But Set was already riding restlessly down the shore.

Min looked out across the water, searching again in vain for some hidden sign that her sister had stood there.

Lu, where are you? I've come to bring you home, she thought, but the words felt hollow somehow. Even if Min was able to convince her to surrender, then—what, exactly?

As long as there's breath in her body, she'll come for me. The echo of Set's words chilled her now.

Her sister would never be content to spend out her days in court with no hope of ruling, Min realized. To Lu, that fate would be no different from death. Worse.

But perhaps . . . Min frowned at the still water. Set might not allow Lu to return to court, but perhaps he would allow her to live the rest of her days in exile or sequestered somewhere well outside the capital.

She could stay at the Eastern Palace, Min thought with renewed hope. *She always loved it there, swimming in the lake . . .*

Min was the *key*, Brother had said. Set needed her. She could use that, surely, leverage herself to win clemency for her sister.

But was she enough? What was she here, in this barren and desolate place, all on her own? Without a city. No mother, no shins, no ammas to train her, to shame her. Here, she was just a girl—flesh and blood and bone. A body.

And locked within that body, a secret. Her curse, her gift.

I've brought you here, she thought. *It's your turn. We had a deal, so where are you?*

"You already have all you need, silly girl." The shamaness's voice was fainter than it had been before. She sounded almost tired. Min found it somehow frightening. *"Don't you see? I'm already here, already in you."*

Min frowned. *But I don't know what to* do.

"You will."

When? She demanded. *You're the one with the magic, you're the one who does . . . everything.*

"I am just an echo, girl," said the voice with a sigh, thin as mountain air. *"I am what she chose to leave in you. You control me, not the other way around. I suppose it's easier for you to pretend otherwise . . . "*

Min turned at the sound of footsteps crunching over the stones and met the eerie piercing eyes of Brother. The old man's face slid into an oily smile.

"You look well, Princess," he told her. "Each step we draw farther north, you seem to grow stronger. Surer of yourself."

She didn't *feel* strong, just stiff from riding all night. She stepped back, a hand going to the bandage plastered to her throat like a choker.

The monk smiled, all understated sorrow and manners. "I do apologize again for that—you must know I would never have actually hurt you."

But you did hurt me. You made me bleed. And Set . . . Set had told him to do it. But, no. Hadn't she already decided not to think about that?

Brother stepped closer and she smelled the stink of his sweat. None of them had slept more than a few hours at a time since they left the capital, and there had been no opportunity for washing. "There was once a physical gate here—you can see the remains of it if you look closely at the ground," he told her. "My research suggests the Yunians placed these gates at points in the earth where the barrier between our world and the next is thinner, more penetrable. Do you sense something?"

"No—I don't think so," Min admitted. She didn't even know what she was meant to feel.

Set approached astride his stallion, followed at a distance by a small group of his men. "Well?" he called out.

Min's body relaxed at the prospect of no longer being alone with Brother. But she recoiled as Set drew closer. His handsome face was strained and sweaty, and his eyes wilder than she had ever seen. She'd been wrong earlier; despite his outward restraint he looked even worse than he had the night before. Loose hairs fell from his normally immaculate plait. But something else was wrong, too, something deeper than all his frayed trappings. He was changed—changing—as sure as she was.

It's Lu, Min realized at last. *She's not obsessed; he is.* The thought made her stomach tighten with anger . . . and an odd twinge of jealousy. If only Lu wasn't so *difficult.* Min was trying to help, but how could one help someone so set against helping herself?

"Patience," Brother told Set, his eyes still trained eagerly on Min. "Give her time to gain a sense of this place. She is untrained, but I trust it will speak to her yet." He licked his lips.

Min looked down, watching the water lap benignly at the shore. Once more, she saw Lu, diving into the unknown deep of that other silvery lake years ago. Swimming away from her.

She'd wanted to follow, Min remembered suddenly. How had she forgotten that? But she hadn't followed; she'd been too afraid. Of the void under the mirrored surface of the water, of the punishment that would await when they returned.

And in that moment, she'd hated her sister for not being afraid, for believing there was something in that unknown beyond, something that she deserved to discover. Her sister . . .

Liar. She felt the presence then, the other, the something else—someone else—flare in her blood. And she knew.

Lu is not my sister, Min realized—admitted—at last. *Not fully. Not truly.*

The thought should have made her sad. Instead, she felt an odd sort of relief. It all made sense now. They no longer belonged to one another, and they never had. Lu owed her nothing, and she owed nothing in return. They were two tangled strings that had finally come unknotted. She was free—and she could be who she wanted, who she was meant to be all along. She would no longer be defined in relief with a sister. She would be defined only by herself.

Min shivered and closed her eyes. Forced herself to burrow

down into the seat of her rage, where that seed was planted. To follow its ravenous growth, radiant and consuming as fire, all through her bones. To the tips of her fingers, the ends of her hair. The whole of her hummed with it. Energy seeking release. Absently, her hand went again to her chest, clutching the crystal pendant that rested there. It felt hot to the touch, warmer than flesh.

"It may help for you visualize the gate," Brother was saying. "Just look, wait for it to come to you—don't be afraid."

"I am not afraid," Min said sharply, dropping the crystal back down to her chest. Her eyes were open. There was no need to visualize the gate. She could see it now, shimmering at the water's edge. A rupture in the air. A gesture at all the unknown energy—the opportunity—that lay beyond.

She raised her hands and *pulled* the energy toward her. It hit with the force of a boulder, a wall of blinding light made solid and also not—something beyond materiality. Pure sensation. Hot and cold all at once. Her blood was afire, her veins were starlight. She felt it enter her, an ocean surging through the flesh of her palms and flooding deep down into her core. It filled her to brimming and overflowed back out a hundredfold.

The stones beneath their feet blew like dead leaves. The air twisted around them in a suffocating tornado. Behind her, the horses reared. Someone screamed, and perhaps it was she, or perhaps it was all of them.

Through the pandemonium she heard Set's voice, so clear it seemed to be right in her ear. "Gods, what has she *done?*"

She did not flinch. She did not lower her hands. As ever, the voice inside was both hers and not, but it belonged to her all the same.

What has she done?

What I was born to do.

CHAPTER 33

The Blue

Lu dismissed her Yunian handmaidens at the door of the apartments she'd been sharing with Nasan. The women left as commanded, but Lu couldn't quite shake the feeling they'd have preferred to stay and watch over her. The Yunians had all been consummately polite—there was no question whether she was their guest or their prisoner—but she could sense that they did not quite trust her.

Fair enough, she thought, not without some bitterness. Between them, Nasan, and everyone from there to Yulan City, she was growing accustomed to the feeling. Seeing the damage her father and his father before him had wrought, she could hardly blame them. It was exhausting, though, this constant scrutiny.

She watched the handmaidens disappear down the corridor before closing the large wooden doors behind them. She sighed and stepped into a large common room, spacious and clean, its cream-colored marble floors and stone walls softened by a cozily lit fire pit at the center. Crowded around it were tuffets and heaps of shaggy carpets.

Beyond the fire pit stood a long stone table, laden with trays of rice and dumplings and cakes, unfamiliar fruits, and an array of colored liquids in crystal decanters. They never saw who brought the food or who took it away. It simply appeared around mealtimes, then vanished while they were asleep. Nasan found it spooky. Lu thought it not so different from the silent manner in which the servants would bring her dinner at home.

No wonder Nasan didn't trust her. No wonder *Nokhai* didn't trust her. She inhabited a different world than they did, one where plenty was so ubiquitous as to be invisible.

Or perhaps there was something ill in her. Something inherently untrustworthy. Nasan seemed to think so. Certainly, Prince Shen and Priestess Vrea had done nothing to assuage that feeling today.

As for Prince Jin, was he as stalwart an ally as he let on? Could he be as naïve and well intentioned as he seemed? Had the Triarch schemed together to produce the outcome he'd offered her? Or did he have a deeper, private scheme at play?

Maybe he's just sick of all the gray here.

Behind her, the doors opened with a groan.

"Princess! You shouldn't have gone through all this trouble!" Nasan said, waving toward the food.

She made the same joke every day. Lu rolled her eyes. Then Nokhai slunk in behind his sister.

He looked even thinner up close, and his black eyes were sunken, rimmed, but alert as ever, roving around the room, as though seeking out missed dangers.

She wanted to run to him, she wanted to hold him, she wanted—but it didn't matter what she wanted anymore. She'd already made her choice, even if it had felt like she didn't have one.

"You look well," she told him.

Nokhai's mouth jerked up at the corner. "Do I?"

"He's hard to kill." Nasan took the room in a few bold strides and snagged a golden-skinned fruit from the table. "Runs in the family," she added, flinging herself onto a pile of carpets by the fire and taking wet, noisy bites of fruit.

Nokhai followed her, sitting on an overstuffed cushion. Not wanting to be left out, Lu toed off her slippers and joined them, her bare feet clammy against the radiantly heated stone floors.

"So," Nasan said as Lu sat. "I think that Prince Jin likes you."

Lu flinched, hazarding a glance at Nok, but he was studying the carpet.

"You should have seen the way he looked at her when we first came upon you two on the beach," Nasan told her brother. Lu flushed, wishing more than ever that she would shut up. "It was like he'd never seen a girl before."

As Nasan spoke, she walked back and forth between the table and where they sat, ferrying trays of food and drink with her. Once, she laid a plate of savory pastries upon Nokhai's lap, but he only stared at it.

It worried Lu—he ought to eat as much as he could, in his state—but she thought she understood how he felt. The aromatic foods stirred nothing in her, either. There was too much happening to focus on something as mundane as eating. She turned her palms toward the flames. The heat felt nice, at least. Nokhai didn't move, but his eyes flicked up, tracking her movements.

"So, you've got what you wanted now, don't you?" Nasan said. "Yunis in your pocket, an army at your back."

"And a prince at your side."

Lu's head jerked up at Nokhai's words. The silence that hung between them was metallic, ringing.

"Well, let's have a toast to the future Emperor Lu," Nasan said, stooping to fetch one of the decanters by her feet. She took a messy swig before thrusting it into Nok's hands. He considered the amber-colored liquid before taking a cautious sip.

His face crumpled. "Oh gods. That tastes awful."

Nasan just laughed and plucked the bottle from his hands. "You'd never guess, but these Yunians know how to make a hard brew."

"To Emperor Lu!" she proclaimed, taking another brazen swallow. She handed the bottle to Lu with an exaggerated bow.

Lu raised it, essaying a wry smile. "And to both of you." Then she drank.

Fire tore through her throat, pricking tears into the corners of her eyes. "Oh . . . my," she choked out. They laughed.

"So," Nasan said, reclaiming the decanter. "When does our army leave?"

Lu arched an eyebrow. "Our army?"

"Yes, *our* army. Our armies, if you prefer."

Lu let it go. They had a good deal of negotiating and planning to do between them; the last thing they needed was to quibble over language. "The Triarch and I still need to sort out the details—"

"And when are we going to do that?" Nasan interrupted, thrusting the decanter back into her hands.

Lu took a perfunctory sip. *It's just language*, she reminded herself, but she could not stop from repeating, "We?"

"Yes." Nasan swiped the decanter back again and drained the last of it. "*We*. I'm not getting edged out just because you found yourself a bigger, shinier army to help you. Our deal still stands."

"Of course it does," Lu said with forced calm. "I keep my word."

"That's good to hear, Princess. That's very good to hear. Because your people don't exactly have a reputation for it."

Before Lu could formulate a response, Nasan stood, fetching a stack of brass-plated cups into which she poured sloppy, generous slugs of garnet-colored wine.

The room felt overly hot, stifling. An effect of the alcohol. Agitated, Lu stood and unclasped her fur mantle, letting it fall. Then she shrugged off the floor-sweeping outer layer of her scarlet robes, leaving only loose-fitted trousers and a sleeveless tunic that belted tightly at the waist.

As she sat again, she caught Nokhai's gaze skittering down her bare arms, before his eyes disappeared beneath the dark fringe of his lashes. Nasan watched him watching her; she raised an eyebrow, but for once made no comment.

"Are you sure you're up for all this, Princess?" she asked Lu, shoving a cup of wine into her hands. "You're putting a lot of lives on the line for a pretty crown and a fancy title."

Annoyance flared in Lu's chest. "Of course I'm ready. I was born for this. Duty demands it of me—it's not just about a title. My cause is just. I will save lives that Set would just as soon—"

Nasan snorted. "Your cause? Please. And when has your empire ever done justice to anyone? Everything it—everything *you*—stand for is counter to it."

Lu took a calming breath. "I am trying to rectify our past crimes. I will return your lands, and make certain nothing like what happened to you ever happens again."

"Things like what happened to us happen all the time, every day. What makes you so special that you could turn it around?"

It felt as if the other girl were taking a prybar to the door Lu had tamped down over her impatience. She forced her voice steady. "If you have such little faith in my abilities, then why work with me at all?"

"Because you're the only chance I've got. And *I* have an actual cause, Princess. I'm trying to save my people. Get back our land. We know what we're fighting for. What we're prepared to die for. I have to know that you understand the stakes as well."

Lu stared, disbelieving. "This isn't just about my life. Which—I don't think you fully appreciate—is on the line as well. This is about the fate of the empire and everyone in it."

"I'm not sure you even know what that means," Nasan said flatly. "The lives of others? Your title, your station—your very existence—is built on the subjugation, on the suffering of others."

"That—that's not me," Lu frowned. "That isn't what I want."

"Doesn't matter. You're playing a game and asking your new friends to sacrifice their lives for it. It comes naturally to you, to demand everything of everyone else."

Nasan took a swig of wine straight from the bottle, the cups she'd just poured apparently forgotten. Then she thrust it at Nok. He took it but did not drink, black eyes dithering between his sister's face and Lu's own.

"The way I see it," Nasan continued, "you and your cousin are no different than you were when we were kids—just two royal brats running around where they don't belong, fighting over who has the bigger stick. Not caring if everyone around you gets hurt, too."

Seeing Lu's reaction she smirked. "Oh, that's right, I remember what you did when we were kids. I was little, but I was old enough. I remember how you got my brother in trouble."

"Got him in—that was Set! I was trying to protect him!"

"He wouldn't have needed protecting if he hadn't gotten mixed up with you in the first place."

Lu looked at her disbelievingly. "I hardly see how befriending someone is—"

"Oh, 'befriending.' Is that what you city dwellers call it?"

"What's that supposed to mean?" Lu demanded.

"I don't know; what's it mean to you? What does my brother, or anyone you use along the way, mean to you?"

"I don't *use* anyone!"

Nasan scoffed. "You use everyone! Nok, the Yunians. You're using me—and I'm using you right back, but I'm out of options. At least I have the honesty to admit what I'm doing. You, you just draw people into your schemes, blackmail my brother with promises of saving his apothecarist friend. You agreed to *marry* some poor infatuated boy of all things—"

"I'm doing what needs to be done!" Lu stood so fast her cushion tipped sideways, knocking over a bowl. It shattered across the stone floor, sending candied nuts and shards of crystal skittering.

Lu leaped to the side to avoid cutting her bare feet and swayed—the drink was stronger than she'd thought. Her head rang with it, but she straightened. "How dare you presume to know anything about my life—"

Nasan stood and moved in on her. "I presume nothing, Princess. You're completely obvious—"

"Obvious?" Lu barked. "What happened to me being deceitful?"

"I never said you weren't a liar—just a bad one."

Lu shook her head. "If this is how you treat your allies, don't expect to get very far."

"Oh, should I do as you do and spread my legs for—"

"*Excuse me?*" Lu said, and surged toward her.

"You heard me," Nasan spat, not backing away. "Prince Jin fell for it, so I guess whatever works, right? And I see the way you look at my brother. Tell me, do you expect to keep him as a consort once you marry, or—"

Lu slapped her. Not hard—openhanded. Nasan turned with it to lessen the blow. Then lunged forward, shoving at Lu's shoulders, screaming incoherently in her face. Lu shoved back, refusing to give her any ground.

"Enough!" Nokhai yelled. He was between them, wedging them apart. "I'm right *here*. And I don't appreciate being used as some kind of bargaining tool"—he caught the sneer on Nasan's face—"by *either* of you."

Lu took a step back, breathing hard. That had been small of her, she knew. Beneath her. *The wine,* she thought.

"No," she agreed aloud. "Of course not."

"You're completely gone for her, aren't you?" Nasan said to her brother. "When I told you to live, I didn't mean you should do it as an imperial lapdog."

Nokhai flushed. "It's not like that, Nasan—"

"She's just going to hurt you, you know," Nasan interrupted, all agitation. "That's what people like her—that's what imperials do. That's what they *are.* I thought you of all people would know that by now."

When Nokhai didn't reply, Nasan shrugged coldly. "I can't listen to this. I'm going for a walk."

The heavy doors slammed behind her, leaving Lu and Nokhai alone in the cold silence.

Lu slumped down into her overturned cushion, dropping her head into her hands. She felt rather than heard Nok sit beside her. He didn't touch her, but she could sense the heat of him. The hair on her arms prickled with it.

"Nasan's afraid," Nok said. "She thinks now that you have the Yunians you'll abandon your deal with her."

Lu sat up with a ragged, desperate breath, like surfacing from a too-deep dive. "I told her I wouldn't," she said, begging him, at least, to believe her. Believe in her.

"I know," he said. "It's just . . . well, you know."

"How am I supposed to work with all these people if none of them are willing to trust me?" she asked.

"I don't know."

She resisted the urge to cover her face again with her hands and settled instead for rubbing them up and down her arms. Her fingers caught over the scar from the crossbow bolt she'd taken the day they'd met in the forest. They'd left the stitches in too long according to Nokhai, and it had healed puckered and jagged. She worried the skin with her nails, and his eyes drifted down, drawn by the movement.

It struck her then, how long they'd been traveling together— long enough for the blood flowing from the wound to slow and clot, for the wet, open flesh to mend and gnarl and harden. So much had changed since then.

"Do *you* trust me?" she asked.

He turned to her in surprise. "I . . ."

She smiled ruefully, casting her gaze back at the dying fire before them. *Never one for lying.*

"I trust . . . I trust your heart," Nokhai said after a breath. "Nasan's right. You can do a lot of harm without meaning to."

"Isn't that true of everyone?"

"I suppose." He grimaced. "You just happen to have a lot of power."

Your title, your station—your very existence—is built on the subjuga-tion, on the suffering of others. The specter of Nasan's words hung between them.

"What about you?" she blurted, sounding more accusa-tory than she intended. "You can change *shape*, Nokhai. You have a power—magic—that's all but lost to the rest of the world."

It wasn't the same, and she knew it. He must have as well,

but all he said was, "I know," looking down into his lap. "I-I'm trying to figure out what to do with that."

There was more. A weight in the gut, a pinch in his forehead, a taut wire pulling his shoulders in tight. She hadn't noticed it earlier, had been too caught up in her own worries, but now she couldn't see anything else. "What is it? What's happened?"

The question caught him off guard. Perhaps that was the only reason he answered honestly. "Vrea—the Oracle. She wants me to stay here. Learn from her how to care for the beast gods. Become a Pactmaker."

"What about Omair?"

He looked startled again, as though he hadn't expected her to remember. "She says he can come, too. Once we free him."

"That's good," Lu said. "That's—incredible. That would mean . . . you could bring the Gift back to Nasan, to your people. Not just your people—all those Gifted, too. That's— you could change everything."

He sighed, looking somewhat less delighted by the notion than she did. "Yes, I know."

She nodded slowly. "That's a lot of responsibility."

"It's just . . ." He hesitated. "It just seems too big for one person—for *me*. I never asked, never wanted to be . . . this."

"But it's good, Nokhai. How could anything but good come from this?"

He shook his head, frustrated. "You don't know that. I don't know that. Why couldn't it have been Nasan?" He laughed wryly. "The gods got it all wrong."

Lu grabbed his hand. "No," she said firmly. "Nokhai, you're as clever and thoughtful and clearheaded as anyone. Much more so than most. That you take this power so seriously shows the gods chose correctly. Wisely."

He was looking at their joined hands. "But I don't know what to do."

"You—you should do what you think is best. For *you*," she told him. "Do what will make you happy."

"Is that what you did? Did you choose what will make you happy?" There was a hint of venom in his voice. He didn't let go of her hand, though.

"You deserve to be happy, Nokhai," she said, not rising to the bait.

He met her gaze for a long moment before he slumped, the fight leaving him with a sigh. "Deserve?" He smiled sardonically. "That doesn't mean anything. People don't get what they deserve in this world. Things just happen, whether you earn them or not."

"It doesn't mean you have to punish yourself for every bad thing. It doesn't mean you have to push away every good thing."

"Is that what this is?" he asked, looking down at their linked hands. "A good thing?"

This time when she kissed him, he sank into it, like surrender, like it was a relief. His hands, tentative and gentle, found her face, brushed the hair from her neck. He let her push him back down into the cushion until she was on top of him. She put her hands on him, moved them over his shoulders, across his back, down to his waist. Felt him shift beneath his tunic, felt the heat of his skin beneath, felt the muscles contract beneath the skin—

"No, I can't," he mumbled, the words moving his lips out

of the kiss. "We can't." Renewed resolve wove threads of steel through his soft voice.

Lu drew back, lowered herself to the floor beside his knees. "Because of Jin?"

He looked away. "This was never going to be anything real, I know that. I'm not stupid. But I can't just . . ."

The air trembled, dissolved his words like salt in water. For a moment, Lu did not understand, and then she did: a sound. A roar. So big, so loud it exceeded what her ears could comprehend. Terrible and wrong and physical. She felt it everywhere, in the cold stone floor beneath her, in her teeth, in her blood. Every part of her shook with it.

It was gone as quick as it had come, replaced by a stillness near as terrifying—silent but for the high ringing in her head.

An earthquake? But Lu already knew the answer in her heart—nothing natural had moved the earth that way.

She had fallen over, but she stood now, reaching out instinctively to help Nokhai as he struggled to his feet. His lips were moving wordlessly. It took another moment, a hard shake of the head, for her hearing to return. Even when it did, his voice was dim and distant.

". . . you hurt?"

Lu shook her head again, half in an answer, half to clear it. "You?" She had the feeling she was shouting, but from the look on his face she could tell he couldn't hear her well either. He shook his head.

"What was that?" she said.

"Nothing good. We need to find Nasan," he said tersely. "She couldn't have gotten too far."

They went to the door, Lu grabbing her sword along the way. They moved stooped and cautious, wary of a second attack. With each moment that passed, none came, and soon enough they were trotting down the corridor, side by side. It wasn't unusual for the passageways to their apartments to be empty, but the silence chilled her now.

When they opened the doors that led out onto the Heart though, all was chaos. Streams of panicked people running, children and bundles of their most prized possessions in tow. They were making for the main temple—the most secure of the large buildings, shored against the mountain.

"Lu!"

She stopped at the sound of Nasan's voice and saw the girl standing at the top of the temple steps, Vrea at her side. Lu must've been easy to pick out in the crowd—the red slash of her tunic sticking out amid the gray.

"Come on," she said, grabbing Nokhai by the hand. They ran to the others, dodging the panicked Yunians dashing into the open temple doors.

"What's happened?" Lu looked between Vrea and Nasan.

"The city is under attack," Vrea said. Her face was calm, tracking something in the sky that Lu could not see. "They have found one of the gates."

"Who has?" Lu demanded. "My cousin?"

Before anyone could answer—was there even an answer to give?—Prince Jin ran up to his sister. "Shen gave orders for everyone to shelter in the temple. I'm sending soldiers to check all the homes, to make sure the elderly and sick are helped."

"Do you know what's happening, Jin?" Lu interrupted. "Who is behind this? Is this Set's doing?"

Before he could respond though, the second attack came. This time the roar was punctuated by a deafening crack, followed by a cacophony of screams from the Yunians flooding past them. Lu ducked, throwing her hands over her head.

Madness, she thought as the earth shook around them.

When she tried to stand, she found Prince Jin covering her, as though he meant to shield her with his own body. She gently pushed him away and saw the others were safe as well.

"It is time," Vrea whispered, almost to herself.

"Time? Time for what?" Lu barked.

Beside her, Jin gasped. "It can't be."

"It is," Vrea said, maddening, insistently placid. "It has come to pass. Look for yourself."

"Look at *what*?" Nokhai demanded. "What's happening?"

Jin pointed upward, his already pale face gone milk white with terror. "The gate to the Inbetween, the seal between the worlds! It's been destroyed."

Lu followed his gesture and saw it then: a slash of eerie, earthly blue in the gray Yunian skies.

CHAPTER 34

The Temple

Nok watched, scarcely understanding, as fingers of blue sky bled through the gray.

"Get them inside, Jin," Vrea said. For the first time, Nok detected an edge to her voice. Not fear—not exactly. But a strain. "Get them to safety, then meet me and Shen in the Heart. We cannot hide any longer. It is time." And then she was gone.

The temple was eerily quiet, though not silent. Half a thousand Yunians huddled around the edges of the stone chamber, whispering among themselves. Somewhere, a baby wailed. When they saw Prince Jin, though, dozens leaped to their feet, a few half bowing but most disposing of decorum to shout at him.

"What's happening?"

"Is it the Hu? Have they found us?"

"I can't find my son, has anyone seen—"

"I saw the blue in the sky!"

"Where is Vrea?"

Prince Jin held up a hand. "There has been a breach in the gate, but my brother and sister have gone forth to reseal it. Please stay calm. The mountain and this temple are wrought through with extra protections—Vrea's spells, and some things that are older. It will protect us from—"

"What is *she* doing here?" someone—Nok couldn't see who exactly in the press—demanded. Prince Jin held up his other hand.

"Please, we must have calm."

But Nok saw amid the concerned, fearful faces more than a few hostile ones. Of course. These were people like him. People who had lost everything at the hands of the empire. He saw that Prince Jin realized it, too—or, perhaps he had been mindful of this all along.

"Your Triarch will protect you," the prince said, stepping between Lu and the encroaching Yunians.

Nok glanced over his shoulder. Lu was watching the crowd, calculating and doubtful and proud, without the sense to be afraid yet. He moved closer to her.

"She's the one they want," a man snapped, and there was no question of whom he spoke. "Send *her* out there. Don't leave her here with us!"

"You're afraid, but losing our heads will make matters worse," Prince Jin said sternly. Some of the angry faces looked shamed by his words, but more than a few scowled deeper. "Stay calm. I must leave to join Vrea and Shen. We need you to keep the peace in here while we maintain the gate. Any able-bodied adults who wish to help protect our people can join me—the soldiers will provide you with arms. Decide among yourselves; I will return."

He steered Lu and the others toward a massive brass-plated door at the rear of the temple.

"Quickly," he said under his breath as he unlocked the door and ushered them through it. "You'll be safer here, in the sanctum."

Nasan went in, but Lu stopped, clutching the edge of the door in one hand. "Your people—they're right," she said. "It's me my cousin wants. Let me face him."

"No," Prince Jin said, holding up a placating hand as Lu flared. "Whoever broke the gate must wield terrible power. You cannot fight it with a sword. It is better for you to stay here."

"But he'll come looking for me."

"We will stop him before it comes to that," the prince said grimly. "Stay and protect your friends. Let us do our work."

"Come on," Nasan said, reemerging to tug Lu by the arm. "The prince is right. You don't know what's out there." The princess favored her with a withering glare.

"Lu, let's just do as he says," Nok said quickly. "The people out there are ready to skin you alive."

She frowned but finally nodded. Nok slipped in after her, and the door slammed, heavy and sullen at his back.

The sanctum was dark, lit only by a series of small windows near the high ceiling. The walls were so tall as to make the windows little more than pinpricks from where they stood. As his eyes adjusted, Nok saw they were in an expansive cavern, nearly as large as the main room of the temple had been, but completely empty. He recalled that from the outside, the temple had been a massive square building butting up against the mountain. The main room of the temple had been square; this sanctum must be carved into the mountain itself.

Nok took a step forward and the sound of his footsteps echoed through the still. The silence that followed was so complete as to feel like an absence.

Lu paced along the perimeter of the cavern like a caged animal. "This isn't right," she said irritably. "I should be out there to meet Set."

"You don't know it's him," Nasan countered.

"Who else would it be?" Lu snapped. "It's him. Him and his cursed monk . . . magician. Creature."

Nok slumped against the wall, his weakness catching hold now that they were safe. The wall was warm as skin against his back. Warmer, even. Where was that heat coming from?

"The Triarch will know better than us how to defend their own borders," Nasan was saying. "Magic, gates between realms—this is outside of our purview, Princess."

"Nothing's outside *my* purview," Lu shot back, but Nasan just snorted.

Pain swept over Nok, so great and whole he could scarcely tell it had radiated from his side. He lifted his shirt to check the wound for fresh bleeding, but his bandages remained clean and dry. Whatever the Yunians had given him to dull his senses was beginning to wear off. He turned against the wall, tried to focus on the stone against his cheek, the warm pressure an anchor holding him fast against the waves of pain and nausea.

Nokhai.

He started, the sound jarring his concentration. He looked around but found no source for the voice.

"I'm counting to a hundred, and then I'm leaving," Lu said.

Nokhai.

Nasan snapped a retort back at Lu, but he didn't hear it; he was too focused on locating the voice. This time he realized: it was coming from behind the wall.

Only, the wall wasn't a wall. It was the mountain. The voice was coming from somewhere inside that dense, ancient stone.

Nokhai, the voice repeated, and it sounded farther away—like it was moving. The strident tones of Nasan and Lu's arguments dampened, as though they were the ones he was hearing through a wall.

Nokhai, the voice insisted.

Unbidden, he followed it, an ear pressed to the stone, to the rearmost wall of the sanctum. The light from the windows did not reach here, and he sank into shadow.

Nokhai, the voice said, and this time he thought he knew it—but only for an instant, more as the physical sensation of recognition than comprehension.

All at once, the wall fell away, and he stood alone in utter darkness.

There was silence, then a flare, like someone lighting an enormous torch. He smelled sulfur, felt heat against his skin.

An enormous flame rose before him, twisting and roaring. Only this fire was black as midnight, spitting silver sparks like dying stars.

He staggered back and fell. His body was illuminated in

indigo light. The fire surged forward, and he threw up his hands to shield his face, useless—

Nokhai, the fire thundered.

As he lowered his hands, the fire cleaved down its center, becoming two: a towering column of black and one of deepest violet.

"What are you?" he whispered, voice shaking.

What are you? the flames repeated back.

Nok closed his eyes. He was dying. His wound had split, or it had gone toxic, flooding his blood with poison. This was a fever, this was death, this was his end.

No, the flames said as one. *It is not.*

They sounded very certain. Reluctantly, he opened his eyes. "Are you real?"

The black flame leaped and flared. *What is real, I wonder?*

Nok sat up, still weak. The pain in his side had abated to make room for fear, but it bit back into him as he moved. He winced. "I've had enough riddles for today. If you're going to kill me, do it quickly."

The column of Violet trembled and flickered, almost like laughter. *Our little wolf is brave.*

And it has a smart mouth, the Black mused.

"Are you one or two?" he asked.

The twin tendrils of flame rippled in unison. *Humans,* the voice of the Violet scoffed, but there was a softness in its voice. A fondness.

One, two. There is no difference. We are.

In unison, the Black and the Violet shot toward the ceiling, straight and thin as ribbons, then began lacing and twisting about one another. It was beautiful, fearsome, their motions as violent and feral as they were graceful. They danced, wilder and harder, until Nok could see no difference between them, only a void as cold and absolute as a desert night. All at once, they split apart, became one Black and one Violet again.

He understood then. "You're—you're the *gods* Vrea speaks to. The Ana and the Aba."

We are known as such, to some, the flames conceded.

"I thought you were meant to be like parents," he said. "I thought you'd be . . . human."

We are not of your realm. We are hard for people to understand. And people fear what they do not understand, said the Violet.

They understand a mother and a father, continued the Black. *They can love a mother and a father. But they cannot love what they fear—not truly. They can obey it, they can even admire and revere it. But fear sucks away the air that the flame of love needs to flourish. In the end, fear becomes revulsion, rejection. Always.*

As they spoke, their twin flames intensified. Inconceivably, the air grew hotter, and Nok flinched. He was going to burn, his hair would catch, the fibers of his clothes—the fire. *Fire.*

"The First Flame," he blurted. "Did it come from you?"

Long ago, the Violet murmured, and their heat abated, as though they were distracted by the memory. *A gift to the Hana. Though they have forgotten what it meant. Their bond to us. Their Pact. Long ago for them, for you. For people.*

Though not so long for us, continued the Black. *We have not forgotten. We, who have created so much . . .*

"Fire doesn't create," Nok said, remembering the soldiers that rode down his parents' tent, that of the elders', razing the whole camp as their scarlet tiger banners snapped in the dry wind. The goats had panicked, stampeded in the fray, some of them lying crushed, unable to move as they burned, too. He remembered the screaming. The stench of seared flesh in the air.

"Fire doesn't create," he repeated, louder now. "It doesn't *give*. It only destroys."

The flames crackled at that, like laughter. *Spoken like a true child of your gods,* said the Violet.

"What about my—what about them?"

Your gods—the ones that gifted you—they were born of the earth.

"The Hu were Gifted—born of the beast gods, too," Nok pointed out. "They had their tigers. Before they went south to conquer the Hana."

They had their tigers, agreed the Violet. *And then they adopted the fire of the Hana. The First, it is called, but it was not. Humans always want to be the beginning of all things, but they never are.*

Distantly, there came a rumble. It was soft, like far-off thunder, but Nok recognized it all the same: another attack.

Yes. It is time for you to take what is yours, said the Violet. *Your kind—your gods, they cannot stay here in the Inbetween. They are of the earth.*

Nok winced, trying to think, trying to take all of it in. If beasts came from the earth, then what of fire? He thought of kindling, of coal, of burned hair, of seared flesh. But that was just fuel.

A story from his childhood came to him then—a wayward girl who found a cave so deep she wandered into the center of the world. A core of molten oceans, of bright ever-burning trees . . .

"What of you?" he demanded. "Are you from this place, this Inbetween?"

Again, the flames crackled. *No one is* from *the Inbetween,* said the Black. *That is why it is in between. It is neither here nor there. It is a no-place. And when it falls, we will go . . .*

"Go where?"

Where forgotten things go.

In the silence, he heard another distant rumble—farther away now. A summer storm receding.

They come.

"They? Is it Set?" he asked.

The one you call Set, confirmed the Black. *And the one who seeks the knowledge of the beginning of all things, and the one who is their weapon. The Girl. She is the deadliest of all, though they do not know it yet.* She *does not know it yet.*

"The girl?" he repeated. "What girl?"

An inversion, hissed the Violet. *With a sweet face and gray eyes. The one born of vengeance. She is a sword wrought in the flames of hatred. Forced. She is disharmony. She is their counterfeit key. It was she who unlocked the gate.*

Confusion gave way to frustration. "Please, Nasan and the others—I have to go."

Go, echoed the Violet. *It is too late for us, but it is not too late for you. For your gods. You have languished long here already—nearly too long. Perhaps you were here even before you arrived. But now you must take your patron and return to where you belong.*

"My patron?"

The paintbrush strokes of the Black and the Violet parted like curtains, sweeping light as a kiss across his face. Nok flinched against the flaring heat of them, burning so hot and fleet and clean it felt almost like cold, like freezing. He closed his eyes.

And when he opened them again, the flames were gone. In their place stood the wolf. His wolf.

Nokhai, the wolf murmured. Its voice was warm and languid, seeming to emanate from the walls of the sanctum cavern like steam. But he felt it come from within as well, rumbling through the thin, quivering flue of his own throat.

"We have to go," he said.

We? the wolf repeated, and now its voice quivered apart like music, harmony—each note sung by a different voice. All at once, he heard Nasan's hoarse lilt, his father's stern, stolid rumbling. There were others, too—Elder Pamuk's imperious croak. The jeers of Karakk and the other Kith boys. And lingering after all the rest, his mother's low, sweet cadence, familiar as a childhood lullaby. Painful as a kick to the chest.

"I need you," he whispered, and his own voice sounded tinny and small. "I need you to tell me what to do. I need . . ." The words died on his lips. *Why won't you come to me?*

I'm here, the wolf said, and again Nok heard the tumbling chorus of his half memories, his ghosts, the many in that one voice.

I'm here. Are you?

He understood then. Suddenly—and also not. He'd known all along, hadn't he? This was all that remained, all they had left him. For years, he'd ignored it in favor of his disbelief, his resentment, his fury. He'd let all that coil around it like a knot of scar tissue, calcify into a shell. Kept the whole thing like a stone in his gut, named it grief. But he saw the truth at the core of it now, clean and swift. It felt like emerging from a long dream in which he'd been someone else.

This was all there was. And what had wrought it was hateful and cruel and wrong—a wrong that would never be reversed—but it, the thing itself, was blameless. It was simply all that remained. *He* was all that remained.

He, and the wolf.

He swiped an arm across his face, found it wet with tears. When had he begun crying?

"Come to me," he said, and though his voice quavered, it held, the words a rope of steel buried in the heart of all that dust and grave dirt. "Come to me, now."

And the wolf came.

This time when it swept over him, warm as summer wind in the steppe, he felt something catch. Knit in place.

It hurt—a harsh clicking pain, deep in his bones, a sharp itch in the marrow. He closed his eyes and accepted it. The pain passed, and then came something new. It spread through his veins, swift and effervescent, gleeful in its quickness, its rightness. He felt buoyant, as though he'd spent his whole life with a boulder lashed to his back, and someone had just cut the ropes. His face twitched and all at once he barked out a laugh—

Joy.

He'd forgotten joy.

He opened his eyes again and found himself alone in the cavern. All that remained of the Black and Violet flames was an ambient warmth, a hint of sulfur in the dead air.

No wolf, either. But he could sense it all the same, the way when he went still and quiet, he could feel his own heartbeat.

He stretched his arms in wonder. The pain and exhaustion weighing down his muscles had disappeared. He walked forward and discovered a new power left in their absence, a singing in his blood, a new strength. The dark of the cavern had receded, too. He blinked. Finding no source of light, he realized that his vision had altered.

The wolf, he thought. He now saw with the wolf's eyes as well as his own.

Walking faster, he reached the end of the cavern and, estimating the place where he'd entered, he pressed his hands to the wall. The stone was still warm to the touch, and he ran his palms over the coarse bite of stone.

"Nok?"

"Where did he go?"

"Where is there *to* go?"

Voices. Human voices, now. He could hear Nasan, and—

"Nokhai!"

Lu.

"Nok?" They were calling louder now.

He pressed again at the wall and this time the stone parted soft as water, and he was stumbling, falling—

"Nokhai!"

Strong arms engulfed him, pulling him upright. He could smell the oil combed through her hair, the perfume they'd dabbed along her collarbone—a combination of sandalwood and something sweet and floral. Citrus blossom, maybe. He opened his eyes.

Lu was holding him, staring down in concern. She looked,

he thought, like fire. Vast and all-consuming and furious. Bigger than fire. She looked like the sun. Beautiful—how could he not have noticed before? But of course, he had.

"Where were you?" she demanded, shaking him a little, because for her, even love would always be a bit bound up with anger.

It made him laugh. It made him want to kiss her. And he would, he resolved. When this was all over, he would kiss her again and again . . .

Nasan cursed. "Is his fever back?"

Lu squinted into the dark behind him. "Nokhai, did you just come out of that *wall*?"

"Don't be stupid!" snapped Nasan. He recognized the particular impatience in her voice, though—his sister was afraid. "It's just a trick of the eye. It's too damn dark in here to see anything. I mean, where would he have gone?" she said, rapping the stone wall with the butt of her fist. "The room ends right there, see?"

Lu shivered—the barest tremor around him. "I don't think it does," she said softly.

Nok sat up. "We have to go. They've broken through the gate."

"How do you know?" Nasan demanded.

"The Ana and the Aba—I had a vision," he blurted. "It's . . . just, trust me. We have to go help the Triarch."

"Not you," Nasan said. "You're in no condition to fight. You can barely stand."

His lips parted to object, but he hesitated. It was an out. No more killing, no more bloodshed, no more terror. He wasn't made for it. Unlike his sister or Lu, he wasn't a born warrior. He didn't even have a weapon.

Only, that wasn't true anymore.

Nok surged to his feet. "I can stand. And I can fight. I—I have my caul now." They stared at him as though still unconvinced he wasn't in the grips of some feverous hallucination.

"You said you can't control when it comes and goes," Lu said carefully. He looked at her, at that stern, stately face. In the flinty copper of her eyes he saw the soldier whose head she'd stung an arrow through to save him, the pale, blood-drained slip of a boy she'd killed in the wood. But he saw exhaustion there, too, and a profound animal fear kept just at bay. Maybe no one was a born warrior.

"It's different now," he told her. "Look . . ."

He closed his eyes, and though he had no way of knowing whether it would work, he knew all the same. Perhaps the whole thing had been one fever dream, perhaps there was no Black and Violet, no fire born from the core of the world, but this much he knew was real. This much was his.

This time, there was no sensation of wind sweeping over him. Instead, the warmth surged from his chest, through the marrow of his bones. He could feel it down to the soles of his feet, in his scalp, in his teeth.

When he opened his eyes again, the room looked bright as day. The others were staring down at him. Nasan in wonder and Lu with something like relief, and something else like pride. The wolf stretched, and Nok felt power course down his spine.

His sister shook her head to dispel the shock on her face, as though embarrassed by how pure it was. Then she grinned. "Well. Let's go kill some imperials."

"Is it Set?" Lu demanded. "Did Set break the gate?"

Set is there, Nok told them. *But he's not alone—he's not the one who broke the gate.*

Lu frowned, the thoughts racing behind her eyes. "Who, then? His monk? Brother?"

No. A girl, Nok said, remembering suddenly. *The Ana and the Aba, they said it was a girl. That she was their key, their weapon. Maybe a Hana nun?*

Lu was shaking her head. "Set didn't bring a girl with him to the capital. And the Hana nuns—they just do rites. Ceremony. There hasn't been anyone with knowledge of magic since they executed the Yunian shamanesses. Are you sure you remember correctly?"

They said it was a girl, Nok repeated stubbornly. And then he remembered the rest. *They said she had gray eyes . . .*

"Your mother has gray eyes," Nasan interrupted, looking at Lu.

"Yes," Lu agreed doubtfully. Then she froze, and Nok saw understanding on her face—then a cavalcade of urgency, of fury, of fear. "My mother," she whispered. "And my sister."

CHAPTER 35

The Fall

Chaos greeted them as they ran out onto the temple steps. Lu could see the battle had reached the far end of the Heart: a horde of blue-clad mounted Hana troops clashing against no more than a dozen Yunians.

There was no sign of Set. Or Min. Her sister couldn't be in that terrible crush of men and horses, could she?

Overhead, the sky still bled, the blue now nearly overtaking the gray. The light was different, too. At first Lu thought it was just her eyes adjusting from the dark of the temple, but no, the whole Heart was changing. Even the trees looked strange, their dull gray-green leaves turned garishly verdant. The long foggy morning of the Inbetween was ending, and the sun had come out harsh and overly bright.

Lu unsheathed her sword, wished for an elk and armor. She looked to her right and saw Nasan heft her staff in both hands. To her left, Nok's wolf bristled, drawing its lips around massive white teeth. They weren't much, but they would have to be enough.

"Let's go," she told them. They ran fleetly down the temple steps.

The noise was horrific, engulfing them as they approached. The copper tang of blood filled the air along with the cloying stench of burned flesh. Where was that coming from?

The Hana troops were bottlenecked at the entrance of the Heart, and for a moment Lu couldn't understand why they weren't advancing. Then she saw Vrea in front of them, pale and still. Shen and Jin rode up to flank her, Jin's paltry army following suit, swords in hand. Vrea's hands were empty, but raised.

Lu was close enough to make out individual faces when one Hana rider made a break toward the Yunians.

All at once the air crackled and flared between Vrea's outstretched hands and the soldiers. A lance of light—no, *lightning*—shot from her palms.

It struck the horse full in the chest, and Lu saw its skeleton, radiating white-hot from the inside out. The shock traveled up into its rider. Man and beast flew back with the force of it, like they were nothing more than dolls.

The horse landed hard and stayed down, a heap of blackened flesh, but the soldier screamed. His helmet fell, and Lu saw the charred dome of his head, then the white of his skull as his burned scalp sloughed away.

"What was *that*?" Nasan demanded.

Lu shook her head numbly. She understood now where the smell of burned flesh had come from.

The horses were stamping and rearing, but Lu could see

the soldiers trying to drive them back into formation. There was no panic in the ranks. Military discipline was one thing. These men did not have the air of soldiers riding to their deaths; they believed they could win against this unnatural terror.

They knew something she did not.

"Princess Lu!"

She tore her eyes from the Hana. The Yunian princes had noticed their presence.

Jin started toward her. "Princess, you shouldn't—"

"Get back to the temple!" Shen shouted.

"I can't do that," she called.

What are the Hana waiting for? Nok's voice sounded in her head. *They're just standing there.*

"Would you want to be next to get roasted like a goat?" Nasan retorted, but her voice shook.

"No, it's not that," Lu said. "Nok's right. They should either charge or retreat and regroup. They're . . ."

The Hana parted ranks. Lu recognized the horse before she saw the rider: a white stallion, armored in finely crafted plates of blue and silver. Upon its back sat her cousin, lean and tall and proud. His sword was drawn. Close beside him rode Brother, small and out of place.

Then came a third horse, also white. And its rider—

"Min!" Lu yelled, but her voice was lost to the fray. Her sister reined up, then dismounted clumsily, staggering forward on bowed legs.

Her sister, and yet, not.

Min's normally sweet, round face was gaunt, webs of delicate veins stark beneath thin, gray skin. Her long black hair had fallen from its upsweep, hanging in dusty hanks like moss off a tree. She was hunched, as though someone had kicked her in the belly, but she lurched inexorably toward Vrea.

"Min, what are you doing?" Lu shouted. "Get back!"

The priestess considered Min as she approached, like a cat sizing up a wounded mouse. She raised her hands.

Lu lunged forward. "No! Don't hurt her! She's only a—"

Lightning shot from Vrea's palms. Min threw out her own hands in helpless defense—and caught the lightning in her grasp.

Vrea's face tightened. She thrust forward harder, but the lightning only built against Min's palms, a spitting, crackling ball, burning so brightly Lu was forced to squint.

"Impressive," Vrea called, her voice melodic and lilting, though ragged at the edges. "What Yunian shamaness taught you our ways?"

"Don't talk to her, Min!" Set barked. He leaned forward in his saddle, greedy gray eyes flashing white from the glow of the lightning.

"I heard your father killed all our shamanesses," Vrea continued. "Those poor girls. Those hostages your kind promised to protect."

"She's trying to distract you!" Set snarled.

Min did not reply, but instead thrust forward hard with the whole of her little body, screaming with the effort. She sounded like a wild animal. The ball of lightning shot back at Vrea and shattered against the priestess's hands in an explosion of white sparks. A boom like thunder threw them all to the ground.

Lu staggered to her feet, ears ringing again. She picked up

her fallen sword. The air was coarse with fine gray dust. She coughed, eyes stinging with grit and tears.

Where Vrea had stood there was now a smoking, blasted-out crater. Deep, crooked cracks emanated from it. The priestess herself had landed some distance away, thrown by the impact, but as Lu watched she climbed to her feet with little more than a tremble in her arms. She dusted off her robes with a misplaced air of quiet dignity.

Lu stepped forward to join Shen and Jin in flanking her, but Nok blocked her path.

Wait, he said. *Look!*

One of the cracks emanating from the blast site widened. As they watched, a slab of paving stone the size of a man's torso broke free and tumbled down into the crevice—leaving in its place a patch of empty, endless sky.

Lu's breath caught in her throat. She could see the stone, still in free fall miles below, until at last it was swallowed by distance and the ether.

"The separation between our realms has been corrupted," Vrea told Min. "Yunis is crumbling. Falling back down to earth. We will fall with it, unless you think you can stop it."

Set laughed, steering his horse daintily back from the slow-spreading cracks in the ground. "You can drop the stern teacher act, Oracle. My little bride broke your gate, dismantled your pitiful spells of protection. You can't overpower us. Whatever you've made she will unmake."

"Destruction is easy," Vrea said, her voice sharp. "This child has strength enough for that. But I wonder, does she have the skill to mend? To create? If not, what is to prevent you from being killed along with the rest of us?"

Fear swept across Set's face, brief as the shadow of a bird overhead.

"Don't." The voice was ragged. Min shoved her long hair back roughly, glowering at Vrea. "Don't speak of me as though I weren't *here!*"

She lashed out a hand and struck Vrea full in the chest with a blast of white light. The priestess bowed around it, manipulating it with her hands, absorbing it into her body. She stumbled, her brow creased in effort. Prince Shen stepped forward as though to help her.

"Get back!" she told him.

"Don't kill the Oracle!" Brother rode up to Min. His stallion stamped in wide, nervous circles and he flailed at the reins to still it. "We need her knowledge. She knows the secrets of this place—I need that *knowledge!*"

"I *am* the knowledge," snarled Min, raising her hand again. "And I don't need anything."

"Min!" Lu screamed, and this time her sister heard, turning like a hound to a whistle.

"Lu?"

Nasan tried to grab her, but Lu ran forward. Min put up a hand.

Lu willed herself not to flinch, not to think of the damage that hand had only just wrought. There was no lightning, no intent behind the gesture. A defensive reflex only. And this was her little sister, after all. Min wouldn't hurt her. She wouldn't.

The two of them stared at one another, breathing hard. At their backs, the two sides faced off warily, neither moving. Vrea's hands were up.

"Lu." Min's voice went soft. "You cut your hair."

"You . . ." The words died on Lu's lips as she searched Min's face. It wasn't just her sister's skin. The tiny veins in her eyes had run up to the surface and burst, flooding the whites of them red, turning the irises into hazy gray islands in a sea of blood. And there was nothing in them, Lu realized with a jolt of terror. No familiarity, no fear.

"Min, what *happened*?" Lu whispered. "What has he done to you?"

Set laughed. A cruel, scraping sound. "I've done nothing. This is what she is. She said it herself: this is what she was born for."

Lu ignored him. "Min, this is madness. Come with me. Let Vrea—help Vrea—salvage whatever's left here. We're all in danger. Whatever's happened, whatever you've done, we can fix it, we can forgive—"

"Enough," Set interrupted coldly, sliding down from his horse and striding forward. "Min is my wife. She is the empress. You speak of forgiveness? Well, she's not yours to forgive."

Lu met his gray gaze, then raised her own sword. "I'll kill you," she said, voice trembling. "Whatever you've done to her—I'll kill you for it."

Brother stepped forward. "Emperor Set, please take care—"

Set's eyes never left Lu. "Min, my empress, burn alive the next person who dares interrupt me and your sister, would you?"

Brother did not speak again.

Set sneered at Lu. "Are you so stupid you don't understand what this is, cousin? You lost. I won."

"Not yet you haven't," Lu said. She flexed her hand around the pommel of her sword, feeling that weight, as familiar as one of her limbs. "Not while I'm alive."

She didn't hear Nokhai approach so much as she felt him. He stopped protectively beside her, his wolf's body taut and bristling.

Set's lip raised in disgust. "What is that thing?"

Don't you remember me? Nokhai's voice trembled in their ears. *You tried to kill me when we were children. I looked a bit different back then, admittedly . . .*

The haughtiness slipped from Set's face. "Ashina? That's not possible. Your Pact was broken—we killed you all!"

Not all.

Set's gray eyes narrowed. His sword flashed in the strange light as he raised it. "Then I'll finish the job now."

"No," Lu snapped. "Nokhai, get back."

Lu . . .

She met his wolf eyes, golden and fierce, and yet still somehow familiar. "I have him," she said, "go help the Triarch. Let me end this."

He fell back, but kept a close distance.

"You and me, cousin," Lu told Set. "Come. Let me teach you one last lesson."

Her words broke something in him; he came at her hard and furious and impossibly fast. She barely had time to parry. Their blades met, the cold bite sending tremors through her arms. She could still feel the Yunian liquor coursing in her blood, and her muscles were weak with disuse.

It has been too long, she realized wildly.

Warriors don't make excuses, Yuri's voice scoffed in her head. *They find what scraps they can in a bad situation and build it into victory.*

They pulled apart with a chime of steel. Lu circled her cousin, searching for weaknesses. His face was livid. Dark shadows rimmed his eyes, and his handsome face was blotched with dirt and dust. He spat at her feet and—was that wine she smelled on his sour breath?

He was as unprepared for this fight as she was, Lu realized. They were well matched in training and skill, but also exhaustion. The outcome would go to whoever could last longer.

She lunged, keeping her eyes trained at his neck as though she meant to strike there. He moved to block her and at the last moment she bobbed and swung low, toward his gut. He spun, and her blade swiped empty air—but just barely. Not giving him a moment's reprieve, she closed the distance between them and thrust her sword at his chest—

He moved, and her blade glanced off his breastplate. She heard the metallic shiver of chain mail beneath. She was suddenly keenly aware of her own bare arms, the thin silk tunic that was the only barrier between his sword and her flesh. Panic prickled down her spine as they pulled apart.

"Surrender and I'll let you live," he panted.

Lu laughed, sounding stronger than she felt. "You expect me to believe that?"

Set feinted, bounced back on light feet as she parried. "Maybe you're not as dumb as I thought. It's true you're not much use to me alive anymore."

She lunged toward his back leg, forcing him to pivot.

"I already have your empire," he continued, jaw tight. "I have your crown. Your sister. But I bet I can find more to take from you. It might be fun to try."

As he spoke, his gaze flicked behind her. Before she could understand, he lunged for Nokhai.

A wordless scream tore out of her. Set brought down his blade in an inelegant hack. It clashed against the stone floor; Nokhai had leaped out of the way. In a flash, the wolf rebounded and lunged. He caught her cousin's forearm in his jaws, teeth screeching against Set's armor.

"Nokhai, get out of there!" she yelled.

The wolf wouldn't be able to pierce the armor, no more than she'd been able to. But perhaps piercing it wasn't the answer . . .

She ran at Set, swinging wildly at his chest. He whipped around and blocked her.

"Leave Nokhai alone," she seethed.

"I'll kill you *both*!" he shrieked, hacking at her.

"Are you sure about that? You can't even seem to manage one of us. Not back then—and not now." Lu blocked his blade with a hard parry, sending him reeling past her.

She spun to face him as he aimed a wild slash at her belly. She leaped back, using the agility that was her only advantage, all the while picking apart his armor with her eyes.

The knees. The gaps at his knees.

He raised his sword and came. "Why can't you see you've *lost*?" He punctuated this last word with another slash of his blade.

She blocked it and forced herself to grin, easy and cruel. "That's not how it works, cousin. In order for me to lose, you have to win. And you're never, ever going to win. It's not in your nature."

He ran at her with a wild, animal cry of rage. She waited until the last possible moment, then slipped to the side. As he passed her, she swung hard and true—fitting her blade into the gap in his armor, just behind the knees.

Her cousin screamed as he went down, blood soaking his golden breeches fast and red.

"No!" The anguished cry came from far off—Lu didn't take her eyes off Set, but some part of her registered it was Min's voice.

The scream died out and the only sound left was Set's furious gasping—a terrible, primal hybrid of seething and weeping. His fingers clawed at the stone floor of the Heart.

She walked over to him, the roar of blood growing in her ears. There was movement among the Hana now, but it felt impossibly far away.

Lu put a foot to his shoulder and gave a hard push, rolling him over onto his back.

"What's wrong with you?" he gritted out, his face so contorted with rage and pain she scarcely recognized him. "Why are you like this—?"

Lu bent over him. He fought as soon as she was in range, flailing his arms, getting in a solid punch that bloodied her lip. But she managed to yank off his helmet. Loosened his gorget. She replaced it with her foot, crushing his throat, pinning him to the ground. His eyes bulged, and his pale lips fluttered—a comical fish's gape. Breathing hard, Lu stooped again to pull the ornate dagger hanging from his belt, considering its ruby-and-carnelian jeweled handle for a moment. She let off her foot and crouched beside him.

Breath rushed back into Set's body with a ghastly wheeze. "Why did the gods make you like this? Just to torment me?"

Hot fury lanced her gut. "I wasn't made to torment you," she snarled. "I wasn't made for you at all. I was made for me."

She plunged the dagger into the exposed base of his throat. Yanking it free took more effort; she felt the hard, grainy crunch of his trachea, the sucking clench of muscle as it withdrew. Blood shot like a fountain from the hole she'd made.

Easy, she thought deliriously, watching the color drain from her cousin's face, the life ebb from his eyes. His flailing faded into a full-body quake into a tremor into nothing. *Too easy.* She almost wanted to do it again, just to be sure. Just to be certain she'd truly—

Lu, watch out! Nok's voice rang in her head.

The boulder caught her in the side. Heat exploded through her arm and ribs like rogue fireworks. Panicked flares of red and violet and silver lit the back of her eyelids.

What . . . ?

Min hurtled toward her. Her sister's hands were outstretched, clutching a second chunk of paving stone, this one larger, wrapped in a dense web of crackling light. She was sweating, her chest heaving with effort, as though the weight of it was too much for her.

"Min?" Lu whispered. *Why?* The question screamed inside her. She couldn't find the breath to ask it, though.

Vrea leaped forward, lightning stretching from her hands toward Min. Min pivoted and released her stone toward Vrea.

The shot went high; Vrea's blast of energy shattered it in mid-flight, raining debris down upon them.

With Vrea distracted, the Hana army charged. Vrea scarcely had time to redirect her focus from Min toward the advancing soldiers, shoving them back with small, directed blasts of energy.

Nok's wolf dove into the fray. It latched its jaws around the throat of the nearest horse and gave a terrible shake. Both beast and rider fell screaming, bowling over several of their nearest compatriots. One of the fallen men struggled to his hands and knees, but Nasan's staff caught him across the jaw, snapping his head back with a sickening crack.

Lu closed her eyes, struggling to breathe. Her body felt undone, taken apart and thrown back together in a heap. In the aftermath, pain began to seep in, flaring from her side, the ball of her shoulder. Around her the battle seethed. The clashing of steel, the braying of horses. Men wailing and dying.

She tried to sit up, but her left arm was dead. She couldn't feel her hand, her fingers. Just a screaming, mindless pain. Her sword was gone, lost to the fray.

It doesn't matter. I'll never wield it properly again. The thought sent a shock of grief through her already splintered heart.

"Lu." Min's voice was improbably quiet, close. Lu opened her eyes and found her sister standing over her, searching her broken body with startled eyes, as though she hadn't been the one to break it.

"Help me, Min," Lu whispered. "You're my sister—"

"Sister?" The word seemed to catch her off guard. She cocked her head and looked into the distance, seemingly oblivious to the wild battle at her back. "Am I?"

"What . . . ?" Lu stammered. "What do you—"

"Isn't it strange," Min said, "the way mother always hated you, and father always ignored me? I confess, it never occurred to me to think anything of it. It was simply the way it was. But it was strange, wasn't it? We never did anything to deserve it, we were just . . . born. It was a mystery."

"Min—"

"Our family was a mystery, and I solved it, Lu." Min turned solemn gray eyes back on her. "We were born to the wrong mothers. Me, to the wife our father hated. And you, to the woman he wasn't allowed to love."

Lu gaped at her. Had her sister lost her mind? "What woman?"

Min shrugged, slippery and slight. "A shamaness. A Yunian shamaness—isn't that strange? Her name was Tsai."

Tsai . . . where had she heard that name before? And then she remembered. Back in Omair's quaint little home in Ansana, the old apothecarist had said it.

Tsai. Slight, almost brittle to look at, but that exterior hid immense power. A star crammed inside a soap bubble.

"It makes me feel better, in a way," Min said. "It explains why we're so different. When we were little, I cursed the heavens for making you so strong, so clever, so beautiful. They gave it all to you and left nothing for me, I thought."

"That's not true, Min. You know it's not—"

"You're right," her sister said. Lu looked up at her in surprise. Min nodded once, as though making a decision. "You're right. It turns out I do have something you don't."

"Min, please—"

"What I have," her sister continued, "isn't from the heavens, though."

"It doesn't matter," Lu slurred, trying to focus past the pain, past her confusion. "Set's gone, you're free now. Whatever it is, I can fix it."

"*No!*" Min shrieked, her hands going to her ears as though she meant to cover them against the sound of Lu's voice. "*I* was going to fix it! I had a plan. I was going to make it all better! I was going to win, and I was going to give Set sons, and I was going to let *you* come home, but you ruined everything!"

Lu licked her lips, tasted blood and dust. "Min. What did Set do to you?"

"You don't understand," Min seethed. "He didn't do anything! It was *me*, it was supposed to be me this time, but you took everything away!" Rage contorted her sister's tired little face, turned it feral and unfamiliar. *Wrong.* This wasn't her sister. Not the one she'd left behind.

Min raised her hands.

A fresh flush of tears stung Lu's eyes. She struggled to keep them open. It would be better if she could stand. But no matter. She was a warrior. She would not flinch at death.

Her sister—for that was what she was, even now, Lu thought, even if what she was saying was true, even with her hands raised like that—her sister's face swam before her, dappled in sparks from the ball of energy building in her hands. It was as though Lu were seeing her from underwater.

She had a sudden memory. The Eastern Palace, some summer, years ago. She had tried to coax Min into the lake, so cool and inviting. Lu had swum out until her feet couldn't touch anymore, then turned back to wave at the shore. *See?* she had called. *It's safe. Just jump in. I'll watch out for you.* There had been longing on her sister's face, but it had been overtaken with fear. She'd always been so afraid. And so Lu had continued on her own, until without meaning to, she had swum so far she couldn't see Min at all anymore.

I love you, she thought. But that wasn't right—that wasn't what—

"I'm sorry," she whispered. Min's eyes widened.

A blur of blue-gray sailed between them, and Min was gone, bowled over by Nokhai's mammoth wolf.

Lu! his voice rang out in her head. *Go!*

"Don't hurt her!" she cried.

Wolf and girl tumbled apart. The ball of energy flew from her sister's hands, but her aim was off, and it missed Nokhai, blasting a hole into the ground where he'd been half a breath earlier.

Nokhai rolled, coming to a graceful, deadly crouch. Min landed on her belly, then struggled to her knees.

She lifted her hands toward Nokhai. There was no hesitation in her face anymore. Just fury. Seething and single-minded.

She never saw Vrea coming. The blast took her hard in the back. Min went rigid with it, her arms thrown out like a scarecrow's. She screamed, barely audible over the electric sputter of the lightning.

"No!" Lu cried. "Vrea! Wait!"

The Oracle dropped her hands and Min fell forward like her spine had been cut. Ropes of white-hot energy still whipped wild around her torso, her arms. They hissed as they lanced in and out of her.

Min lay still, her breath shallow and fast. Then, incredibly, her sister rose up on one leg, then the other. She turned toward Vrea.

The veins spidering across her face had gone deep purple. A patch beneath one eye had burst into a dark splotch like spilled ink. The reddened whites of her eyes were darkening at the corners, the black bleeding inward, making the hazy gray of her irises look white by contrast.

"*Enough*," said Vrea, and her voice filled the air, firm and solemn.

"Not quite," Min said flatly. She flexed her hands, watching the lightning lick around her fingers like flames on kindling. "You're tired, old woman. You spent your strength destroying our army. Do you think you have enough left for me?"

"The corruption in your soul is consuming you," Vrea said, thrusting out an arm. "Look! Look around at the madness you've wrought."

Lu rose up on her good arm and followed the Oracle's gesture. Around them, the walls of the Heart crumbled, billowing dust in their wake like a sandstorm. The trees planted along their edges flared green, then alarmingly greener, so bright it hurt her eyes. Then they dimmed, went golden, then black and gray as though they'd been charred. Their leaves dropped, drifting on the air, white and soft as ash.

"If you don't stop, we will *all* die," Vrea continued. "Help me put an end to this, before it's too late."

"It's already ending," Min said. "It's already too late."

She lunged forward, thrusting with both hands. The energy crackling around her disappeared into her body, sucked down under the skin. There was a pause, and then an enormous ball of light shot out through her palms. It shattered into Vrea's chest and the priestess flew through the air, limp. She hit the ground, dead weight, and did not move again.

"No!" She could hear Prince Shen's roar over the melee. "No! Vrea!"

Lu closed her eyes.

There was a rumble—so close, impossibly close, a thunderstorm beneath their feet—followed by a deep moan, as if the world itself were grieving. Half the stone floor fell away, replaced by a terrifying maw of sky.

In an instant, two hundred imperial soldiers on horseback were tumbling down into that abyss of benign, placid blue. The remaining soldiers reined up their horses and broke rank, stampeding away in terror. Most were headed out of the Heart, back from where they'd come, but some were trapped on the other side of the split.

Jin directed what was left of his tiny army back from the widening seam. Lu covered her head with her good hand as they stampeded past. *How stupid, after everything else, to die crushed under a pack of panicked horses,* she thought.

"Get to the temple!" Jin hollered. "The ground won't hold without Vrea! Do you hear me? Get to the mountain! To the temple!"

Prince Shen drew Vrea's broken body tight to him. Thin lines of blood ran from her nose. They left red streaks against Shen's tunic as he clutched her close.

Jin ran back toward him. "We have to go!"

Shen shook his head. Lu could barely hear him. "She's gone. She was all we had, and she's gone."

Lu looked behind her as yet more pavement crumbled. Set's body was still lying there. For a moment, she met his dead, unseeing eyes with her own.

Then a crack widened beneath him and he too was gone.

"Can you stand?" Jin stooped at her side. His face was twisted in grief and all at once, Lu saw the old man in it, the young man, and the little boy—so many faces flickering like candlelight buffeted in the wind. She looked to where he'd been and saw Shen still crouched on the ground, holding Vrea.

Lu struggled to her knees.

"No time." Jin's face resettled into the one she knew as he lifted her into his arms.

"Wait!" she shouted, struggling against him, but he was already running in retreat. Pain seared from her shoulder, through her ribs every time his feet slammed against the ground. "Wait, wait. Put me down! The others—Nokhai!"

"They're coming," Jin panted.

Lu looked over his shoulder and saw Nasan blazing on their heels, her face twisted, straining. Her staff was clenched in her right hand, and in her left, Lu saw the glint of steel. Her sword.

"Retreat!" The cry came from the remaining Hana soldiers. "Retreat! Back to the gate!"

Lu, Nokhai's voice came urgent in her head. She cast about wildly for him, then saw him standing by Min—near the epicenter of the crumbling ground.

Lu, I don't think she can walk—

"Nok, don't be an idiot! Leave her!" Nasan waved at him frantically with her staff.

"Let me go!" Lu pounded on Jin's back with her good hand. "Let me go! My sister—"

He stopped, but before Lu could free herself from his grasp, a stallion thundered up alongside Nokhai and its rider slid off. A small figure in dun-colored robes. With some effort, he lifted Min into his arms. As he turned to regard Nok, his hood slid off.

Brother.

"*Him*," Nasan cried in shock, and it took Lu a moment to understand she was talking about the monk, not Nokhai. "It's him! That monster . . ."

Nokhai and the monk stared at one another, man and wolf. Two sets of keen, watchful black eyes. As though they had reached some unspoken agreement, the monk threw Min onto his saddle and clambered on after her. A blink, and his stallion was riding away across the fast-disintegrating ground.

"Nokhai, come on!" Lu shouted as Jin began moving again.

The wolf jerked, finally turning from the place where the monk had been, and ran.

They were halfway up the temple steps when the widening split in the ground reached them. Jin stumbled as the stones beneath his feet began to break, to dissolve and fall away. Lu staggered out of his arms, barely kept her balance, ran for her life.

"Faster!" Nasan shouted from somewhere beside her. Pandemonium. Lu could scarcely see anything in the blanketing dust, could scarcely sense anything but the consuming roar of the world breaking around her. Of the made being unmade.

She looked back for Nokhai and saw the dark shape of his wolf leaping its way up the collapsing stairs.

Up ahead, Jin pulled open the heavy doors to the temple. "Get in!" he bellowed. Nasan glanced back, but Lu waved her on.

"Go!" she screamed.

"My brother—"

"I've got him!"

Nasan hesitated, then nodded. "You better, Princess." She raced through the doors as Lu turned back down the stairs.

"Lu, no!" Jin called.

"Nokhai!" Lu ran toward him. The wolf was close now, wending a twisting path over what ground remained. One more leap and he would . . .

The stones beneath his feet caved.

A cry tore itself from Lu's throat, but as Nokhai jumped through the empty air, his shape changed. The wolf twisted, and all at once the dark fur drew back, the claws retracted, and Nokhai grabbed the bottom remaining stair with two human hands, breaking his fall.

"I've got you!" Lu shouted, taking the stairs between them in a single leap, falling to her knees. She extended her good hand to him, felt his fingers catch, tangling hot and urgent against her own.

The stair dissolved.

He didn't scream. The weight in her hand was there, and then it was too much, and just as fast, it was gone.

"Nokhai!"

She stared into the empty air, disbelieving. Some part of her registered the stone beneath her giving way. In a moment she too would fall. *Good. It's what I deserve. It's—*

"It's too late!" Strong hands grabbed her.

"No!" She kicked and writhed, but Jin hauled her into his arms and held fast.

"We have to go. It's too late."

"No!" she insisted, her voice breaking. But he was running again, toward the temple, racing the disintegration. But that was wrong, she thought—Nokhai had gone the other way.

"We have to go back!" she screamed. *"Nokhai!"*

"It's too late, Lu," Jin whispered into her hair as they passed into the temple. "I'm sorry. I'm so sorry."

He laid her on the floor, pulling the door tight behind them. The roar of the breaking pavement dulled. Lu blinked in the darkness, saw the vague shapes of people crowding around her. Stupidly, desperately, she searched for Nokhai, but he wasn't there.

He wasn't ever going to be there.

"What should we do, Jin?" Nasan was asking. "How— where . . . where's my brother? Lu? *Lu!* Where's Nok?"

She should stand. She should open her eyes. She needed to face Nasan. Her body wouldn't move, though. She swallowed hard, unable to hold back the tears streaming from her eyes. "Nokhai. He's—"

The temple plummeted.

CHAPTER 36

Disintegration

*T*he ground was still moving. Min's body seized with the expectation, the terror. The earth was breaking apart, and it was all her doing—she had to stop it. Couldn't. How could she—

She sat up and found herself in the small box of her carriage. Beautifully appointed as ever, with its silk-upholstered walls and gilded hardware.

It felt like a coffin.

"You're awake."

Panting, Min threw off the covers and found Brother sitting across from her. Butterfly was crouched at his side, pale and shivering despite the heat.

"*Shh*," the old man tutted, pressing Min back down. "Rest. You must rest."

"No!" she cried, recoiling at his touch. The ground was still shaking—she had to get *out*. Had to get away, had to go, had to run, had to find Set. Only Set was . . . he was . . .

"There's nowhere to go," the old man said softly. Perhaps he meant it as a comfort; it felt like a threat.

Min's heart still raced. She felt the force of it alone might throw her off the bed. Someone let out a sob. Butterfly. When Min looked at her, the nuna buried her face into the filthy orange sleeves of her robe.

"None of that," Brother snapped. It was the harshest voice Min had ever heard him use. "You're upsetting your princess. Go—tell the driver to halt the column."

The nuna ran to the front of the carriage. Moments later, they slowed and stilled.

"You're disoriented," Brother said. "I'll give you something to help you sleep."

It wasn't an offer. He looked tired, nearly as dazed as she felt. She wanted to kick him in the throat. Lu would. Lu would—

Lu.

All at once she remembered her sister's face, the way the older girl had looked at her. Her shock. The sense that all she had held to be true was unmoored.

She'd looked at Min like she was someone—something— she didn't know anymore. Didn't recognize.

You never knew me at all, sister. But no, not sister anymore.

What have I done?

Brother placed a cup in her hands. She looked down at its milky contents and recalled the poison her mother had forced her father to swallow. It hadn't been a dream; she could admit that much now. She looked up at the monk. He had cut her with his knife, made her bleed.

He had also saved her. Clumsily thrown her up onto his saddle. Ridden her through the gate between this world and the Inbetween, just before it collapsed behind them.

There had been such terrible noise, and a break in the ground that looked like the sky, and everyone had run. Everyone except her. And the wolf. The boy. She wondered vaguely what had become of him.

"Set is dead," she whispered. There had been blood coming out of his neck. So much blood.

"Yes," Brother sighed. "He is."

What will happen now?

"The terrain has changed," Brother said as he drew back a curtain and looked outside. Min flinched at the flare of daylight.

"How long have I been asleep?"

"Not long enough. You need more rest, Princess."

Empress, she thought. But was she? With her husband dead, what did that leave her?

The Girl King, Min thought deliriously. Ridiculous. They'd never let her rule in her own right, not truly. Even if they did, she wouldn't want it—would she? How could she? She didn't know the first thing about ruling, leading. Not like her sister...

"Do you think—is it possible she survived?" Min blurted.

"Lu? It's possible. The Yunians surely had protections for themselves. And since she was under their care, well ..."

Lu is alive. Min was sure of it. *If there was ever a chance, Lu found it.* It frightened her that she didn't know how that made her feel.

"Your claim is safe," assured the monk, misreading her

thoughts. "Even if Lu survived, she has nothing now. Fewer than a handful of broken-down soldiers at her back and the alliance of a city that doesn't exist anymore. The remnants of which we destroyed."

You don't know her.

"What's important now is that you heal," the monk continued. "You have exhausted yourself. Set—we—asked too much of you, too soon. You can build your strength up at your aunt and uncle's estate before we head back to Yulan City, where we will learn to better control your powers."

Min shuddered. She wasn't sure she ever wanted to use those powers again—not after all that had happened. Besides, what good would it be? Set was dead, Yunis had collapsed into ruin, and—

"What about the prophecy?" she blurted. "The prophecy foretold—"

"Prophecies," Brother said, "can be malleable. In accordance with what is needed. As the world changes, so does truth."

Min wasn't sure what to say to that.

"Perhaps your cousin's reign was never meant to be," Brother continued. "Perhaps he was merely a tool of the heavens, to bring me to you. Who's to say?"

Me?

"Poor Set," the monk sighed. "I thought his passion, his fervor for what was *real* could sustain him. But he was young and reckless. In the end, he was seduced by the promise of fast power. Of revenge on your sister. He wanted that short-term, earthly glory too much. I thought he wanted to plumb the depths of what time has forgotten. What men have lost, and what they have yet to discover. Power like nothing the world has ever seen ..."

His dark eyes fixed beadily on her. Min folded her arms protectively across her chest.

Me. I am the knowledge. I am the power. He wanted what she had. Wanted what she was.

What about what I want?

She didn't say the words aloud, though. It wouldn't be fair. Asking him a question to which she knew there was no answer.

Brother bowed his head. "If you'll excuse me, I need to speak with the captain—I will return shortly. In the meantime, drink that draft I gave you and try to rest, Princess."

When he'd gone, she set aside the draft and lifted the curtain hanging over the window by her bed. Outside, she counted perhaps thirty soldiers on horseback. Thirty men out of near a thousand.

Brother's stallion had stumbled. As they'd ridden back out of the glowing slit she'd rent in the air, where the lake met the shore, the horse's hooves had scrabbled for purchase. When Min looked down she'd seen the stones below were slick with blood. Blood, and lumps of something soft and pink and boneless—for that was what remained of men when they fell from such a great height.

Was Set's blood, his bits of flesh, among them?

She closed her eyes.

What have I done?

What you were born to do.

The voice was thin this time, too weary for mocking. Min

hadn't even felt her appear, as though she hadn't come at all—or as though she had been present the whole time.

"Tsai," she blurted aloud, not caring if anyone heard. Butterfly hadn't returned, and Min suspected she wouldn't until she was forced to. "You're her mother, aren't you? You're Lu's mother but you let me . . . do that to her."

"*I told you,*" she murmured. "*I'm not her anymore, not truly.*"

"I know!" Min snapped. "You're an echo, a shade, a memory. But why would you help me hurt her daughter?"

There was a pause. "*It's funny, isn't it? Tsai cursed you out of love for her child, but all that remains is me. A thing that seeks revenge like a snake seeks the warmth of a beating heart. I was born out of love. I was born of rightful fury. But what does that become when the love is gone?*"

Min didn't know. "I don't care," she said, and realized it was true. "Why do you sound so weak?"

"*I just told you. What I am wasn't meant to last in this world. I'm tired.*"

"Why don't you leave me, then?" Min demanded. "Our deal was that I would bring you to Yunis—but I'm headed back home now, and you're still here."

The shamaness laughed. A sad, little sound that dissolved like sugar into water. "*You have to release me. And for all your talk of sons and happiness and a kind soul, you don't* want *to let me go.*"

"Of course I do," Min cried. "Why would I—"

Liar.

And this time it sounded like her voice, and hers alone. The shamaness was gone—and also not. She could not feel her any longer, but then, she could no more feel her own lungs, her own heart.

What have I done? The question was contemplative this time. And she knew the answer.

Not nearly enough.

⚜

When Brother returned, Min was sitting up.

"You haven't drunk your medicine," he said, gesturing to the cup she had set on the floor beside the bed.

"No," she agreed. "And I won't. I've slept enough."

"I really think—"

"Go tell the captain to get us moving again; we are wasting time."

"Yes, of course, but—"

"And send Butterfly back in here," she commanded. "I should like a change of clothes and my hair brushed."

"Y-yes, Princess," Brother stammered. "Of course."

"And Brother?"

"Yes?"

"You will address me as 'Empress' from now on."

Something like fear rippled across his face as he bowed. "Yes, Empress." When he stood again, it was gone.

Min smiled toothily, and the fear returned.

"Good," she said.

CHAPTER 37

Crowned

*T*here," said the healer. Lu felt the woman's energy, cool as water, withdraw from her body. "That's as much as I can do for now."

As Prince Jin looked on anxiously, Lu rotated her shoulder. It ached down to the bone, but dully now. Whole once more. She ran a hand over her ribs, bruised but whole as well. "Thank you," she said to the healer.

The healer ignored her and instead spoke to Prince Jin. "The shoulder will take some time to finish mending. The bones were splintered, and my powers are weaker down here."

She hates me. Rushing into battle in their defense had clearly not won Lu any new love from the Yunians.

"You did your best," Jin told the healer.

"Yes, well. Vrea could have done more, perhaps ... I'm sorry." The woman brushed tears from her eyes.

Vrea. They would find a way to blame her for that death as well, and likely Prince Shen's, too. Perhaps not unfairly.

Lu flexed her good hand, felt the phantom brush of Nokhai's fingers slipping through it.

After it fell to earth from the Inbetween, the temple had reappeared protruding out of the mountain's broad face. Right by the lake where Jin had welcomed her to Yunis just days ago—a lifetime ago, it seemed now. Jin had explained that because the temple had been first built on earth, then raised into the Inbetween, it was spared the violent reentry into the physical realm that the Heart had endured. Like welcomed like, he had said.

Everything else had been built there. Gone were the houses, the loosely manicured gardens. Gone were the walls and the paving stones, the component parts of the Heart.

And gone was Nokhai.

Lu had told Nasan herself—she could give her that, at least. The Ashina girl fell upon her before she could finish her words. For once, Lu hadn't fought back, just let the other girl's fists rain down. That had been fine—almost a relief. Tangible. The pain small and sharp enough to keep her anchored in her body. But the other girl's screams had cut deeper.

He trusted you! I warned him, I told him—but he trusted you, and you threw him away like he was nothing!

Her eye throbbed where Nasan had punched her. It would bruise, if it hadn't already. Lu clapped a hand over her face, waiting for the pain to subside.

"I could try to fix that swelling around the eye if it's bothering her," the healer said reluctantly.

"No." Lu lowered her hand and stood. "No. It feels fine."

Someone—she couldn't remember who—had given her a shawl. She shivered and wrapped it tighter around her shoulders. It smelled like someone else, someone unfamiliar. Perhaps that person was dead now. She fought the urge to shrug the shawl off. She would need it come nightfall.

Once Jin deemed it safe, they had all set out to wander the lakeshore. To look for survivors, they told themselves. But of course, there were none. Nasan, Jin, his shrunken army, and the few hundred Yunian civilians—were all that was left.

And Lu. She'd forgotten to count herself.

There weren't even bodies to speak of. Instead, the shore was stained red for as far as she could see. Those who hadn't made it to the temple in time had fallen, as though from the sky. The impact had reduced them to wide splotches of blood, like enormous poppies painted across the land. Here and there, she recognized things. The tattered tunic of a Hana soldier. A gleaming helmet, perversely untouched. Half a horse, gone boneless and soft as jelly.

They had little hope of identifying anyone based on these grisly clues. At first, Lu tried to look for the gold of Set's armor. Then she saw a gleaming white femur sticking straight up in a heap of gore, as if it were calling for help. She tried not to look too closely after that.

Occasionally she would catch glimpses of Nasan farther down the shore, staring off into the water, or tending to someone. The Ashina girl never met her eyes. Sooner or later they would have to speak again, but for the time being Lu left her alone.

It occurred to her to look for some hairpin or scrap of cloth she might recognize as belonging to her sister.

No, she told herself. *Min made it out—you saw Brother come back for her. They made it out. Min couldn't be . . .*

Min. Had she truly wrought all this? Lu remembered the rage contorting her sister's face, the black blood in the whites of her eyes, her awful grief over Set's death.

Who would rule with Set gone? The role would default to Min, but in name only. Her sister's power could never truly be her own. It would be granted to whoever wheedled their way into marrying her next, and in the meantime taken up by the strongest, greediest voices in court. Perhaps that sinister monk Brother, perhaps their—no, *Min's* mother. Not Lu's.

Tsai.

Could there be any truth to Min's revelation? Of all the people to birth a Hu princess of the empire, a shamaness. An unclean, unnatural wielder of magic. A hostage. A prisoner.

And yet, some childlike part of her thrilled at the notion. Surged with hope. *That's why my—why the empress never loved me. My real mother would never have hated me so. My real mother would love me.* Wouldn't she?

A star crammed inside a soap bubble.

Omair had known her mother. Omair would know the truth. Omair, whom Nokhai had pledged to rescue.

Whom Nokhai would never see again—

Her hand clenched around open air, around nothing. *No.* She shut the thought out. If she gave in to it now, if she fell into that hole, she would never claw her way free.

"Princess?"

She started and turned toward the voice. Jin stood there, weary in the dying light.

"Princess, it will be dark soon. We should gather everyone inside the temple for the night."

They're your people. You tell them. But of course—

"Our Pact," she said. "Our marriage agreement—"

"It still stands," he said firmly. "That is—if you want it to. I no longer have much of an army to offer you, but what I have is still yours."

"No, of course. It's only, the terrain has changed. Your need is greater now. And even with Set gone, there's still my sister and mother and who knows who else to contend with. And I'm still here—far away from the throne, without an army. I don't know that I have much to offer you." She smiled ruefully. "Perhaps I never did. Only my claim. My dream. It seems childish now, after everything that's been lost."

"All we need is you," he said. "Your leadership, your heart."

"*I trust your heart.*" Nok's words shivered through her. Her jaw clenched as she pushed them away.

Jin placed a tentative hand on her shoulder. Her good shoulder; he was always mindful, deliberate. "You have all you need within you. I believe that. I believe in you."

His eyes were earnest. But what was left of her to believe in? She had lost her chance at the throne. She'd lost her father. Her sister.

For weeks, she had thought of nothing but reaching Yunis, of reaping an army, storming back to Yulan City wreathed in righteous triumph. That dream had kept her feet moving forward, kept her heart pumping. And Nokhai, with his single-minded desire to free Omair, had been the sole witness to that. Together, their entwined missions had made the dream seem like a reality.

Now her army was lost. And Nokhai was gone.

"I should gather people up for the night," Jin said. "Will you—"

She waved him off. "Yes, I'll come help you in a moment. I just need . . ."

He nodded and began to walk off. Then he paused. "Nokhai must have believed in you, as I do. To have fought by your side to the very end."

Lu watched him go. *Nokhai never believed in me. He fought for Omair.*

Omair, who would remain languishing in prison. Another promise broken.

If only she could just reach the capital . . .

But the fact remained that she had no *army*.

Over Jin's shoulder, Lu saw Nasan helping an elderly woman sit on a fallen log.

Jin might not have an army anymore, but Nasan did. Not an army that was big or strong or well equipped. But a capable one. Despite their numbers, they'd managed to infiltrate a heavily guarded labor camp. And those camps . . .

Lu walked toward her.

The Ashina girl gave Lu's swollen eye an appraising look. She had the grace not to look proud of it, but neither did she apologize.

"What do you want, Princess?" she asked instead.

"We need to get everyone inside before nightfall," Lu told her. "Can you help?"

Nasan's mouth tightened. "Now? Sure. Tomorrow? I need to get back to my own people."

There it was. "We have a deal."

"We *had* a deal," Nasan corrected cagily. "That deal was, I help you get to Yunis, you get a real army, which you then use to overthrow your horrible cousin and regain the power to grant my people back our land. But I don't see an army anymore, do you?"

"I've seen yours."

"Yes, and that's the last you'll see of them," Nasan said warningly.

"Set's dead; we're closer now than when we began," Lu pointed out. "And besides, you swore on your honor."

"Well, the terms changed a little when your crazy sister put a split in the world and broke an entire plane of existence."

"I thought you wanted to protect and help your people," Lu said with exaggerated surprise.

"I certainly do," Nasan replied flatly. "*My* people. These aren't my people."

"Nokhai—" Too late, she realized she should not say his name so soon, but Nasan barely flinched. Lu surged on. "Nokhai told me that the Gifted never saw themselves as unified, as one. But the way you live with your people, you call them all your own, no matter the Kith from which they came."

"Of course."

"And so, if no god or tradition or name binds you, what does?"

Your title, your station—your very existence—is built on the subjugation, on the suffering of others.

Nasan frowned as though she saw where this was going. "We all suffered the same under your empire."

"Exactly. These Yunians are no different."

"It *is* different," Nasan persisted. "These people . . . they can't—they aren't Gifted."

"Neither are you," Lu said boldly. "Not anymore."

"We might've been. Nok was a Pactmaker. But he's gone now, isn't he?" the Ashina girl snapped. "You let him die."

I lost him, too. But Nasan would not understand that; she didn't want to. Lu squared her shoulders. It was fine. She could let the other girl have that much. "We are not talking about what might have been. We are talking about what is."

Nasan's black eyes narrowed. "You still don't have an army. That's what *is*."

"I still have my claim," Lu said, threading steel through her voice. *Don't let her see you blink.* "And I *know* you want that land. I can still give that to you once I've reclaimed my throne."

"That land is ours by right."

"And I'm sure whoever ends up pulling my sister's strings would be happy to grant it back to you if you ask nicely."

The other girl's mouth set in a tight line. "My people alone won't be enough to win against the imperial army."

"No," Lu agreed. "But your people are capable of infiltrating and liberating labor camps, are they not? You've done that before."

Nasan scowled. "What's your point?"

"How many people would you say each camp holds?"

Understanding flickered to life behind Nasan's eyes. "Those people aren't warriors," she protested. "Most of them are half-dead with starvation or disease. I don't know what they tell you in Yulan City, but slaves aren't exactly coddled."

"How many?" Lu repeated.

"In each camp? On average, a few hundred, give or take."

"What about the largest? Camp nine, say?"

"A thousand. Easy. But like I said, they're no soldiers."

"Maybe not. But they're angry, and they hate imperials. They might not win a war alone, but by sheer numbers, they could certainly cause damage. They could burn a city. Start enough trouble to let a smaller party—say, us, and no more than a dozen of your best people—infiltrate the palace."

"Of course, because the palace isn't defended by highly trained armed guards and enormous walls."

Lu forced herself to smile. "The thing about being a princess is, you grow up in the palace. It's your home. And you know all its secrets, all its weaknesses."

Nasan pursed her lips, but Lu could see the idea taking root in her mind. "You're crazy," she said, but that was fine. A person like Nasan, with the vision to break into an imperial labor camp—a prison of death from which there should be no feasible escape—that was a person to whom crazy wasn't such a bad thing. Nasan wasn't through arguing, though. "Who's to say the prisoners won't just kill you straight off, considering they hate imperials so much?"

"What would they stand to gain from that? Kill me and

there's no overthrow, no change in the empire at all. Fight with me, and I will alter the whole face of the North."

"They may not hear that argument so well while they're busy tearing you to pieces."

"I'll have Prince Jin by my side, and you—the great liberator. They've surely heard rumors about you and your people by now. You can help them see reason."

"And how do you expect to keep a thousand sickly people alive all the way down to the capital? People have to eat, you know."

Lu hid a smile. They were arguing on her terms now. "The soldiers running the camps have food and medicine. Weapons, armor, horses."

Thoughts were racing behind Nasan's clever eyes. Lu had her. "We'd have to strike fast, and hard," Nasan murmured, almost to herself. "If even one imperial slips out, we'll have the whole army coming for us before you could blink."

"So, we won't let even one slip out."

"What you'd be asking of these prisoners—you'd be sending most of them to their deaths. Maybe all of them."

"Once we've taken the prison, they'll be free to choose. They could follow me or go on their way."

"Some choice," the other girl scoffed. "Die of freezing or starvation in the empty desert or become your foot soldier. Out of one prison, into another."

Your title, your station—your very existence—is built on the subjugation, on the suffering of others.

Lu hesitated. *I'd be giving them the opportunity to fight for themselves—for their freedom.* But somehow the words would not leave her tongue.

Nasan didn't comment on her silence. Just licked her lips, then cast a look down the darkening shore. "It'll be bloody," she warned. "Bloody and ugly."

Nearby, two small children were splashing and giggling in the shallows of the lake, seemingly oblivious to the clouds of blood pinking the waters. Someone—a parent, maybe— shrieked at them to get out. Lu watched them run up the rocky shore, chagrined.

"I'm up to my ears in bloody and ugly," Lu said.

"You don't have to tell me."

"So." Lu gathered herself. "Does our deal stand?"

Nasan scowled. "It's getting dark. Let's get these people back inside."

"Do we have a deal?" Lu repeated, louder.

Nasan sighed. "Tomorrow," she said at length, turning toward the temple. "Tomorrow we march back to fetch my army."

"And then?" Lu persisted at her retreating figure.

Nasan didn't stop. "Then we head to the camps."

⁂

They were ready to go before dawn, a few hundred hunched survivors with little more than the clothes on their backs, and what life still fluttered in their tired hearts. They had put the weakest—the elderly and small children, of which there were more than Lu would have liked—on horseback. The rest of them would walk.

Lu stretched as she gazed out onto the lake for the last time, trying to ease the stiffness that persisted in her shoulder. She touched the hilt of her sword, secure once more at her waist.

Goodbye. She sent the thought skipping across the water like a stone. She would not miss this place in all its bleak, morose beauty, but she felt the need to honor it all the same. And again, this time for the many souls—and one soul in particular—that now lingered lost beneath that mirrored surface:

Goodbye, Nokhai.

Prince Jin walked up and stood at her side.

"Do you think," she asked hesitantly, "they'll wash up, eventually?" She did not have to say of whom she spoke.

Prince Jin grimaced. "The lake behaved . . . differently in the Inbetween. I do not know about this lake. They may be lost to us for good."

He didn't say what they were both thinking: that even those that had landed in the lake were likely not intact. That there would be no bodies to wash up at all.

Lu felt the sensation of Nokhai's mouth against her own. The way he had moved beneath her hands. How easy it was to take the living flesh, the blood, the bone for granted. How callously ungrateful it was to be alive and not recall at every moment that so many were not.

"We need to keep moving," Nasan said, walking up beside them.

Lu drew a shuddering breath. She would be glad to be away from this place.

Jin held up his hands and called for the Yunians to gather.

They did, with the halting, distant air of sleepwalkers. People who believed they were already half-dead. People who were sure there was nothing left to live for.

"We have suffered tremendous loss," Jin told them. "But our fallen fathers and mothers, our sisters and brothers, and indeed, my sister Vrea, my brother Shen—they would all want us to endure. And we will. Together, Princess Lu and I will lead you to safety. Those among us able and willing shall reclaim what has been taken from us by the old emperors, and by the false Emperor Set. Together, we will build a new homeland, one governed by wisdom and justice."

He took Lu's good hand in his own, then raised it overhead.

"All hail my future wife, Princess Lu, rightful ruler of the empire, and queen of Yunis!"

Looking past Prince Jin and his watery, sanguine smile, Lu saw little enthusiasm among the Yunians. They clapped dutifully through their weariness and suspicion.

Your title, your station—your very existence—is built on the subjugation, on the suffering of others.

A few of the Yunians, though, met her eyes and nodded, as though communicating that they would give her a chance. To hope against hope.

What other choice did they have?

Lu tried to speak to those few as she addressed them. "I know you do not love me as your own yet. I understand. I hope that I will have the opportunity to win your trust and your respect in the days to come."

An anxious, fragile silence followed.

Then Nasan shouted, "All hail the Girl King!"

The crowd murmured amused assent, and Nasan flashed her a wry grin.

Behind the Ashina girl stood a Yunian orphan child, not more than five years old. Her black eyes were two dark pits of mistrust. Lu looked away, tried not to take it for a portent of what was to come. What they were about to face allowed no room for uncertainty.

"All hail the Girl King!" shouted the crowd.

Lu straightened her shoulders, hiding the lingering stiffness in the left. She forced herself to smile, closed-lipped and benevolent and appropriately, faintly mournful. Ready to assume the role for which she had been born—all that she was ever intended for.

EPILOGUE

Awake

*T*he fog is too dense. Nok can barely breathe. Even his limbs seem inhibited by it; his movements indolent, disobedient. He keeps on, forcing one foot in front of the other, feels himself move forward. When had he started walking? When did he get here? How?

Someone is just ahead of him. As he closes in, he recognizes her. She moves like mist, slow, there but not quite. Distant as a star. But he recognizes her in spite of it. Perhaps because of it. Perhaps that vagueness of body, that inbetweeness is as much a part of her as the cool eyes, the close-shorn hair.

The wolf huffs at his side. Nok strokes the creature, fond and absent. His hand passes through it like water. The wolf is not of the Inbetween, but it too has some inbetweeness in its nature. Neither here nor there, not quite spirit, not quite flesh.

And what of me? What am I made of?

There is no answer. He walks.

Vrea seems to sense him trailing behind her. There's something almost amused to the set of her shoulders—he can imagine the quirk of a smile upon her wide mouth.

They're silent for a time, and then he asks: "Where are we?"

"Nowhere at all, I fear." She stops walking, turns and waits until he and the wolf are at her side. "We are in the remains of the Inbetween."

"I thought it had been destroyed? Isn't that what happened?" Odd; he can't remember.

"That which was Inbetween is gone, but the space holds," Vrea tells him. "It has simply been . . . emptied. Remade. Wherever there are two, there must be something dividing them."

Are you one, or two? He asked that to someone, something, once.

"Not the Ana and Aba," he says. "They are both."

"Yes," she agrees. "They are both one and two. They are harmony. But we are not."

He's silent at that, and she lets him think. He feels he could think for a lifetime, for the span of kingdoms, long enough for stars to blaze into creation and collapse in upon themselves, and still she would wait.

Maybe he will. He feels . . . unhurried. He would feel nothing at all were it not for the nagging in his heart. A finger worrying some loose thread there. He's forgotten.

He remembers. Not everything, but it's something.

"Are we dead?" The thought makes him sad—but only vaguely. From an arm's length.

"Not quite dead," Vrea says. "Not yet."

He thinks on that, his hand stroking through the wolf's there-and-gone-again fur. He looks down and sees the path has disappeared. They're standing on stone. No, rocks. The shore of a lake. That seems familiar, somehow. "Not dead," he repeats to himself.

Vrea toes off her sandals and sits. "Do you want to be?"

He thinks about that, too, as he sits. "No. I thought— but, no."

She nods seriously. "A good choice for you."

The wolf lies down next to him, pressing warmly against his thigh. He feels a relaxed sigh shudder through it, no different from a sleeping dog. "Do we get to choose?"

"Right now, you do."

"And you?"

Her mouth makes the saddest smile. "I'm afraid not. I've lived too long as it is."

He remembers something else. "You seemed certain it would end. You said that Yunis's time was coming to a close. But . . . " He understands now. "You still hoped, didn't you?"

"I thought we might have a chance. To stay. Or to go elsewhere. The Ana and the Aba, they told me the way was unclear. That there might be another. Or that's what I believed they said. It's hard to know for certain. Perhaps I only heard what I wanted to hear, because I was afraid to die, after all."

"I thought you were supposed to see the future," he says. "Isn't that what an Oracle does? Know all our fates? Or are you saying fate isn't real?"

"Oh, fate is real, Nokhai. Those of us with the Gift see it the way you see light—simultaneously washing over and penetrating all things. But like light, it can play tricks on the eye. Sometimes it can be manipulated. Sometimes it can blind the seer. And sometimes the thing that sways it cannot be foreseen."

"So," he says. "What you're telling me is, sometimes you just get it wrong."

Vrea smiles faintly at him. "Sometimes we just get it wrong," she agrees.

The soft light emanating through the fog shifts, almost imperceptibly. Bluer. Cooler. And now he can hear water. Like the Milk River lapping against its retaining walls. Jostling boats in the Yulan City harbor.

Nok's sense of unease grows. The loose thread in his heart is now a pinprick hole. Perhaps that thing he's forgotten isn't so unimportant, after all.

"What am I supposed to do now?" he asks.

Vrea stands, brushing invisible dust from her robes. The water-smoothed rocks beneath her feet clink together. She squints out toward the water. There's a boat in it now, floating toward them. Two figures sit inside, and he recognizes the closer of the two as Prince Shen. The other is only a purpled shadow. It is wearing a hood, but Nok suspects that even if it weren't, he wouldn't be able to see its face.

"It is my time," Vrea tells him. "I am no longer of this place. I am on to your . . . what was it you said? Your nothing. On to the unknown."

"What am I supposed to do?" he repeats.

"What it is you were meant to do," she tells him.

"But I don't know what that is," he protests, standing.

"You do," she says. She makes as though to step into her

sandals, but seems to think better of it and leaves them on the shore. Then she wades out into the white surf. He follows her, but stops halfway between the boat and the shore. The water is cool against his ankles.

Vrea turns back to him. "You do. Or at least, you will. Goodbye, Nokhai. You are an interesting person. I am glad to have met you, even if our time together was so brief."

She gives a little wave of one hand. Nok watches her climb gracefully into the boat. He feels bereft and yet calm. He feels there is something else he is meant to say now, some final words to send along in the modest wind pulling her boat farther and farther from shore, but he can think of nothing. And then, the boat is gone.

Foam churns on the lake surface, like cream on whey. Fog still shrouds the shore, but whereas before he could scarcely see more than an arm's length around him, now there are shapes and shadows to decipher into trees, distant mountains. Quiet and awesome and vast.

It is so still here. So empty that there is nothing for time and perception to cling to. He has the sense of an entire day passing as he draws a single breath.

There is movement at the corner of his eye, and he looks back to the shore, expecting to see his wolf. He does, but now there are new figures emerging from the fog, lining up like they are on display. The first that comes clear into view is a spotted deer with a rack of silvery antlers. It gingerly appoints its delicate feet amid the smooth rocks. Nok's heart leaps as his wolf looks toward it, but the deer shows no concern at all.

Next comes a tawny cougar, followed by a glittering blue-green cobra, a boar, a black panther, a white owl riding upon the back of a wild ox—more and more, until Nok can scarcely name them as quickly as they appear.

For a moment, he thinks he sees the stark black and orange stripes of a tiger moving behind a dun-colored coyote, but then it is gone again, vanished amid the wall of fur and flesh before him.

He knows them, though some are creatures he has never seen before. Knows them even before the golden eagle of the Iarudi sails down from the sky and lights upon a log of drift-wood, talons seizing it in a shower of splinters.

Gifters. Gods. Each the patron of a Kith. And every pair of eyes—golden to black to green—are upon him. Waiting.

He steps forward.

The golden eagle comes at him first, swooping from its perch, that curved, cruel beak aimed for his face. Nok throws his hands up, but the eagle is like smoke, like wind. It breaks over him—through him. He feels it settle deep inside, its airy energy spreading buoyant through his bones. A red bear charges next, its great paws kicking up stones and surf.

It is too much. They slam through him, one after the other, and his body hums with it, a cacophony of power and energy. He feels too small, like there's too much blood beneath his skin. His heart bangs against his ribs, bursting with it . . .

He's stumbling backward into the brackish water, only now there is none. Only open air, through which he plummets like a stone.

He awoke drowning. A gasp like a scream tore out of him as he broke the surface of the water. *Air,* Nok thought, sucking it in, greedy. *Air.*

So caught up in the animal joy of merely breathing, it took him a moment to realize he was alone in open water. He cast about for the shore, but there was none to see. Fear lanced through him then, cold. His muscles were aching—for how much longer could he hope to tread?

I'm going to die, he realized.

Something prickled his scalp—a half memory.

Am I dead?

No. Not dead yet. *Focus.*

He could make out a lumpy shadow far off on the horizon. Land. A strip of it beneath the bright blue sky. *Blue.* No longer was he in the Inbetween. This was the earth, and he, like any other earthly thing, was alive.

So he swam. Until his hands felt as cold and heavy as stone, until the muscles in his shoulders spasmed and seized, he swam. Past weakness, then the end of weakness, then the point where his body felt consumed by pain, and then *was* pain, and then the blazing absence, the nothing that followed.

Still he swam, until his hands were paddling against stone.

He threw himself upon the shore, choking and sputtering water from his belly and his lungs. Every part of him ached— cramps seized his calves, his guts, his hands. As the feeling returned to his cold-numbed fingers, it felt like his flesh was afire. Violently, viscerally alive.

He'd never known anything sweeter.

ACKNOWLEDGMENTS

Any creative work requires the wisdom, cooperation, and labor of unseen dozens to make its way into the world, and the romantic myth of the individual artist executing a finished work on her own is just that—a myth. Nothing makes this more apparent than publishing a book. Experiencing *The Girl King*'s long journey from start to your hands, reader, made me wonder why we elevate the myth at all; the reality is far more magical.

To that end, I would like to thank the following people from the bottom of my heart. Their work and support is woven through every page, in every serif, in every neatly patched plothole, every correctly placed comma, and I am humbled by their contributions.

I am eternally grateful to my all-star agent, Beth Phelan, for taking a chance on me and *The Girl King*. This would never have happened without you. Thank you for your savviness, persistence, boldness, and the speed with which you reply to emails—in short, thanks for possessing all the qualities I wish I had. Thank you also for your patience; wry humor; early editorial acuity; kindness; and your fondness for dogs, which is equaled perhaps only by my fondness for cats, and thus makes me feel better about being a pet weirdo.

Thank you to my deeply insightful and casually brilliant editor, Hali Baumstein. I kind of knew you were the one for this project when you didn't flinch at my wildest, most incendiary plans for this series, and I definitely knew you were the one when you dropped a Taylor Swift reference in my first edit letter. I can't imagine having done *The Girl King* with anyone else, and I'm so excited to crack open book two together.

My gratitude is also owed to the whole amazing team at Bloomsbury for their kind support; I feel very lucky and honored to publish my debut with such a special and talented group. Thank you to Cindy Loh, Sarah Shumway, Diane Aronson, Melissa Kavonic, Donna Mark, Cristina Gilbert, Lily Yengle, Beth Eller, Brittany Mitchell, and Alona Fryman. Special thanks to Lizzy Mason and Anna Bernard in publicity, Erica Barmash and Emily Ritter in marketing, Cindy (again), and everyone who made my first BEA experience a terrific one.

Many thanks to copy editor Juliann Barbato and proofreader Linda Minton, who continually amazed me with their breadth of knowledge and attention to detail. I still don't really understand where commas go, but you both definitely do, so I can sleep at night.

Thank you to illustrator Tommy Arnold for bringing Lu to life through his beautiful cover and to Danielle Ceccolini for her lovely, complementary design. Thank you also to (supremely talented artist) Alexis Castellanos for designing the ARC.

Special thanks also to my UK and Australia/New Zealand editor Rachel Winterbottom for her invaluable input in shaping *The Girl King*. Thank you to the whole team at Gollancz for their work bringing Lu, Min, and Nok across the pond(s), in particular Alex Layt, Jennifer McMenemy, Paul Stark, Paul Hussey, Jo Carpenter, Kat Lynch, and Brendan Durkin.

Thank you to the Bent Agency for their work in getting *The Girl King* out into the world. Special thanks to Molly Ker Hawn for her work in facilitating its publication in the UK and Australia/New Zealand. Thank you to the team at the Gallt & Zacker Literary Agency for their support, and to film agent Mary Pender Coplan at UTA.

Thank you to teacher and mentor Marjorie Liu and the incredible writers of the VONA Popular Fiction classes of 2014 and 2015. Already several amazing books and short stories have emerged from our cohort, and I fully expect more to follow. Marjorie, thank you for your quiet warmth and your insight and for challenging us to dream and create big.

Thank you to all the wonderful writers and artists I've had the opportunity to meet either in the flesh or virtually while getting this book out into the world. I will always treasure your advice and kindness, and I hope I have the opportunity to pay them forward. Special thanks to my blurbers Cindy Pon, Kendare Blake, Heidi Heilig, Marjorie (again), and Julie C. Dao and also to my brilliant, funny agent siblings of the #beoples group on Slack.

I owe an unpayable debt of gratitude to all the YA writers of color who have come before me. Without their hard work and vision, *The Girl King* would never have made it onto the page, let alone a bookstore shelf.

Special thanks to my very smart friend Naomi Cui for providing invaluable linguistic advice and feedback for many of the names and places in this story.

I listened to a lot of music while brainstorming (and sometimes, procrastinating) about this book. I like to think it all had some purpose. Each character has their own playlist so the entire soundtrack would be too long to list. Instead, here are some of the most important albums: Okkervil River's *Black Sheep Boy*, Ramesh's *The King*, Kate Bush's *Hounds of Love*, White Sea's *In Cold Blood*, and The Killers' *Day & Age*. Thank you to those artists.

Thank you to my umma and appa for raising me with every opportunity they never had, and for supporting me on the slow, plodding path toward making this book a reality, no matter how bemusing and financially insoluble it must have seemed. Appa, I can't express how much it meant when you read an early version of the manuscript. Thank you for making note of those little typos and continuity errors, which of course you did. Thank you, Umma, for making visits to the Seneca Falls Library—our version of church—checking out weekly stacks twenty books deep, heedless of the librarian's disapproving stare.

Thank you to my brother Joseph for the hand-me-down *Star Wars* action figures, giving me *A Game of Thrones* when I was far too young, and all the long late-night holiday conversations about books and movies. You fostered and encouraged my love of sci-fi and fantasy first, when no one else got it.

Special thanks to Tracy for listening to me spout the very earliest version of this plot on the drive to Jamaica Bay and telling me Min was her favorite character. I regret we didn't know about mosquito season in Queens before we made the trip, but I'm grateful for the car ride, and your brilliance and feedback. Thank you also to Carly for live-texting me your reading of an early version of the manuscript, and your enthusiasm for my loving descriptions of gore.

Thank you to Dr. Shinhee Han, without whom I would undoubtedly still be the saddest, least-qualified bookkeeper in all of Manhattan.

Much gratitude goes to my in-laws, especially Kate and Bruce for their unquestioning acceptance of and enthusiasm for my dreams from day one. Their generosity of spirit remains breathtaking. And thank you to Lola, because I'm not above shameless ploys like putting your name in a book to make a play for favorite aunt status.

My mother will be very angry to find me thanking my pets, which honestly is at least 40 percent of the reason I'm doing it. Thank you, Dr. Watson, Pamina, Ásdís, Heathcliff, Squirrel, and little Steven. I would get so much more done without you in my life, but I'm very glad you're here. I'm fairly confident at least half of you can't read, but perhaps one of the others will tell you about this if they're feeling charitable.

Most of all: Kevin. My first editor, first fan, and fiercest advocate, who believed in this book long before I ever did. I look forward to reading your multivolume Snowdrop fan fiction. Thank you for your unrelenting, vigorous validation, and several hundred expertly crafted peanut butter sandwiches. Every day you restore my belief in the human capacity for kindness, honesty, wit, compassion, devotion, self-betterment, and curiosity. You are my inspiration in all things, my one true love.

MIMI YU is the author of *The Girl King*. She was born and raised in rural upstate New York and she is an alumna of VONA/Voices. She received a BA from Sarah Lawrence College and an MFA from the New School/Parsons School of Design. When she's not writing, she enjoys gardening, quilting, boxing, and fostering kittens. Mimi has five cats, one dog, and four planets in Aquarius. She currently resides with her family in Chicagoland.

www.mimiyu.info
Twitter and Instagram: @baby_ajumma